D0049668

Enter by the Narrow Gate

Enter by the Narrow Gate

A Christopher Worthy/Father Fortis Mystery

DAVID CARLSON

coffeetownpress

Seattle, WA

coffeetownpress

Coffeetown Press
PO Box 70515
Seattle, WA 98127

For more information go to: www.coffeetownpress.com
www.davidccarlson.org

This is a work of fiction. Names, characters, places, brands, media, and incidents are either the product of the author's imagination or are used fictitiously.

Cover art: *Narrow Gate*, watercolor by Kathy Carlson from a photograph by Susie Fleck
Cover design by Sabrina Sun

Enter by the Narrow Gate
Copyright © 2016 by David Carlson

ISBN: 978-1-60381-391-4 (Trade Paper)
ISBN: 978-1-60381-392-1 (eBook)

Library of Congress Control Number: 2016940165

Printed in the United States of America

"Enter by the narrow gate; for the gate is wide and the way is easy, that leads to destruction, and those who enter it are many. For the gate is narrow and the way is hard that leads to life, and those who find it are few."

Matthew 7:13-14 RSV

ACKNOWLEDGMENTS

———◆———

To KATHY, MY WIFE AND EDITOR, I owe the most. She believed that Christopher Worthy and Father Fortis would one day have their chance to solve puzzling murders. I thank her also for the cover art. My sons, Leif and Marten, also artists, were among the first to encourage me to keep writing. To them, I add Amanda, my daughter-in-law, an avid reader and supporter of this series. Sara Camilli, my literary agent, has from the beginning been an enthusiastic fan of Worthy and Father Fortis. I also wish to thank Jennifer McCord and Catherine Treadgold from Coffeetown Press for their patience and invaluable assistance with this book and series.

Various others offered encouraging words that helped me more than they know. To my sister, Ruth, to Susie, to John, to Tim, and to Bill—thank you.

I wish to thank Franklin College, a gem of a liberal-arts college and my academic home since 1978. Through Franklin College's support from the Dietz Faculty Travel Fund and the Charles B. and Kathleen O. Van Nuys Deans Chair in Religious Studies, I was able to travel to New Mexico and to Venice, Italy, to conduct research for this mystery series.

CHAPTER ONE

———◆———

Sister Anna stared in disbelief at the rusty lock dangling from the latch. How could this have happened? She'd left the remote retreat house before noon, as she had every day that week, and was absolutely positive that she'd locked it. Every day, when she'd returned from her painting forays into the surrounding canyons of New Mexico's high desert, she'd found the place locked up tightly. Until today.

In the gathering darkness, her fingers found the latch and rested on the two loose screws. *Just the crazy summer wind*, she thought with relief.

She laughed lightly as she opened the door and stepped inside. "A couple of screws loose. How perfect." Those were exactly the words her father had uttered when she first told him of her decision to become a nun. *Too bad he isn't still alive to hear I'm leaving the order*, she thought.

With each step down the narrow hallway, she expected to see the faint gleam of the battery-powered lamp in the bedroom. But there was no light.

"I know I left that on," she muttered. But the lamp dimmed last night, she recalled. Maybe the battery had finally given out. *Just as well*, she thought. *Tomorrow I leave and then it's a whole new beginning.*

Loose screws and dim bulbs. Like the punch line of a bad joke. Her fingers found the mattress, then the nightstand and the matches upon it. She lit the candle and sat down wearily upon the bed.

"Tomorrow, a whole new beginning," she repeated, as she lay back on the pillows and stared up at the gnarled log rafters. The place had been her home for the week after Easter, and here she'd decided to end her religious vocation. The decision had come gradually but with increasing waves of relief. She would use the inheritance from her grandmother to rent an art studio, maybe still in New Mexico, and begin her life yet again. She knew it was the right decision to leave St. Mary of the Snows, but that didn't mean there wouldn't be painful conversations ahead.

She would begin by telling Abbot Timothy, not just to follow monastic rules of respect, but because Abbot Timothy deserved to know first. It had been he, on his annual supervisory visit to her convent in Oklahoma, who had found her languishing in the infirmary. Blathering as was usual for him—always calling her Sister Annetta—he'd seen what she couldn't have admitted to herself at the time, that her desire to be both a nun and artist was never going to be acceptable to Abbess Cecelia. He'd invited Anna to return with him to St. Mary of the Snows, where she'd stayed for the past two months while her strength returned.

My decision will be a slap in the face, she thought.

A scurrying sound from the other side of the retreat house interrupted her thoughts. Yawning, she sat up. That pesky red squirrel again. She made a mental note to tell Father Bernard about the uninvited visitor so a trap could be set before the next guest arrived.

She looked down longingly at the pillow. "I'll be back after my prayers, so save my place."

Taking the candle, she retraced her steps down the hallway toward the chapel. A tightness gripped her stomach at the prospect of explaining her decision to Father Bernard, her spiritual director for the past two months.

"Maybe he already suspects," she mumbled to herself. Their most recent meetings had become games of twenty questions, and she hadn't been winning. Father Bernard seemed to have some hidden agenda for her, one that shifted without rhyme or reason. His adamant opposition to her initial request for a retreat had inexplicably given way to enthusiastic consent the next day. "Talk about a hard guy to figure out," she said.

Hearing more rustling sounds from down the hallway, she stopped and felt her spine tingle. The red squirrel was getting bolder, or maybe more than one had found a way in. She tiptoed gingerly to the doorway of the room and peered into the darkness. She heard nothing.

"You rascal, you know I'm here, don't you?" she called into the gloom.

Again, she heard nothing. The tingling along her backbone persisted as she edged into the room, the candle held out in front of her. *What's making me anxious,* she told herself, *isn't the pesky squirrel but the knowledge that Father Bernard will be tougher on me than Abbot Timothy.* The abbot would simply look older and sadder as he called her Sister Annetta for the last time. But Father Bernard would stomp around, his hair flying, as he pummeled her with question after question.

Kneeling before the altar in the dark chapel, she offered a prayer for the last person at the monastery she'd have to tell. Abbot Timothy's disappointment and even Father Bernard's anger would be easier to take than Brother Andrew's tears. Her partner in the monastery's print shop for the past months, Andrew had grown too fond of her. The two of them were among the few under thirty at St. Mary's, so perhaps his attraction had been inevitable. But his plea of undying love, delivered with a rose two weeks before, had strained their easy friendship.

She gazed down at the flickering candlelight on the floor and groaned. Did she need to tell Brother Andrew first? If someone else told him of her decision to leave her order, he'd be sure to misunderstand and assume she'd accepted his harebrained plan to run off together.

Over the past week, she'd half-expected Brother Andrew to find his way over the twenty miles that separated the retreat house from the monastery. But, then, she'd feared the same from Father Bernard. She was sure that it was crazy thoughts such as these that had made her believe she was being watched over the past two days.

As she tried to restart her prayers, the truth hit her: she'd established deeper roots in her two months at St. Mary's than she had in her last three years at her home convent in Oklahoma. The only monk at St. Mary's who'd be happy to see her go would be the coward who'd kept leaving her notes. *You don't belong here. You are not wanted here.* And that last one: *You will have to answer to God for what you are doing to St. Mary's.*

Behind her, from the back room, she heard the rustling sounds again. Only this time the commotion seemed too loud. Her whole body tensed as she realized that the source was no squirrel.

"Oh, Lord," she whispered, "the open door." So what was behind her—a cow, coyote, or rattlesnake? *Not a snake,* she concluded. *A rattlesnake would only rattle.*

She considered forgetting the prayers and running back to her room. *I could leave the outside door open again,* she thought, *so the uninvited guest could leave. Or another could come in.*

To fight back the panic rising in her stomach, she gazed up at the altar and searched in the gloom for the statues of the suffering Christ and the Virgin Mary that flanked the cross. Why did the altar seem so bare? She rose to one knee and reached for the candle to shed more light on the matter. It was then that she saw the confetti strewn on the floor to her left.

Just a squirrel after all, she thought with relief. "Shame on you, you little rascal."

She brought the candlelight down to the mess and gasped. The statues from the altar, broken in pieces before her, were surrounded by bits of paper.

She reached for the shredded bits, only to recognize familiar lines and words from her journal.

"Mary, Mother of God, have mercy on me," she whispered as the paper fluttered from her hand to the floor.

She sensed rather than heard the movement behind her. Still kneeling, she turned and saw a hooded figure coming toward her out of a dark corner. The knife's blade tore into her back, was yanked out, and stabbed her again.

Sinking to the floor, she tried to form words of a prayer. Her lips moved, but the only voice she heard came from the one standing over her.

"Fallen, fallen is the whore of Babylon."

CHAPTER TWO

---◆---

O N A WARM MORNING IN LATE April, Father Fortis was drumming his fingers on the library table. *Thump, thump, thump,* two quicker thumps and then a flourish of four final beats. He stopped and pondered the sound. His fingers hadn't erred, but the meter couldn't be right. The sequence violated the pattern of every Byzantine chant he knew.

Flipping back to the beginning of the article lying open in front of him, he reread Father Linus's opening argument. The work was the most respected treatment of Roman chant to come out in the last thirty years, and the presence of the elderly Father Linus at St. Mary of the Snows had been, in fact, the reason Father Fortis had chosen the New Mexican Trappist monastery for his sabbatical.

Father Fortis saw his work on ancient Roman chant as his small contribution to the slow journey of reconciliation between the Orthodox and Catholic churches. He had detractors at his own Orthodox monastery in Ohio who denounced his sabbatical at the Catholic and Trappist monastery of St. Mary of the Snows as "too ecumenical."

Too ecumenical? Father Fortis wanted to remind his critics that Ecumenical Patriarch Athenagoras and Pope Paul VI had embraced in 1964, ending the schism of the previous millennium and setting the two churches on the road to reconciliation. He bristled at the notion that his love of his Orthodox heritage was compromised by his willingness to admit that Catholics could be equally devoted to their own rich tradition.

Closing his eyes, Father Fortis whistled the line. *No, that meter is not possible,* he concluded with a firm shake of his head. *I must discuss this with*

Father Linus when we meet. He inhaled deeply to whistle the line again when a bony hand clamped down on his own.

"Silence!"

He looked up into the jowls of an elderly monk, the same monk who'd been napping at the head table when he entered the library.

Chastened, Father Fortis frowned and whispered an apology. Glancing around the room, he saw a novice and three monks of various ages working at separate tables. He offered a nod of regret in their direction, but they all acted as if they'd heard nothing.

It was then that he realized the old monk still held him firmly by the hand.

"I want you to leave," the monk whispered, saliva flying from the corners of his mouth.

"What?" Father Fortis asked, pulling his hand free.

"Leave!"

Father Fortis heard a cough emanate from one of the other tables. "I'm here for research," he whispered in explanation.

"What research?" the old monk demanded.

"Roman chant with Father Linus."

Straightening up, the old monk folded his arms. He continued to stare down at Father Fortis. "Then do your whistling in Linus's room. This is my library."

Father Fortis gathered his books, paper, and pen. *Like being back in high school*, he thought.

Out in the hallway, he found a drinking fountain and took a long drink. *Nice beginning to my stay*, he thought, as he wet his hands and wiped his face. Turning, he saw a novice standing awkwardly behind him.

"Brother Elias is a bit upset today," the young man offered, pulling at one of his sleeves. "We all are. Please forgive our manners."

Father Fortis nodded as he patted his face with a handkerchief. "Certainly, certainly, my son. Sorry if my whistling disturbed everyone. Quite thoughtless of me."

The novice raised his hand. "No, no, not at all." Extending his hand, he added, "I'm Bartholomew, just a brother, not a priest. You're the Orthodox monk staying with us."

With a slight smile, Father Fortis lifted his arms above his massive torso to let the black silk of his robes hang like wings. "I must look like an overweight Batman in this get-up, but please call me Father Nicholas."

The novice returned the smile. "Ah, the winged avenger. I collected Batman comics as a kid. How long will you be with us?"

"My sabbatical is for six weeks."

The novice's face beamed with pleasure. "That's wonderful. Maybe they'll ask you to speak in one of our chapter meetings. The Orthodox are our sister church dating a long ways back, as Pope John Paul II made clear. We had a Buddhist monk stay with us for a week. That was a couple of months ago, but I'm still reading books that he left."

"An Orthodox monk and even a Buddhist monk? St. Mary's must be a very open place."

The two walked down the hallway toward the dormitory. "Yes and no," the novice replied. "Not everyone approved of the Buddhist being here."

"I suppose that means the old monk in the library didn't let him whistle either."

The novice laughed easily. "No, Brother Elias is definitely old-school. He probably thinks of you Orthodox as heretics."

"Not a big believer in Vatican II, then," Father Fortis mused.

"I'm not sure he believes in Vatican I," Brother Bartholomew replied with a smile. "But you're lucky to be working with Father Linus. He's just the opposite."

"Well, I hope to be working with Father Linus. I arrived five days ago, but we haven't had much chance to dig into the research. Father Linus was down with a cold when I first arrived and now, as you say, everyone is a bit preoccupied. After all, her funeral was just yesterday."

"Yes, Sister Anna's death—her murder—is a terrible tragedy," the novice said, his voice thick with emotion. "She was one of us at St. Mary's, strange as that may seem. No one can believe she's actually gone. Did you meet her?"

"No, she'd already left for her retreat when I arrived last week. But I was here when they brought back the terrible news." Father Fortis paused in front of his guestroom and fished out his key. "In times like these, a community relies on its abbot."

He looked up and caught the pained expression on the novice's face.

"Abbot Timothy is a good abbot, St. Mary's superior for over two decades, and a holy man," the novice whispered, as he glanced down the hallway in both directions. "There's no doubt about that, but he seems …."

"I sense that he's a bit overwhelmed," Father Fortis offered. "Quite understandable, really."

The novice shrugged. "That's a kind way of putting it. Some of the older brothers say the abbot has been eccentric for some time, but this week it's much worse."

Father Fortis remembered his first meeting with Abbot Timothy on Wednesday, when he'd stopped in to formally introduce himself and thank the monastery for its hospitality. But it wasn't clear how much of what he'd said had been heard by the old man, who sat slumped to one side in a chair. Wednesday had been the same day that the news of Sister Anna's death had been shared with the community, so Father Fortis had simply given the abbot the benefit of the doubt.

But the next morning, when news crews began arriving from Santa Fe, Father Fortis saw a side of the abbot that supported Brother Bartholomew's concern. From his window, he'd observed the monks as they returned from their chapter meeting. They'd walked with heads down, their sandaled feet sending up small clouds of dust. Without warning, a photographer had moved toward one of the novices, someone who seemed even younger than Brother Bartholomew. The poor boy raised his hood and shied away from the raised camera, but this only drew more attention from the rest of the news crew.

Abbot Timothy stepped forward to intervene, but was pushed aside and nearly fell in the process. Another monk, a burly one with a nimbus of wild gray hair, stepped into the fray and pushed the photographer back with a mighty shove. The photographer went down in a heap, his camera flying. More dust. Abbot Timothy teetered for a moment, his hand covering his mouth, before turning on his heels and scurrying away.

What a zoo, Father Fortis had thought at the time.

Father Fortis inserted the key and turned the doorknob of his room. "Well, Brother Bartholomew, we know what we must do. We must all pray for the abbot," he whispered.

"And we must all help him where we can," the novice added cryptically. He nodded and continued down the hall.

Entering the room, Father Fortis placed his research on the bedside table. Staring up at him was the newspaper that he'd bought the day before when last in town. He sat on the bed and reread the account of how one of the novices had discovered Sister Anna's body in a remote retreat house owned by St. Mary's. He wondered if the novice had been Brother Bartholomew or the poor boy who'd been harassed by the photographer.

Next he reviewed the coroner's brief public statement. Sister Anna had been stabbed twice in the back, with either wound capable of being fatal. But the evidence pointed to something quite strange that had occurred later. Dead or dying, Sister Anna had been stabbed repeatedly in and between her breasts. Father Fortis pulled on his beard and pondered the odd detail. Was the attack sexual? He couldn't deny that St. Mary's tragedy intrigued him. Why had a nun stayed in an all-male community in the first place? That had to be irregular, even in post-Vatican II days. From an oblique comment in the paper by one of St. Mary's leaders, a Father Bernard, he gleaned that Abbot Timothy had rescued Sister Anna from some crisis at her convent in Oklahoma. What had that been?

The newspaper account reported that the nun had stayed at St. Mary's for nearly two months, time enough for the tight community of monks to learn all about her. Had they all accepted her? He couldn't imagine Brother Elias had embraced her warmly, but Brother Bartholomew had clearly been fond of her. Had someone in the community loved her too much? From the picture in the newspaper, Father Fortis found the prospect believable. The woman had been truly beautiful—a curse for a nun.

Father Fortis looked up to the crucifix above the bed. He thought of the novice's comment—"and we must all help him where we can."

"Holy God, Holy Mighty, Holy Immortal, you know me better than I know myself," he said. "So if you've brought me halfway across the country to a place where a terrible murder has been committed, does that mean I'm supposed to do something?" He paced the room, keyed up by the thought. His mind gradually quieted as he considered the trauma that St. Mary's would now undergo. Monasteries had been honed over their seventeen-hundred-year history to withstand a wide variety of storms such as low vocations, poor leadership, shortages of funds, disgruntled monks, and petty jealousies. But the murder of a nun in a community of monks wasn't the kind of storm the ancient monastic founders had in mind when they penned their early rules.

Add to this the fact that neither the media nor police had any experience separating what constituted normal from abnormal life in a monastery, and any monk would admit that a monastery could be as fragile as an orchid.

Father Fortis gazed up again at the crucifix for a moment before returning to the newspaper. *Yes,* he thought, *a murder with the spice of sex could destroy St. Mary's in a matter of weeks.*

On Saturday, after his meager evening meal of rice, refried beans, and Jell-O, Father Fortis retraced his steps of three days before to the abbot's office and knocked on the heavy door. A tired voice bade him enter.

Father Fortis stood in front of the desk and looked across to St. Mary's spiritual leader. Bread crumbs peppered the abbot's white beard.

"Abbot Timothy, I'm sorry to bother you again, but I'm wondering if I might have a brief word."

The abbot looked up from a ledger of figures and squinted through half glasses. For a moment, Father Fortis thought he would have to reintroduce himself.

"Father Nicholas, our Orthodox guest, isn't it? My, my, you are a big man, aren't you? You'd give Father Bernard a fight, I'd imagine. Oh, where are my manners? Yes, yes, please sit down." The abbot began to rise from his chair, but Father Fortis waved him to stay seated. Behind the abbot and through a massive window that looked out on a canyon wall, a hawk ascended on an updraft past the ancient cliffs of brown and red and pink.

Hoping the abbot hadn't heard about the incident in the library, Father

Fortis launched into his offer. "I believe I might be able to help you, Abbot Timothy."

The old man glanced down at the figures and then back up at his guest. A puzzled expression crossed his face. "Help me?"

A new realization crossed Father Fortis's mind. Given that he'd brought the nun to St. Mary's, the abbot would be the most distraught of anyone by her death. But of all the members of the community, he was the only one who had to balance his grief with worries about the financial difficulties that the tragedy would bring to the community.

"Abbot Timothy, I think we both know that the police, and certainly the press, will have difficulty understanding life at St. Mary's. They'll assume from the rules that all kinds of secrets are being hidden, just because our way of life is so foreign to them."

Abbot Timothy placed his glasses down on the papers and stared at Father Fortis. Knuckle joints tortured by arthritis bulged beneath a thin layer of flesh.

"I suppose that's true," he muttered in a tired voice. "Yes, of course it is, but I don't see how that can be avoided."

Father Fortis sat forward in the chair. "I believe there's something I can do to help. I'd like to invite a friend of mine to stay here at St. Mary's. Just for a few weeks, you understand."

The abbot rubbed his forehead for a moment. "Requests for guests must go to Father Cornelius. He's our guestmaster, you see. Now, if you'll excuse me—"

"No, Abbot Timothy, I don't think you understand. My friend is a policeman, a detective from Detroit."

The abbot seemed confused by the new information. "Why would a policeman come all the way from Detroit?"

"Actually, I have word this morning that he's arriving today on another case. He'll be in Santa Fe searching for a missing college student."

Abbot Timothy rose slowly from his chair. He moved behind it, and folding his arms, hid his hands up his sleeves as if to warm them. "Father Nicholas, I don't know if we've ever had a policeman here on retreat. At least not one from Detroit."

Brother Bartholomew was right, Father Fortis thought. The abbot was more than a bit eccentric. "No, Abbot Timothy, my friend wouldn't be at St. Mary's on retreat. If Lieutenant Worthy could simply stay here, he'd bring a set of trained eyes to your problem. And of course, I'd help him understand things here." Father Fortis sat ever further forward in his chair and pulled on his beard. "What I'm trying to say is that Lieutenant Worthy is an exceptionally talented man, very intuitive. And a highly decorated police officer, I might add. I'm honored to say that he's confided in me on several occasions."

Technically true, Father Fortis thought, *although it would be more truthful to admit that I'm the one who usually pumps Worthy for details of his cases.*

Abbot Timothy resumed his seat and rested his hands on the desk. His eyes wandered down to the figures before him, but after a moment he looked up. "But aren't you from Ohio, Father Nicholas? How do you know a policeman from Detroit? I'm sure I wouldn't know a policeman from Detroit if I were a monk in Ohio."

He has the attention span of a child, Father Fortis thought.

"Our acquaintance is a bit odd, Abbot Timothy," he began, speaking slowly. "You see, we got to know each other when a tragedy struck my monastery of St. Simeon several years ago."

"Oh? I guess I didn't hear about that," the abbot said.

Father Fortis sensed that if he went into the details of that case with Abbot Timothy, he might never get the conversation back on track. But Father Fortis had to admit that the case had certainly changed his own life. As the monastery's novice master, he had found himself working closely with Christopher Worthy, a homicide detective from Detroit, where the murdered novice had been from. Together, they had uncovered how and why a novice of St. Simeon's had died in an Ohio cornfield. Their friendship, now in its fourth year, had eventually led to Worthy telling him how his older daughter Allyson had run away, only to walk back into the house five months later, offering no explanation. Not at the time, and not since.

He paused for another moment as he remembered Worthy's confession that although he could solve complicated murders, he hadn't found the first clue about Allyson's whereabouts in those months.

Well, that's one on me, he mused. *Why didn't I think of that before? Worthy's here to find the missing girl because of Allyson.*

The abbot pulled down on an earlobe.

"Perhaps we should discuss this another time, Father Nicholas."

"Reverend Father, I know it's a bit hard to follow, but what I'm requesting boils down to this. Lieutenant Worthy could stay here at St. Mary's—with your permission, of course. Most of the time he'll be in Santa Fe, busy with his missing person's case, but when he is here, the two of us would do what we can … to help St. Mary's, I mean."

Abbot Timothy's jaw sagged, and for several moments he was silent. Father Fortis studied the furrows rising and falling across the abbot's brow and tried to predict the question forming in the old man's mind. He was prepared to deal with any concern about Worthy's discretion. He was also prepared to explain what he'd meant by saying that he'd assist Worthy. He was even ready to suggest how Worthy's presence at St. Mary's could be sensitively explained to the local police.

"I do have one concern, Father Nicholas."

"Yes, Reverend Father?"

The abbot leaned forward and trained a bloodshot eye on Father Fortis. "He'll pay?"

"What?"

"For room and food. Your friend can pay for them?" the abbot asked.

Father Fortis laughed nervously. "Of course, of course. I'm sure he'll be happy to pay."

"Hmm. He won't be shooting off his gun, will he? I won't allow target practice. You can understand that, can't you, Father?"

"Indeed I can," Father Fortis said. With a straight face he added, "I've known Lieutenant Worthy for several years, and I can vouch for the fact that he's very careful about target practice."

"Hmm." The abbot repositioned his glasses on his nose and returned to his figures.

Father Fortis sat silently, waiting for a decision. After a moment, he coughed. "So, it's all right if my friend stays here for a few weeks, Reverend Father?"

The abbot looked up again as if he'd forgotten he had a guest. "The policeman? Yes, yes, of course. I'm sure I said that. But remind him about the target practice."

✝

HAVING NEVER TRAVELED OUT WEST BEFORE, Lieutenant Christopher Worthy had bought a travel guide to New Mexico at the Detroit airport. In flight, he studied photos of desert landscapes, petroglyphs, snowy mountains with ski lodges, dried riverbeds, dancing Native Americans, Hispanic markets, and cowboys herding cattle. In short, he found the images confusing. To his Michigan eyes, New Mexico did not seem so much a state as a country, and a foreign country at that. As his plane descended into Albuquerque, he looked down with curiosity on a snowcapped mountain range that suddenly gave way to an arid valley peppered with buildings, homes, and roads that stretched to the western horizon.

Nothing looked like home to him, but then again it felt good to be away from Detroit and his assignment at the police academy.

Christopher Worthy now rested his foot on the baggage carousel, his arch still throbbing where the stewardess's cart had run over it. His new chukka boot was definitely scuffed.

He glanced around the Albuquerque airport with its cactus plants and wondered if anyone had been sent to meet him. He guessed not. Local law enforcement must have taken the fax about his arrival as an insult. Who wanted an outsider butting in on a simple missing person's case?

Other passengers from his flight mingled along the edge of the carousel. Some, judging by the logos on their jackets and their odd metal suitcases, were bowlers in from Detroit and Lansing for a tournament. In a row of chairs nearby sat a lone woman, absorbed in a *Women's Health* magazine. He lingered a few seconds on the shiny dark hair that framed the stunning face, then exhaled slowly.

As he watched the luggage roll like boulders down the chute, he remembered his vague promise to call Susan upon arrival. Funny what practices survived the end of a marriage. He looked around for the familiar bank of telephones, but saw only the dreaded cell phone variety plastered to the ears of five or six fellow travelers. How anyone could talk into one of those devices when others, perfect strangers, could overhear every word was a mystery to him. And those phones tended to ring at the oddest moments. At a funeral he'd attended a year ago, one pallbearer's phone chimed out, "Oh say, can you see" just as the casket was being lowered into the ground. Worthy had been the last in his precinct to relinquish his pager for the new technology, and after managing to lose three cell phones, his captain had let him return to the pager. His daughter, Allyson, called him a Luddite, which once she'd defined it struck him as a compliment. As long as he promised to keep his captain informed of developments, he was free to conduct his investigations without that dreaded beeping interrupting everything.

He lifted his two bags—neatly pressed shirts and trousers in the one and legal pads and gear in the other—and meandered toward the car rental desks. Ordinarily, he'd have followed procedure and rented the economy model, but the father of the missing girl from Detroit was the city's third largest car dealer. One of his last sights in Detroit had been Arrol VanBruskman's face smiling down at him from a billboard. "Are You Ready to Step Up to a Lexus?"

Maybe I am, Worthy thought. He passed the woman with the *Women's Health* and noticed her turquoise necklace, shaped like a string of teardrops. Out of the corner of his eye, he saw her close the magazine. Was she checking him out? He tried to imagine how he would look to a beautiful woman as he listened for trailing footsteps but heard none. She probably saw him as tall, given his height of six feet, two inches, and lanky. He hoped she couldn't see the gray strands that were still outnumbered by his fair, blond hair. *Perhaps I look a bit better than the bowlers from Michigan*, he thought, *but then again, why do I think she's looking for any man?*

He chose the line for Hertz, set down his bags, and was glancing around again for the telephones when he realized the dark-haired woman was standing directly behind him.

"Excuse me, but I saw you come in on the Detroit flight," she said, her eyes, nearly as dark as her hair, holding his gaze. "Are you Lieutenant Worthy?"

He reached into his sports coat, fumbling for his identification. The woman glanced at his offered picture, then again at his face.

"I guess you're you, all right," she said with a smile as she offered her hand. "I'm Lieutenant Lacey, Santa Fe Sheriff's Department."

"Nice of you to come. I was wondering if you were looking me over."

She dropped his hand.

"I meant it as a compliment, about your skills," he blurted out. "You could have been anyone, reading a magazine, waiting for your husband … anyone."

"Except you knew right away I'm a cop," she corrected him.

Excellent beginning, he chided himself.

Looking past his shoulder, the policewoman asked, "By the way, could there be a priest with a ponytail looking for you?"

Worthy turned to see Father Fortis, looking like a Sumo wrestler on a rampage, lumbering through the door, his beard flying in the breeze. The priest's huge smile gave way to a boisterous laugh as he lifted Worthy off the ground in a bear hug. Worthy detected the telltale smell of a spearmint on Father Fortis's breath. Others in line for a rental car turned to take in the odd sight before quickly looking away.

"How wonderful it is to see your pale, anemic face, Christopher," Father Fortis exclaimed, stepping back to look Worthy over. "You need some sun, my friend, and you've come to the right place."

Father Fortis removed his black cap and bowed toward the policewoman. "My apologies, my dear. You must be Susan. Christopher wrote me the good news, but that was months ago! How beautiful you are, my dear, and how marvelous that you're back together!"

He punched Worthy's arm playfully before taking a step toward the policewoman.

This is my fault, Worthy thought, his face reddening. Sent two months ago, his letter to the priest must have exaggerated his renewed hope for the marriage.

"I'm Lieutenant Lacey, Father," she said, offering her hand.

"Oh, dear, I'm so sorry. How very stupid of me. Yes, quite thoughtless," he said, pumping her hand.

After an awkward silence, Father Fortis grabbed Worthy's arm, pulling him out of line. "Well, here we all are. But what are you doing in this line, Christopher? You're staying with me at St. Mary's."

Worthy's brain snapped to attention. Four days before, in the middle of another long week with police academy recruits, he'd read about the murder of the nun at a remote monastery in New Mexico. When would he be given a shot at another homicide? His last case had improved his status in the department, not to mention returning him to the media limelight. That moment of favor, however, brought an immediate reassignment to the academy, as if the department were protecting him from another setback.

Then, the day before yesterday, Worthy had been handed a missing person's case, a rich girl from Detroit who'd walked away from her college spring break trip in New Mexico. Instantly, the memory of the nun's murder had returned. But it wasn't until he'd found Father Fortis's last letter, informing him of the sabbatical at a Trappist monastery in New Mexico, that he wondered if his friend could be staying at *that* monastery.

A quick call to Father Fortis's home community in Ohio had confirmed it. Nick, as Worthy had been invited to call him, had indeed gone to St. Mary of the Snows and arrived a few days before the nun's body was discovered. It would be the type of coincidence that Father Fortis would call providential.

"You say you want him to stay at St. Mary's? Why's that?" the policewoman asked.

Worthy suppressed a smile as Father Fortis pulled out a handkerchief and wiped his brow.

"My dear, you must think I never make sense," the priest stammered. "Would you be so kind as to remind me of your name?"

"Lieutenant Lacey from the sheriff's department, Father," she replied.

"Yes, yes, that's right. Forgive me, Lieutenant Lacey, but it's really quite simple. When I received the message that Christopher would be in Santa Fe on a case, I gave in to a very selfish thought. You see, we monks have few opportunities to visit with close friends. I couldn't see how it would hamper his work if he stayed with us. He'd have use of one of the monastery's vehicles, and I promise that we go to bed very early. Oh, and did I mention, St. Mary's is near Santa Fe, just out by Truchas?"

"I know where St. Mary's is, Father. It's nearly forty miles from Santa Fe, but since you drove down from there you already know that."

"Is it really that far, my dear? My, my."

The policewoman gave Father Fortis a withering look. "What surprises me is St. Mary's permitting guests right now, especially a homicide detective from Detroit."

Father Fortis shook his head vigorously. "No, no, please don't connect my offer with the terrible tragedy. The last thing the police need is a couple of meddling outsiders."

With the words "meddling outsiders," Worthy noticed a slight twitch at the corner of the policewoman's mouth. Yes, it was just as he had protested to his captain back in Detroit. *How would we feel if a detective from Santa Fe barged in on one of our cases?*

The policewoman seemed to ponder Father Fortis's explanation, but gave no indication that she was convinced. She reached into her shoulder bag for a folder and handed it to Worthy. "I work Child Protection, Lieutenant, which is why I was assigned this case. The children I look for are usually a lot younger, but Ellie VanBruskman is still technically underage. What's in there," she said, nodding toward the folder, "should bring you up to speed on everything we know so far."

She started toward the exit before looking back over her shoulder. "I assume we'll see you in the morning after your restful night at St. Mary's?"

"I'll be there by nine," Worthy replied. "I'd like to meet your boss, if that's possible. I feel a need to explain why I'm here."

The policewoman faced him. "I can't promise that everyone's going to welcome you with open arms, Lieutenant, but Sheriff Cortini is a decent man. Turn around, will you?"

Puzzled, Worthy did so. Something flat pressed against his back, then a sharp point slowly etched down his spine before traversing several times from shoulder to shoulder. As the policewoman continued to draw what Worthy took to be a map, he felt the hair on the back of his neck stand up. It had been a long time since a woman had touched him.

"What about you?" he asked boldly. "Is my being here a problem for you? I mean, it's really your case."

The pen stopped its movement. "We were told the girl could be sick. Is that true?" she asked.

Worthy noted that she'd evaded his question. "Is Ellie VanBruskman really sick? Well, we know she was diagnosed about two years ago as bipolar, but we also know she likes to squirrel away her pills. So it's hard to say if she's in serious trouble or laughing at us from some motel in Vegas."

The pressure on his back lifted, and Worthy faced the policewoman.

"Being a mother myself, I tend to assume the worst, Lieutenant," she said. "Let's say this girl is sicker than either of us can imagine. That means we have to find her as soon as possible, and who gets the credit doesn't really matter, does it?"

She handed Worthy the map, nodded toward Father Fortis, and walked out the door. Her suit looked less professional from the back, the skirt stretched tight across her narrow hips as she hurried across to the parking lot. Her hair swayed from shoulder to shoulder, her earrings sparkling in the late-afternoon sun. Just before disappearing behind a concrete pillar on the other side of the road, she glanced back and caught Worthy's eye.

He blushed, as he had since grade school when the cute girl would make that last check to see if the boys were watching, and so he was surprised by the look on her face. Was it suspicion, or something more?

He turned back toward his bags, saw the bank of telephones to his left, and remembered his promise to Susan. *Tomorrow*, he thought; *tomorrow's good enough.*

He felt Father Fortis's huge hand slap his shoulder. "The Jeep is parked outside, my friend. What do you say we take a little detour and see where the body was found?"

CHAPTER THREE

---◆---

THE JEEP RUMBLED ALONG HIGHWAY 503, rising from the Rio Grande valley and leaving the noise of the freeway behind. Mountains, many with snow still on them in early June, loomed ahead above the piñon forests.

At the top of a rise, a collection of weather-beaten buildings could be seen.

"That's Truchas," Father Fortis explained. "Not much of a town. Little more than a couple bars and an old church, really."

He thought of his own introduction to Truchas just days before. He'd been on his way into the general store, trying to buy dental floss and mints, when a derelict grabbed him by the pectoral cross hanging from his neck.

"You a priest?" he muttered.

Father Fortis freed the cross from the derelict's grip. The woven design of a roadrunner on the front of the man's serape was covered with greasy stains. "Yes, my son. Can I help you in any way?"

The derelict's eyes had danced as he inspected Father Fortis's ponytail and long flowing robes before returning to the enamel cross. "You say you're a father. Not *my* father," he said, as he spat at Father Fortis's feet before crossing the street.

Father Fortis shook off the memory and took his foot off the accelerator to let the Jeep coast. "Get ready for a bumpy ride."

He turned off the asphalt onto a deeply rutted dirt road that worked its way toward the piñon trees above. Father Fortis fought to keep the Jeep's narrow wheelbase from falling into the ruts from other vehicles—those of food suppliers, guests, and more recently, police vans.

"I suppose you've already taken a look around the place," Worthy said.

"I've been here less than a week, Christopher. So, no, I haven't."

The Jeep jogged left at a fork in the road. "But you seem to know where you're headed, Nick."

Father Fortis offered a sly smile. "I never said I hadn't studied maps of the grounds. And by the way, when we get to St. Mary's, say nothing about our little trip out here, okay?"

"Understood. But they do know I'm a cop, don't they?"

"Of course. Sometimes the best disguise is the truth. And the truth is that you're in New Mexico to find a missing college girl."

"And even if they suspect otherwise, you're left to poke around while doing your research. How's the sabbatical going, by the way?"

Father Fortis sighed heavily as he swerved to avoid a boulder in the road. "I can't say I've gotten very far. My research partner, Father Linus, is a bit of an old kook. Our research time together means he's allowed to talk freely, still a bit of a rarity for Trappist monks. So he talked nonstop at our first meeting this morning. Unfortunately, our project never came up."

"You came out here to work on some sort of music, as I remember."

"We're working on very old music called Roman chant. Ecumenically significant, you might say, given that the chant shows eastern Christian influence. Father Linus wrote the definitive monograph, but that was decades ago. To be honest, I think he misrepresented matters when we first communicated. You see, he assured me that he was very keen on my particular theory on the problem. He wrote that he found my Orthodox ideas a fresh new angle. I'm sure they were fresh. I don't think he's thought about his research in years."

Coming to an unmarked crossroads, Father Fortis slowed, looking left before turning right onto an even rockier road. At the bottom of a hill, he slowed the Jeep to a crawl before edging through a shallow creek. On the other side, the Jeep bounced along as if on a washboard while Father Fortis craned his neck to follow the tire prints ahead.

"How many ways are there out to the place?" Worthy shouted over the whining motor.

"The retreat house? I saw only the one on the map. I can't see how anyone could make their way cross-country, can you?"

"No. That means that unless the killer hiked in or came by horseback, he probably used this same road. Did they find any prints at the place?"

Father Fortis shifted into low gear to negotiate a steep rise, propelling rocks, like bullets, off to the side. They were in the thick piñon trees now, and he wondered how even a horse could pass anywhere but on the road. "I've heard nothing about prints, but the police have been tight-lipped. I don't think even the abbot knows exactly what they've found."

The vehicle hit a massive hole, throwing the two men to the right. The

Jeep, its transmission whining, lurched out of the pit and climbed toward the next rise.

"Have you read anything about the nun's murder?" Father Fortis asked.

"A bit. Her body was mutilated, right?"

"Yes, indeed, it was. I'll show you some photos the abbot gave me. I have to say they're pretty grisly. You see, she was stabbed repeatedly. First in her back, and then, from what I was told, she was stabbed in the heart."

"Her heart? Whoa! And she wasn't sexually assaulted?"

"No, her underclothing was undisturbed. It seems to be a very odd and a very sad murder."

"They always are, Nick."

Just when Father Fortis was sure that the side trip had been a mistake, the Jeep rounded a final set of rocks, standing like sentinels, and faced a squat adobe building. A one-story L-shaped structure, with broken log ends protruding from the top, the retreat house made no more sense to the priest now than it had in the photos. It looked more like an old garage from the forties, its small windows set too high on the walls and too opaque to let in much light. There was nothing of the modern lines of St. Mary's sanctuary here.

Father Fortis brought the Jeep to a full stop. Both men sat for a moment in silence as they studied the odd building before them.

Worthy turned around in his seat and drew a flashlight from his suitcase. "Well, as long as we're here, I suppose it won't hurt to take a look around."

Exiting the Jeep, the two men passed under the yellow tape cordoning off the building. With a handkerchief, Worthy pushed against the building's wooden door, but it didn't open.

"See if there's a screwdriver in the Jeep, will you, Nick?"

Father Fortis returned to the vehicle and rummaged through a toolbox.

"Here's one," he called to Worthy as he jogged back.

"I think the lock is only an old latch on the inside." Worthy pushed against the door again, creating a slight opening. With one upward thrust of the screwdriver, he sprung the primitive lock.

Instead of following Worthy into the gloomy retreat house, Father Fortis paused for a moment to study a statue of the Blessed Virgin, arms outstretched, that stood guard in the dirt yard. From the canyon below, darkness rose like mist. He crossed himself and said a brief prayer for the woman who'd died inside. From the ghastly photos, he recalled the look of bewilderment on Sister Anna's face. What words had she prayed as she looked into her killer's eyes? Did she know that face?

He tried to recall the faces of the twenty-nine professed monks of St. Mary's, plus the three younger novices and the one old hermit. Could one of them have come out to this remote retreat house, a good twelve miles from the monastery itself, without being missed? Or had the killer been someone from outside, perhaps a guest who'd visited the monastery over the past two months? If so, how would a guest know of this place?

As if he'd been listening in on his thoughts, Worthy called out from inside the building, "A nun living with a bunch of monks is a bit odd, isn't it?"

Father Fortis entered the door and walked down a hallway toward Worthy's flashlight beam. "I don't know much more than what was in the paper. About two months ago, Sister Anna returned with the abbot from his pastoral visit to one of St. Mary's foundations."

"What's a foundation?"

"In this case, it's a convent, a daughter house in Oklahoma under the spiritual care of Abbot Timothy. What Father Linus told me was that when Sister Anna arrived at St. Mary's, she could barely walk and only spoke in whispers. Everyone thought she was sick."

Something metal hit the floor in the room in front of him, causing Father Fortis to jump.

"Sorry, Nick. Just an old shovel. I'm over here."

Father Fortis moved into a second room and found Worthy aiming the flashlight around the perimeter of the room. The beam illuminated the crease where the wall met the floor, but aside from a small wagon filled with potted plants, the room seemed bare.

"Susan sends her greetings, by the way," Worthy said. "Actually, she asked me to give you a hug, but don't hold your breath."

"It would be nice to finally meet her someday. That way I won't confuse her with policewomen. But I hope she's well. More importantly, how is Allyson?"

"I'm not sure what I can tell you about Allyson," Worthy replied. "I solve mysteries for a living, but that daughter of mine is unsolvable. I guess I'm too close to things. And Susan can't take her eyes off her when I'm around. I guess she's afraid I'm going to say something, and Allyson is going to bolt for the door again."

"But that's how you got this missing-person's case, right?"

Worthy grunted an assent.

"That's a bit of a change for you," Father Fortis added.

Worthy gave a sharp laugh. "You mean it's beneath me, don't you? The truth is that I managed somehow to solve a high-profile case four months ago and got my name back in the paper. Now I'm a departmental trophy, Nick, something that's safer if kept on the shelf. They're afraid I'll dent the shiny finish if I'm given another real case. Hello, what's this?" Worthy's flashlight beam had moved to the center of the room to two dark stains, eight feet apart.

"Your nun must have bled to death right here, but I'm guessing from this trail that she was stabbed over there." He aimed the beam at a smaller spot near an empty altar. "Now, was there a struggle, or was she dragged unconscious to where I'm standing?"

Father Fortis bent down and looked at the stains, then at the thin maroon line leading back to the center of the room. "So much blood. It's hard to believe a frail body could hold so much."

"That's what you get when you puncture the heart."

Father Fortis rose to his feet, only to feel a wave of nausea rise as well. "Christopher, I'm feeling a little woozy."

"Sorry, Nick. I assumed you'd seen all this in the photos. Kneel down and put your head between your knees."

Father Fortis obeyed, but it took a few moments for his head to stop spinning. "Those were just photos, Christopher. This is a bit too real." He turned so that he couldn't see the stains and took several deep breaths.

"When you can, tell me what you remember from the photos, Nick. Besides the body, what else was here when the police first arrived?"

Careful to stay clear of the stains, Father Fortis picked up Worthy's flashlight, shining the beam from one wall to the other. In a recessed alcove were white planks and old shelves with books stacked haphazardly.

"I think the shelves and books are the same in the photos. There were also bits of paper, like confetti, strewn all over the floor. The police must have all that."

"And the body, what did she look like?"

Father Fortis closed his eyes, trying to recall the photos, but all he could think about was the young woman dying in this very spot, with her last breath crying out, asking "why" of her killer, or perhaps of God. He'd been told at the monastery that Sister Anna had been on retreat to pray for guidance, to try to discern the path ahead. Instead, her path had ended in this pool of blood.

"Sorry, Christopher, I don't seem to remember the details. Can't this wait until you see the photos in my room?"

"No, Nick, it can't. I don't mean to be a jerk about it, but we're here now, and who knows if we'll ever be back? Just tell me anything that comes to mind. God knows, the local guys purged this place."

Father Fortis took another deep breath. "As I said, there was confetti everywhere, even on her. Wait a minute," he added, looking up. "I think she was also holding something in one of her hands."

Worthy smiled. "Good, good, Nick. What was it?"

"I'm not sure. It could have been another piece of paper—only it wasn't shredded."

"Huh. It would be nice to know what that was."

Father Fortis felt another wave of vertigo and closed his eyes again until the spinning stopped.

Worthy took the flashlight back and bent down to inspect a small area to the left of the larger stains. "Nick, look at this."

Father Fortis looked down. "I don't see anything."

"I wonder if the local guys caught this. There's a single nick in the floor, and it's fresh. See how much cleaner the wood is in the cavity?"

"Her fingernails, maybe?" Father Fortis asked.

"Not likely. Too deep. No, a very sharp knife was stuck in the floor right here."

"The weapon?"

"Maybe, but why isn't there any blood in the hole?" Worthy inserted the edge of the screwdriver in the floor wound.

"If there's no blood, wouldn't that mean that the killer stuck the knife in the floor before he stabbed her?"

"Maybe," Worthy said. "But how about afterwards? Didn't you say she was stabbed in the back, then in her heart?"

"That's right."

"Okay, so what about this? The killer stabbed her in the back and then wiped the knife blade clean before sticking it right here in the floor."

"But why?" Father Fortis asked. The new clue had banished his lightheadedness.

"I think he sat right about where you are, Nick, over her dead body, and thought about what he wanted to do next."

"Before he stabbed her in the heart?" Father Fortis asked.

"Yes. I think so. And that means the wounds to the heart were an afterthought. So what does that tell us? That's something that would be interesting to find out. Interesting, that is, if I weren't here on another case."

Father Fortis rose and tested his legs. He looked up at the tiny windows and realized that the sun had set. "Time to go, my friend, if we don't want to drive off that road in the dark."

Worthy grunted noncommittally. He swung the beam around the room again before rising.

Outside, Worthy reset the primitive lock with a flick of the screwdriver. The two stood for a moment and looked up at the first stars blinking overhead.

"This place is a taste of meat to a starving guy, Nick. And oh, what a taste it is. I should be working a case like this, not tracking down a college girl off on a lark. With my luck, we'll find her tomorrow, and by the end of the week I'll be back doing jail time at the academy."

The two walked slowly toward the Jeep. Father Fortis rested his hand on his friend's shoulder. "Allow me a pious reflection, Christopher. Consider for a moment the two of us—a homicide detective and an overly curious monk from the Midwest. And where do we both find ourselves? In New Mexico, less than a week after a brutal murder. Trust me on this one, my friend. We're here for a reason."

Chapter Four

————— ◆ —————

THE FOLLOWING MONDAY MORNING, WORTHY PULLED into the sheriff's department parking lot. He reread the note at the bottom of Sera Lacey's map. "Don't expect me until after 9:00. I have to drop my son off at school."

He stepped out of the Jeep and gazed up at the brilliant blue sky. Detroit would kill for a day like this. And the scenery .... Color surrounded him, from the snowcapped mountains reaching up into the clear air to the green forests that surrendered at the lower elevation to the desert floor.

Inside the one-story building, Worthy waited patiently as the receptionist handled a call in a mix of English and Spanish. Between callers, she responded to Worthy's request by pointing down a sunny hallway. He found the door for the Child Protection team and read the name, Lieutenant Sera Lacey, stenciled below it.

S-e-r-a? He thought again of the policewoman's flashing black hair and wondered about the name. Was it Hispanic or Native American? A silhouette appeared behind the frosted glass, and suddenly the door swung open to reveal the striking woman of yesterday.

Smiling, she ushered him in to where a short, muscular, middle-aged man was rising stiffly from a chair. With a strong grip, Sheriff Cortini introduced himself. He sported a flattop military style, but his shirt was open. On his feet were cowboy boots tipped with polished silver. Worthy sat down, the knot of his tie pulling on his neck.

"Welcome to Santa Fe, Lieutenant. First time out here?"

"It's my first time out west, period," Worthy replied.

Sheriff Cortini leaned back in his chair. "Now, my family is from Chicago, originally. My dad was stationed out here after the war, and then they stayed. That makes me still a newcomer."

It was all easy talk, but Worthy could feel Cortini sizing him up.

"Sera tells me you're staying out at St. Mary's. Seems you got a friend out there."

Worthy nodded. "A monk from Ohio. He's out there on what they call a sabbatical."

"Ah, an academic. My momma always told me I should be a teacher. Lately around here, I think I should've listened. I've never been up to St. Mary's myself, but I hear it's beautiful." The sheriff took a moment to rub the knee of a trouser leg. "Lots of commotion up there right now. Could be interesting, don't you think?"

Worthy paused, weighing his words. "Other than Sunday services yesterday morning, it's been pretty quiet up there. No one knocked on my door to turn himself in."

Cortini laughed easily. "But you are a homicide detective, right?"

And based on this interrogation, so are you, Worthy thought.

"What I am is a cop who's been poorly assigned," Worthy replied. "The father of our missing girl happens to be a big shot in Detroit, so he threw his weight around. And here I am."

The sheriff eyed him for a moment before nodding. "Parents go pretty nuts when a kid runs off. I don't care how old she is. Which brings us to your fax, Lieutenant. We're not quite sure how this Victor Martinez ties in."

"Actually, I'm not sure he does. The girl's mother caught me just as I was leaving for the airport, all excited because she'd remembered that this Victor Martinez lives out here."

Sera leaned forward in her chair. "Your fax said Victor and the VanBruskman girl were students together in Detroit. Does the mother think they were more than that?"

Worthy shrugged. "Lovers? I don't know. She didn't say."

"Well, that's the first that we heard about Victor Martinez. Do you believe the mother, Lieutenant?" Cortini added.

It was both a perceptive question and one that invited Worthy to offer an opinion. *This guy is good*, he thought.

"Her story sounded a bit convenient, that's all," Worthy replied. "The father hands me a credit card, and my captain tells me to take the first plane I can get. I'm rushed off before I can even go through the girl's room, and then at the last minute the mother waltzes into my office and hands me this name."

Worthy wondered if he sounded like a whiner. "I don't do missing persons, so maybe I'm wrong, but shouldn't we be looking into why she might have run away in the first place?"

Sera Lacey answered. "So when the mother told you her daughter was running toward this Victor Martinez, you wondered the opposite, right?"

"Exactly," he said. "I want to know is if she's running from something in Detroit."

Cortini rose and walked to the window. "That means Victor Martinez might be a false lead. Yet you're here in Santa Fe, not in Detroit." He looked over in Sera's direction. "Where should he begin?"

"I think Chimayó," Sera offered. "It's the last place the group visited. Besides, one of the other students said he saw Ellie looking out the door a couple times."

"And, according to the folder, she vanished the next morning," Worthy added. "So we start at this Chimayó place. Are you coming along?" he asked the policewoman.

Sera Lacey started to answer when the phone rang. Excusing herself, she turned away from the two men.

Sheriff Cortini leaned against the wall. "Sera interviewed the professor and the other college students before they flew back. And she's checked all the hospitals and clinics to see if the girl could have shown up there under another name. But nothing. Then, let me see. Yes, she called all the other places the group visited."

Worthy knew all this from the folder, but recognized the message of support. His own captain in Detroit could learn a lesson or two from this guy.

Cortini shook his head slowly. "Hell, I saw that professor. He was one sorry sight, let me tell you. A real young guy. He could have been a college kid himself. I suppose he's in a shitload of trouble. Maybe I should be glad I didn't become a teacher. But anyway, you might pick up something else out at Chimayó."

Sheriff Cortini pushed himself from the wall and approached Worthy. "It was good to meet you, Lieutenant. You probably want to get back to your family, so let's all hope we find the girl soon."

Worthy rose to shake the captain's hand. "What is this Chimayó—an Indian site, some museum?"

"Well, now, that's an interesting question. Chimayó is a bit of a lot of things. It's a small town, even by our standards, but it also has a very unusual church," the sheriff said. "People react to it in all sorts of ways."

Sera Lacey hung up the phone and rose to her feet. "Sorry. My son forgot his lunch. I caught a bit of what you were talking about. I'd say Chimayó is whatever people allow it to be. For some, it's a freak show. For pilgrims, it's a place of healing." Worthy caught the challenge in her voice as she added, "You'll have to decide for yourself, Lieutenant."

The sheriff raised his hands in mock surrender. "Like I said, Chimayó is controversial. Me, I'm just an outsider."

Which means the policewoman isn't, Worthy thought. Cortini and Sera waited, as if it were Worthy's turn to choose a side. Cops had a habit of disagreeing over the smallest matters, from advancement test questions to personal weapons preference, but an old church?

He looked out the window at a car-shaped cloud disappearing over a mountain crest.

"All I care about is what Ellie VanBruskman made of the place," he said. "By the way, what did you decide about coming with me?"

The woman's eyes fell to her desk. "Why don't we do this, Lieutenant? You check out Chimayó, and I'll run out to Acomita, where the Martinez boy has some family. If the two kids are lovers, someone has probably seen them together. Families are pretty tight out here."

Worthy left the office with the sheriff. He had a good feeling about this man, that he was the type of superior who said what he was thinking, someone not threatened by his arrival. But with Sera Lacey, he felt like he'd just failed a test.

✝

A HAND-PAINTED SIGN GREETED WORTHY AND FATHER Fortis as they pulled into the parking lot of El Sanctuario de Chimayó. "Lock Vehicles. Do Not Leave Valuables in Sight." *Pretty slim pickings today*, Father Fortis thought as he glanced over at the only other vehicle, a rusted VW bus with Colorado plates.

"This isn't exactly what I expected," Father Fortis said as he peered up at the adobe church with its corrugated roof and cramped courtyard. El Sanctuario had been described in a brochure at the monastery as the "Lourdes of North America," and so he'd anticipated something more along the lines of the stunning Saint Francis Cathedral in downtown Santa Fe. It was hard to imagine this small church holding more than eighty to ninety people, yet Father Fortis knew from the brochure that pilgrims from as far away as Guatemala made the journey during Holy Week, when crowds swelled into the thousands.

"The church is in better shape than the town," Worthy added, nodding toward the adobe houses and dusty streets.

"I'm not so sure," Father Fortis disagreed. In Greece, even the smallest and poorest villages basked in the glow of a whitewashed church set on the highest point. The town of Chimayó, however, with its shacks and trailers, seemed intent on dragging the famous church down into the dirt—miraculous dirt though it might be.

It had been a desire to escape from the monastery, as much as his own curiosity, that had prompted Father Fortis to accompany Worthy to Chimayó. Only that morning he'd found a handwritten note in his mail slot, reading, "You are not wanted here. You are not needed here."

What troubled him the most was not the sentiment. Much as at his own St. Simeon's, there were always hardliners who opposed ecumenism. It had only been since 1964 that the Orthodox and Catholic churches had dropped their long-standing anathemas against each other. Fifty years was a long time for most institutions, but not for the church. What bothered him about the note was the knowledge that whoever wrote it had to know of his conversation with Abbot Timothy. He'd wanted to keep his eyes open around St. Mary's. But now, he realized, someone had an eye on him.

The two men entered the church through its two carved doors and immediately found themselves crammed into a small anteroom. Overcome with a wave of claustrophobia, Father Fortis pushed against a smaller, inner door, and the two entered a dim, windowless room.

Even before his eyes adjusted to the gloom, Father Fortis felt the cold of the stone floor. Then, as if emerging from a fog, his eyes found the ornately carved altar at the front. Tall spines of red and pink, like barber poles, framed compartments from where saints peeked out. In the altar's center, in a small opening, a slumped Christ, bathed in his own blood, hung suspended in death. Above the crucifix was a painting, unknown and puzzling to Father Fortis, portraying two forearms crossing each other, both hands bearing bleeding nail wounds.

Worthy was gazing at other statues on the side wall.

"A penny for your thoughts, my friend," Father Fortis whispered.

"Not with those folks able to hear."

The priest peered forward and realized his friend was right. Three people, a couple and a nun, were talking quietly by the side of the front altar. Anticipating a wait, Father Fortis ducked into the back row of benches, knelt, and crossed himself.

The strange note under his door clouded his thoughts, and he prayed fitfully, his words like heavy boulders refusing to budge. In the middle of his petitions, he caught a bit of the nun's presentation from the front. "El Sanctuario was built in 1810, although it had been a sacred site for the Indians ...."

He shifted his knees on the cold floor and started his prayer again. But as before, his intentions were trumped by voices, this time from the young woman. "Sister, we're not Catholics and don't know how this works."

Father Fortis peeked toward the altar, where the silent member of the three, a man with shoulder-length hair dangling over his denim jacket, had encircled the taller woman's waist with an arm. The woman leaned on him, as if she might faint.

Father Fortis glanced at Worthy, who was sitting a few seats down the row and seemed to be inspecting the carved ceiling. What brought people to places like this was desperation, something too close to superstition for a man with Worthy's stance on faith.

Up at the front, the nun edged toward a side door, stammering a bit as she explained that the miracles of Chimayó, as at any holy place, were rare and followed no set rules. The couple, however, remained planted by the altar.

"There was this one crippled child, a real wailer, about three weeks ago," the nun said, speaking from a tiny doorframe. "His family couldn't budge him from this room in here, which is where the blessed dirt is. My Spanish isn't great, but I could tell he was begging Jesus and Our Lady to heal him."

"Go on, Sister," the woman pleaded breathlessly.

"Nobody was with the boy at the time, but apparently he came out crying and threw himself down in front of the altar."

Worthy cleared his throat before rising from the pew. He walked toward a table in the back that was stacked with books.

"I'm not sure we understand, ma'am," the man said.

"What I'm saying is that the boy walked into this room on crutches, but came out without them."

The woman hurried to the door and peeked into the room, as if the boy were still in there. Father Fortis hoped Worthy wasn't listening.

But the nun's next comment surprised the priest. "I must tell you that the boy's crutches disappeared the next day."

The nun paused, but the couple stood motionless before her. "My dears, what I'm trying to say is that nobody can predict what happens here. Yes, some people are healed, and only God knows why. The reality is that most people experience nothing in terms of physical healing or maybe just a temporary remission—"

"But you said the boy ran to the altar!" the woman protested, grabbing the nun's arm as if to save them both from falling over a cliff. The nun patted the woman's hand, edging the couple through the doorway.

Father Fortis and Worthy approached the altar, even as the nun's voice echoed from the side room.

"You have to believe me," she said. "I have absolutely nothing to do with what happens here. It's your faith that's important, not me." The couple didn't respond, and the nun added curtly, "Please don't feel that you have to take so much of the dirt."

Father Fortis studied the altar before him, noting the votive tokens, the tin and brass arms, legs, and hearts that littered the floor.

"When I think of all the people who come here, my friend, and why they come, I can't help but feel we're standing in a very sad place. A very sad place, indeed," he whispered.

Worthy didn't respond.

"Perhaps the church is a bit overdone. Yes, I admit that," Father Fortis continued, sensing Worthy's objections. "But when I look at these little trinkets and all the people needing a miracle, I see how close hope is to despair. Yes, sometimes they are frighteningly close."

Again, Worthy said nothing.

The nun popped her head out of the side room and rolled her eyes at Father Fortis. Worthy broke his silence by introducing himself and Father Fortis and explaining their mission. The nun seemed disappointed as she walked toward the front bench and sat down wearily.

"As I told the policewoman on the phone, you're asking about a day during Lent. Good Lord, it's wall to wall in here from February to April. All I remember from those days is the crowds waiting outside and the smell of the people jammed into this old place. It gets pretty ripe." The nun's nose twitched at the memory.

Worthy reached into the folder and drew out Ellie VanBruskman's picture. "Do you remember this girl?"

The nun took the photo and shook her head. "No. Sorry. I can only imagine how worried her parents must be."

"She's not exactly a child, Sister."

"Lieutenant, have you ever run away and not known where you're headed?"

Worthy looked away for a moment before answering. "I noticed the guest books on the back table. Do many visitors write in them?"

"Some pilgrims do, but most don't take the time," the nun replied. "I already looked through them after the policewoman called, if that's what you're getting at. I didn't find anything out of the ordinary."

"Fine, but can I look at the pages for April eighth?" Worthy asked.

The nun moved briskly to the back table, returning with a large blue, cloth-covered scrapbook. Sitting down and opening the book on her lap, she began humming off key, turning pages until stopping at one.

"Here it is."

As Worthy sat down on the other side of the nun and the three scanned the page, Father Fortis noticed that most of the entries were in Spanish. Only at the bottom did he see the name of a Professor Wormley from Allgemein College. Next to the name was the comment, "Thank you. My students found El Sanctuario provocative."

Below were two other comments in English, both apparently from students in the group. Each suggested that their professor tended toward overstatement. The first, "This place is friggin' cold" was followed by "I'm still an atheist."

"I guess I missed those," the nun confessed. "Is one of those from your missing girl?"

"It's hard to say," Worthy replied. The policeman studied the entries and then turned to the next page, which Father Fortis saw was again filled with Hispanic names. Turning a third page, Worthy's finger rested on a penciled, unsigned entry at the very top. From where he sat, Father Fortis could just make out childish loops and pencil smudges.

"I wonder ..." Worthy began.

"But that's from much later in the day," the nun insisted. "Look at all the names in between."

"Unless she accidentally turned two pages instead of one," Worthy replied.

"What does it say, Christopher?" Father Fortis asked.

Worthy angled the book to catch the meager light from the altar and showed the words to the priest. "I like the brite colors and holey picturs. Some day, I maybe come back."

"That's not from a college student!" the nun declared.

"Maybe from this one," Worthy replied.

"But even if she did write it, what does it tell you?" Father Fortis asked.

"I'm not sure."

Father Fortis cleared his throat. "May I have a look?"

The book ended up like a Bible in Father Fortis's lap. He gazed down at the childish script, recalling from yesterday's drive to the monastery Worthy's uncertainty about the girl's true medical condition. If the VanBruskman girl had indeed written this message, did it hint at genuine emotional limitations or trickery? He began a silent prayer for the girl's recovery and instinctively rubbed the loops of her handwriting with his forefinger.

His hand stopped. "Unless I'm wrong, something else was written beneath this." He returned the book to Worthy, watching intently as his friend traced the childish words with his forefinger.

"Nick, I think you're right. Something's been erased, then written over." He angled the book up again toward the light from the altar. "And, unless I'm mistaken, I think I can read the name Victor."

CHAPTER FIVE

———— ✦ ————

WORTHY GLANCED TOWARD THE BACK OF the church where the door was swinging gently in the afternoon breeze. In a matter of minutes they'd be out of this stuffy hole and on their way. For the life of him, he couldn't understand why Sera Lacey had made such a big deal of the place, or why Father Fortis seemed so intent on defending it. Unlike St. Mary of the Snows, whose architecture had impressed him with its austerity and subtlety, the famous Church of Chimayó seemed like a carnival warehouse.

But as he had tried to explain that morning at the sheriff's station, all that mattered was what Ellie VanBruskman had made of the place. Perhaps what was written beneath the childish words in the book would provide an answer to that question. But then again, the skeptical nun might be right. There was no guarantee that the comment was from the missing girl, and even if it were, the underlying words might be just as pointless.

"Where are you going with that book, Lieutenant?" the nun asked as he started for the door.

"I'm sorry, I thought you knew that I'd need to take it back for processing."

The nun frowned. "If you must, you must, I suppose. It's just that people like to read about the miracles."

Promising the book's return within a day or two, he made a second attempt for the door.

The nun, however, still had Father Fortis pinned down in the front row. "The policewoman said the girl might be ill. Can you tell me a bit more? We'd like to pray for her, you see."

Father Fortis patted her arm. "Yes, of course, my dear." He looked up at

Worthy, a twinkle in his eye. "Worthy, you can share that with sister, can't you?"

Worthy glared at his friend, but complied. "She's been diagnosed with something called bipolar disorder, which is a form of—"

"Of depression," the nun finished. "That happens to be one of Chimayó's specialties, along with paralysis of the legs." She shrugged toward Father Fortis. "Don't ask me to explain how those two connect."

Worthy motioned toward the door, but the nun intercepted the message.

"Father can't leave without seeing our main attraction," she commanded, her face aglow. "You, too, Lieutenant. Your missing student must have taken some of the dirt."

The priest grinned mischievously before ducking his huge frame through the portal.

Reluctantly, Worthy followed, passing into what could have been a theater prop room. Crutches and braces hung from the rafters above, while on the walls saccharine prints of Jesus and the Virgin Mary stared out, their hearts visible and rosy. Rosaries hung like clumps of seaweed from other framed pictures, these of saints, their eyes gazing dreamily toward heaven.

To the right, in an even smaller and darker room, Worthy spotted the couple, arm in arm, huddling over something on the floor. Father Fortis walked to the far wall, bent down to kiss an icon of the Madonna and Child before crossing himself. Worthy heard the nun's tremulous sigh and thought if his friend wasn't careful he'd have her swooning at his feet.

He checked his watch. If they could break free in fifteen minutes, there would be enough time to drop Father Fortis off at the monastery and still get to the lab before it closed. He paused in front of a glass case set in the center of the room and peered in at a kewpie doll bedecked in purple velvet. The floor of the case was littered with the tiny tokens he'd seen by the altar, some in the shape of cars, candles, crosses, as well as miniature arms and legs. Fighting an urge to smile, he stooped to study handwritten notes that had been slid through the case's small opening. One, in English, prayed for a happy marriage, another for a son in prison.

"Those are milagros," the nun whispered, standing close to him. She explained that each represented a request for healing or thanksgiving for a blessing received.

Oh great, Worthy thought, detecting the note of zeal in the nun's voice. *Another person trying to save my soul.*

The nun continued in an animated whisper, "For example, that little leg could mean someone has had an operation, but it could also symbolize something like the 'leg' of a journey. Quite ingenious, don't you think?"

"I suppose you sell these trinkets?"

The nun reared up as if struck. "Absolutely not. The pilgrims bring them or buy them in town, but not here."

From the innermost room, the woman, her voice shaky with emotion, called out. "Sister, would you please come in here?"

As the nun obeyed, Father Fortis turned and smiled, his eyebrows raised. Worthy gestured toward his watch.

"Soon," the priest mouthed. "I'd like a bit of the dirt."

With the couple trailing behind her, the nun returned to the room of crutches and braces. "Really, I'm forbidden to do that," she said, shaking her head. "I'll pray for you, but please, trust in our good Lord and His loving mother."

The woman wept softly as the man thanked the nun and ushered his companion back into the church proper. An open sob echoed through the sanctuary.

"They want too much," the nun whispered to Father Fortis. "They imagine that if I'd only rub the dirt on them, then God would have to … heal them, or in this case, give them a child."

Father Fortis nodded sympathetically. "A healing site attracts desperate people, like those two."

"Sometimes it's worse," the nun whispered, coming closer to the priest. "This couple isn't Catholic. When I claim to have nothing to do with what happens here, Catholics think I'm just trying to be the humble nun. That's when I can almost hear the devil laughing. As we both know, when all else fails, Satan can latch onto us with pride."

Worthy cleared his throat. "The lab closes at five, Nick."

"Not before Father takes some dirt," the nun stated, guiding the priest into the inner room.

Worthy watched Father Fortis cross himself, kneel, and reach down for the dirt. With smudgy fingers, the priest crossed himself again and remained on his knees.

The nun scurried over to a weather-beaten cupboard before returning to the priest. As she handed a small sandwich bag to Father Fortis, the priest whispered a thank you. Worthy could have sworn the nun's knees buckled.

For the first time since Worthy had been in this odd church, he felt overcome with fatigue. Perhaps it was the circle of mounded dirt on the floor, his friend on his knees, and the clucking of the nun. Or perhaps it was the endless pages of names in the book he held in his hand, the thousands of people who dragged their hopelessness into this tiny room and polished the stone floor with their knees, never noticing that the dirt at their feet was the same color as the soil outside, never wondering how each new day, no matter how many hands scooped out mounds from the day before, the well would be always brimming.

He felt the nun's gaze upon him. "You don't like it here, do you, Lieutenant?" Before he could answer, she continued, "To be honest, sometimes the place gets to me, too. Just don't make El Sanctuario harder than it is."

I don't need this, Worthy thought, scrambling to find some way to extricate himself. "I just need to get the book back to Santa Fe and find out if it means anything," he repeated.

Father Fortis met Worthy's eye and seemed to plead for forbearance. *Don't worry*, Worthy thought, *I never insult someone I might need to re-question.*

Worthy had turned back toward the room of crutches, hanging like old bones, when he felt the silken coolness of a sandwich bag slip into his hand. "Turn off your head, Lieutenant, and pray with your knees," she whispered.

Worthy looked down at the bag, wondering if the nun felt it her duty to coerce every visitor. Old images of his youth came flooding back, the town drunk crying at the Sunday night altar, his father and the pitiful few in attendance pretending the scene didn't happen four times a year. He turned the bag over in his hand, searching for a way out, before realizing that if he refused, the nun would turn him into a prayer concern, a new bead on her rosary.

He moved quickly to the hole, crouching rather than kneeling. After filling the bag, he took out a felt-tip pen to print "Chimayó, May 4, Ellie VanBruskman." It was an action he'd done a hundred times before—labeling small containers of bloodstained clothing, hair, human tissue, or even dirt like this.

And yet something troubled him, something more than the eyes of the nun and Father Fortis on him. He wanted to tell the nun that this was simply routine police work, but instead he rose quickly, slid the bag into his right-hand pocket, and left the room.

✝

WORTHY DELIVERED THE BOOK TO THE lab ten minutes before five and got the clear impression that his demand for immediate analysis wasn't appreciated. Wandering outside, he found a public phone and called Susan just as the sun was setting over the mountains. The conversation was brief, and as was typical, focused entirely on Allyson. Hanging up the phone, he remained for a few moments in the cool breeze before walking dejectedly back to the policewoman's office.

Sera Lacey sat behind her desk as she briefed him on her trip to Acomita. "Victor Martinez hasn't been seen since February, and now the boy's mother doesn't seem to be around. The poor woman left a ton of bills unpaid and no forwarding address."

"Any other relatives?" Worthy asked.

"I did manage to track down the grandmother's address. Grandmothers are the key out here."

Worthy glanced down at a picture on the desk of a smiling Little Leaguer, a boy of nine or ten, with red hair and freckles but also the black eyebrows of his mother. Somewhere in his apartment in Detroit was a photo of Allyson at the same age in almost the same pose, a soccer ball cradled under her arm.

Susan had spent the first two minutes of their phone conversation talking excitedly about Allyson, who'd finally agreed to go back to Rachel, her therapist. Even more surprising, their older daughter had spent a half hour alone with Rachel.

Something in his ex-wife's voice—something besides the whispering that always signaled Allyson was home—had made him uneasy. Then it came. After Allyson's session with Rachel, the therapist wanted Susan to relay a message to "the father." Allyson's running away had come after she'd returned home from school one day to find him—her father and the man her mother had divorced six months earlier—sitting across the table from Susan, drinking coffee and talking just like old times.

"Rachel says it confused Allyson, so for the time being, Chris, you're to call before you come over." Worthy held his tongue. It had been Susan who had invited him over that day, she who had made the coffee and the fudge brownies, his favorite. Yet now he'd become the criminal in Allyson's eyes. She had run away the next day, her disappearance a headline story in the local papers. Five months later, she had come back. Little wonder the VanBruskmans thought he could find their daughter after the initial police assigned to the case failed to turn up a clue. What he would have told them, if they had bothered to ask, was that he hadn't had anything to do with finding Allyson. No one had. She had come back on her own, without apology or explanation.

"So how was Chimayó?" Sera asked, breaking into his thoughts. "Did you see the room in the back, the one with the sacred dirt?"

"I got the grand tour," he replied. "A nosy nun made sure of that."

Sera Lacey's face reddened. She returned to the files on her desk, and after a moment of silence, reached for the phone. Worthy turned back toward the window, where the last pink rays shone feebly over the mountains. He had failed another test with his new partner, and maybe he had wanted to. It hardly seemed to matter. How was it possible that Allyson had run away because of him?

"The lab tech thinks he'll have your results in about half an hour," Sera reported. "I can fax them to the monastery, if you'd like."

He sighed. The morning had begun with a new sense of lightness, of being where no one but Father Fortis knew him—or resented him. People even seemed to want his help. But now his new partner clearly wanted him to leave.

"I guess I'll take a walk and come back."

"Suit yourself," she replied, not bothering to look up.

He left the station and headed for a cluster of shops down a side street. He needed to shower, to grab some sleep, to recover his bearings.

He passed a store specializing in ceramic tiles, one window filled with squares of smiling suns, moons, and signs of the zodiac, while in another, an entire bathroom—the flooring, the walls, and even the sink and shower—was composed of tiles. In the corner was a clay fireplace studded with more tiles. A fireplace in the bathroom?

He came to an alley and crossed the street to start the slow trek back. In the window of a travel agency was a cutout of New York City's skyline at night. Bright lights, shiny steel and stone, rain-soaked streets. He had intended to walk those streets with Susan on their twentieth anniversary trip. That had been his plan, at least. *This is what we would have seen*, he thought. *This is where we would have walked.*

At the sound of running footsteps, he turned to see the policewoman jogging toward him. Her black hair swirled around her face with each step, while in her hand she waved a white piece of paper. She beamed as if she'd recalculated his score and he'd passed the test after all.

"Well, Mr. Detroit, I think you've found our trail."

He bent down to read the real message from Chimayó: "Victor, I missed you. Someday I will find you."

Here it was, his first view into Ellie VanBruskman's true state of mind. What else could the statement "someday I will find you" mean but that Victor Martinez was indeed the reason she'd run away? What else did the missing girl's second message mean, the childish scrawl written on top, but that she was more cunning than anyone realized?

Worthy handed the paper back to the policewoman. "Let's go talk to that grandmother."

CHAPTER SIX

———◆———

FATHER FORTIS SAT ALONE OVER BREAKFAST. He took a long sip of coffee and sighed, pondering the mysterious action of mercy. His prayers the evening before had been plagued with self-recriminations, due to what he'd allowed to happen at Chimayó.

Of course, the nun at El Sanctuario had come on too strong, treating Worthy as if he were an errant confirmation candidate, but hadn't he also let his friend down? He'd thought it funny to egg the nun on and perhaps to show his friend that he was still capable of flirting. But when she started grilling Worthy, he hadn't interceded, hadn't escorted the nun into the back room to let his friend escape.

He had been prepared to apologize to Worthy, but that was before his friend had appeared in his room late last night bearing the evidence from the lab, a huge smile on his face.

"Don't you see, Nick? Chimayó was their pre-arranged meeting place," Worthy had explained, too excited to even sit. "Ellie VanBruskman isn't as nutty as she wants everyone to think."

"But doesn't her message—the real one, I mean—prove that the rendezvous with this Victor never occurred?"

The question didn't even dent Worthy's smile. "The Martinez kid probably forgot what day it was, or maybe the college group came in the morning instead of the afternoon. Either way, we know some things that Ellie VanBruskman doesn't want us to know. We know she's clever, and we know where she was headed."

"Which means you could be done with the case pretty soon."

Worthy had shrugged. "Maybe, but I don't think so. These two kids had a plan, and for all we know it's working."

Father Fortis took another long sip of coffee and watched the sun's rays play on the rough-hewn refectory tables. *A monastery refectory is truly a wonder*, he thought. Most refectories he'd visited, whether Orthodox or Catholic, in Europe or in the States, were surprisingly similar. Huge rectangular rooms of brick, wood, or in St. Mary's case, adobe, they all seemed to feature long wooden tables and sturdy benches. Had it not been for the simple crucifixes or icons on the walls, a monastery refectory could be confused with a training table for athletes—a comparison that struck Father Fortis as oddly appropriate.

And the food was always plentiful, even in a Trappist community that forbade not only meat, but also fish for most of the year. Cheese was the monastic replacement, and Father Fortis had visited enough monasteries to know that many gourmet cheeses had been created by inventive monks over the centuries. As any honest monk would concede, fasting did not always mean deprivation.

And best of all, conversation was forbidden in a refectory. The only voice permitted at mealtime was that of the one monk assigned to intone the wisdom of the church Fathers. Blessedly, even that wasn't happening this morning at St. Mary's.

He picked up the final morsel of wheat bread from his plate and wondered again why eating couldn't also be considered prayer. Didn't food, properly taken, promote recollection, the tastes exploding in the mouth calling forth gratitude for the bounty of creation? Couldn't swallowing, when the food passed the heart and lungs, become a plea for strength to do God's will? Easy for a fat monk to say, he realized, but wasn't something similar written in the *Philokalia,* an ancient book of Orthodox monastic wisdom?

Father Fortis rose from the table. *Yes, I will have another bowl of the muesli and a few more fresh berries. Imagine. Fresh berries in the desert.*

Just as he sat down again at the table, he saw Worthy enter the room. His friend's starched Oxford-cloth shirt in the midst of the Trappist robes made him look like someone who'd dropped in from another century. The smile from the night before still played across his friend's face. The priest motioned silently for Worthy to join him and was surprised when two arms waved back. Half-hidden behind the tall policeman was the slight, hunched-over Father Linus, his research partner.

The man's face reminded Father Fortis of their upcoming work session that afternoon. *More incessant chatter*, he thought. A knife clattered to the floor, and a blushing novice stooped to retrieve it.

A monk with a knife. Was it possible that one of the men in this very room had wielded one against Sister Anna? In the days since the murder, he had wanted to believe that the killer was someone from outside. But then again, maybe Sister Anna had also received a note in her mailbox, telling her that she, too, wasn't wanted or needed.

He gazed around the room at the monks' faces, some diligent, some merely exhausted, and recognized their counterparts back at his own monastery, St. Simeon's in Ohio. There were the old monks whose hands shook as they brought spoons to their mouths and who stood with difficulty through the community services. Not likely that one of them had gone out to the remote chapel and killed the nun.

Then there were the seven or eight monks of middle age, those in leadership positions who stared beyond their breakfast to the pressing worries of a monastery. They had greatest access to the vehicles and were capable of the crime, but what would have been the motive?

Finally, there were the three novices, the young men clearly prone to hormonal rages and fully capable of finding the pretty nun a temptation. What fantasies had danced in the dark of the novitiate dormitory while Sister Anna was living among them, eating with them, walking in the cloister below their windows, even working with them shoulder to shoulder? But would not the crime then have been sexual, rather than some form of ritual?

Setting down his plate across from Father Fortis and Worthy, Father Linus waved a bony forefinger at the two men and pointed in the direction of the dormitory. Father Fortis felt his heart sink. *Now my entire morning is shot*, he thought.

Twenty minutes later, the two visitors were sitting on a threadbare sofa in Father Linus's simple quarters. Across from them, the old monk sat in a straight-backed wooden chair, his fingers tapping on the armrests. According to the abbot, Father Linus had a heart condition. Father Fortis had also been told that the old monk refused to slow down.

"I passed through Detroit once, when I was young," Father Linus said to Worthy. "It was during the Depression, when I was riding the rails, and I am happy to report that the jails were very clean in the Motor City. Do they still call it the 'Motor City?' "

Father Fortis rose and began to pace the room. *We're going to get his entire life story*, he thought. He knew he should simply accept it, offer the pointless hour as a penance.

He found himself drawn to a primitive painting of the Virgin Mary on the far wall, depicting her sorrow with daggers protruding from her heart. It reminded him of something. An icon from Greece, perhaps?

"You like *santos*, Nicholas, our Hispanic Catholic depiction of the saints?" the old monk asked.

"This one is very compelling. It definitely interests me."

"It's a *retablo* from my village," Father Linus said, his voice excited.

"And what is that?"

"A retablo is a depiction of a holy person painted on wood, not to be confused with a three-dimensional carved saint, which is a *bulto*. I have always thought of retablos as Hispanic icons."

"Yes, I was thinking the same. But I'm not the art expert," Father Fortis said, nodding toward Worthy.

The old monk's dancing forefinger picked up its beat on the armrest. "Ah, are you an artist as well as a detective?"

"Hardly," Worthy protested, shooting a glance at Father Fortis. "Art history was my minor in college, but that was a long time ago."

"Still, it is very interesting," the old monk said as he rose and walked toward the back room.

In a low voice, Father Fortis said, "Sorry, my friend. We'll have a cup of coffee and be going."

"Why not play along? Maybe the old guy knows something about the nun," Worthy whispered back. "Anyway, think of it as payback for yesterday with that nosy nun."

"Oh, Christopher, that is beneath even you!"

"Relax. When it gets to be too much, I'll tell him I have to leave for Acoma."

"Did I hear you say Acoma?" The old monk shuffled back into the room, a framed painting in his hand. "The Pueblos are New Mexico's jewels, Lieutenant. Nineteen tribes, their ancestral lands are not reservations, no, not reservations. Each pueblo is a country within this country. There is nothing like them in the world. Nothing. And Acoma is one of the finest and best preserved."

Father Linus placed the painting on a coffee table in front of Worthy and padded back to his chair. "I've put some water on for tea. So let us talk art. Did you know that Georgia O'Keeffe visited us once?"

And off we go on another tangent, Father Fortis thought.

"Are you saying this is an O'Keeffe?" Worthy asked.

Father Fortis gazed down at the canvas, and found to his consternation that it interested him. His eye was first drawn to the huge sun in the center of the canvas. Everything in the painting from the sharp-edged trees to the mesas to the crowd of people off to one side had a bright orange or purple cast from the sun's fading glare. One object alone, a crucifixion in the foreground, was shaded in black.

The old monk laughed dryly. "No, no, my mistake. How could a monk afford an O'Keeffe? No, what you're holding is simply a reproduction, and not even one of hers. It's by Ernest Blumenschein, a member of the Taos school. I'm curious what both of you think of it."

Ask me if I care, Father Fortis thought. But Worthy accepted the invitation, lifting the painting from the table and pointing to the figure in the foreground. "Shouldn't there be three crosses instead of one?"

The old monk leaned his head back, his knee bobbing as he stared through feverish eyes at Father Fortis.

"Your friend has a good eye, Nicholas. I wonder if you would agree that art is sometimes like crime. It's often the outsider who helps us see what is right in front of us. Hmm?"

Father Fortis paused, wondering for the first time if he'd underestimated the old monk. But before he could respond, Father Linus turned back toward Worthy and broke out in laughter.

"What in the world are you doing, Lieutenant?"

"I'm turning the painting upside down, and I'm squinting," Worthy replied.

"I can see that. But why?"

"It's one of the few things I remember from my art courses. If you want to see a painting, sometimes you have to dismiss the details and find the underlying structure."

"Ah-ha! I didn't know that. And what does your squinting tell you?"

Worthy shifted in his seat. "It tells me the shape of the crowd on the right side balances almost perfectly the shape of this mound on the other. Here, take a look."

The old monk accepted the painting, removed his glasses, and squinted. "Mound? Ah, you mean the mesa. Yes, I see what you mean. Quite amazing. Nicholas, do you agree?"

"Yes, I suppose I do. I mean, I see what he's saying. But Father Linus, I wonder if the water's boiling. Worthy has to be leaving—"

"In a minute, Nick," Worthy interrupted. "What I don't understand is why the sun is the focal point of the painting instead of Christ on the cross."

Father Linus handed the painting back to Worthy and turned to his other guest. "Nicholas, would you be so kind as to get the kettle? The tea and the cups are already on a tray. And when you return, I want to hear what you see in the figure on the cross."

Father Fortis walked briskly into the kitchen and in a moment was back with the tray. *Whatever game we're playing here,* he thought, *let's get it over with quickly.* He let Father Linus pour the tea while he took another glance at the painting. "I agree with Christopher. It's odd where the painter placed our Lord."

"Ah, but the answer to that is simple," the old monk said. "The figure on the cross is not our Lord."

Stunned, Father Fortis stared again at the painting. How could the figure not be Christ?

"You're looking at the Brotherhood of Our Father, Jesus the Nazarene. Don't tell me you've never heard of the *Penitentes*, Nicholas." He sat straighter in the chair before adding, "The Penitentes kept the Christian faith alive in New Mexico when priests were few and far between. They still do." He paused as he looked down at the canvas and then back at Worthy. "Blumenschein has portrayed what we call a *Calvario*, just like the English word 'Calvary,' " the monk said, his forefinger aquiver on the policeman's knee. "That was who I was."

Father Fortis felt a weight drop heavily into the pit of his stomach. He'd read about the Penitentes in seminary, how their extreme mortification reclaimed some practices from medieval times, if not the earlier Desert Fathers. But how could Worthy possibly understand? And what possible reason could Father Linus have for raising this bizarre subject?

"So you're saying we're looking at a passion play," Worthy suggested.

Father Linus looked over toward Father Fortis even as he answered Worthy's question. "The Penitentes are devout Catholics who feel compelled to share in Christ's suffering. The man chosen to be *Christo* in this painting is literally suffering with Christ—suffering *as* Christ."

As if the painting had bitten him, Worthy let it drop to the coffee table. "What are you saying? What kind of sadistic …?"

For the first time, the old man sat calmly, his fingers quiet on the armrest, as Worthy stared at him. "Lieutenant, Lieutenant, please let me explain. Every man in that crowd wanted to trade places with the Christo; every boy wanted to grow up to be him."

Worthy stood abruptly. "But real nails?"

"Of course, but there is no permanent damage," Father Linus explained.

Father Fortis saw Worthy's jaw muscles clench.

"Don't try to tell me this man was envied?" Worthy asked, looking down on the old monk. "No child grows up dreaming of nails being hammered through his hands. What's going on in that painting is not religion. I don't give a damn what you say."

In a moment, Worthy was out the door, leaving the two monks alone.

Father Fortis stood. "I believe you owe my friend an apology, and you owe me an explanation."

The old monk looked sharply at his guest. "I owe *you* an explanation? I'd say it's the other way round. You could start by telling me what the abbot told you about the murder."

Father Fortis stared at the old monk. "What? You've completely lost me."

Father Linus rose slowly, painting in hand, and shuffled to the far wall. He hung the offending scene on a hook before moving to the balcony door. Closing it, he drew the curtains.

"All I know about the murder is the trivial bits that the abbot and Father Bernard have decided to tell us in Chapter," he hissed. "Unlike you, I've not been invited into his office to discuss the details."

Father Fortis studied the monk's trembling mouth. "Let me get this straight. You're jealous because the abbot told me things about the murder? And that's why you scared my friend off with this crazy painting?"

"So it's crazy? Is that what you've decided?"

Father Fortis started for the door, but the old man blocked his way with surprising speed. "Sit down, Nicholas. Please," Father Linus asked in a calmer voice. "We must talk."

Father Fortis remained standing in the center of the room. "No more pointless stories, or I leave. Do you understand?"

The old monk shuffled hurriedly to the wall and removed the santo of the Virgin Mary. "What was it you said about this when you came into my room?"

"I'm not sure I remember," Father Fortis replied. "Didn't I say something about the santo being beautiful?"

The monk placed the santo on the table before returning to his seat. "No, you said you found it interesting."

"So?"

"There are few secrets at St. Mary's, Nicholas. That's why I knew you had met with the abbot, and I've even seen the photos you were given—don't ask me how. But then you come into my room with your police friend and immediately walk to this particular santo. What did you mean by *interesting*? What does that mean?"

Father Fortis pulled on his beard for a moment as he studied the santo. "I meant just what I said. The grief in her eyes, yet the calmness, it's ... arresting. What did you think I meant?"

As the old man stared at Father Fortis, his eyes seemed to soften. "That's all?"

"Yes, of course."

"Nicholas, if I trust you now and I'm wrong, many people will suffer for that mistake." The monk took off his thick glasses and rubbed his eyes. He brought his watch to his face to check the time before folding his hands beneath his cassock.

"You gave me quite a fright this morning," he said. "I'd been hoping that you might trust me with what the abbot knows, but when you walked directly to my santo, I thought you, or even worse, the abbot, had figured things out."

Father Fortis glanced down at the sorrowful image before him. He shrugged and waited for the old man to explain.

Father Linus motioned behind him toward Blumenschein's painting on the wall. He pointed to a small building to the left of the bright sun.

"That building is a *morada*, Nicholas, a Penitente meeting place. The brothers agree to stay there during Holy Week. Everyone, including the women and children, come on Good Friday to see the Christo on the cross."

The old monk leaned toward Father Fortis and continued in a whisper, "The police think Sister Anna died in our retreat house, but the place wasn't always that."

Father Fortis nodded. "So that's what this is about. It was a morada, then. "

"One abandoned long ago, maybe forty years or more. It didn't even show up on our property maps when we bought the land. Father Bernard accidentally found it several years ago when he was on one of his runs. Abbot Timothy thought it might serve us as a type of hermitage."

"Sister Anna went out there to pray for direction, didn't she?"

The old monk leaned back in his chair and closed his eyes. "She was one of the first to use it after the renovation. Did the abbot tell you what she was holding in her hand when she died?"

Father Fortis thought for a moment. "It was a piece of paper, wasn't it?"

"Sister Anna was an artist. She was holding one of her drawings, the only one not shredded by the killer. It was a drawing of a santo of the Virgin Mary."

"The same as this?" Father Fortis asked.

"Nearly."

"It must have meant a great deal to her."

The old monk reached over and grasped his guest's wrist. The next words were even fainter. "Did they tell you about the marks on her body?"

"I know she was stabbed in the back and then, for some reason, she was stabbed repeatedly in her heart."

" 'For some reason,' you say," the monk muttered. "Yes, that's the problem. How long will it be before they think they know that reason? Did you notice the pattern of her wounds, Nicholas?"

"Pattern?"

"Sister Anna was stabbed precisely seven times. Four wounds here," he said, pointing to the right side of his chest, "and three on the other side."

The old monk turned the santo toward Father Fortis. "Now count the knives protruding from Our Lady."

CHAPTER SEVEN

———◆———

WORTHY'S THIGH MUSCLES BURNED AS HE hiked up the road to Acoma where Victor Martinez's grandmother lived. Ten yards ahead of him, Sera Lacey, without a hint of fatigue, was telling him about the ancient city.

"Some pueblos in New Mexico are completely closed to outsiders, even to police. Others are open only on certain feast days. Acoma is open nearly year round. You see, the tourists like their pottery, and the Acoma tribal people need the money."

Worthy gasped. "So what do they do if they have a serious crime?"

"They have their own police. Of course, they can always request outside help, but I'm telling you this for a reason. We have no jurisdiction in Acoma. You can't throw your weight around up here, and neither can I."

Worthy stopped to catch his breath. *Is that how she sees me?* he thought.

"Even some Anglos who've lived out here for twenty years don't know that the Pueblos are all autonomous nations that just happen to be within New Mexico. That's why we had to sign in at the visitors' center down below."

"An old monk at St. Mary's told me something about that this morning," Worthy said. He pushed his sunglasses up his nose and gazed out across the valley to other mesas, all barren. Nature here seemed to bear a grudge against the land, blistering it with heat strong enough to crack boulders. Only the squattiest scrub brush grew in the sand.

"I understand why their ancestors lived on top of these mesas for protection, but why don't these people move down?"

"Tradition doesn't have much to do with convenience," Sera replied. "Once we reach the top, we'll be in the oldest continuously inhabited city in North America, Lieutenant. I bet you didn't know that. There's no electricity or running water. That and the heat make life pretty rough, but they wouldn't think of insulting their ancestors."

She pointed to another mound perhaps a mile away. "See that mesa over there? It's called the *Mesa Encantada*, the Enchanted Mesa. It looks like it would offer even better protection, right?"

Worthy nodded, glad for the rest.

"Long before the Franciscans arrived—no one knows for sure just how far back—the ancestors of the Acoma lived over there. But one day a horrendous storm destroyed the only pathway to the top. The men were on a hunting party over there by Mt. Taylor." She pointed out a snowcapped peak to the west. "When they came back, they could hear the cries of some of their women."

"But they couldn't get to the top," Worthy said.

The policewoman didn't say anything for a moment. "The women had to choose between jumping to their death and waiting to starve on top."

"And the men? What did they do?"

"They mourned their losses, then married women from neighboring pueblos. Life started over on this mesa, practically next to the other one."

His partner's words made him think of what Father Fortis had told him over lunch, about Father Linus's santo and the nun's wounds. The past in New Mexico cast a long shadow, rearing up and colliding with the present.

Silently, the two trudged the remaining hundred feet to the top and walked to a small adobe house that bore a tour sign. While the policewoman went inside to present her credentials, Worthy remained outside, trying to catch his breath in the thin air.

Their ride from Santa Fe had gone smoothly. Sera pointed out major sights as they drove west from Albuquerque, the petroglyph-embellished canyon walls near the Rio Grande River as well as the bleached-white church of Laguna Pueblo.

At her initiative, the conversation turned to family, and Worthy offered a hurried account of his divorce, the more recent thaw, and finally his daughter Allyson's running away.

When he finished, Sera caught his eye. "So the VanBruskmans choosing you to hunt down their daughter wasn't exactly a coincidence."

"No, no accident. But to tell you the truth, I never knew where my own daughter was hiding out. One day she just came back to the house and went up to her room."

"She's never told you or your wife—your ex-wife—where she'd been?"

"No, and why would she? She's got that over us. She came back on her own, and she can run away again on her own." Maybe he should have told the VanBruskmans that, he thought.

"So tell me about your kids," he asked.

Sera produced a wallet photo of a boy kneeling in his Little League uniform, a smaller version of the one in her office. "That's Felipe, my one and only."

"He definitely has your eyes."

"Actually, he looks more like Stephen, my late husband."

Worthy winced. "Oh."

Sera didn't say anything for a moment. "It happened five years ago. It was Christmas, with the rush and all, and he was driving for UPS up by the Colorado border when he hit a patch of black ice. Stephen was an Anglo," she explained, "which is where I got the name Lacey. My maiden name is Ortiz."

"Spanish, right?"

"Yes, Spanish," she'd said, laughing. "You really aren't from around here, are you?"

"Obviously not. But I thought the way you spelled your first name must be ethnic."

She laughed again. "I was supposed to be a boy, and then I would have been Felipe. My parents already had eight girls, so they couldn't think of a name for me for three days. Then my mother remembered that my father's one good Sunday shirt was by Sero. You know, the shirt company. So I became Sera. That's a true story."

Waiting outside the tour office for the policewoman to reappear, Worthy looked over toward the other, tragic mesa. Those ancient people thought they'd built a place of safety. Instead, they'd built a tomb.

As if on some cue, doors of the adobe houses opened along the main dirt road of Acoma. One by one, women emerged from their homes, boxes in hand. Setting them down, they brought out pieces of pottery and arranged them on old card tables.

"What's your ex-wife like?" Sera asked from behind him.

"What?"

"Come on, Lieutenant, it's a simple question. What's she like?"

He shrugged, aware he was blushing. "I'd say she's tall, blonde like me, a bit shy. She was pretty …. Actually, she still is."

Sera laughed as she picked up a stone and turned it over in her hand. "No, silly. What does she *like*, not what does she look like. I mean, if you're still trying to work things out, why not surprise her with some pottery?"

Still blushing, he looked away toward the distant Mt. Taylor and thought of his phone conversation with Susan the day before. "Before the divorce, I always brought her back a gift. Now, after Ally's trick, I'd better not."

"Oops. Sorry for butting in."

"Don't worry about it. By the way, you should lead when we talk to the grandmother."

Her eyes studied his face. "Why?"

"Like you said, I'm not from around here. And there's something about this place, the quiet of it. There's just too much I don't know."

Sera caught a stand of hair and hooked it behind her ear.

"I guess we can try that," she replied as they began the trek down the road. The women nodded to Sera, but said nothing as the two walked in silence to the end of the path and then turned left. They approached a brightly painted blue door where a fringe of newspaper strips dangled above it as a wind stop. Sera mounted the two steps and knocked softly before stepping down to where Worthy waited.

The door opened, and an old, bowlegged woman looked down on them. Her face was creased with deep lines running from nose to jaw, like someone who'd lost her teeth. Her hair, weightless with age, danced in the breeze. Her left arm shook at her side.

Sera introduced the two of them and then waited again. The woman paused before motioning them inside, as if it took extra time for the words to travel the ten feet between them.

The room was dark as a cave, with only a small fire of twigs lighting a corner fireplace. Smells of resin and something fried hit Worthy. He removed his sunglasses and realized that his head was only inches from the gnarled log beams holding up the floor above. Not until Sera bowed to a corner of the room did he realize that another woman was sitting by the fire, knitting needles in her hands.

The grandmother pointed to a pair of chairs, but the policewoman remained standing until the old woman sat down in the rocker.

"Thank you for inviting us into your home, Mrs. Tambo," Sera said.

"My family and my ancestors welcome you," the old woman replied, bowing slightly.

The four sat quietly. The only sounds were the clicking of the knitting needles and the occasional hiss from the fire.

"Lieutenant Worthy has come from Detroit in search of a missing girl. Her name is Ellie VanBruskman."

The grandmother looked Worthy over as if weighing the policewoman's words. Just when he thought his partner would have to repeat the introduction, Mrs. Tambo spoke.

"How did the girl lose herself?"

Sera turned toward Worthy and waited. The other woman's needles stopped as she reached down to a basket on the floor for another ball of yarn.

"We believe she ran away to find Victor, your grandson," Worthy said, surprised at how loud his voice sounded in the room.

The old woman continued to study Worthy, then turned back toward Sera. "Is the journey so far that the father and mother cannot come, or are they too old?"

"Actually, the reason I'm here … the reason we're here …" he began before catching himself. "The truth is, Lieutenant Lacey knows more about this case than I do."

Sera held his gaze for a moment before answering the grandmother. "If we don't find the missing girl, I'm sure the mother will come."

The old woman rocked slowly, her one hand shaking rhythmically in her lap.

"Is this man her kinsman?" the grandmother asked.

Sera waited, as if testing Worthy's decision. "He carries the parents' worry," she said.

"But you said he was a policeman. They must be a poor family."

A log popped in the fire. The other woman poked the coals with an iron rod.

"You may be right, Mrs. Tambo. The family must be poor to send him first," Sera answered.

Mrs. Tambo stopped rocking. "Victor said a girl by that name shared her books with him. Victor said these books were more expensive than my pottery. Victor said the girl had plenty of money. Now you say the mother is too poor to come."

Sera nodded. "I'm glad you know what good friends the two of them are. We fear she may be in trouble, perhaps lost in the desert."

The other woman stopped knitting and stood abruptly, holding onto the mantel for support. For a second, Worthy thought she would speak, but she only knelt down to jab again at the coals.

The grandmother grunted, taking something from her pocket and putting it into her mouth. Her toothless gums mashed for a moment before she spoke. "The girl took pills that hurt her. So Victor said."

Worthy sat forward, glancing over at Sera, but the policewoman's gaze remained on the old woman. In his last-minute meeting with Mrs. VanBruskman, he'd had the feeling he wasn't being told everything. Was it drugs the mother had covered up?

A sigh, then a hurried cough, came from the other woman by the fire.

"Was Victor talking about illegal drugs?" Sera asked.

"The mother gave her pills," Mrs. Tambo replied.

Worthy watched the woman's jaw rise and fall with each chew, the wrinkled skin on her neck lagging a half-beat behind.

"Victor said she couldn't laugh," the grandmother continued. "I do not trust a woman who has money for books and for laugh-stop pills, but no money to find her daughter."

Of course, Worthy thought, remembering the file. The grandmother was talking about the anti-depressants. Ellie VanBruskman must have been taking the type that locked her into an emotional middle range, lopping off the highs and the lows. Spontaneous laughter would have been rare. He also knew that when the girl's pills were finished, if they weren't already, she would probably soar for a while before crashing.

The old woman's rocker stopped. "Victor is a good boy."

The other woman poked again at the fire, sending sparks up the chimney.

"We found a note left by the girl at Chimayó. It was addressed to your grandson. Victor hasn't done anything wrong, but we do need his help," Sera replied.

Worthy felt a change in the room. Everyone seemed to be waiting for something.

"Mrs. Tambo, may I speak … to her?" Sera asked, gesturing to the other woman.

The grandmother gazed down at the floor as she said something in her native language. The other woman responded in the same low voice, and Mrs. Tambo nodded to Sera.

The policewoman rose and approached the fire. She reached out for the woman's hand, and when she spoke, her voice was soft, hardly audible over the fire's hissing.

"Mrs. Martinez, I am a mother, too, and I know what it is to worry about a son. If something has happened to Victor, please let us help."

The woman seemed to crumple, hiding her face for a moment.

"He said someone was following him in Detroit," she said, her voice shaking. "After he was here for a few weeks, he said he was being followed again. That was when he went to his uncle's in Chimayó for Holy Week. He's done that before, but this time he didn't stay for more than a few days. Now we don't know where he is."

"When was he in Chimayó?" Sera asked.

"The end of February, maybe March, I think," the mother answered.

But that would mean Victor Martinez had left Chimayó weeks before Ellie VanBruskman's visit, Worthy realized. No wonder Ellie had missed him at the healing church and left her message. But where was she now, and was it still worth searching for Victor?

Sera knelt and patted the woman's arm again. "Maybe he's taking care of her right now. When we find them, I'll tell him his mother is worried. Okay?"

The mother drew out a handkerchief and wiped her eyes. "Tell my *padrelito* that his mother misses his gentle smile."

"I will."

As Worthy and Sera started to leave, the grandmother handed Sera a box. The policewoman raised it to her face and inhaled. "It smells delicious. Thank you, Mrs. Tambo."

Five minutes later, Worthy sat next to Sera on the steps of Acoma's seventeenth-century church.

"What's padrelito mean?" he asked.

"My little priest. It's her nickname for Victor, I guess."

He wrinkled his brow. "Little priest? I wonder what that's about," Finding Ellie VanBruskman suddenly seemed even more of a challenge.

"Here, have some fry bread."

As Sera handed him a piece, she squeezed his hand. "Thanks for what you did in there. Even Cortini would have tried to force the interview."

Worthy shrugged. "It was tempting, but I would have ruined everything. Detroit and Acoma exist in different worlds. Tell me how you knew about the mother."

Sera tore a piece of the fry bread in half and looked at it. "Every time Victor's name was mentioned, her knitting needles stopped or speeded up."

"I missed that," he said. "I'm probably going to miss a lot."

"I don't know. Cortini told me who you are."

Worthy gazed toward the valley and the distant canyon walls beyond. "Which version did he tell you, the flake or the super cop?"

"Not the flake. You'll have to tell me about that yourself. No, he said you're one of the most decorated detectives in Detroit. So you letting me handle the interview my way is very special."

"Any more bread?" he asked, trying to change the subject.

Sera reached into the box, but her hand stopped abruptly. She gasped as she lifted the napkin carefully from the bottom of the box, exposing several letters held together by a ribbon. Rising to her feet, she looked back toward Mrs. Tambo's house.

"They're from Ellie VanBruskman," she said in a low voice. "The grandmother wants us to have them."

"Well, open them."

"No. Not here. I don't think the mother knows she gave them to us."

The two said nothing as they walked to the road leading down off the mesa. In some of the windows, Worthy could see kerosene lamps burning, but there was no sign of the women or the pottery. He thought of the box in Sera's hand, the letters from Ellie to Victor. Had Victor seen them before he left for his uncle's? If not, what help could they be?

As they reached the edge of the mesa, Sera stopped.

"Can I show you something?"

The question took him off guard. "Sure."

Sera led him to a worn path running alongside the last house. The path seemed to end at the edge of the ancient mesa, but then veered sharply down and to the left, forming a snaky route through the rocks to the valley below.

"It's the old way down," Sera explained. "Are you game?"

Not waiting for his reply, she led the way, the box of bread and letters gripped in her hand. Worthy followed gingerly until a huge boulder obstructed their progress. Without hesitating, Sera turned right as if to leap into open air, then reached out at the last second for a smoothed-out handhold in a rock.

"How old is this path?" he asked.

"Only six or seven hundred years old," Sera said as she disappeared around another rock.

Worthy followed cautiously, aware that one false step could mean a drop of over a hundred feet to the rocks below. He called down again, hoping to slow Sera's progress. "Do you think the path on that other mesa was like this? With handholds, I mean?"

Her footsteps stopped below him. "It had to be. They didn't want their enemies to have an easy time."

They finished the descent, with Sera laughing as she encouraged him to jump the last four feet to the valley floor. He let go of the handhold and landed softly in the sand.

"Not bad," she said.

"For an old guy, you mean."

"No, for an Easterner," she said, grinning.

Worthy studied the crooked path that they'd descended. "I'm trying to imagine what it would be like to hear your wife and children crying and not be able to do anything."

"I'll tell you what I believe happened. Those who jumped thought that love would give them wings. Those who stayed on top chose to die where they'd always lived. Love versus security."

Worthy stamped the dust from his boots. "That's not enough of a choice."

Sera looked at him for a moment before beginning the walk back to the parking lot. "Those were the only choices life gave them."

And what choices did Ellie VanBruskman see before she ran away? he wondered. Was she running to Victor, this "little priest," in hopes of finding love, security, or something else?

✝

IN THE DARKNESS FOLLOWING THE NIGHT service of Vigils at St. Mary's, Father Fortis remained in his assigned stall and watched as the columns of monks processed toward the sanctuary altar. Each bowed deeply from the waist before the abbot, then turned to the icon of the Virgin Mary to bow again before filing out into the night.

He picked out the distinctive slap of Father Linus's sandals at the rear of the line, and the old monk's parting words from that morning came to mind: "Sister Anna's murder was terrible, but you need to know that it wasn't the only attack that has taken place on one of our old moradas. But please. I ask you to say nothing about the santo until next week."

"Why next week?" Father Fortis had asked.

"I want you to meet the *hermano mayor*, the governing brother at a morada, a Penitente meeting house. Please, it's only a few days."

Father Fortis's heart had skipped a beat at the time, but now he wondered if it would take the police that long to link the murder with the Penitentes. A routine search at the county courthouse should show that the retreat house had previously been a morada. And how long would it take the police to figure out the meaning of the seven wounds between Sister Anna's breasts?

Sitting alone in the dark, he gazed out of the massive window at the rock face. Moonlight promised to break free of the crest line at any moment and illuminate the room. As he rose from his seat with thoughts of returning to bed, he heard a faint creaking sound from the balcony above. That was the area reserved for guests, but the monastery had closed its guesthouse to all but Worthy and himself until the investigation was over.

He sat quietly, half expecting to see a sneaky reporter's head peeking over the railing. He saw and heard nothing, yet something or someone was definitely there. He could feel it. Rising silently, he edged his way to the back of the chapel and to the stairs leading up to the balcony.

He ascended cautiously, wondering if he was overreacting. Couldn't the sound simply be the evening breeze as it flowed down the valley?

He reached the top stair and peered into the dark balcony. He waited, but again heard nothing. At that moment, the moon broke free of the canyon wall outside and flooded the chapel with light. In that flash, Father Fortis saw three things. One, exploding in the clear desert night air, the bands of color on the far canyon wall. *How odd*, he thought, *to see pinks, reds, even browns at this time of night.* Two, in the same instant, he saw that the balcony was empty, its rows of hand-hewn benches bare except for a stack of daily missals. And three, he saw the door at the other end of the balcony swaying slightly.

He hurried between the rows of benches, his robes sending the missals flying. Pushing on the door, he saw the top of another stairwell leading downward into an even greater darkness. Somewhere below, he heard another door close and a key turn in a lock.

CHAPTER EIGHT

———— ◆ ————

C*AN'T REACH YOU. STILL SAY YOU don't need cell phone? Return ASAP for consultation with VanBruskmans. New evidence. —Captain Spicer.*

Worthy stood under the flickering light in his room and reread the fax. *What new evidence?* he asked himself. In the bathroom, he poured a glass of water and looked at his reflection in the mirror. Grimy streaks of dust from the Acoma mesa lined his forehead and a band of salty perspiration coated his starched collar. "What new evidence?" he repeated, this time out loud. *Dammit, I've been here less than a week, and I'm the one with new evidence.*

Worthy knew that his frustration was partially his own fault. Captain Spicer's terseness was his way of making Worthy pay for refusing to use a cell phone. Spicer hated faxing as much as Worthy hated cell phones. He undressed, and stepping into the shower, stood under the stream of water as he tried to guess what his captain was referring to. Ever since the Church of Chimayó, he'd suspected that he'd have to go back to Detroit. That is, unless the VanBruskman girl turned up in a hospital or had simply been on a lark and now wanted to be found. But now Ellie's letters to Victor suggested that Detroit held clues to the boy as well.

The first letter, a Christmas card written within weeks of Victor's late-semester withdrawal from Allgemein College, had hardly been noteworthy. Ellie wrote that she missed Victor, that she hoped she had passed her Spanish final without his help, and that she wanted to hear from him soon. The only puzzling line had been Ellie's statement that she dreaded the upcoming Christmas break, when she had to spend time with "these old people pretending to be parents."

Worthy turned off the water and grabbed a towel. The girl's comment could mean nothing. It was the type of crack his own daughter, Allyson, might make about him.

Brushing his hair, he turned his thoughts to the second letter. Written on pink stationery with a unicorn at the top, the letter had shared the girl's excitement about joining the college trip to New Mexico. The date of the visit to Chimayó was underlined twice in the itinerary, and below that Ellie had added a postscript: "You were right to leave. The college will never admit a thing."

"What's that about?" Sera had asked after he read the line to her in the car. The postscript made it sound as if something had happened to drive the boy away from Allgemein, a prestigious private liberal-arts college. He wondered if the grandmother knew the reason and had chosen not to tell them. He ruled out the mother knowing. A parent as worried as she would have told them everything. That meant that Worthy would have to find the answer in Detroit.

After a restless night of sleep and an early breakfast in the refectory, Worthy sat on the balcony of Father Fortis's room and shared the news. Below the balcony, two monks approached from opposite ends of the cloister and passed each other with only a brief nod before proceeding on their separate ways.

"Let me drive you to the airport," Father Fortis whispered. "There are a few developments I want to share with you. Privately, I mean."

"Of course."

Father Fortis's hand stroked his beard before coming to rest on his pectoral cross. *Something is troubling him*, Worthy thought. And it wasn't hard to understand why his friend didn't want to say anything here. Initially Worthy had been impressed by St. Mary's quiet and solitude, but with each hour spent here, he sensed that people were listening in on that silence.

Father Fortis crossed his arms and stared out at the desert. "And how long do you think you'll be gone, Christopher?"

"I'd say it's going to take two days, three at the most, to finish the interviews. Beyond that, it all depends on what the hell the fax means by 'new evidence.' "

"You say that as if you don't believe it. Are you still suspicious of the parents?"

"If I am, I'm not sure I have a right to be," Worthy replied. "The mother put us on the track of Victor Martinez, and that turns out to be a real lead. So why don't I trust her? I don't know. Maybe it's because she reminds me of my ex-mother-in-law."

Worthy looked out at the huge white clouds building over the mountains and a path leading from a cloister gate into the desert. Perhaps the path led to the retreat house, the murder site, a good twenty miles, according to Father Fortis's map. Much too far to walk. He thought of the nun out there alone for nearly a week. Someone had driven her out there. Could it have been the same monk who'd found her body?

In the Jeep, Father Fortis said nothing until they hit the smooth blacktop of Route 503, a good six miles from the curious ears at the monastery.

"You'd tell me if I were making a fool of myself, wouldn't you?" he blurted out.

For the second time that morning, Worthy saw worry on Father Fortis's face. "I think you'd better tell me what's going on."

Father Fortis hit the steering wheel with the palm of his hand. "All of a sudden, it's like I have a sign around my neck. 'Father Nick—boy detective.'"

"Slow down. What happened?"

Father Fortis took a deep breath. "It was after the Compline service last night. I stayed for a few minutes so I could pray alone. That's when I heard someone above me in the balcony."

"Are you saying someone was spying on you?"

Father Fortis shrugged, the grip on the steering wheel turning his knuckles white. "I think so, but they were gone by the time I got up there."

Worthy considered the news. "So it was someone who could move quickly. Not one of the older monks, then."

"I hadn't thought of that. But the mystery man clearly knew his way around."

The Jeep struggled as it tried to pass a semi and succeeded only when Father Fortis punched the accelerator. The engine registered its protest.

"And there's something else," Father Fortis said. "I stayed and talked with Father Linus yesterday after you left."

"I know. You already told me. That business about the nun's wounds and that weird group."

"There's more, Christopher. What I didn't tell you was that he asked me not to say anything about the whole business until next week." He gave Worthy a panicky look. "Good Lord, my friend. You didn't say anything to that policewoman about the Penitentes, did you?"

"No. But what's the big deal about next week?"

"I'm to meet one of the old leaders of the group."

"Oh, God, Nick. You know he's going to be as crazy as Linus, don't you?"

"No, I'll meet with him," Father Fortis replied firmly. "Linus knows something. But here's my problem. If the police do their job, they're going to figure out the connection pretty quickly. So part of me wonders if I'm making a mistake not telling someone—such as the abbot. If I don't tell him and he finds out that I already knew, he'll think I betrayed him. But if I tell him, Linus won't ever trust me again."

Worthy pondered his friend's dilemma. "Okay, here's a thought," he said.

"After dropping me at the airport, you're going back through Santa Fe, right?"

"Yes. Why?"

"Why not stop by Sera Lacey's office and ask her advice?"

Father Fortis shot an angry glance at Worthy. "Your partner? But she's a cop. Didn't you hear a word I said?"

"Calm down, Nick. Sera will know what to do with the information. My guess is that she'll honor your secret."

"You sound pretty sure about that. How do you know I can trust her?"

"Because I do," Worthy said. "It's the first thing you figure out about a new partner."

Father Fortis was silent for a moment before sighing deeply. "Okay, then, I will. Thanks. That's one less thing to worry about."

"You have more?"

"Not exactly a worry, and I'm sorry about snapping at you. No, it's simply another note I found this morning, this one from the abbot. He wants me to meet with Sister Anna's confessor, a Father Bernard. He's one of those tall, lean monks with this head of wild hair. He looks a bit like an old rock star. Handsome, I suppose, in his way, but not in your league," Father Fortis said with a smile.

Worthy narrowed his eyes on the road ahead as he played with the new idea. Why hadn't he thought of that before?

"Did you hear me, Christopher?"

"What? Yes, I heard you. You said Sister Anna had a confessor. Every Catholic has to go to confession, right? And really devout Catholics go regularly, don't they?"

"Of course. Confession is standard procedure for monks and nuns. So I'm sure Sister Anna—"

"I'm not talking about Sister Anna," Worthy interrupted. "Did I tell you what Victor Martinez's mother calls him?"

"No."

"Padrelito. Sera tells me it means 'little priest.'"

Father Fortis pulled on his beard. "Ah-ha. The faithful altar boy type, the kind mothers and priests mark for the priesthood. You think the boy's priest out here might know something?"

"Not here, Nick. Back in Detroit. Something happened, something pretty major it seems, at the college. Whatever it was, it drove the boy back here." Worthy paused. "Victor also told his mother he was being followed. I'm thinking a boy with that kind of nickname would have run right to his priest in case of trouble."

"At the college, you're saying," Father Fortis said.

"Right. A Catholic chaplain, if Allgemein has one."

"Given the number of Catholics in Detroit, they must. But good luck getting him to talk, Christopher. Confessors promise confidentiality, you know."

Worthy's brain was already spinning with plans. His plane wouldn't land until after eight o'clock, Detroit time. First thing in the morning, he'd head for the college to interview Dr. Wormley, the professor who'd led the group. It should be easy to run by the chaplain's office after that. The meeting with the VanBruskmans could wait.

"Christopher, I swear your brain is already back in Detroit. I said you're going to have a tough time getting around the vow of confidentiality."

Worthy sat up, narrowing his focus on the highway, as if to urge the plodding Jeep forward. Gone were any regrets about having to go back to Detroit. In forty-eight hours, he would very likely have answers to both mysteries—Ellie's and Victor's.

✝

TRUST IS A CHAIN FORGED A *link at a time*, Father Fortis told himself as he knocked on the door of the Child Protection Office. Father Linus had trusted him with the clue about the santo, he had trusted Worthy, and Worthy had encouraged him to trust Sera Lacey. But wasn't a chain only as strong as its weakest link? How could a conscientious policewoman not pass the clue along?

The door opened, with Sera Lacey's face showing surprise. "Father Fortis?"

"Am I disturbing you, my dear?"

"Not at all. Please come in."

Her office struck him as small, not much more than a desk, two filing cabinets, and three chairs, but the walls were brightly decorated. His eye immediately lit on a primitive crucifix surrounded by faded photos of old men, women, and children. Below the cloud of photos was a delicate tile of the Virgin of Guadalupe. He sighed deeply and felt his body relax into the chair. Yes, he knew something important about this woman. Perhaps he could leave his secret with her.

"I assume Chris got off okay," she said as she made her way to her chair behind the desk.

"Chris? Oh, you mean Christopher," he replied. "Yes, yes. No problem. In fact, by the time we reached the airport he seemed eager, almost excited, to get back for his interviews. And you? What will you do while he's gone?"

"Tackle these," she replied, pointing to a stack of folders. "They're the more normal runaways, if any child can be called that. And I'm going out to Chimayó to interview Victor Martinez's uncle." She caught Father Fortis's eye. "Chris told me you went out there with him."

"To Chimayó? Yes, I did. Not the kind of place a person forgets."

"Not everyone takes to it," she said, her gaze still on him. "I understand you had a hand in finding the book—the one with the girl's message to Victor."

He felt his face redden. "Oh, I think it's fairer to say the book wanted to be found."

The two sat in silence for a moment before Sera smiled. "Okay, Father. Why don't you tell me why you're here?"

Father Fortis gripped the prayer cord on his wrist and gazed up again at the crucifix. "Christopher said I could trust you with something, something I know."

Sera leaned back in her chair. "Something about the murder, maybe?"

Father Fortis nodded. "I can see from the crucifix and the Virgin of Guadalupe on your wall that you're Catholic. Perhaps you've heard of a group called the Penitentes."

Sera rose and closed the door before moving to the lone window.

"Chris said that you should tell me something about the Penitentes?" she asked, her back to him. "I'm surprised."

Father Fortis shook his head. "No, I heard it from someone else. I'm sorry, but I don't think I'm at liberty to tell you that person's name. So no, it wasn't Christopher. In fact, it would be fairer to say that he had a pretty tough time with something he heard about the group."

Still with her back to him, she said, "What exactly did he hear?"

"Someone at St. Mary's took it upon himself to tell him about their Good Friday practices, at least the practices of the most traditional brotherhoods."

"Oh, I see," Sera said softly. "Yes, that would be tough for Chris. I get the feeling that there's a lot in New Mexico our friend is going to struggle with."

"No doubt, my dear, but you should know something about Christopher. He'll always tell you exactly what he thinks, and he isn't afraid to change his mind. I'm wondering if your colleagues down the hall would be as fair."

Sera didn't respond to the challenge as she returned to her desk. "Am I to understand that you have information linking the murder with the Penitentes?"

Father Fortis took a deep breath and plunged ahead. "The place where her body was found, the retreat house, was once one of their ... I forget the term."

Sera leaned forward. "A morada, Father. I wondered about that when I saw the windows in the photos. It may take the guys on the case a while to make the connection—that is, unless the Penitente brothers left something behind."

"Things left behind? But we found nothing—"

He stopped himself too late. Had she just tricked him into revealing that they had already snooped around the murder site?

The policewoman slowly shook her head. "Your secret is safe with me, Father. A lot of moradas lie empty around these parts, all the way up into Colorado. When the old Penitente brothers stopped using one, they liked to believe that they were just leaving it for the next generation. You may have noticed large crosses in a backroom, perhaps some whips and rattles."

"I did see some white planks stacked together, white ones. I guess they could have been crosses," he said. "So you think some of the brothers may have been secretly coming back there?"

Sera shook her head. "I told you what the old Penitentes hoped for, Father. Their faith is strong, but not very realistic. The young don't think much of the old ways. No, I don't think it's all that damning that the murder site was once a morada." She paused. "Is there something else?"

He pulled on his beard. "Is it that clear from my face? Yes, well, then, here it is. My anonymous source told me that the marks on Sister Anna's body, the stab wounds, were all in this area," he said, pointing to his heart.

"That's right."

"Well, yesterday, my dear, I was shown a favorite santo of the Penitentes. The Blessed Virgin Mary bears stab wounds exactly in the same place."

The policewoman exhaled slowly. "That's a bit different, isn't it? I don't think they know that."

Father Fortis noticed she said *they* instead of *we*.

"Father, you've trusted me, and now I have to trust you. First of all, I'd like you to promise that you won't tell Chris what I'm about to say."

Father Fortis looked up. "May I ask why?"

"I'm not sure how much he would trust me if he knew that my father and grandfather were both Penitente brothers."

"Oh, I see. But certainly if the Penitentes are involved in the case in any way, you can't simply cover that up."

"Of course not, Father, but Worthy isn't working that case, is he? Don't bother answering that. I'm not that stupid. But I see no reason to force him to deal with something so far outside his reality."

"Yes, I can see that," he said, remembering his friend stalking out of Father Linus's room. "May I ask what you're going to do with what I've just told you?"

Sera paused. "People come for confessions in the Orthodox church, am I right?"

"Same as in yours, Lieutenant."

"Consider what you've told me your confession, Father. Now it's in my hands. Will you trust me?"

"Yes, yes I will. If you're going to wait to tell your superiors, rest assured I will as well."

Sera shook her head. "No, Father, you don't understand. Very soon, maybe by tomorrow or the next day, they're going to stumble onto this. You simply have to trust me, no matter what happens."

CHAPTER NINE

———◆———

DESPITE HIS FLIGHT INTO DETROIT BEING delayed, Worthy was at the college by ten o'clock the next morning. Entering the social science building, he followed the sign up to the anthropology department on the third floor. On his way down the hallway, a display in a glass case caught his eye. Pottery, much like he'd seen at Acoma, and striped blankets were arranged neatly beneath printed cards. On one card were the words, "Purchased with Allgemein Funds on the Spring Break North American Anthropology Trip, led by Assistant Professor Samuel Wormley."

"Assistant Professor" meant Wormley was new. *New and unlucky*, Worthy thought. The professor's statements in Santa Fe as well as Detroit were completely consistent. Ellie VanBruskman had given no warning before running off. She'd been, in fact, a model student without "typical college issues," the file reported, which Worthy took to mean she hadn't gone out drinking every night of the trip. A slight man in a wrinkled shirt answered Worthy's knock on the door. Much as Sheriff Cortini had said, the professor looked more like a student than faculty. Worthy introduced himself and was ushered into the office, the door closing quickly behind him. He sat and watched as Wormley strode indecisively between the window and the cluttered desk. In the end, the professor slumped into the chair behind his desk, his hands on his temples, as if he understood perfectly what private colleges like Allgemein did to new faculty who lost daughters of the rich and powerful.

While Worthy explained that he'd just returned from New Mexico, the professor sat back and stared at the ceiling.

"I don't know what's going to go first, Lieutenant, my job, my health, or my m-marriage," he stammered, forcing a laugh. "It's not as if I had the fifteen pounds to lose. And as my students will tell you, I can't lecture for shit. Perhaps I never could." He paused, rubbing his hands together. "Can I tell you something that's driving me crazy?"

"Of course."

"I keep thinking that there's some simple answer to the whole mess." He took off his glasses and stared with bloodshot eyes at Worthy. "But I'm wrong, aren't I?"

"To be honest, her disappearance isn't looking all that simple. That's why I'm here."

"Of course," Wormley replied dejectedly. "How can I help?"

"You said in your statements that Ellie came to see you in December about the trip. Was there anything unusual about that?"

"Do you mean her applying so late? Maybe a little, but she said she'd just spotted the posters around campus. She claimed she'd been interested in the Southwest for a long time."

"She said, 'a long time'?"

"Yes, I'm sure she did, although I can't vouch for my memory any longer."

It was going to be hard, Worthy realized, to keep the professor from falling into his private pool of despair with every question.

"What did you think of Ellie—at first, I mean?" he asked.

"She dressed a bit funny, old-fashioned in a way. I mean, how many college students wear barrettes anymore, much less one with a pink unicorn on it? I remember thinking that she seemed the kind of student I wouldn't have to worry about. Ha!" He slumped farther down in his chair and continued rubbing his temples.

"How much did you know about her medical condition?"

Wormley's face brightened. "I followed all the rules on that. Every student filled out the standard medical permission slip. And the mother called me—twice if I'm not mistaken—to tell me that Ellie needed to take her medication daily. Ellie wasn't the only one in that situation. I reminded her the first couple days, but then it didn't seem necessary." A cloud returned to his face. "I suppose I was wrong about that, too." He sat forward in his chair, his eyes pooling with tears. "Nothing, Lieutenant, you've found nothing?"

"We think she ran away in search of someone, a boy she knew from her first semester here," Worthy replied. "Did you know a Victor Martinez?"

Wormley jumped to his feet. "Really? That's good, isn't it? That means she could be okay."

"If we can find Victor Martinez, we'll have a better idea. Did you know him, Professor?" Worthy repeated.

"Native American, wasn't he? He wasn't in any of my classes, but I met him at the reception in September for new faculty and students." Wormley paused, as if stuck in the memory. "That seems a long time ago. Victor seemed bright, very eager, as I remember."

"Did he ever say he wanted to go on the trip?"

"No, I'm sure he didn't. He'd have made a good assistant, I guess. I wonder why I didn't ask him."

Worthy tried to pull Wormley back to the case. "After this reception, did you see him?"

"Maybe once or twice in the halls, but not with Ellie, if that's what you mean."

The professor picked up a fountain pen from his desk and began to twirl it in his hands. "Wait a minute. I saw him a couple of time in Stott's office, but when was that?"

"Who's Stott?"

"He's God around here," Wormley replied, his face serious. "He's my department chair, one of Allgemein's big names. Central American anthropology, especially Mayan. I thought everyone in Detroit knew Stott."

"And Victor was one of his students?"

Wormley shrugged. "He must have been. No one goes to Stott's office for sympathy."

Worthy jotted the name down. "Let's talk about Chimayó. Did Ellie act differently in any way when you were there?"

"At Chimayó? No. Like I told them in Santa Fe, Ellie went off by herself, but that wasn't unusual." The professor paused for a moment. "I talked to a policewoman, very kind. She was the only one who didn't make me feel that I should be jailed right then and there." He paused. "I don't suppose you've met her."

"Yes, I have."

"Tell her … I don't know. Forget it."

"I'll tell her that you remember her. Now, Professor, you said Ellie had a tendency to go off by herself. What did she do? I mean, did she just sit and stare off in space, watch the other kids, sneak a smoke?"

"Chimayó, Chimayó …." Wormley looked out the window for a few seconds before turning to face Worthy. "She sketched. Yes, she had a sketch pad."

"Really," Worthy said. "We didn't know that. Did she ever show you her drawings?"

"Not exactly, but I did catch a glimpse of one she did on Acoma. That's a Pueblo community."

Worthy nodded. "I've been there."

Wormley winced. "I suppose you're revisiting every place we went."

"Why don't you just tell me what happened at Acoma."

"I remember walking over and watching her work. She was drawing the railing on the Spanish commander's headquarters."

"How would you describe her work? Childish, perhaps?"

"Childish? No, not at all. She had real talent, real feeling," the professor said dreamily. "I'd say polished. I just assumed that she'd had art lessons."

"The two of you didn't talk much, then," Worthy commented.

Wormley gripped the arm rails of his chair and looked down again. "Why did I ever think I could handle fifteen kids on my own? They'll say it was bad judgment, and they'll be right. Three partiers kept me pretty sleepless."

Wormley wanted to be helpful, but Worthy could tell that the professor's self-loathing had worn a groove in his memory.

"Just one more question, Professor. After Ellie ran off, what did the other students say?"

Wormley sighed heavily as he leaned back in his chair. "Oh God, the plane ride back, after the police questioned them all, was sheer hell. My guess is that they were too scared to talk seriously about it, so they made it into a big joke. Some turned it into an abduction story—Ellie being taken by aliens to Roswell! Others said she'd split for Vegas on her daddy's money. She's rich, you know."

"Yes, I know."

As Worthy rose to go, the professor remained seated, looking up sheepishly at him. "Can I tell my wife what you said?"

"About what?"

"About Ellie running off to find the Martinez boy. It would be more help to her—to both of us—than you know, Lieutenant."

As he headed for Dr. Stott's office, Worthy wondered if the interview with Wormley had been little more than a charity call. Ellie VanBruskman had made herself the kind of student easy to overlook. With other more typical spring break problems to deal with, the hapless professor had clearly done just that. Would this Stott know more about Victor?

Dr. Stott was trim and middle-aged, his long gray hair gathered into a ponytail like an old hippie. Standing in the doorway to introduce himself, Worthy smelled the faint scent of furniture polish.

"You can have ten minutes, Lieutenant," Stott said, motioning Worthy in. "Unless, that is, you've come to arrest me. Come to think of it, please arrest me. Jail would be better than the faculty senate. At the lowest rung of hell they're doing curricular reform. Trying to get that done before summer school."

"Can't help you today, Professor. I'm here inquiring about Victor Martinez."

Stott leaned back in his chair and balanced effortlessly, his sandals dangling off the ground. He looked over his half glasses and pursed his lips slightly.

"What's Victor got himself into now?"

"Maybe nothing. We're looking into the possibility that Ellie VanBruskman, the missing girl from Allgemein, ran off to find him."

"Ay yai yai," Stott replied as he stared at something on his computer screen. "Mr. Martinez was what we academics call a colossal disappointment, Lieutenant. That means he really screwed up. Victor came to Allgemein on a free ride, which is nothing to sneeze at, by the way. That's roughly one hundred sixty grand over four years. And the first decision he makes as an adult is to throw that all away. Not just my class, but all of them. As I remember, he didn't even bother to finish the semester."

Stott stopped speaking, his eyes squinting at his computer.

"Could you speculate as to why he did that?" Worthy asked.

"Oh, it's quite common, Lieutenant," the professor replied without looking up. "It's very politically incorrect for me to say it, but he lacked two key background traits. One, no one in his family had been to college. So Victor was probably a big deal back home, a prima donna. Second reason. Kids such as Victor lack the stamina. College is hard. You have to work, meaning you have to do more than just live off cheap small-town laurels. Victor came from some podunk town in Arizona and tubed out, *comprende*?"

Worthy sensed Stott was the type who enjoyed sitting behind his polished desk and glancing over his half glasses at disappointed parents, explaining how their son or daughter had let everyone down.

"New Mexico. Victor is from New Mexico," Worthy corrected.

Stott glanced up briefly from the computer screen.

"How bright is Victor?" Worthy asked, the question making him sound a bit like a devastated parent himself.

"Very bright. That's why it's such a shame. He wasn't one of those minorities we accept so we can plaster his picture on future admissions brochures." Stott looked over his glasses at Worthy. "I told him that, by the way."

"When was that?"

"Sometime in November, before Thanksgiving if I'm not mistaken. He sat right where you're sitting, and I told him his type pisses me off. I shared some things I know about the scholarship's donor, trying to make him feel guilty for the waste of it all. He didn't even have the courtesy to answer me. So when I heard he left a week or so after … well, I guess you could say I saw it coming. And now, I've got to go."

As the men parted in the hallway, Stott called after Worthy, "If you find our young friend, tell him that Stott says to shape up and think about what's best for his family."

Worthy walked down the hallway past Wormley's dark office and stopped again in front of the display case of pottery and blankets. Worthy imagined the man already home telling his wife about Ellie and Victor. *How odd*, he thought. Wormley couldn't have been more worried about Ellie VanBruskman. Professor Stott hadn't even asked about the missing girl.

CHAPTER TEN

———◆———

FATHER FORTIS SAW THE FLASHING LIGHTS of the police cars long before he pulled into the monastery's parking area. *Lord, have mercy, now what?* he thought. Sera Lacey had predicted that it wouldn't take the police much time to put the pieces together, but he'd envisioned several days, not one.

As he walked hurriedly toward the dormitory, an ambulance emerged and roared past him. Its siren echoing off the canyon wall made it seem as if St. Mary's was under attack.

Father Fortis steadied his pectoral cross as he hurried through the doorway. Immediately, Brother Bartholomew blocked his way.

"Abbot Timothy needs to see you, Father."

"Of course, of course," he said, his heart racing as he tried to keep up with the novice. "What's happened, my son?"

Brother Bartholomew shook his head. "I'd better not say."

Father Fortis entered the abbot's office and found it bursting with monks. On one side of the room sat Father Linus and the old librarian, Brother Elias. Linus sat rigidly in the chair, his knee bouncing, while Brother Elias eyed Father Fortis warily. On the other side of the room, to the left of Abbot Timothy, was a young man, notebook opened in his lap. The badge in his suit's lapel pocket indicated he was from the police. Behind Abbot Timothy, leaning against the windowsill, was a middle-aged monk with wild, bristling hair. Father Fortis recognized him as St. Mary's spiritual director, Father Bernard.

Abbot Timothy motioned Father Fortis toward the only empty chair remaining, the one next to the policeman. "Father Nicholas, good, I'm glad it's you. I was worried when we couldn't find you."

"I'm sure I told you this morning, Reverend Father. I was in Albuquerque at the library—"

"This is Lieutenant Choi," the abbot said, as if he'd heard nothing.

The man next to Father Fortis reached over and shook his hand. "Afternoon," he said in a soft voice before returning to his notes.

The monk who'd been standing by the window came over and stood behind Father Fortis. In a smooth West Texas drawl, he said, "I don't think we've met yet, Father. I'm Bernard."

Father Fortis turned to shake the man's hand. The power of the grip reminded him that Father Bernard had been the monk who'd pushed the photographer to the ground days earlier. Most monks seemed to shrink within their robes, but Father Bernard's white cassock hung as tightly on his shoulders as a military uniform.

"Father Nicholas, St. Mary's has had another tragedy," the abbot said, his eyes gazing wearily at the ceiling. "Perhaps you've already heard. No? Oh, dear. Forgive me, everyone, but I'm still in a bit of shock. Bernard, would you kindly explain to Father Nicholas what's happened?"

"Of course," the spiritual director said. "To be blunt, Brother Andrew tried to kill himself this morning. He overdosed on medication, actually, but by some miracle, he was found by one of our suppliers, lying unconscious on the floor of the print shop."

"Horrible, horrible," the abbot added. He looked over at Father Fortis and seemed to wait, as if for some response.

"I'm sorry, Reverend Father. Have I met this Brother Andrew?"

The abbot gave him a quizzical look. "You haven't met him? Brother Andrew worked in the print shop with poor Sister Annetta."

"Anna," Father Bernard corrected.

"What?" Abbot Timothy asked, turning around in his chair.

"Not important," the spiritual director said.

Lieutenant Choi cleared his throat. "From what we've been able to determine, no one saw Brother Andrew at breakfast this morning. But since he's had a tendency to miss breakfast, no one paid much attention."

"Horrible, horrible," the abbot repeated, rubbing his one hand with the other. "And such an odd coincidence," he added, looking at the policeman. "It's as if Brother Andrew knew that you were coming back today to interview him again."

A snort escaped Father Linus.

Abbot Timothy looked around the room. "What?"

Father Fortis caught the shake of Bernard's head in Linus's direction.

Lieutenant Choi turned back to Father Fortis. "We're searching the print shop and his room right now."

"Looking for what," Father Fortis said, "a note?"

"Maybe," Choi responded evasively.

"Father Nicholas," the abbot said, "how could anyone not hear the commotion when the ambulance arrived?"

"As I tried to say before, I was in Albuquerque at a library."

"We haven't seen your detective friend around. Did he find his missing student, then?" Father Bernard asked.

Father Fortis noticed the sudden interest in Lieutenant Choi's eyes.

"No, the girl hasn't been found," Father Fortis clarified. "Lieutenant Worthy flew back to Detroit yesterday for a few days of consultation. Now, about Brother Andrew. I'd like to help, but as I said, I don't think I'd even know what he looks like."

"Of course you would," Father Linus said acidly. "He's Hispanic. Dark complexion, shifty eyes. The look of a killer."

"Linus, please," Father Bernard scolded.

"Well, the police interviewed me," Brother Elias grunted. "And I'm Irish."

Father Linus spun in his chair and stared at his fellow monk, a wry smile forming at the corners of his mouth. "Yes, you're the one exception. That's a bit curious, don't you think, dear brother?"

Brother Elias's face reddened. "I'll have you know I wasn't the only one who saw Brother Andrew's moony look whenever she was around."

Father Linus's eyes narrowed as he glared at the other monk. "What would St. Mary's do without her vigilant librarian-slash-guardian angel, Brother Elias? Always ready to share every wild suspicion, aren't you?"

"Really, that's enough, Linus," Father Bernard said.

Lieutenant Choi remained silent, though Father Fortis noticed that his eyes keenly followed the exchange.

"And this Spanish connection ..." Father Fortis said. "I still don't understand."

Choi turned a few pages in his notebook and cleared his throat. "That's what I was about to share when you arrived." He nodded at Father Fortis. "The retreat house where the nun was murdered once belonged to a Hispanic religious group. They call themselves the Penitentes. I assume you've all heard of them."

"Of course we have, Lieutenant," Father Bernard answered. "But the brotherhood of the Penitentes has all but died out. Surely you don't think they had something to do with this."

Father Elias raised his hand like a schoolboy. "Actually, the notion of the Penitentes being a thing of the past isn't completely—"

"Oh, do tell," Linus interrupted.

Abbot Timothy turned toward the policeman. "I should say that Brother Elias's hobby is to keep—"

"Abbot Timothy, please," Brother Elias broke in. "You gave me that as an assignment."

"An assignment, then," the abbot said. "Elias keeps us informed of the activities of the more extreme religious groups in the area, particularly those who hate our church."

Father Fortis twisted in his chair so that he couldn't see Father Linus's face. Outside, a cloud moved over the rock face and deepened the gloom in the room. Was Choi suggesting that Brother Andrew was a Penitente? If so, why hadn't Father Linus told him that?

He decided it was less suspicious to ask the question directly. "How would Brother Andrew know about these Penitentes?"

"We aren't sure he does," Choi replied. "You see, we didn't know about the retreat house's previous owners when we first talked with him."

"But even if there is some connection, Lieutenant, I can't see why a Catholic group would want to harm St. Mary's," Father Bernard said.

"No one is saying any group did," Choi replied. "As I was saying earlier, we came out today simply to follow up on our new information."

Which means the police don't yet know what Sister Anna's wounds mean, Father Fortis realized.

His thoughts were interrupted by Father Linus. "And is Father Fortis here because he's been working with me, a dangerous Hispanic?"

"Don't look at me." Lieutenant Choi shrugged. "The abbot mentioned that he might be able to help."

Abbot Timothy leaned forward in his chair, his hands clasped before him on his desk as if he were about to offer a prayer. "I'm sure Father Nicholas knows why he's here."

"But I don't, Reverend Father."

"What? But what about the folder I left for you to read?"

Puzzled, Father Fortis shrugged. "I don't know what folder you're talking about."

A vein stood out on the abbot's forehead. "I'm talking about the one I put under your door last night."

"Don't you mean the note you left asking me to meet with Father Bernard?"

"No, no, no. I'm talking about the folder that was with the note," the abbot snapped impatiently.

"But there was only the note."

The abbot sat back as if struck. "Oh, good heavens."

"What was in the folder?" Lieutenant Choi asked.

"Only a copy of Sister Annetta's journal. Oh, my."

Oh, my, indeed, Father Fortis thought. He'd found the abbot's note on his bed after Vigils. Had Brother Andrew entered his room and taken the journal? If so, did that mean it had been Brother Andrew spying on him from the balcony?

The abbot turned to Lieutenant Choi. "Of course, it was only a copy. You have the real journal," he said with a forced laugh. "Nothing incriminating. No, nothing at all."

Choi closed his notebook and rose. "The EMT says we'll be able to talk with the young man tomorrow. He can explain himself then. My advice to you all," he said, directing his comments at the abbot and Father Bernard, "is not to blame yourselves for what happened. Young people try to kill themselves for the oddest reasons."

"No doubt that's true," Father Bernard agreed, "but at St. Mary's we take the command to be our brother's keeper quite literally."

Father Fortis sat quietly, wondering why everyone in the room was assuming that Brother Andrew had tried to kill himself. "What if there's no suicide note?" he asked.

"I never said there would be," Choi replied. "They're not a requirement, you know, except in novels."

After Choi left, the abbot asked Father Fortis to stay. As the others filed out, Father Bernard leading the pack, Father Linus tugged on Father Fortis's sleeve, mouthing the words "see me" before he closed the door behind him.

Abbot Timothy sighed deeply. "You promised that you would help, Father Nicholas. Now might be a good time."

The abbot still had his lucid moments, Father Fortis acknowledged. Should he tell the abbot about the knife wounds? Since Choi knew about the morada, what sense did it make to withhold that piece of information any longer?

As Father Fortis absentmindedly popped a spearmint into his mouth, he noticed the abbot reaching into his desk and pulling out a mint of his own. The abbot's fingers fought at the cellophane, resulting in the mint dropping to the floor.

No, Father Fortis thought, *let's not tell the abbot about the knife wounds yet.*

"I'm only too happy to help," he said, "once we find something truly important."

The abbot found the mint and popped it into his mouth. "What's that? You want to help? Fine, fine. Well, why don't you meet with Father Bernard. He was Sister Annetta's confessor, you know. Oh, I just remembered. He has another copy of her journal."

The sun broke clear for a moment before quickly disappearing behind another cloud.

"Brother Andrew, *dear* Brother Andrew. What did we miss?" the abbot said, looking around his study as if the walls would know.

"The lieutenant said that he'd interviewed Brother Andrew before. What do they suspect?" Father Fortis asked.

The abbot shook his head slowly. He worked on the mint for a moment before answering. "Father Bernard doesn't believe that poor Brother Andrew had the slightest thing to do with Annetta's death. You see, Father Bernard has talked to the boy many times. But now this. Promise me, Nicholas, that you'll talk with Bernard. And read her journal. Yes, that would be good."

"Of course, Reverend Father, but I can't believe I'll find something her own confessor missed."

"But Father Bernard requested it himself. He's a very wise man," the abbot said, his eyes fixed on his hands. "The type to succeed me. Perhaps you've heard the rumors, Father?"

"No, not at all," Father Fortis replied.

"Well, you should know this. Talk like that doesn't bother me. Being an abbot is a heavy cross, and my shoulders are too weak. I'm the shepherd of this community, and with Brother Andrew I've perhaps lost a second of my flock." The abbot's mouth quivered. "Sorry, Father Nicholas, I seem to be filled with self-pity tonight. That's hardly helpful."

No, Father Fortis thought, *but it's blessedly normal. And this community needs her abbot to be normal right now.*

The abbot looked up and caught Father Fortis's eye. "I'd like to tell you what Father Bernard said when I told him that you wanted to help. He said you weren't the type to miss much."

The comment surprised Father Fortis. When had St. Mary's spiritual director had a chance to observe him?

The abbot clasped his hands in front of him tightly. "I think I should also tell you that Father Bernard is Brother Andrew's confessor as well."

"I'll see him today," Father Fortis promised, even as another plan was forming in his mind. Brother Elias, the suspicious and nosy librarian, wasn't the type to miss anything at St. Mary's. He'd noticed or imagined something between Brother Andrew and Sister Anna. What else had he seen?

✠

WORTHY'S STOP AT THE CHAPLAINCY OFFICES at Allgemein College found the Catholic priest already gone for the day. No, the student receptionist said while she chomped her gum, she had no idea where Father Veneri was. Would Worthy like to leave his card and come back tomorrow?

So it wasn't until the next morning, June 1, after a night of sorting through old mail in his apartment, that he returned to the Student Services building at the college. In the chaplain's waiting room, he found the same student receptionist playing solitaire.

"Father P should be finished in a couple of minutes," she said. "He knows you're coming."

Worthy sat in one of the soft chairs and looked around the room. A diploma from the Gregorian University in Rome hung center stage with the name *Abel Pius Veneri, S.J.,D.Min. Ph.D.* in bold letters. Photos of students surrounded the diploma, one of a group in front of the Vatican, another of students kneeling beneath a Habitat for Humanity sign. Dead center in both photos was a bearded priest smiling beneath the same Detroit Tigers baseball cap. *Father P, no doubt,* Worthy thought.

Full ashtrays and cups covered the coffee table in front of him. Beneath the glass was an assortment of quotations and yellowed cartoons. He leaned over and studied one of a pope standing dejectedly in front of the heavenly gates while St. Peter chatted with a haloed Che Guevara.

The door to the priest's office opened slightly, releasing the sound of moving chairs. Three females filed out into the waiting room, the last struggling to gain control of a backpack.

The priest from the photos stood in the office doorway and called after the retreating student, "Remember what I said, Mickey. Cajole, request, twist an arm, beg on your knees, but get those two guys for the seven-thirty summer masses. Tell them there'll be a plenary indulgence of a thousand years plus beers at Chiggers if they play two numbers each week. *Capisce?*"

He didn't catch the female student's reply as two other students pushed past the priest and headed for the door. One yelled back a plea for prayer to get into a summer chemistry class before disappearing down the hallway. Father Veneri scooped up a pile of pink messages from the desk. "Jani, I know the semester is over, but remember that the term 'work-study' doesn't include playing cards." He flashed Worthy a broad smile and directed him into the office. Seeing him close up, Worthy noticed that the priest wasn't the young Tom Selleck lookalike from the photos. His beard was full and curled on the sides, but thin strands of hair had been trained to cover a balding forehead. The white tab of his Roman collar was missing, leaving the shirt open casually.

"Pardon the smoke, Lieutenant," the priest said as he fanned at the air of his office and opened a window. He sat down in one of the chairs at a long table and motioned Worthy toward another. "I let the kids light up when we're planning the weekend Masses." The priest shook his head. "This place has to have the most idiotic smoking policy. The dorms are all smoke-free while faculty can do whatever they want in their offices. So, duh! Students are suddenly visiting their profs like crazy. I'd say that was the method to the administration's madness, but that would suggest intelligence."

Worthy glanced around the smoky room at the crowded bookshelves. Various athletic trophies shared space with stacks of books and CDs. The only religious symbol he could find, a small cross with an abstract Christ, peeked out from behind an autographed football.

"So tell me, how I can help you, Lieutenant?"

Worthy handed a photo of Ellie VanBruskman across the table.

"Ah, the missing girl. Sorry, I don't know her. I'm pretty sure she isn't Catholic."

"How about this one," Worthy said, handing across a photo of Victor Martinez.

The priest rubbed his chin. "Yes, I know Victor. But are you saying there's some connection between the two?"

"We're not sure, but we'd like to talk with Victor. We think he may have some information about the girl."

"I wish I could help you," Father Veneri said, "but I haven't seen Victor at Mass for a couple of months."

"I assumed you knew. He withdrew from Allgemein in November."

Father Veneri folded his hands in front of him on the table, a large redstoned ring glistening in the light. "Well, that would explain my not seeing him. When did you say he left school?"

"Late November."

"Okay. I guess it has been that long."

"And you never saw him with a girl at services?"

"No, Victor was a real loner. Not even a roommate, as I remember. Do you mind if I smoke?"

"It's your office."

The priest laughed. "Good point." He lit the cigarette and sent a plume of smoke toward the ceiling.

Worthy leaned forward in his chair. "Did Victor come to you for confession, Father?"

Father Veneri rested the cigarette on the lip of an ashtray. He offered an apologetic grimace as he said, "I'm really sorry, but I can't answer that, Lieutenant."

Worthy held the priest's gaze. His father being a minister, Worthy had grown up around clergy and mainly felt pity for them. But there was something about this guy he didn't like. "I wish you'd reconsider that, Father. The boy may be a key witness in a missing person's investigation."

The priest's face contorted into a frown, but his voice remained firm. "It's simply not that easy." He raised his folded hands in front of him, his index fingers pointing up like a church steeple. "Simply not that easy," he repeated.

"Okay, let me start over. Tell me what Victor was like," Worthy asked.

The priest let his hands fall. "Yes, well, I don't see any harm in that. Victor was by far, bar none, the most traditional student I've ever encountered at Allgemein. My God, he wanted confession in one of those old booths with a mesh grill!"

Father Veneri paused to take another draw on his cigarette as he studied the missing girl's photo. "VanBruskman. I guess I never made the connection. I bought a car at one of her dad's places."

A headache began to pulse behind Worthy's eyes. *Welcome back to Detroit,* he thought, *where nothing is ever easy.* "Did Victor ever mention problems he had at the college?"

The priest shifted in his chair. "Remember, Lieutenant, I didn't know he'd left the college until three minutes ago. But, if you're talking about classes," he added, "I'd say no. Someone told me Victor is pretty smart."

Worthy waited silently, the pain radiating out toward his temples. Finally he said, "How about outside of class?"

"How would I know—"

"You see, Father," Worthy said, "Ellie VanBruskman is a very sick girl. She needs medication to stay in touch with reality. Victor could be our only way of finding her."

"But I already told you that I didn't even know the two were friends. And from what I can tell, you're not even sure she's with him," the priest added quickly, his nostrils flaring.

"And that's all you can tell me?"

"Look, Lieutenant, this isn't a Catholic college, and I have a responsibility to my flock. If any of them found out that I spill their secrets to every policeman who asks me to break confidence, I'd be through."

The two men sat in the silence before Father Veneri stamped out his cigarette and looked over at Worthy. "Why don't you ask me specific questions? If I can answer them, I will. If I can't, well—"

"All right, here's a question," Worthy said, cutting him off again. "How often did Victor come to see you?"

Father Veneri sighed heavily. "He was a regular at Mass, until November, apparently. But in terms of confession, I'd say more than a few times."

"Did he come to talk with you regularly or more toward the end of the semester?"

The priest started to speak, but stopped. "I can't answer that."

Worthy fired back another question. "Did he ever seem especially troubled when he came?"

The priest's face reddened. "Students who bother with confession are usually troubled. So yes, you can assume that."

Hardly letting the priest catch his breath, Worthy pushed ahead. "Did

Victor ever say Allgemein had let him down for some reason?"

The priest rubbed his forehead briskly, as if he were the one with the headache, and smoothed the thin strands of hair over the bald spot. Staring down at his hands, he said, "It's the rare student who admits they've let their profs and classes down, and not the other way around."

"So, I can take that as a yes," Worthy countered.

Father Veneri paused. An odd smile slowly formed. "Here's something I can tell you. I made a point of specifically inviting Victor to sign up for my class on Modern Catholicism. It's not only Catholics who take it, thank God," he clarified, "but it does give my tribe a chance to rant about God and the old church a bit."

"Was Victor ranting?" Worthy asked.

The priest laughed. "God, no, but I wish he had. Victor needs to find out that the sky won't fall if he drops his childish way of looking at the world."

He's trying to tell me something, Worthy thought, *but he wants to play the hip priest later with students, tell them how he stood up to the "man."*

"I'd put it this way," Rev. Veneri continued. "As a Catholic, Victor was living in the nineteenth century. No, I'll revise that. He was living in the Middle Ages."

Worthy wondered what this college chaplain would make of the monks at St. Mary's. "Tell me what you mean by 'childish,' " he requested.

Father Veneri dug out another cigarette and lit it. "The boy was loaded with a ton of guilt—the details of which I'm not free to share. But the guilt arose over things a reasonable person would not give a second thought about." The priest raised both hands as if to indicate that was all he could say.

Worthy ignored the red light and pressed forward. "Are we talking sex, drugs, booze, cheating, what?"

"No, no, nothing as normal as that. God, how can I put this?" He sucked on the cigarette and sent another ribbon of smoke toward the ceiling. "Okay, how's this? Let's say someone ran into this office and told us a tornado had just touched down over in East Lansing, killing scores of people. What would you consider to be a normal human reaction at that moment?"

"Shock, I guess, and sadness," Worthy replied.

"Especially if we knew some of the victims, right? But what if I heard the news and began beating myself up, saying that I should have prevented that tornado? Lieutenant, that was Victor."

Veneri sat back in the chair and stared at Worthy. "I told Victor to let go of the things he can't control and focus on his studies."

"It doesn't seem like he took your advice," Worthy replied. He remembered the worried look on Victor's mother's face. "Did Victor ever mention being followed?"

Father Veneri picked a bit of tobacco leaf off his lip before consulting his watch. "I need to be going, Lieutenant, but I'll tell you this. Do you want to know what was chasing Victor? It was his own fear, fueled by a massively distorted sense of guilt. That's all."

Worthy stood, certain of one thing. Victor had told this priest about being followed. But by whom, and for what reason?

CHAPTER ELEVEN

———◆———

O N THE WAY TO HIS CAR, Worthy passed a group of guys sporting identical fraternity T-shirts.

"Fuck him if he can't take a joke," said the smallest of the three. "Man, I say, fuck him. Giving me an F in an intro class. What do profs think we do all night in the dorm? Study?"

The student cringed when he saw Worthy suddenly turn and stare at him. But Worthy would have only thanked him. He felt his headache lift slightly. Maybe he'd been asking the wrong people about Victor Martinez. It wouldn't be professors or even a chaplain who would know him best, but the guys in his dorm.

A half hour later, after checking at the Dean of Students office, Worthy was knocking on the door of the resident assistant of Shirk Hall. A bleary-eyed, skinny student in a Pistons jersey opened the door. When the resident assistant realized that Worthy wasn't conducting a drug search of the floor, he calmed down and answered his questions.

"Yeah, Victor lived here first semester, but I never heard why he dropped out."

Worthy looked down the hallway at the pizza boxes on the floor and the blinking fluorescent ceiling light, its cover cracked in half. "Tell me how Victor got along on the floor. Someone told me he had a single room."

The supervisor wouldn't look Worthy in the eye. "His roommate moved in with another guy after the first week. It happens."

"Any particular reason?"

The R.A. shook his head and looked down the hallway in the other direction.

"Was Victor the only minority student on this floor?" Worthy asked.

"Probably," the R.A. admitted. "Something happen to him?"

"We'd just like to ask him a few questions," Worthy hedged. He could make out a message in spray paint at the end of the hall that hadn't quite been masked by a coat of new paint. *Fuck Allgemein. They fuck us.*

Nice neighbors for a padrelito, Worthy thought.

"My college dorm was a lot like this," Worthy said. "We used to pull a lot of pranks. You know, against the dorks on the floor. That ever happen to Victor?"

The student nodded toward one wing of the hallway. "Cravitz can be pretty rough on some of the guys," he whispered.

"Rough? How so?" Worthy asked.

"Jesus, it's not my fault, okay? Allgemein expects too much from RAs," he whined. "What's Cravitz, a second-year jock, doing in a fucking freshman dorm anyway?"

"So this Cravitz is a bully. How about some specifics?"

"He's got something on everybody," the RA explained, folding his arms tightly in front of him, his shoulders hunched. "You know the type?"

"Sure. What did he have on Victor?"

"It was the gay thing."

"Gay?" Worthy asked.

The RA leaned against his door frame and ran a hand through his disheveled hair. "It was just a stupid joke," he said, his eyes pleading as if Worthy could arrest him for complicity.

Worthy waited silently.

"There was this younger kid, another Indian, who came to see Victor in the afternoons sometimes. Cravitz started calling Victor 'Gayronimo' and the other kid 'Chief Feather Fuck.' Everything's a joke to Cravitz," the RA repeated.

"How did Victor take it?" Worthy asked.

The RA shrugged. "It was weird. When it first started, Victor seemed to look right through Cravitz, like he didn't see him. Kind of spooky."

"And later?"

"Cravitz finally got to him. He jacked off in a condom and tacked it up on Victor's door. With a note, of course, saying it was from Chief Feather Fuck."

"What did Victor do?"

"Well, hell, we were all there when he came back to the room. He didn't say a word. He just went into Cravitz's room, and we could hear Cravitz call him a 'fudgepacker.' Shit, before you knew it, here's Victor flying at him with a knife. I mean a big knife, and he goes right for Cravitz's balls. That's right, his balls. Thank God, somebody grabbed his arm. But I can tell you, it freaked the hell out of me."

"Did you report it?"

"I was going to, but then he left school. Sort of settled things, you know?"

"So that happened in November, then?"

"Yeah, right before he left."

"And this other Indian student, what happened to him?"

"I don't know. He'd already stopped coming around, though. Maybe Victor did have something going with him. Maybe that's why he freaked. Gay lovers' quarrel, you know?"

WORTHY KNEW HE COULDN'T PUT IT off any longer. Every hour that he didn't report in to his precinct would mean a bump in his captain's blood pressure. Spicer knew he was back, which meant the VanBruskmans did as well. They'd expect a report, and he would hear about the "new evidence."

With a sense of dread, he started toward the precinct, then on impulse turned around and headed in the opposite direction. If he had to face the lot of them, why not surprise them a bit, face them on his own terms?

The rain was slanting off the lake as Worthy headed through early rush-hour traffic toward Grosse Pointe and the VanBruskman home. He exited the freeway and drove up Jefferson Avenue, struck by the scarcity of neighborhood businesses. In Grosse Pointe, it seemed the affluent lived above the ordinary human needs of food and clothing, requiring only tree-lined boulevards. Even the lone filling station that was nestled by the freeway, with its small pharmacy and dry cleaners alongside, was hidden behind a colonial façade. So where did a kid like Ellie VanBruskman hang out around here?

He drove down brick-paved streets until he came to a massive French Provincial with VanBruskman on a brass plate out by the street. Driving up the circular driveway, Worthy parked as close as he could to the house, but even so, he still had to sprint thirty yards through heavy rain to reach the front entrance.

Mrs. VanBruskman opened the door almost immediately. She clutched the neck of her silk robe and pearls as she stared at the policeman. "Lieutenant Worthy?" She reached for her hair, which looked as if it hadn't yet been combed.

"May I come in?"

Without speaking, the woman led him through the open foyer to a room off to the left, a dark-paneled study that was clearly a man's room. A brace of antique shotguns hung above the stone fireplace. On either side were lit bookcases full of trophies, semi-deflated basketballs, and footballs. One basketball's lettering boasted of a championship thirty years before.

Mrs. VanBruskman chose the leather couch, where a brimming ashtray balanced precariously on one arm.

"Well, Lieutenant Worthy, you've taken us by surprise," she said, pulling her robe over a tanned knee. Her slippered feet, tiny like a child's, peeked out from below. "I don't remember that we were to meet you here. Should I phone my husband?"

Worthy remained standing. "Before you do that, Mrs. VanBruskman, could we talk for a few minutes?"

"No, I think I'd better call him first," she said, a tight smile trailing her as she left the room. "You know, Arrol is most anxious to see you," she called from the hallway. "Sit, sit, Lieutenant. I'll be right back."

Worthy removed his raincoat, setting it down on the carpet next to the chair. On the opposite wall was a collection of seascapes. In one, several old sailing vessels were struggling through storms, while in the other, two ships, their cannons blasting, were fighting at close quarters.

Mrs. VanBruskman tiptoed back into the room and reclaimed her seat on the couch. She lit another cigarette and re-crossed her legs. Worthy noticed that she'd combed her hair.

"Arrol will be here soon, but he has to pick up something on his way home. Now, what is it you wanted to ask me?"

"First of all, I suppose I want to thank you. It's seems you were right. Your daughter might have run off to find Victor Martinez."

"Did you find him?"

"Not yet, but we did find some letters Ellie sent to him beginning last December. Do you know if she ever received any mail from him?"

Mrs. VanBruskman inhaled deeply. "Well, of course, I'd know. And I know that she didn't. Ellie received little mail, Lieutenant. An occasional notice of something at the college and a birthday card from her cousins, but no, nothing from that boy." She glanced at her watch before flicking the ash into the ashtray.

"A diary, perhaps? Lots of girls keep them," he said, even as he remembered that Allyson hadn't.

"No, Lieutenant, Ellie's never been much of a writer. She always got so nervous about book reports. But she did like to draw little pictures—cartoons really, nothing serious."

Nothing serious? So Ellie had hidden her sketches from her own mother.

"Can you tell me how Ellie and Victor became study partners?" he asked.

"Now that's all my husband's doing, Lieutenant," she answered abruptly. "When we got Ellie into Allgemein this fall, Arrol met with one of the deans over there. After her troubles, we wanted her to succeed, you see, to get a good start. Victor came highly recommended, a bright boy on scholarship."

"What exactly did his help entail?"

"I believe Arrol paid him for six hours of tutoring a week, always here at the house. That was our rule. Usually they worked here in Arrol's study, but sometimes they were in Ellie's room. The boy would occasionally stay for dinner. He had good manners, which makes things very pleasant, I always think."

Mrs. VanBruskman spoke deliberately, as if she were pacing herself. After a moment, she twisted on the sofa and tapped her cigarette again on the ashtray. "I should tell you that Arrol found the boy a bit proud, although my husband would put it more strongly. You see, Victor would never let him call a cab. The boy insisted on walking the six blocks to catch the bus back to the college. The bus, for God's sake. A bit odd, don't you think?"

Worthy put the pieces together. In such a mansion, Victor must have felt that he was indeed the "boy" hired to help their struggling daughter. His grandmother's entire house on Acoma could fit within this one room. But he had his pride, something that undoubtedly bothered the rich car dealer.

"How long did the study arrangement last?" he asked, as if he didn't already know the answer.

"As I remember, Victor didn't come around much at the end of the semester. Ellie's grades were good—surprisingly so, I thought—so it didn't seem to matter."

Worthy felt a wariness in the woman whenever her daughter's name came back into the conversation.

"We think something happened in late November, Mrs. VanBruskman, something that brought a big change in Victor. We think your daughter knew some secret—"

He paused when he saw the look of alarm on the woman's face.

"No, I'm sure there was no secret between them," she said, studying her cigarette. "You see, I would have known something like that. We're very close."

So close she ran away, Worthy thought.

"Before your husband arrives, I was wondering if I could take a look at Ellie's room."

Mrs. VanBruskman hesitated, but then rose, steadying herself before leading him down a carpeted hallway. To his surprise, she opened a white door, but then walked slowly back toward the front of the house.

As he entered the bedroom, he heard her voice from down the hall. "Can I get you something to drink, Lieutenant? Or is it like in the movies. You're 'on duty.' "

"Something like that. So, no thanks."

Worthy entered what could have passed for a motel room. The desktop was bare except for a small vase of blue plastic flowers, the single bed neatly made with a stuffed poodle posed on top. On a small white table against the wall sat a flat-screen TV. It was only when he moved to the desk that he saw the half-empty glass next to the bed. He picked it up, smelled the scotch, and recognized the color of the lipstick on the rim.

He sat and opened the desk drawers. Instead of makeup and pictures of friends, Worthy found neatly stacked paper and pens, some still in their packaging. The second drawer held plastic unicorns, pink and blue, crowded together as if in a corral. A nineteen-year-old girl cherished these toys? *Maybe she used them for babysitting*, he thought. He remembered from Ellie's files that before being hospitalized, she'd babysat in the neighborhood. Children loved her because she would sit and play with them for hours.

In the third drawer, hidden beneath several Allgemein notebooks, was what he had hoped to find. Eagerly, he lifted the stack of sketchpads out before noticing that the top one was unused. He opened the second and saw more unicorns, some romping through woods while others were jumping fences. The last drawing—signed by Ellie in 2008, when she would have been twelve—was of a unicorn on a drawbridge, scampering away from a dark castle. *Unicorns, then hospitalization for depression*, he thought.

He opened the last sketchpad, wondering if his instincts had been wrong. After several more pages of unicorns, he turned a page to see a credible rendering of Victor Martinez. The boy was standing at attention, like a soldier, holding something in his hand. Worthy looked more closely and recognized a crucifix, drawn in great detail. The drawing seemed years beyond the unicorns. Victor held the cross out solemnly toward the viewer. Below it, someone had written the words *ENTER BY THE NARROW GATE*, accompanied by the date of November seventh.

On the following page was another crucifix, drawn with rays of light radiating from it. The crucifix looked vaguely familiar to Worthy, the arms and shoulders of the dead Christ making a perfect V as the head slumped lifelessly on the chest. Drops of blood fell to the ground from the head, hands, feet, and side. Below it were the similar words *THE NARROW GATE*.

Worthy flipped quickly through the rest of the pages, all blank, until he came to the last page. Here, in a far more amateurish hand, was a drawing of Chimayó, its unmistakable garden wall, old doors, and squat towers.

He looked out the window to the rain falling on the manicured lawn. *Victor must have drawn this*, he thought. He turned the page over. On the back was another, more flowery, handwritten note, *CENTER OF THE WORLD*. Worthy closed the sketchpad and slipped it into his sport coat pocket. He needed to take it with him, but would the VanBruskmans let him?

He heard heavy footsteps coming down the hallway and knew they were Arrol VanBruskman's. But he was only half right. The father's angry face shared the doorway with Captain Spicer's.

"Jeez, Worthy," Captain Spicer said, as if he didn't know what else to say.

"I'll say this for you, Lieutenant," Arrol VanBruskman said, pushing past him. "You've got balls coming into my house after the way you've screwed things up."

He turned on his heel and like a magnet led the two policemen back to the study where his wife sat curled up on the couch, a glass in her hand. Arrol VanBruskman remained on his feet, pacing, while Captain Spicer sat on the other end of the couch. He chewed furiously on his nicotine gum as Mrs. VanBruskman sent a stream of smoke in his direction.

Worthy returned to the chair and waited for Mr. VanBruskman's opening blast. He understood now the wife's odd smile. What her husband had "picked up on his way home" had been Spicer.

"Let's start with your stupid-ass emails, Lieutenant," the car dealer fumed. "What the hell do I care about some Mexican kid? I sent you out there to find my Ellie."

"Victor is from New Mexico, not Mexico, darling," Mrs. VanBruskman corrected.

"I said I don't give a damn about the kid and that includes where he's from," Arrol said, staring at his wife. Mrs. VanBruskman's smirk didn't budge as she swirled her drink.

"And here's my second goddamn problem. You were told to get your ass back here because of new evidence, and now I find out that you've been back since yesterday morning. Where the hell have you been?"

"Conducting interviews, ones I should have done before I ever left Detroit. And about Victor Martinez," Worthy replied patiently, "it was your wife who suggested he could be important. And that turns out—"

"My wife isn't running this case, Lieutenant," Arrol VanBruskman blurted out, leaving little doubt as to who was.

"With all due respect, Mr. VanBruskman, I think that's going a bit too far," Captain Spicer interjected, his eyes intently studying the weave in the carpet.

"All right, all right. But I'm the one paying for this circus, and by God, if you did work for me, I'd fire your sorry ass."

Worthy waited a few seconds before speaking. "I was at the college interviewing people who knew your daughter and Victor Martinez. And before you start in on Victor Martinez again," Worthy said, ignoring his captain's look of alarm, "I'd like to finish what I was trying to explain. We've confirmed that your daughter did run away to find Victor Martinez. We don't know if she found him, but it's possible that they're hiding in some remote house that the boy knows about. New Mexico is a huge—"

"Ah, Chris," Spicer broke in, his eyes still studying the floor. "There's some new evidence."

"Well, will someone tell me what it is?" Worthy shot back.

Arrol VanBruskman walked to stand over Worthy. He started to say something, but instead walked away. "You tell him, Spicer," he commanded.

"No, let me," Mrs. VanBruskman said, smiling at Worthy. "Ellie sent us a letter."

Worthy felt the blood draining from his face. "What?"

"It's postmarked five days ago, from Santa Fe. Would you call Santa Fe remote, Lieutenant?"

The room was suddenly silent.

"I'd like to see this letter," Worthy asked in a deadpan voice.

Mrs. VanBruskman looked to her husband, received a nod, and picked up some papers from the end table next to the ashtray.

She's good, Worthy thought. *She could have shown me the letter the minute I arrived, but she didn't want to spoil her husband's thunder or give me a chance to collect my thoughts.* She handed the letter to Spicer, who rose and carried it dutifully across the room to Worthy.

As if in a fog, Worthy studied the crumpled and stained envelope before reading the one line on the thin sheet of paper. *I'll be okay unless you try to find me. Goodbye forever, Ellie.*

"When did you say you got this?" Worthy asked, his eyes still on the single page.

Arrol VanBruskman had his back to him, and it was his wife who replied. "It arrived three days ago."

"But that doesn't make any sense," Worthy said, leaning forward.

Captain Spicer spoke in a rush, as if to cut off Arrol VanBruskman. "Nor to any of us, Chris. How did she manage to send this from Santa Fe when you say there's been no trace of her?"

Worthy turned the paper over in his hand. "You can verify the handwriting?"

"Goddammit, we know what our daughter's handwriting looks like," Arrol said.

"You're not going to like my first impression," Worthy continued. "This looks like something she wrote when she first ran off, not five days—"

Arrol VanBruskman wheeled about, his face beet-red. "Damn it all to hell! Our Ellie walked to a mailbox in broad daylight five days ago or into a post office, with her picture probably plastered all over the fucking place, and she sent it!"

"Arrol, please," Mrs. VanBruskman interrupted, tapping a new cigarette on the box. Spicer cleared his throat, and the VanBruskmans turned toward him as if expecting some wisdom. Worthy knew better. He continued to inspect the crumpled envelope, especially the odd dusty stains along one edge.

"If your daughter's medical condition is as serious as you've told me, she couldn't have sent this letter—not five days ago, anyway."

"So help me God, if you start trying to tell us Victor Martinez sent this, or we need to run some fancy checks on what kind of paper it's on, I'll have your badge," Mr. VanBruskman fumed. "Find our daughter. Our daughter, Lieutenant, not goddamn Victor! Can't you see she's laughing at us?"

Worthy looked up from the letter to study the man. He was breathing heavily, his fists clenched. *So that is it?* Worthy thought. *They aren't worried about their daughter, but angry at her. She's gotten free of them.* He didn't expect Spicer to see the point. The captain was only here to do what he always did—to smooth things over with the public.

"Did the letter come this way, with all these stains and creases on it?" he asked.

"Of course," Mrs. VanBruskman replied, as if offended at his insinuation. "But you know how the mail service is these days. And who knows what care they take in New Mexico."

Worthy turned toward Captain Spicer. "I assume it's been checked for fingerprints."

"The only clear prints were Mrs. VanBruskman's."

Worthy turned the envelope over in his hand again. "It looks so old, like it's been lying around some place."

"We're not going to sit here and listen to your lame excuses," Arrol VanBruskman said from across the room. "You've had a week on my dollar, and I hope you've enjoyed the pool at the hotel. Against my better judgment, your captain has gotten me to pay for two more. But if you don't find something by then, your free lunch is over. Shit. First the police out there fail me, and now you. I could have hired any private detective I wanted, but they said you were better. Ha!" The car dealer stomped from the room, causing his wife's ashtray to tumble to the floor.

Mrs. VanBruskman turned and gave Worthy her biggest smile. "When will you fly back, Lieutenant?"

"Tomorrow," he replied, standing to put on his coat. He hoped no one would ask why he wasn't leaving for the airport right then. He had no desire to explain why he needed to see his own daughter before flying back to look for theirs.

CHAPTER TWELVE

———— ◆ ————

FATHER FORTIS STARED AT FATHER LINUS, who was standing in his doorway. "We're going to the morada now? You said next week."

Father Linus closed the door behind him. "I need to warn the Brotherhood," he whispered. "As you just said, that nosy lieutenant knows too much."

"How could I hear anything Lieutenant Choi was saying with you spitting like a rattlesnake? You need to remember your heart."

Father Linus glared angrily at Father Fortis. "Who told you about my heart?"

"It doesn't matter. I say it for your own good. You're pushing yourself too hard."

"Nonsense. I feel fine. And about that Lieutenant Choi … you give him too much credit. He doesn't know what he's doing."

"Why? Because he's quiet?" Father Fortis asked. "Listen to me, Linus. Choi didn't miss a thing that happened in that room, especially your tantrum. You might as well have worn a Penitente T-shirt."

"My friends are waiting at the morada," the old monk replied, glancing at his watch. "Are you coming or not?"

"The abbot has asked me to meet with Father Bernard."

"Do that later. Bernard is a good man—and for an Anglo, no enemy of the Brotherhood—but what he can tell you about the murder is small potatoes compared to what you'll find out if you come with me."

"Won't our absence be noticed?" Father Fortis asked.

"Noticed? Of course it will be noticed. You can count on Brother Elias for that. But on the form, I've checked us out to Santa Fe. I said we were going in for our research. You are on sabbatical, aren't you?"

"Not that I can see," Father Fortis replied.

"It isn't a complete lie. We'll talk about our research on the way," the old monk promised.

But they didn't talk about Roman chant, not for the entire forty-five minutes that it took to drive to a small adobe building on the outskirts of Mora.

As the Jeep turned in behind the building, Father Fortis caught a glimpse of a life-sized statue of Jesus kneeling in prayer by a rock. *Jesus in Gethsemane*, he thought, noticing the bright red paint flowing from Christ's brow.

Three men appeared from the doorway of the building, all three versions of one another—old, wearing faded long-sleeved plaid shirts and straw cowboy hats, and walking with their eyes fixed on the ground. The white mustache on the man in the middle fell like a waterfall over his mouth.

Without a word, Linus shook the hand of each before embracing the last man. In the flood of Spanish that passed among the four, Father Fortis heard his name mentioned. One of the men, who had a milk-white cataract in his left eye, stared at Father Fortis's pectoral cross and suddenly bent down to kiss it. The others followed suit.

Linus spoke little, his usual bluster gone, as if he considered himself outranked by the leathery-faced men. After a pause in the conversation, the man with the cataract led the guests toward the morada.

"I told them they could trust you," Linus whispered. "I hope I'm right."

Father Fortis stepped into a dark room, expecting to see something like the retreat house where Sister Anna's body was found. But when one of the other men lit a lantern, he found himself in a smaller version of El Sanctuario de Chimayó. A wooden railing set off an altar area where a plain white table held a jumble of statues. Two dominated in size, one of the Virgin Mary with her arms outstretched in grief, painted tears flooding her face, the other a bleeding and bound Christ in a red robe, his head bowed. The hair beneath his thorny crown looked real, as did the drops of blood that angled down the face, onto his robe and hands.

Father Linus crossed himself and bowed to the altar before moving back toward Father Fortis.

"Being allowed to see this is a rare honor," he whispered.

The two sat on the front bench while the old man with the cataract returned from behind the altar with a large manila envelope. His gnarled hands shook as he fumbled with the clasp.

"Their English is poor, Nicholas, so I'll be translating," Father Linus said.

With a slight nod, Linus accepted a stack of photos and papers before addressing one of the other men. The man moved to one of the small windows set at the top of the wall and pulled back the curtain. A glimmer of light lifted the gloom of the place and revealed clouds of dust still settling after their intrusion. Father Fortis noted that the floor was made of uneven wooden planks, while the walls were bare adobe except for the stations of the cross and a few tin crucifixes. From the ceiling's wooden beams hung a simple two-armed candelabra in the shape of an X. Wax pooled on the floor, evidence of fat white candles recently being burned.

"Nicholas," Father Linus said, "I believe these pictures will prove that Sister Anna's killer couldn't possibly have been one of us." He still gripped the papers tightly in his hand.

The silence of the three men bore down upon Father Fortis like a suffocating blanket. He took a deep breath and waited.

"These first photos show what this morada looked like less than a year ago," Linus explained.

The first photo revealed the room they were in, spray paint covering the walls. Two others showed the altar in shambles. The saints were smashed on the floor, while the statue of the Virgin Mary was decapitated.

Father Linus studied the other photos in his hand, pointing to some pencil marks on the back side of one as he spoke to the others in Spanish.

"Sì sì," he said after listening to the leader's explanation. "They tell me these other photos are of two old moradas from up in Colorado. The vandalism up there is more recent, from just two months ago. Unfortunately, our brothers and sisters can't afford the repairs yet. Look at them closely, Nicholas."

Father Fortis felt all eyes on him as he scanned through the new photos.

"The writing on the walls ... does it mean the same thing?"

"No, some are pentacles, satanic markings. The police told us that gangs often leave them. It shows they're tough guys. But we're sure no gang did this."

"Why?"

"Look at the photos again, Nicholas."

"What am I looking for?" he asked. "Did the vandals steal the same sort of things, like santos?"

One of the men whispered to the elder. Father Linus heard him out before speaking.

"The answer is yes and no. Something important was taken from one of the moradas up in Colorado."

"So, two months ago," Father Fortis figured.

Father Linus spoke rapidly to the oldest man, who nodded back. Turning to Father Fortis, he said, "I have permission to tell you this. Santos aren't the only type of Penitente art. They can be bought in forty shops in Santa Fe alone. No, what these people took from the morada in Colorado was something different, something much rarer. Have you ever heard of a death cart, Nicholas?"

Father Fortis noticed the buzzing between the three men. "Are you talking about something used at funerals?"

"Not just any funeral. One funeral. It's used in our Good Friday processions."

Father Fortis considered the explanation. "Ah, I think I understand. Orthodox in Greece process the icon of the dead Christ through their villages on that day."

"But that's not how we use this cart, Nicholas. It doesn't carry Christ. It carries Death itself. Ah, I see that puzzles you. Our cart carries a skeleton, but rest assured, it is only a wooden one."

"Oh. Then you're mocking death on Good Friday," Father Fortis surmised. "Yes, I see the symbolism."

"It's our way of remembering that our Lord Himself was frightened by death, just as we are. But he conquered death for us."

"And you say this cart was stolen from one of the moradas in Colorado?"

A new tension in the room suggested to Father Fortis that his English had been understood.

"Yes. It was a great loss," Father Linus replied. "Especially with *santeros* being so very rare."

"Santeros? "

"Trained woodcarvers, Nicholas. Fewer and fewer continue the old ways."

Father Fortis restudied the photos in his hand. "Tell me about the roof. How was this hole made?"

Father Linus posed the question in Spanish to the older man. "It must have been done with a sledgehammer. We believe it made an opening for a ladder. Then they used the sledgehammer to destroy the wooden beams. My brothers don't think a gang did this damage," Linus explained. "We know gangs have vandalized our moradas. That's an old problem. But whoever did this wanted to make sure no one would ever use this place again."

"They were wrong," the third man declared, his voice strong and clear.

Father Fortis felt the pride of these men. They were too defensive about the Brotherhood to be objective, he thought.

"With respect, I don't see why that necessarily rules out a gang," he said.

"Why would gangs go to the trouble of removing their tire tracks? Gangs like to advertise their presence. But there is more, much more, you need to understand." Father Linus handed him another two photos. "Study these, please. Especially the floors and the walls."

Father Fortis compared the photos. The floors were littered with pieces of statues of saints—arms and heads broken off the bodies. Not one seemed to have survived the attack intact. Littering the floors were also layers of shredded paper, some as small as confetti. On the wall in each photo was a plain cross.

"I see what you mean," Father Fortis said. "Sister Anna's body was covered with bits of paper like this, wasn't it?"

Father Linus's head bobbed excitedly. "Think how long it would take even a group of people to tear paper into pieces that small and scatter them all around. Do gangs do that? No. Now, Nicholas, what do you notice on the walls?"

"The crosses ... but why would they leave them on the wall after destroying everything else?" In the background, the whispers of the three men grew louder.

"Look again, and you'll see that the crosses aren't exactly unmarked," Father Linus said.

Father Fortis held the photos up to the meager light. On the floor below each of the crosses was the broken-off figure of the crucified Christ.

"They removed our Lord, but left the cross alone. How strange."

"Strange indeed," Father Linus replied, looking pleased. "The police dismissed that, said it wasn't important. Hah! The Brotherhood is devoted to the suffering of our Lord. It is our very reason for existing."

Father Fortis stared again at the photos. Father Linus had made a good point, but it did not explain everything. Who but a Penitente would mutilate a nun's body to mimic a favorite santo of the Brotherhood? He looked up to find the elder's milky eye boring into him. He looked down at the man's hands and saw the telltale nail prints.

"Father Linus, you said a moment ago that there's more these men want me to know?"

The old monk gave him a searching look. "Do you believe us, then?"

"I can't say that. But I want them to know they can trust me. Please tell them that."

Father Linus's eyes filled with tears. "Nicholas, I thought you could tell. The old one is my brother. I mean my real brother."

Father Fortis looked from Father Linus to the one with the cataract. *Yes, of course*, he thought. There were marked similarities between their faces.

In a low voice, Father Linus spoke in Spanish with his brother and the others. The four whispered together; then Father Linus's brother stepped forward.

"They have *carreta* and *La Muerta*," he said in a wavering voice.

"What does he mean?" Father Fortis whispered.

"The Death skeleton and the cart. The ones who vandalized the place in Colorado stole them both," the old monk explained.

"But you already told me that," Father Fortis protested.

"No, you don't understand, Nicholas. La Muerta is still missing, but the police … they have the cart in their possession."

"What?"

"Thank God they don't know what it is. If they did, they'd draw the wrong conclusion."

A shadowy memory rose in Father Fortis's mind. "What does this cart look like?"

"Wooden, with railing all around it. Wooden wheels, too."

"About four feet long?" Father Fortis asked.

"Yes. I was wondering if you'd remember seeing it."

"It was along the back wall in the photos of Sister Anna."

"The killer put flower pots in it! The *bastardo* steals from us and then puts the cart near her body. Just to incriminate us!"

And he's doing a good job, Father Fortis thought. Didn't Father Linus realize that the clue proved the killer had to be some twisted Penitente?

"But Linus, how can you be sure it's the same cart?" he asked. "Maybe the one in the retreat house was left there years ago."

Father Linus looked up at his brother. "No, the one next to Sister Anna's body was from that morada. My brother and I have known that cart our entire lives. You see, we helped our father build it."

CHAPTER THIRTEEN

———◆———

WORTHY DROVE SLOWLY THROUGH HIS OLD neighborhood. The trees that the neighborhood association had planted in the boulevards had noticeably grown since he'd last been here, and judging from a tricycle in the neighbor's yard, old Mrs. Davis had finally sold her place.

He glanced briefly at his old house and continued down the street. There were still fifteen minutes to kill before he'd said that he'd arrive. He drove by the grade school where he'd attended PTA meetings for both Allyson and Amy. That seemed a lifetime ago.

Circling the block, he parked in front of his house and walked slowly to the side door. He stopped to kick at a tuft of crabgrass growing in a crack in the driveway. Was it too much to hope for, after dealing with the VanBruskmans, that Allyson would be civil to him?

For some reason, he thought of the santo of the suffering Virgin Mary in Father Linus's room. A mother with knives piercing her heart. What a perfect description of a divorced parent.

To his relief, it was Susan, not Allyson, who answered his knock. "You're early," she whispered with a slight tremor in her voice.

Worthy took a step back on the stoop and gazed down at his dusty shoes. *A bit of New Mexico*, he thought. "Is it a crisis if I'm five minutes early?"

Susan blocked the way into the house. "Are you in trouble, Chris?"

"Not all that much. Why?"

But he knew. After leaving the VanBruskmans, he'd had to endure ten minutes in Captain Spicer's car. Assuring Worthy of his continued confidence in him, Spicer had managed to make it clear that the letter from the missing girl concerned him.

"The letter has to be bogus," Worthy replied. "Ellie's face is plastered everywhere out there."

"But the handwriting matches."

"I'm not saying she didn't write it. What I'm saying is that the girl isn't somewhere right under our noses in Santa Fe. Hell, I've only been out there a week. Give me some time to prove it."

"Chris, Chris, forget VanBruskman's comment about the two weeks. I never agreed to that," Spicer assured him.

No, Worthy knew the deadline had indeed been promised. And because of that, he'd stopped before coming over to his old house to call Sera. But even that hadn't gone right. The policewoman wasn't in her office, so he'd left instructions on an answering machine for her to check all the area post offices. "Ask them if they remember a letter turning up with smudges all over it," he'd said.

"Are you sure you're not in trouble?" Susan repeated.

"Spicer called here, didn't he?"

"This morning," she said, still standing in the doorway. "He said he knew you were back in town, but you hadn't checked in."

He felt his face flush. He couldn't believe Spicer had called his ex-wife. "Look, I've seen him, and we're just not the best of friends. Okay?"

Susan opened the door and led him toward the kitchen by the back way, avoiding the stairs.

"I'm not trying to be difficult, Chris, but I just got home myself and don't know what mood she's in," Susan whispered. "All I know is that she's leaving for work in a few minutes."

So if I hadn't come early, I'd have missed her, Worthy reasoned. Allyson had planned things pretty well. As he entered the kitchen, his younger daughter, Amy, jumped up from the table and threw her arms around his waist.

"Daddy, Daddy, show me what you brought me."

"Easy, greedy Gus," he teased, squeezing her tightly. "How are you, pumpkin?"

Before she could reply, another voice spoke from behind him.

"You're early."

He turned to see Allyson leaning, arms folded, against the doorway to the kitchen. He hardly recognized her with the short hair and dark eyeliner. Had she finally realized how much she took after his side of the family?

Allyson gave her sister a look of utter boredom. "Amy, you are such a child. No one gets a gift without some reason."

Amy disentangled herself from her father. "A trip is still a reason. Isn't it, Daddy?"

"Sure, sure, pumpkin," he said. "I got you something."

Allyson walked to the refrigerator. "You don't get it, Amy," she said, turning her back on both of them to hunt for some food. "Dad doesn't bring us presents because he takes trips, but because Mom lets him come back over here." Yogurt cup in hand, she faced Worthy. "Mom says you've been looking for another missing girl."

He sat down at the end of the table but decided to leave his coat on. Here they were, the four of them, sharing the same room, just as they had not long ago. Even the tension in the air was the same, except it used to come from Susan. Now it was from his older daughter. Would Amy be next?

He waited for Susan to say something, to show him how things worked with Allyson these days. Instead, his ex-wife left the room, calling back to Allyson to let her know when she needed to leave.

Amy plopped down on her father's lap and scrunched up her face at her sister.

"I don't care what you say. Daddy always brings me a present."

Allyson rolled her eyes and turned back toward the refrigerator.

Worthy reached into his pocket and brought out the small wrapped box. "Sorry, honey, it's only something small from the airport gift shop."

Eleven-year-old Amy tore the treasure open, laughing victoriously as she held up the small porcelain horse. "See, Ally, see? Thank you, Daddy. Did you ride one in Mexico?"

Worthy laughed despite himself and despite Allyson. "Believe it or not, they drive cars out there. And I was in New Mexico."

Susan poked her head back in the room. "A horse? Oh, that's cute, sweetie." Jangling her car keys, she said to Allyson, "Time to go?"

Allyson walked past her father without speaking, but stopped and whirled about in the doorway. Worthy braced himself.

"Dad didn't ride a horse because that would mean he took time off work." She paused for a second to reload. "If you got me the matching cowgirl, I don't want it."

Without thinking, Worthy reached into his pocket and threw the plastic bag halfway across the room. It landed at Allyson's feet with a soft thud.

"What's this shit?" Allyson asked, standing motionless.

It felt a scene out of an old home movie, all of them in the same old space, only this time he couldn't remember his part. "It's a bag of dirt."

Bewilderment crossed Allyson's face, even as she reached down and picked it up. Worthy caught Susan's panicked expression even as he felt his own heart pounding up into his throat. *What am I doing?* he thought.

Allyson opened the little bag and reached in, as if looking for something buried. She extracted a dusty finger and held it up for her father to see. "So you got me a bag of dirt and Amy got a stupid horse?"

"It's magic dirt from a place called Chimayó. Although I guess magic isn't the right word," he muttered. He took a deep breath and pressed on, "People out there call it healing dirt. They come from thousands of miles away for it." For a fraction of a second, he thought he saw pain in her eyes. He looked away, wondering what torture the psychiatrist would make of his impulsive act.

He waited for the door to slam, for a scream, or for the dirt to be poured over his head. Instead he heard a tremor in Allyson's voice. "What's it heal? I mean, are we talking pimples or world hunger?"

Worthy shrugged. His pounding heart made speaking impossible. Amy twisted off his lap and set her horse on the table as if to make it clear who'd gotten the real gift.

"Well, Dad, am I supposed to be impressed?" Allyson challenged as she put the bag of dirt in her pocket.

Susan's hands circled behind Allyson, mouthing to Worthy to please let them leave.

But Allyson crossed her arms and leaned against the door frame, waiting for an answer. Worthy could feel something ready to snap, either in the room or in himself.

"No, not impressed," he managed to say, looking her in the eye.

The exchange seemed to puzzle Allyson as much as it did Worthy. She started to say something, turned as if to walk away, then shot a glance back at her father. "That's good, because I'm not."

"Then it looks like the two of us finally agree on something, Ally," he said, not daring to look up.

A half hour later, Worthy sat with Amy in the backyard swing waiting for Susan to return. When she arrived, she walked slowly out to them and asked Amy to go in to watch TV. Worthy stopped the swing with his legs when his ex-wife sat down at the other end.

"Look, Susan, I don't know why I did that with the dirt," he said. He wondered what his bizarre stunt would cost him. Would the psychiatrist cut him off completely?

Susan sat silently. He imagined old Mrs. Davis looking over the fence and thinking how the two of them sitting in the swing together looked like old times. But Mrs. Davis was gone, and it wasn't old times.

"I honestly don't know what possessed me," he confessed. "I didn't even know I had the bag of dirt in my pocket until I reached in for the horse. "

He looked around the garden, Susan's pride and joy, and toward the fence he'd built to protect the girls from the creek.

Susan cleared her throat. "I want to tell you about Allyson ... what I know, that is. As you can see, she's pretty angry."

If that's supposed to make me feel guilty, he thought, *it worked.*

"The counselor says her anger is a good sign. 'Necessary tension,' Rachel calls it. You got a blast of it tonight, Chris, but I get it almost every day. Amy does, too. I hope Amy understands."

Worthy watched a pair of cardinals fly through the yard. "Still no word on where she ran to, or why?"

Susan shook her head. "That's down below the anger, Rachel says." She pulled her legs up and gripped them with both hands. "What Ally said to you was cruel, but it is strange that you're looking for another missing girl. I know it about killed us, but at least Allyson came back well-fed and in good health."

"I'm still hoping the same will be true about this one."

"You think she could be dead?" Susan asked.

"If Ellie VanBruskman were more like Allyson, I'd give her a better chance. But she seems almost the opposite."

Susan looked over at Worthy. "Are you saying we did something right with Ally?"

Worthy looked over to see tears streaming down her face.

"I think we did a lot of things right," Worthy replied.

From the porch, Amy called out. "Ally called. She's got a headache. She wants you to pick her up in a half hour."

Worthy rose, causing the swing to sway. "Can I ask you something?"

Susan remained in the swing and gazed out on her garden. "If it's what you always ask me, I don't think I can take it tonight, Chris."

"No, it's not about us. I won't do that anymore, Susan."

She looked up at him, puzzled, and he couldn't tell if she were relieved or hurt. "What do you want to know?" she asked.

"Do you remember something happening at Allgemein College last fall, some sort of tragedy?"

Susan shook her head. "No, with Allyson running off, I was scouring the newspapers every day. I'm sure I'd have remembered if something .... Wait a minute. There was that horrible accident out at the Palisades. The Pakistani boy ... wasn't his father a professor at the college?"

Pakistani? The RA had said Indian. *Close enough*, he thought. "Tell me what you remember."

"I think he was a little older than Amy. He fell while rock climbing with some friends. As I remember, he died without regaining consciousness. Did your missing girl know him?"

"I'm not sure, but I'm pretty sure someone else did. When was all this?"

Susan rose from the swing and fanned away a mosquito. Lines on her face, new to Worthy, formed tiny shadows in the evening light. "I think it was a couple of weeks before Thanksgiving."

That had to be it, Worthy thought. Victor knew the boy who'd died. But why had he and Ellie blamed Allgemein?

They walked together toward the house. "Oh, I knew there was something I was supposed to tell you," she said. "Someone called for you a couple nights ago."

"Here?" he asked testily.

"You still get a lot of calls here, Chris. Mostly for better phone service or a new mortgage, but this one was from a woman."

"A woman? Did she leave a name?"

"Cartwright, I think. Dr. Cartwright. I think she said she was from Mercy Center. She asked if you'd call her back. Does that make any sense?"

Worthy stopped in the yard and nodded slowly. Ellie's psychiatrist at the hospital. Why hadn't he thought about that himself? But then again, why hadn't the VanBruskmans mentioned her?

While shaving the next morning—a rainy Sunday in Detroit—Worthy thought about Father Fortis back in New Mexico. Had he followed through and told Sera Lacey about the santo? What would she make of the similarity of the old painting and the nun's stab wounds? *More than I,* he admitted. A cop from the Midwest wasn't going to solve this one.

Once he flew back to New Mexico, Father Fortis would ask him about Allyson. What would he say? He'd have to tell him about giving her the dirt, and he'd have to admit he had no idea why he'd done that. Well, at least Allyson hadn't exploded. Maybe it *was* magic dirt.

Despite the fiasco at the VanBruskmans' house, he considered the time in Detroit as worth it. And before he flew out, he still had the interview with Dr. Cartwright. He wondered what she might know.

As he dried his face, he tried to find a thread of logic in what he knew. Victor had come to Detroit in the fall and had made a good start at a prestigious college. A religious kid, he'd been the helper type. He reached out to the fragile VanBruskman girl and also befriended a Pakistani boy. Despite hazing in his dorm, he managed to impress his professors—until early November. That was when the Pakistani boy had died, and that was when Victor and Ellie agreed that Allgemein was somehow at fault. After that, Victor dropped out of school.

Worthy straightened his tie, admitting that what he knew didn't offer one clue as to the boy's whereabouts. But at least with Victor, he had the beginning of a sequence. That was more than he could say about Ellie. She'd been hospitalized for depression a year ago. She did well in college, thanks to Victor's help, but lost her only college friend in November. In December, she signed up to take the spring break trip to New Mexico—Victor's home. There she ran away, and from that point on, her trail was completely cold.

Had she found Victor? Was she still searching for him? Or was she already dead?

Maybe Ellie's doctor would offer some help. He'd rechecked his files the night before and found, oddly, that Dr. Cartwright wasn't the psychiatrist of record.

MERCY CENTER'S RECEPTION AREA WAS THE sunny sort, with paintings of flowers about to bloom and ducks winging over rivers. The décor reminded him of something the nosy nun at Chimayó had said as they were about to leave the church. "People who come to Chimayó have tried the bright, cheery places. They come here for the darkness," she'd said.

A college-aged orderly escorted Worthy through a series of locked doors and down thickly carpeted hallways. At yet another locked door, the orderly glanced through the small pane of reinforced glass before unlocking the entrance to the adolescent unit. On the left, halfway down the hallway, Worthy was shown the office of Dr. Jane Cartwright.

A middle-aged woman with a stern gaze, gray hair pulled tightly to her head, admitted him into the room. The place seemed made entirely of metal: filing cabinets and a large desk, its top bare and shiny, along with the two heavy steel chairs.

As soon as the psychiatrist had closed the door behind them, she asked, "First, Lieutenant, can you tell me if you think Ellie is all right?"

Worthy remained standing as he explained that Ellie was proving harder to find than anyone had first thought. "She could be in a great deal of trouble, or she could be simply hiding out somewhere," he said.

"Which is why I called, Lieutenant. Please sit down."

As he did so, Worthy wondered if Ellie VanBruskman had sat in his chair, telling this doctor all her secrets. On the chance that she was still alive, Worthy hoped so.

"I appreciate your contacting me, doctor. Ellie is proving a difficult person for us to understand," he began.

Still standing, Dr. Cartwright took off her glasses and let them dangle from a chain around her neck. "In the end, the VanBruskmans and I couldn't work together, so I knew you wouldn't get my name from them. I apologize for disturbing your ex-wife. The whole thing seemed a bit awkward for her."

"It's okay. We still speak."

"Always best for the children when you do," she said. She sat down behind her desk and stared at him for a moment. "I have some information that might help you."

Worthy didn't get his hopes up. He'd heard that promise too many times before.

"But," she added, "for legal reasons I'll explain later, it would be better if you told me what you already know before I comment."

"What we know? That won't take long. We know that Ellie went to New Mexico to find a young man named Victor Martinez." Worthy watched the doctor's face but saw no reaction to the name. "We haven't been able to find him, either, so we don't know if they're together or not. And we know that Mr. Martinez left here last November over some problem at the college. The last thing we've learned is that Ellie was aware of Victor's problem and blamed Allgemein."

Dr. Cartwright jotted down a few notes as he spoke. "Are you at liberty to tell me what you've learned from the college?" she asked.

"People there either don't know anything or they won't tell me."

The psychiatrist sat back and glanced toward the room's only window. "And Ellen? What did you think of her?"

Worthy looked puzzled. "But I said we haven't found Ellie."

"No, no, Lieutenant. Ellen is the mother's name. I see you didn't know that."

Ellen and Ellie—was that supposed to mean something? He scratched his chin. "Mothers don't usually give daughters their own names, do they?"

"It's very rare. Not like men."

"I'm sure that's not the only thing the VanBruskmans have kept from me. Something the father said led me to believe they're angry at her for maybe getting away."

"That's something worth pondering, Lieutenant." Dr. Cartwright opened a drawer, withdrew a folder and laid it on the desk, her hands, palms down, on top of it. "Let's put the parents aside for a while. Are you willing to toy with perjury to learn more about Ellie and Victor Martinez, Lieutenant?"

"Perjury? I don't understand."

"It's simple, Lieutenant. If you're asked in court if we discussed details from this file, are you willing to deny that under oath?"

Worthy pondered the question. "I'd say you're taking more of a risk than me. But yes, if it helps me find the girl, I will."

Dr. Cartwright nodded firmly, put her glasses back on, and began turning pages. "Excellent. Ellie was a patient here from March through May of last year. She then became an outpatient, again under my care, until late December. So you can see that I treated Ellie during the period when Victor Martinez came into her life." She paused on one page. "It looks like I didn't hear the boy's name until September, so I assume that's when they met."

"That's right."

"Here's the way that I'd describe their relationship, Lieutenant," she said, looking over her glasses at him. "In September, Victor was like a third parent to Ellie, but by November he was more like a younger brother."

"Does that mean Ellie was getting better, or had Victor changed?" Worthy asked.

"A fair question, but one I can't fully answer. You see, I was treating only Ellie. Trying to be objective, I'd say that Ellie made good progress on some serious underlying issues during the fall. Her mother thought just the opposite, by the way. I guess we can't talk about Ellie without talking about the mother."

"Ellie and Ellen," Worthy repeated.

"There you are, Lieutenant. Keep thinking about that. But if we're talking about Victor, I'd say that he became needier as she grew stronger. It's a common reaction."

"Were they lovers?" Worthy asked.

Dr. Cartwright looked past Worthy before speaking. "If Ellie had romantic feelings for Victor in September, they would have been infantile and unstable. That's simply another way of saying that I wondered the same thing and worried a bit. Gradually I realized that Victor wasn't that kind of threat. Ellie described him as very religious. Are we still talking about the same boy?"

"All of what you say matches," Worthy replied. "Did she ever mention Victor feeling obsessively guilty about something, perhaps the accidental death of another boy?"

The psychiatrist sat back in her chair and removed her glasses. "In early November, Ellie came in one day and said that she was very upset. It seems that Victor had had several meltdowns, crying fits, in her room when they were supposed to be studying. Now, remember that Victor was her only real friend in college. He'd just told her that he was quitting school and going back home. I remember that afternoon vividly, because I was relieved to see how Ellie handled it. She was sad, which is appropriate under the circumstances, but she wasn't panicky. I also noted in her file that her capacity for empathy was clearly increasing. She truly felt bad for Victor. But she didn't say anything about a boy dying."

"Which means that she didn't tell you why he wanted to leave," Worthy said.

"No, but I remember advising her to encourage Victor to talk to someone at the college."

"I'm pretty sure he did that," Worthy interjected, "but I think it backfired."

The psychiatrist nodded as she returned to her notes. "That seems borne out by something I've written here from two weeks later. That would be about the end of November. Ellie told me that Victor had in fact confided in two persons from the college, but it seems they only made things worse."

Two people? Beside Father Veneri, who was the second? Stott hardly described his meeting with Victor as the boy *confiding* in him.

A new thought made Worthy stir in his chair. "Did Ellie ever tell you that Victor thought he was being followed?"

"No, but it wouldn't surprise me."

"Really? Why not?"

"From the way Ellie talked about Victor, I can imagine that he was disintegrating psychologically, maybe already hallucinating. He could have thought he was seeing the dead boy."

Worthy sat in silence for a moment. Dr. Cartwright and Father Veneri both agreed that Victor had just imagined being followed.

"How else can I help you, Lieutenant?"

There's more, he thought. *She knows more. But what?* He consulted his notes before looking up. "Did Ellie ever talk about running away from home?"

Dr. Cartwright looked at him pensively. "People verbalize a lot of things in therapy, but most never become serious plans. My job is to sift through what I'm hearing and find the patterns. When Ellie stopped coming to me, I had a clear sense of her plan. I knew that the parents were about to terminate treatment, so I asked her to dream out loud, to tell me what she wanted for herself. First on her list was finishing college, which in light of what you're reporting may be important. She verbalized that goal after Victor had left Allgemein."

Worthy's concentration was broken by the sound of running, then shouting, in the hallway outside the door.

The psychiatrist didn't even glance over toward the noise. "That's not unusual, Lieutenant. They'll buzz me if they need my help."

Worthy tried to make sense of what the psychiatrist had said. "What you're telling me only makes things more confusing. You're saying that in December Ellie sounded healthy enough to imagine finishing college without Victor. Yet in the spring she runs away."

"Then perhaps I am at fault," Dr. Cartwright said, looking at Worthy intently. "Ellie may not have talked about running away, but then again she's nineteen. Another part of her plan was to move out of their house."

Dr. Cartwright's emphasis on the word "their" struck Worthy like a brick. A flood of images came to his mind—the angry face of Arrol VanBruskman lurching toward him, the cool wariness in his wife's eyes, the unicorns imprisoned in Ellie's desk, and the empty glass of Scotch on the floor. Last to surface was a memory of the odd line in Ellie's final letter to Victor, "those old people pretending to be parents."

He sat silently, aware that the psychiatrist was studying him.

"My God, Ellie's adopted," he whispered slowly.

Dr. Cartwright put her glasses back on and nodded slowly.

"That's why they fired you, isn't it? You helped Ellie figure that out."

Again, the psychiatrist nodded. The whole world seemed eerily quiet as Worthy sat with his thoughts.

"Maybe there's yet another question you want to ask me?" Dr. Cartwright asked.

Without waiting for a response, she passed two photos across the desk. One showed Ellie on the day of her admission to Mercy Center, and the other was of Ellie on the day of her release. In the first, the girl looked no more than thirteen, hair in pigtails, eyes dull, her face pudgy with acne eruptions. In the second, Ellie seemed older, more alert, even smiling faintly. In the second, she looked less like the VanBruskmans.

He flipped back to the first, sensing he was missing something. He studied the dead eyes of the first one before being drawn to the hair. It was light, not unlike the color of Mrs. VanBruskman's. In the later photo, her hair was black as Sera's.

His heart raced. "Were Ellie's real parents Hispanic?"

The doctor's eyes narrowed. "Don't get too far ahead of yourself, Lieutenant. I'm quite sure she didn't run away to find her mother."

"Why not? It all makes sense."

"First of all, you seem pretty certain that she ran away to find Victor. What would he have to do with a search for her mother? But there's something else. When Ellie told her parents that she knew the big dark secret, they insisted on coming personally with her the next time. That was when they terminated our sessions. Mrs. VanBruskman was livid, claiming they would sue me for ruining their family."

Dr. Cartwright paused to recover her composure. "I was very proud of Ellie, Lieutenant. Mrs. VanBruskman was raging, telling Ellie that she was sicker than when she'd first been hospitalized. Ellie just smiled and then asked to know the name of her true mother. Mr. VanBruskman laughed in her face. 'What? Are you planning on going down to South Miami?' he asked. I didn't get the feeling that he was lying."

Dr. Cartwright closed the folder, took off the half glasses, and looked up. Her eyes were full of pain.

"May I ask you a question, Lieutenant?"

Worthy nodded.

"How did Ellie sound in her letters to Victor? Was her thinking disoriented or loose in any way?"

Worthy looked out the small, wire-reinforced window. To help the Ellies of this city, this woman locked herself up with them. Some got better, and no doubt some didn't. And then some, like Ellie VanBruskman, got too healthy—so healthy that those who signed them in didn't like it.

"Everything Ellie wrote," he told the doctor, "sounded focused. I think she clearly expected to find Victor."

" 'Focused,' " Dr. Cartwright repeated, gazing down at her desk. "God, how I hope you're right. Whenever a client is ripped out of treatment like she was," she snapped her fingers, "we never know for sure if she'll make it. And no one ever tells us."

Worthy stood, but Dr. Cartwright continued to sit at her desk and stare down at the folder.

"Tell me the truth, Lieutenant. Do you think she's alive?"

Worthy thought of the odd note that the VanBruskmans had just received from Santa Fe. "You might know better about that than I. How long can she last without her pills?"

Dr. Cartwright closed her eyes. "Ellie's depression is the type that requires medication, sometimes for the rest of a person's life. The other thing I should tell you is that her medication is maintenance only. She can't possibly improve without regular therapy."

She led Worthy to the door and unlocked it. "This is one of those times, Lieutenant, when I hope I'm wrong. I'm doing my best to picture her doing just fine, wherever she is."

CHAPTER FOURTEEN

———◆———

FATHER FORTIS KNEW THAT EVERY MODERN monastery had a Father Bernard on staff, someone with clinical training in pastoral psychology. These counselors, often serving as spiritual directors, administered the personality tests to novices. They also conducted the sensitive interviews regarding the sexual orientation of the young men seeking admission and were called upon when serious emotional and spiritual ills manifested themselves. In Father Fortis's experience, spiritual directors were rarely promoted to being abbots, perhaps because they knew too many secrets.

Father Bernard opened the door to Father Fortis's knock with a generous smile. "I'd almost given up on you, Father," he said in his West Texas accent. A shock of gray hair made the monk seem even taller than his large frame. The obvious strength of the man gave credence to the rumor that he'd come straight into monastic life from service as a Navy Seal.

Father Fortis remembered the type from his high school wrestling days. As the only heavyweight, he'd been paired with the one guy capable of wrestling him in practice. The guy wrestled two weight classes down but was muscular like Father Bernard. For three years, the two seemed to wrestle one long match, Father Fortis forever trying to use his massive weight to tire his opponent, the other guy countering with his speed and strength. Real opponents in competitions were comparatively easy to defeat for both of them.

"Father Bernard, I apologize for not stopping by sooner," Father Fortis said. "I meant to come by yesterday, but Father Linus and I were off on … research."

Father Bernard ushered him into what looked like a private library. Bookshelves groaned under the weight of heavy tomes, periodicals, and folders. A coffee table was covered with mugs and magazines.

"Let's make a deal," the monk said as he poured two cups of coffee. "You call me Bernard, and I'll call you Nicholas. This 'Father this, Father that' stuff tires me out. And thank you, by the way, for getting Linus away from here yesterday. We're all distraught about Sister Anna, but he's taking matters very personally. And that's not good for his heart."

A similar thought had crossed Father Fortis's mind the night before. When the two of them had been at the morada, the old monk had been as calm as Father Fortis had ever seen him. But the closer the Jeep got to the monastery, the more agitated Father Linus became. By the time they pulled into the parking lot, Father Linus's diatribe against Brother Elias left him gasping for breath.

"Any word on Brother Andrew?" Father Fortis asked his host. "What a terrible time for St. Mary's to deal with an extra strain."

Father Bernard drew up a chair and sat facing his visitor. "We can talk about Andrew in a moment. But as to the community, yes, you're absolutely right. We're fraying a bit, Nicholas. No doubt about that."

"I don't know anything harder on a monastery than the hint of sexual misconduct," Father Fortis offered.

Father Bernard took a sip of coffee. "Ah, yes. Sex. You can't even use the word in a monastery without misconduct being assumed. Yet the truth is all of us, not just Andrew and Sister Anna, are sexual beings."

"I suspect the rules at my monastery are quite similar to St. Mary's," Father Fortis added. "Our sexual energies don't disappear when we become monks, but are to be turned toward God. That's very easy to say, but harder to do. Especially when someone as beautiful as Sister Anna is living in your midst."

Father Bernard knotted his hands behind his head and leaned back in his chair. "I'm not so sure. Once a month here at St. Mary's, we allow female guests to stay with us. So, we've seen beautiful women before."

"But Sister Anna was here every day for two months."

"And as the police find so interesting, she worked closely with Andrew on a daily basis," Father Bernard added. He sat forward and picked a notebook up off the coffee table. "Abbot Timothy and I would like you to read Sister Anna's journal. I think it answers every question you might have about Andrew." He handed the copy to Father Fortis. "But the journal has a much greater importance. I'd say its chief value is being such an honest record of her feelings."

Father Fortis opened the folder and gazed down at the first page. Large exclamation points and question marks dotted the text. "I will be happy to read through this, but you knew the person behind the words. What should I be looking for?"

Father Bernard paused a moment. "The journal wasn't her idea, but mine. I told her what I tell everyone, that if I was to serve as her spiritual director, she'd have to write in it every day. Anna agreed … reluctantly, I might add. The police, of course, were hoping she'd point a finger toward whoever killed her. But in the big scheme of things, what she wrote covers something far more important."

"I assume you mean her life," Father Fortis offered.

"Yes, her journey of faith. Sister Anna was an amazing soul, Nicholas. Full of vim and vinegar, as my immigrant mother would have put it. Actually, that also described my mother. I don't want to say too much and bias your reading, but the first part of the journal describes what brought her to St. Mary's. The rest covers what she discovered while living among us."

Father Fortis flipped to the end of the journal. Sister Anna had written two hundred and forty-five pages.

Father Bernard laughed softly. "Yes, you're right. It's pretty thick when you consider how short a time she was with us."

"And where is Brother Andrew mentioned?" Father Fortis asked.

"It's marked, but the raciest comment she makes about him is to call him a puppy dog. He helped her out in the print shop on most of her art projects. That comment was, and maybe still is, what interested the police the most. But one of our older monks, Brother Caspian, was always in the shop with them."

An old monk with bad hearing could miss a lot, Father Fortis thought. "If the journal exonerates Brother Andrew, why would he try to kill himself?"

Father Bernard studied his hands. The joints of his fingers were massive, strong for someone who spent his days listening to the problems of others.

"The poor kid probably felt like St. Sebastian after the police got through with him. Their questions would have been like arrows to a lad as sensitive as Andrew."

"But he was cleared, right?"

Father Bernard smiled. "Oh, yes, and his alibi is so simple. The boy never learned to drive. Brother Bartholomew gave him his first lesson a week before the tragedy. They'd only driven around the parking lot, and from what Bartholomew told me, Andrew made a mess of that."

Father Fortis remembered the tortuous road to the murder site. "So it's hardly likely that he drove out to the retreat house, the old morada."

Father Bernard ran his hand over his scalp. His hair sprang back rebelliously to its same disheveled shape. "Ah, you know where it is, then?"

Father Fortis felt his face heat up at having so carelessly revealed his visit with Worthy to the scene of the murder. "I saw it on a map. It looked to be a curvy road."

Father Bernard paused and let the awkward silence speak for itself. "That it is. But again, I want to make it clear that Andrew isn't the real reason we'd like you to read the journal. Even before Andrew took those pills, the abbot and I wanted you to take a look at it. As I said before, Anna was a remarkable person."

An amazing soul. A remarkable person. Did such elevated language say more about the spiritual director than it did the nun?

Father Bernard looked down at the magazines on the table. "I take it that you've seen the photos of her body."

Father Fortis nodded.

"The shredded paper all over the floor—those were her sketches. She went on retreat to pray for direction, but she also did a lot of drawing. Literally hundreds of sketches were found in the place, most of them torn to pieces."

"Perhaps her drawings were her prayers," Father Fortis suggested.

Father Bernard looked up and nodded in agreement. "Yes, good of you to see that. I think she would have liked you, Nicholas, and I think after you read her journal, you're going to like her, too."

Ah, but will I fall under her spell as Brother Andrew did, and maybe you? Father Fortis rose from the chair. He offered a quick prayer for forgiveness if he'd judged this man harshly.

"So once I finish reading this, we can talk again?"

"I look forward to it," Father Bernard said as he escorted his guest to the door.

Father Fortis paused before leaving. "Thank you for trusting me with the journal. I keep expecting someone to tell me to mind my own business."

The spiritual director shook his head. "Someone probably will, but read it before you thank me, Nicholas. Her journal won't necessarily make your life with us any easier."

Father Fortis stood in the doorway and pondered the comment. "I'm not sure I follow you."

Father Bernard looked out into the darkened corridor. "Has it ever occurred to you that St. Mary's pain might just be beginning?"

✠

AS THEY DROVE NORTH FROM THE airport, Sera Lacey glanced over at Worthy. "Was it hard to come back?"

Worthy gazed out at the cliffs rising from the Rio Grande valley. Had it rained every day in Detroit or did it only seem that way? He looked toward a tiny cluster of homes set halfway up the mountainside. *It wouldn't be bad to live out here,* he thought.

"Was it hard to come back from Detroit? Are you kidding?" He'd slept well last night at St. Mary's, the first good night's sleep in days. This morning he'd felt euphoric, as if a day so beautiful promised something incredible. "Detroit's a pressure cooker. Spend a few days there, and you'll see why people move out here."

"Huh. Then I guess I misunderstood your message. I got the feeling that you were pleased with the trip."

"Oh, the trip was worth it. At least the interview with Ellie's psychiatrist, and maybe even the one with that lame campus priest. But based on that damned letter, the VanBruskmans are sure I'm taking a vacation out here."

"The letter does make us look pretty stupid," Sera said. "As soon as I got your message, I put the word out to all the maintenance crews at the post offices. Nothing out of the ordinary so far, but then a letter in a post office is a bit like a needle in a haystack."

"I wish I could have brought that letter back. You'd have thought from all the smudges that it was at least a month old."

"Except for the postmark," Sera observed.

"Right," Worthy conceded, "except for the postmark. So what have you got?"

"I wish I had more to tell you, but I did manage to speak with Victor's uncle."

"The one out at Chimayó, right?" Worthy asked.

Sera switched lanes to pass a cattle truck. "That's the one. I wish I could report that he had a lot to say, but maybe it was because I'm a woman. About the only thing I got from him was the name of Alonzo Muniz, one of Victor's close friends from high school up at Española. That's only about an hour up the road. Unless you have a better plan, I thought we'd run up there now. The Muniz boy has a summer cleaning job at the school."

The beauty of the day and the fact that he was thousands of miles away from Detroit made it easy for Worthy to forget about the new deadline set by Arrol VanBruskman. Besides, maybe this Alonzo would have an idea where Victor could be hiding.

As they drove north past the pueblo communities of Tesuque and Picuris, Worthy shared in more detail what he'd gleaned in Detroit. As he'd imagined she would be, Sera was most stunned by the news of Ellie's adoption.

"Those bastards. That's a pretty big piece of the puzzle to keep from us," she said.

"Wait until you see the sketchpad I took from Ellie's room. There's a portrait of Victor, along with a lot of crosses and religious lingo. It makes his mother's nickname for him sound right."

"Padrelito?" Sera asked. "And Ellie's parents—or adoptive parents, I should say—they just let you take this sketchpad?"

"Not exactly, but I can guarantee they'll never know it's gone."

"Ah, I see. Now you're stealing evidence from the people paying your way. This case just keeps getting more interesting. I sure hope you brought back some brilliant theory to pull it all together."

Worthy laughed. "I think I have the beginning of one, but I wouldn't call it brilliant." He turned in the seat toward her. "I do have a new theory about why Ellie ran away."

"Oh? She isn't trying to find Victor?"

"Yes and no. It's something I got from Ellie's psychiatrist. I think Ellie ran away because she was worried about Victor, not because she was hoping he would rescue her."

"Really?"

"All the signs point to him being pretty much of a nutcase by the time he got back here," Worthy explained.

Sera drove without speaking for a moment. "I didn't get that idea from the uncle. Victor left Chimayó before Easter, but the uncle figured he just wanted to hang out with his friends. Like Alonzo, maybe. That sounds pretty normal for a kid that age."

Worthy shook his head. "No, no. Normal isn't close to the way the psychiatrist or the priest remembers him."

"You keep mentioning Ellie's psychiatrist. Are you saying this doctor met him?"

Worthy was surprised by the challenge in Sera's voice. "No, but you can imagine that Ellie talked a lot about his troubles in the fall. Look, once you take a look at the sketchpad, I think you'll change your mind."

"Maybe," she said.

"Okay, I'll give you an example," Worthy said. "There is this odd language, and I'm pretty sure Victor wrote it, because it doesn't look like Ellie's handwriting. He writes about needing to enter by some narrow gate. But what gate? And there's something else. Have you ever heard Chimayó called the center of the earth?"

Sera looked puzzled. "No, not exactly."

"But you love the place, right? Can you think of a reason someone would call it that?"

A slight smile broke out across Sera's face. "Maybe I do. When I was younger, my family drove out there every year." She patted the top of her head. "I always had a new mantilla for Mass, but every year it fell off. My sisters said my head was too pointed."

Worthy chuckled. "My sister always said my head was too big. Come to think of it, I bet she'd still say that. So about Chimayó. Why would Victor call it the center of the earth?"

"Maybe because it's a pilgrimage place. Did you see the milagros when you were there?

"Those little … symbols?" Worthy asked, avoiding the word trinkets.

"My sisters and I were given fifty cents every year to buy one to leave with the Holy Child of Atocha. You simply can't understand the place if you go there as a tourist. Sure, tourists can buy milagros and they can take home some of the dirt, but pilgrims always leave something. If not a milagro, then at least a prayer."

Her fond memories of the place brought a pang of regret to Worthy.

"What I said about the place must have sounded pretty rude," he said.

"Yes, it did."

"I should have stayed more objective." He looked out toward the mountains ahead. "That's my way of saying I'm sorry."

She nodded. "Apology accepted. Objectivity is pretty tough to muster with a place like El Sanctuario. I just figured you weren't Catholic."

"No, not even religious. Although sometimes I think Father Nick still holds out hope for me."

"Does that mean you used to be religious?" she asked.

"Brace yourself, Sera. My father was a minister."

Sera guffawed, a curiously raucous sound for such a poised woman. "Sorry, but I thought you were kidding."

"Not kidding, but that was all a long time ago."

Sera's fingernails clicked rhythmically on the steering wheel. "Do you mind telling me what happened?"

Why did he have the feeling that the question had been waiting in the wings for a long time? And how could he describe the sorry state of his soul to someone who loved a place like Chimayó?

He looked up to the snowcapped peaks, so clear in the morning light. "I don't want you to think I like … not believing in anything."

Now, that's a stupid way to begin, he thought. "Let me put it this way. Some things happened to me, and about the only way I can describe those months is to say that a cloud came down over everything. Eventually the cloud started to lift, but the God I used to believe in was just … gone."

Sera drove in silence for a time. Finally she said, "I've always believed in Him, even when I wished there wasn't a God. I'm not sure that makes any sense." She'd spoken softly, as if confessing a painful truth of her own.

"What I've decided is that losing faith makes no more sense than having it," he said.

"Those things that happened to you … they must have been pretty bad."

"I'm not so sure. Others have dealt with far worse and still believed in

God, but yes, I'd say a big bunch of bad stuff hit me about the same time." He looked down at his hands. "It's not all that interesting, really."

"Try me."

He pondered the invitation and felt something pushing him to say what had been trapped in his mind for over a year. "I was lead guy on the most gruesome murder I'd ever seen—a black teenaged girl who'd been raped at least four times before she died. Within twenty-four hours, a bunch of gang members from another neighborhood—real tough kids—were arrested. That's the way they like to do it in Detroit. Quick arrests. But the neighborhood leaders complained, said it was a cover-up, and about that time I began to wonder about a few things myself. I rearranged some of the pieces, and in the end, we arrested a white kid from a hundred miles north of Detroit. The murder had taken place up there, but he and a buddy dropped the body in a Dumpster in the city."

Worthy paused, caught up in the memory. Sera didn't say anything.

"The kid who did it was an Eagle Scout, headed for college," he continued. "He even said he'd thought about becoming a cop. Anyway, the night of the verdict, the TV news flashed my picture and called me a hero for defusing mounting racial tension. You know how that works."

"No, I can't say I've ever had that problem."

"It was a problem, because I knew I was no hero. The dead girl was Allyson's age, but she was nothing like my daughter. She'd been in jail on drug charges, involved in prostitution for years, the whole thing. Do you know what kept running through my mind?"

"No."

"It was like this huge truth. Maybe it's the cloud I'm talking about. I knew that no one, including myself, would have cared one ounce for this girl if she hadn't been murdered."

Sera groaned. "She was invisible, Chris. That's what most of the runaways are out here. They're invisible until they try to be just that—invisible."

Worthy knew he could end the story right there, but felt an urge to show his partner the rest of his ugly scar.

"So that night, I turned off the TV and just sat there, feeling famous and hollow at the same time. Susan came into the room, sat down at the other end of the couch, and told me she wanted a divorce."

Sera stared over at him. "What?"

Worthy cleared his throat. "I never saw it coming. I swear I didn't. I still don't see it clearly, but I've given up trying."

"And then your daughter ran away," Sera said with a sigh. "I'm so sorry, Chris."

He shrugged. "Like I said, others have dealt with more, plenty more. You, for example. You lost your husband, and you have to raise a boy on your own."

"Losing Steve was awful, but my family was there, my sisters and especially my grandfather. Without them I'd have fallen apart. Who knows, maybe I'd have lost my faith, too." She sounded almost wistful. "Wasn't anyone there for you, Chris?"

Worthy studied the starched cuffs of his shirt and the perfect creases of his khakis. He thought of his apartment, the never-ending stack of DVDs, a different one for each of the seven nights of the week. He thought of the awkward weekly visits to his old house, with only Amy happy to see him. He thought of the payback he'd received at work after his divorce, those who'd resented his meteoric rise now enjoying his stumbling ineptitude. He thought of his first meeting with Father Fortis and his panicky fear that the huge, talkative monk could smother him to death with a hug.

"Until Father Fortis—I mean Nick—came along, I guess there was no one."

"Oh, Chris," she replied. "You were invisible, just like the dead girl."

He turned away and studied his reflection in the window, as it floated like a ghost in front of the boulders and mountains beyond. *And maybe that's like Ellie VanBruskman*, he thought, *living in that mansion with people pretending to be her parents.* She was invisible long before she ran away.

CHAPTER FIFTEEN

———◆———

W ORTHY AND SERA WALKED DOWN THE deserted hallway toward the high school's art room. On the walls, murals portrayed historical scenes of the area. One was a river with native fishermen spearing fish from atop a primitive rocky dam. On the other wall, ancient adobe buildings like those at Acoma were depicted. *The past, always the past*, Worthy thought.

In the car, he had decided to let Sera conduct this interview. After all, it was she who had uncovered Alonzo Muniz's name. The boy was her lead to follow up. But also, Worthy felt he owed her something. No partner he'd ever worked with had understood him half as well or as rapidly. Usually, by this time in a case, his previous partners were complaining about his lack of cooperation. *Perhaps I am changing*, he thought.

In the art room, they found Cesar Muniz, Alonzo's father, leaning over a block of wood with carving tools. Rising from his work stool, Mr. Muniz removed his safety glasses and shook hands with the visitors. Worthy noted a faded tattoo of a bleeding crucifix on the man's right forearm.

"Victor? Yes, my son and Victor have been friends for years," Mr. Muniz said, reaching for a broom. His English was more heavily tinged with Spanish than Sera's. "In fact, they worked together here last summer on the grounds crew. Is Victor in some sort of trouble?"

"We're hoping he can help us find a missing girl from Detroit," Sera replied.

Mr. Muniz began to sweep wood shavings into neat piles on the floor. "Such a shame about Victor dropping out of college. Everyone had such high hopes for him."

Worthy strolled around the room as a means of letting Sera know that the interview was hers. Pots bearing intricate triangle designs sat in rows on a long wooden table, ready to be fired. A mosaic project next to them displayed a sky of stars and moon. He paused in front of another table at the far end of the room, where wooden blocks were pinned in vises. On each of the pillars, Worthy detected the faint outlines of a human form drawn in pencil.

As he looked up to a wall covered with photos of mountain scenes, his eyes rested on what could only be a santo of the Virgin Mary. It looked much like the one in the morada. The female figurine looked down as her feet rested on a crescent moon.

He felt a sudden tingling in his temples. Then the strength of his legs seemed to flow onto the floor. His stomach followed, producing a wave of nausea. He stumbled to a chair and fell as much as sat in it. The ringing in his ears made it impossible to understand Sera's words from the other side of the room. Yet he must have uttered a sound, perhaps a grunt, for Sera and the art teacher stopped talking and looked his way.

Worthy waved them off, as if he had simply slipped. From some of his past cases, the ones that had earned him his commendations, he knew that in two or three minutes the jumbled puzzle pieces in his mind would begin to slowly connect as if on their own. He accepted the dizziness as part of the sudden awareness that the picture emerging was nothing like what he expected.

He looked up at the wall. Yes, that was in fact a santo. He looked down at the blocks of wood in vises and ascertained that the penciled outlines were indeed of the same Virgin Mary. *The past, always the past*, he thought again.

In a moment, he could make out the teacher's voice again. Without understanding how he knew, he was certain that the man was protecting something. But was it his son, Victor, or the Penitente Brotherhood? He breathed slowly. A picture was coming together. Several of the missing pieces of the puzzle of Victor, Ellie, and so much more were in this room.

Worthy felt strength flow back into his legs. Yes, he knew what he had to do. And in that moment, he knew that Sera might hate him for what must come next.

As he waited for a break in the conversation between Mr. Muniz and Sera, he recalled a memory from a weekend at the family cabin in northern Michigan. Saturday mornings in the early fall, before the sun rose, he would leave Susan and the girls asleep to don fishing waders and walk the shoreline. In the pre-dawn light, he would cast the fly methodically beneath overhanging trees, hoping for a rise from a late-season bass. One such Saturday morning before Susan had demanded the divorce, he'd come upon his old neighbor sitting at the end of his pier, nursing a cup of coffee.

"You're about three weeks too late," the old man had announced. He held out a second cup to Worthy and explained that he'd missed the annual rollover, when the upper layers of the lake became cooler than the darker waters below.

The old man explained that when the lake "rolled over, the warmer water rushed to the surface." Everything swimming in the water was caught in the rush. "Right now, the fish are too damned confused to know which end is up," he'd said.

Like those startled fish, Worthy's thoughts swirled as he looked from the blocks of wood to the santo to Mr. Muniz's fading tattoo. The only things missing on the santo, he thought, were the seven swords between the Virgin's breasts.

He cleared his throat and pointed to the wooden pillars. "Do all your students carve these?"

The art teacher shook his head. "No, those are from an advanced summer school class."

Worthy noted Sera's confused look and counted slowly to five before asking, "Did Victor ever carve one of these?"

Sera shook her head at him, then stopped and gazed down at the floor. It was a moment that Worthy had experienced too many times, one that always seemed to present him no choice but to push forward, even though he knew that he was cursed with being the only one in the room who saw the picture emerging.

Mr. Muniz, broom in hand, ambled toward him. "Victor was too busy with his college prep classes and the school newspaper to take my class."

"But he knew how to carve, right?"

"Of course. Actually, his grandfather was ...." Mr. Muniz gripped the broom tightly in both hands and stopped.

"I think you were going to say a woodcarver," Worthy said.

Sera joined the two men and stared blankly at Worthy. *Does she see it?* he wondered.

"Is your son, by any chance, working at the school today?" she asked.

Worthy breathed a sigh of relief. Yes, she must have figured out where their interview was headed.

"He's down in the gym, cleaning the locker rooms," Mr. Muniz replied.

"Can we talk to him, please?" she asked.

Without responding, Mr. Muniz set the broom against the wall and left the room.

Standing in front of Worthy, Sera whispered, "Care to tell me what's going on?"

Worthy's heart sank. He thought she'd understood, but clearly he had been mistaken. He brought a finger to his lips. "I'll explain later. Make sure you ask Alonzo about—" He stopped when a crew-cut teenager in a black No Fear T-shirt swaggered into the room.

"Either of you seen my dad?"

Sera introduced herself and Worthy before explaining where the boy's father was. Then she added, "Alonzo, we're looking for Victor Martinez."

There was a moment of silence before Alonzo asked, "Why?" The boy stuffed his hands in his back pockets and stared sullenly at the policewoman.

"A college friend of his ran away several weeks ago. Maybe you saw the story in the paper or on the news. We're hoping Victor can help us find her."

Mr. Muniz reentered the room, and father and son held each other's gaze before Mr. Muniz picked up the broom again.

"Alonzo, would you like to sit down?" Sera asked.

"I'm okay."

"All right, then. Would you tell us when you last saw Victor?"

The boy shrugged. "Maybe February or March."

Despite his pulse beating like a hammer in his neck, Worthy sat silently, watching and waiting.

"Do you remember if that was before or after Easter?" Sera asked.

The sound of sweeping stopped abruptly, and the boy's shoulder flinched as if he'd been poked by his father's broom. "I said March. Easter's in April."

Worthy tried unsuccessfully to catch Sera's eye. *You have to push back*, he thought. *The kid's trying to intimidate, and you have to beat him at his own game.*

Sera's voice remained calm. "Did Victor ever talk about troubles he had back at the college in Detroit?"

The boy's eyes flitted again to his father before returning to the floor. "Why would he?" Alonzo mumbled. "I didn't see him much after he came back."

"Your father said the two of you were close. We were hoping—"

"Look lady, I said I don't know nothing."

Worthy rose from the chair. "Lieutenant Lacey, let's talk outside for a moment." His voice sounded clipped in his own ears and he suspected the others also perceived it that way. *Just as well*, he thought.

Although surprised, Sera followed him out into the hallway. Worthy shut the door behind them. "This isn't working," he said.

His partner's eyes narrowed. "What isn't?"

"Your soft approach. You have to make this kid jump. And that's not going to happen until we get the dad out of there."

Sera turned away, staring down the long hallway. "So now I can't handle this, is that what you're saying?"

He searched for something to say that would narrow the gulf between them. He folded his arms across his chest, his eyes on the mural of the fishermen spearing a fish. "Can't you see how he keeps looking over at his dad?"

Sera's cheeks flushed. "If we ask the father to go, the boy will have a perfect right to follow him right out the door."

"Not if you tell him to sit his ass down," Worthy said.

Sera's head jumped back as if hit. "God, Chris, the boy hasn't done anything. No, I won't do that."

"Dammit, he knows something important, more than you can apparently see right now. If you won't get the old man out of there, I will."

Sera turned her back to him, but said before opening the door, "With your superior insight, you are obviously way ahead of me. Please show me how it's done."

Through the opened door, she called in, "Mr. Muniz, may we speak with you out here?"

"Dad, don't," Alonzo challenged.

Worthy leaned back against a locker, willing the adrenaline to ease from his head and chest. The boy's macho act would collapse in a second if she just stood up to him.

Mr. Muniz stepped into the hallway. Sera closed the door and waited for Worthy to speak. Worthy waited her out and finally nodded to her.

"Alonzo is a good boy, Mr. Muniz," she began. "I think he's scared, but I can assure you he's done nothing wrong. Now we need to speak to him alone."

No, no, no, Worthy thought. *You don't ask. You tell him.*

To his surprise, Mr. Muniz nodded his head as if he'd expected the request and shuffled down the hall. The two reentered the room, Worthy standing in the doorway. He would let Sera lead, if she would in fact do that.

Alonzo remained where he was, head down. His hands reached deeper into his back pockets. Sera took his arm and escorted him toward a chair by one of the tables.

Sitting next to him, she repeated the question. "Do you know why Victor quit college?"

The boy rubbed a finger over the tabletop, pushing the sawdust into a neat pile. "What's Victor done?"

Oh, yeah, he knows something, Worthy thought. *But this handholding isn't going to get it out of him.*

Sera smiled gently. "I told you the truth before. We just need to talk with him."

The boy shrugged and remained silent.

Worthy pulled up a chair in front of the boy, making sure that the chair clattered as it hit the linoleum floor. He sat forward, his face little more than a foot from Alonzo's. "Listen up, Alonzo. I flew out here last night from Detroit, and I am in no mood for this bullshit act."

"That's it, I'm out of here," Alonzo said, rising from the chair.

"Sit down!"

The boy did so, but turned his entire body away from the two of them.

"Ever see those cop shows on TV, Alonzo? Frankly, those shows don't seem very realistic to me, with that good cop, bad cop routine. You see, in my twenty years as a police officer, I haven't met that many good cops. But today, you're in luck. There is one, but only one, in this room." He leaned in even closer to Alonzo and in a raised voice said, "Do I have your attention, son?"

"Hey, fuck you, man."

The photo of Sister Anna lying in a pool of blood flitted through his mind as he grabbed the front of the boy's T-shirt. "You're not leaving this room until we have some answers." Worthy hoped that Sera had caught up, but her whispered, "Chris, stop it!" as she grabbed his arm told him she hadn't tumbled onto anything.

"See, Lieutenant Lacey is a bona fide good cop. But I'm not," he said, releasing the boy's shirt. "Let me tell you what I already know." Taking a deep breath, he said in Sera's direction as such as Alonzo's, "I know about Victor and the Penitentes."

Sera released his arm as if he had some communicable disease. He felt rage surge up into his chest. *My God*, he thought, *she knew all along.* Had the uncle told her, or had she known even before that?

"How dare you?" Sera hissed. "Alonzo, you don't have to answer that."

Worthy's eyes bored into Alonzo's. "Don't listen to her. She knows you're not leaving until you tell us everything you know."

Alonzo caught the tension between the two of them and turned on Worthy. "Hey, man, I know my fucking rights."

"Chris, you can't do this," Sera protested.

Worthy plowed ahead as is Sera had said nothing. "You and Victor talked when he came back. Just tell me what he said about his problems."

"Fuck you, man," Alonzo repeated, but this time there were tears in his eyes.

"Stop it!" Sera ordered.

He turned toward her. "Leave!"

She rose and walked hurriedly toward the door. His ears burned. Every hair on his head tingled. He wanted to run after her. He wanted to tell her that it was all a game, that he'd only leaned like this on two or three witnesses in his entire career. But most of all, he wanted to explain that Victor was the key to everything, and that they had to find him before matters got worse.

"God, kid, you've put me in a mess of trouble with my partner." He felt like he was playing a part in a play as he gripped the boy's wrist and squeezed. "If I say you threw a punch and I had to break your arm, it would just be your word against mine. So I'm going to ask you one more time. What did he tell you?"

Alonzo muttered something through his sniffles.

"Speak up," Worthy demanded.

"I said, we used to joke about the old ones, their rituals and shit," Alonzo repeated. "Victor made up jokes about what to say to Penitentes."

"But he wasn't doing that when he came back from Detroit, was he?" Worthy pressed.

Alonzo's hand shook beneath Worthy's grip, and he released it. "Oh, yeah. It was Brotherhood this, hermanos that."

"Specifics, Alonzo. Tell me exactly what Victor said."

The boy glanced toward the door. "He said he needed to find a serious Brotherhood, not some bullshit kind, and it had to be by Holy Week."

"So why didn't he talk to his uncle?"

Alonzo wiped away a tear and stared at the wall. "Shit, you have to believe me, man. I had to stop listening to him. He was talking crazy."

Worthy sat back in the chair. "Victor didn't look so good in March, did he?"

Alonzo opened his eyes wide and licked his lips. "He was skinny, like he wasn't eating."

"Or maybe fasting?"

The boy shrugged.

"Where'd he been before you saw him in March?"

Alonzo wiped his nose with his sleeve. "Up in Colorado. He said he was trying to find the right morada."

Out of the corner of his eye, Worthy saw that Sera had returned to the room. She leaned against the wall, her eyes red. "Let me guess. One that would give him the big part on Good Friday. He wanted the cross, the nails, the whole bit, right?" Worthy added.

Alonzo's eyes filled with terror, as if Worthy was reading his mind. "He said a devil chased him out of Detroit. He said innocent blood was crying out from the ground, stupid shit like that. Then he said he'd run into an angel in Colorado. The angel told him to search for some old morada down here. That's when I stopped listening. I mean one minute he was crying, the next minute he looked like he could … I don't know …."

"Harm someone?" Worthy asked.

Alonzo looked up. "Maybe. No, Victor wouldn't do that. No, that can't be true."

Worthy let the protest pass before asking, "Victor told you a devil was following him in Michigan and an angel met him in Colorado?"

Alonzo nodded. "I told you he was out of his head." The boy looked away as tears started down his cheeks again.

Worthy could hear Sera's sigh as she walked toward the door again. *She's leaving*, he thought in disbelief. I show her why I had to push this hard, and she just leaves? He thought back over the case, wondering where they'd gotten off track. In the car, she'd fought against everything he'd said about Victor. And now this.

But he hadn't been all that quick himself in seeing the entire picture. That was despite the fact that nearly everyone in Detroit who knew Victor— Professor Stott, the Catholic chaplain, and Dr. Cartwright—had practically handed him the clue, describing how unbalanced the boy was at the end. *But for some reason, I missed it*, Worthy admitted to himself. And God, why didn't I take the RA's story seriously about Victor trying to knife the bully?

He pictured Sera standing alone in the hallway. Maybe all wasn't lost. Maybe, once the waters had finished rolling over and she saw what he saw, she'd understand that Santa Fe didn't have two mysteries to solve, a murdered nun and a missing college girl. No, there'd been two women in trouble, but only one mystery. And Victor Martinez was the key to it all.

CHAPTER SIXTEEN

———— ◆ ————

IT WASN'T UNTIL AFTER MONDAY'S MEAGER supper and before the service of Compline that Father Fortis was able to find Brother Elias. The old monk frowned at his guest before admitting him into his room. Looking around at the newspapers and file folders piled high on the floor, Father Fortis wondered if the librarian had thrown anything away since his arrival at St. Mary's. The room's peculiar odor seemed to come from the tabby cat that rubbed against Father Fortis's leg.

"Something I can do for you?" Brother Elias asked, his eyebrows darting up and down. Without waiting for an answer, he shuffled to a table and sat before the laptop computer. The monk rapidly tapped a few keys and squinted at the screen.

How odd, Father Fortis thought, *that one of St. Mary's oldest monks would be so proficient with computers.*

"I'd like to ask you about something you said at the meeting with the police," Father Fortis said.

"Oh, did I say something interesting?" Brother Elias grunted as he pointed toward a chair.

Father Fortis removed a precariously stacked pile of folders before sitting down. The adobe walls of the room were bare except for a simple crucifix on one wall.

"You said that St. Mary's has enemies," Father Fortis said. "I'd like to know more about that."

The old monk glanced from the screen to his visitor. "Why? What business is it of yours?"

"We have some similar problems of our own back in Ohio," Father Fortis said. It was a lie. The Amish and Old Order Mennonites who surrounded St. Simeon's had been gracious neighbors, leaving the monks alone. The Amish way of life, monastic in its own way to most Americans, drew attention away from the Orthodox monks chanting and beekeeping farther back in the woods.

Brother Elias turned back to the screen. He was about Father Linus's age, suggesting the two had probably known each other for a long time. *Maybe too long,* Father Fortis thought, judging by the friction between them. Linus had been ordained a priest, while Elias had chosen to remain a brother. Or had he been passed over?

"Your community's problems aren't ours," the old monk grunted.

"I disagree. Monasteries all over the world have quite a bit in common."

A bony finger shot up toward heaven. "Wrong! We're not two different baseball teams," Brother Elias snapped back. "There's our church and yours."

So that was it, Father Fortis thought. The librarian despised him because he wasn't Catholic.

"You scholars are all the same," Elias said in disgust. "It's not good enough being a monk. You think your precious articles and books can change the past. Ha!" The monk's face was a battlefield, columns of skin moving angrily from neck to forehead as he spoke.

"You mean the gulf between our two churches? I believe there's always hope—"

"Ha, and another big fat ha! A thousand years of heresy isn't putty in your hands. An old chant isn't going to resurrect what's dead and gone. What does it matter that Holy Mother church and your church once chanted the same words? What matters is that you rejected the authority of the Pope, an authority given to St. Peter by Christ Himself!"

The old monk pointed outside his window. "See the cliff out there, the one with the cross on top?"

Father Fortis nodded.

"Ever notice those boulders lying at the bottom of the cliff? All good for nothing. Jesus said to Peter, 'Upon this rock I will build my Church.' The cross is still planted in the rock. But you Orthodox chose to split off, go your own way. Then it was the Protestants. Now it's the cults. All useless rubble. You think your chants and fancy monographs can mend damage like that?"

Father Fortis knew he was being baited, but he hadn't come for that fight. "To quote something I received recently, it sounds like I'm not wanted here, and I'm not needed here."

Brother Elias's eyebrows shot up, but he didn't answer. Instead, he snapped his fingers at the cat, which jumped into his lap.

"I bet Sister Anna received a similar message," Father Fortis said.

The cat purred and closed its eyes in meditation as the monk scratched his neck.

"Well, Boniface, it looks like our special guest is on to us," Brother Elias replied. "She didn't belong here, as everyone now knows."

"I'm guessing you did more than send her a note. You shared your opinion with Abbot Timothy, didn't you?"

"Of course, more than once."

"And Brother Andrew? Did you send him notes as well?"

"No. That stupid boy," Brother Elias said with disdain.

"Why 'stupid'? Because he had normal feelings for a woman?"

The old monk's face turned crimson. The cat yawned up at Father Fortis, showing its teeth. "The boy spent a year in our novitiate, and yet the first skirt he sees, he drools like a dog on the prowl. Disgusting."

Father Fortis thought again how wrong outsiders could be about monks. Guests tended to throw all monks into a narrow category—so holy that they were beyond carnal urges. But monks were as varied as any other group. At one end of the spectrum were dried-up old prunes like Elias, who'd forgotten what the appendage that hung down between their legs was for. At the other end were Brother Andrew and maybe Father Bernard, still dealing painfully with the fact that they were men.

The old monk glared up at him. "For the third time, I'm busy."

"Then I won't keep you. Tell me about St. Mary's enemies."

"I just said I was busy." Elias gave him a sly smile. "As they say on the Internet, you'd better narrow your search."

"Okay. Tell me about the groups who've harassed St. Mary's recently. Say, since Sister Anna came."

Lifting the cat off his lap, the old monk pecked nimbly on the keyboard. "You'll see nothing from over there," he muttered.

Father Fortis brought his chair around to the other side of the table.

"The Southwest is full of fanatics," Elias began. He moved his hand on the finger pad and brought a screen up for viewing. "This one insists that Pope John Paul, being Polish, was a Communist spy." He tapped the finger pad again and brought up a second screen. "This one says the church is smuggling Mexicans and Central Americans across the border so she can destroy the English language in America."

Brother Elias tapped the finger pad again, and the screen changed. "None of those had anything to say about our dead nun, but this one did," he said, pointing to the screen.

Father Fortis squinted to see a flag waving behind the words "Fight the Beast." Below the logo was a grainy photograph of St. Mary's, followed by a photocopy of a February article from the *Santa Fe Herald*. Father Fortis scanned the article's description of current building projects at the monastery, especially the architectural plans for the proposed library.

In a caption written below were the words "Celibacy is a demonic and pious charade of Roman Papists to cover immoral practices. A whore is living with the queers at this place."

Brother Elias was right. This wasn't funny. "Do the police know about this?" he asked.

"Of course, but since this site is from Missouri, they said it was too far away to matter. They said the group probably found the story on the newspaper's website."

"But somebody from out here must have alerted them to it. Groups like these tend to network," Father Fortis said.

The old monk's eyebrows jumped, and he looked at Father Fortis with what might have passed for respect. "Harrumph."

Could whoever had sent the article to the group in Missouri have been responsible, even indirectly, for vandalizing the moradas and killing Sister Anna? Such a wacko group would have motive, but how would they know enough about santos to mark the nun's body?

"You talked about other groups," Father Fortis said. "How many are there?"

The old monk leaned forward, his face alight. "Enough for me to put them into categories. Most just love to hate us." He looked out at the rock face again. "Without us, they'd have nothing to attack."

Father Fortis pondered the comment. "It reminds me of that story from Brazil, the one about that TV evangelist who took a hammer to the statue of the Blessed Virgin."

"That's one type. But there are also renegade Mormon groups, the polygamist types who talk big on their websites. We're hated by all sorts."

Father Fortis thought about the wounds left on Sister Anna. It hardly seemed likely that radical Mormons would know about death carts and santos.

"Have any groups trespassed on your property?"

Elias shook his head. "Nothing serious. There was a group of New Agers a few years back. On our property, but not dangerous."

Father Fortis agreed. Why would New Agers mutilate a nun's body?

"One more question, Brother Elias," he asked. "Lieutenant Choi mentioned a group that I can't say I know much about. What was it he called them?"

"The Penitentes," Elias replied.

"That's right. The Penitentes. Could they hate St. Mary's for some reason, enough to kill Sister Anna?"

Brother Elias made a kissing sound and caught the cat as it jumped into his lap. "The Penitentes are just a bunch of old fools. Like Linus." Brother Elias nuzzled the head of the cat. "I saw one of their processions once. It was supposed to scare me. Ha! Just an embarrassment. That's what I think of the so-called Brotherhood. Ask Bernard if you don't believe me."

It was hardly the name that Father Fortis expected to hear. "Why Father Bernard?"

"Well, I do overhear things here. I heard him tell Brother Andrew just a few days ago that the Penitentes would be gone in twenty years. I personally think that's a generous estimate."

"So Andrew is a Penitente, then."

Brother Elias nodded knowingly. "Oh, yes. One of the few younger ones, I suspect."

Puzzled, Father Fortis thought back over the past two days. Father Bernard had mentioned nothing about Brother Andrew being connected with the secretive group. Then again, neither had Father Linus. But what most troubled Father Fortis was this: why had Father Linus suggested Father Bernard was sympathetic to the Brotherhood while Elias had clearly overheard the opposite?

CHAPTER SEVENTEEN

—◆—

"I THOUGHT I'D HAVE TO HITCHHIKE BACK to St. Mary's," Worthy said, trying to lighten the mood as Sera sped along toward St. Mary's. The two-lane road winding out of Española toward the monastery could have come straight out of a TV commercial, the kind where a beautiful woman smiled as her man mastered bridges and mountain passes. This woman wasn't smiling as she spun the wheel first one way, then the other.

What could Worthy do except state the obvious to explain why he'd taken over the interview? She'd been in the room when Alonzo confirmed how crazy Victor sounded when he came home. Did she really think Alonzo was like Victor's mother at Acoma, simply waiting for the right cue to tell them everything he knew? Of course Sera hated his methods. *He* hated his methods. Couldn't she at least concede their effectiveness?

But the set of her jaw and the way her hands squeezed the steering wheel said it all. He wanted to find a way to break the silence, to thank her for bringing him to the art room where all the pieces of the puzzle fell into place. He wanted to give her credit for helping him understand the santos and the wooden blocks. But his partner clearly didn't want to be thanked.

"Look, Sera, I work homicide. We see guys like Alonzo all the time. What other options did he give us?"

"But this isn't homicide. We're looking for a missing college girl."

Oh, it's homicide, all right, he thought.

The tires squealed around a tight turn. "And what did you get with all that tough guy stuff?" she asked. "Let me tell you, Victor being a Penitente explains nothing."

He felt his face burn. "And yet you already knew. So much for being partners."

"Don't lecture me about being partners! 'Sera, get the hell out of the room'? Some partner. Look, I didn't tell you about Victor and the Brotherhood because you wouldn't understand."

"Wouldn't understand? Victor being a Penitente is the single most important piece of the puzzle," he shot back.

"Look, you couldn't even handle the dirt at Chimayó. Believe me, that's nothing compared to understanding the Brotherhood. Besides, your friend said the same thing."

He twisted in the passenger seat. "Nick? You asked Nick?"

"Settle down." She paused a moment. "Yes, we talked about it, and we were right. You say Victor coming from a Penitente family explains everything? Tell me one way that it helps us find Ellie."

Where to begin? He took a deep breath. "It doesn't help us find her. It just explains why we're not going to find her alive."

Sera took her foot off the accelerator and eased onto the shoulder. The car came to a stop at the top of a hill. Below them, children ran in a dirt yard in front of a few trailers.

"You're saying she's dead?" Sera asked, staring at him.

He didn't answer but waited for her to take the next step.

"Good Lord, I should have believed you back at Acoma. You *are* flaky. The next thing you're going to tell me is that Victor killed her."

He looked out the window and didn't respond.

"Oh, no. Are you serious?"

"Sera, I wish I was wrong. I honestly do. Will you let me explain?"

Sera stared straight ahead. "My God, you don't even have the decency to doubt yourself, do you?"

"Just give me twenty minutes."

She pulled the car back onto the road. "Less, if I get to the monastery before that."

The car gathered speed as it shot down the hill toward the tiny village.

"You heard Alonzo," he said. "Victor was crazy, looking for some place to be nailed to a cross."

Sera slammed her hand on the steering wheel. "They don't use nails anymore."

"Maybe not, but Alonzo said that Victor was looking for a *serious* morada, not the bullshit kind. Why did Victor feel he needed to be on a cross? That's the important question we have to answer, Sera."

"You seem to know all the answers. You tell me."

"Okay, and no, I'm not certain. But I think Victor wanted that because of what happened back in Detroit. Remember what I faxed you about the Pakistani boy? Victor couldn't deal with that, and I'm absolutely sure he didn't get comfort from anybody at the college. So I'm picturing him overwhelmed by guilt. It was too much to live with, but what could he do?"

"I just work with runaways. I'm too stupid to follow any of this."

Despite her words, he noticed that she had slowed down.

"Here's this kid who used to make fun of the Penitentes, but in November, after the Pakistani boy got killed in Detroit, he started drawing pictures of himself holding one of their crosses. Then he came home and lived with his mother before trying his uncle. And by the way, don't pretend you don't know that his uncle is a Penitente. Why else would Victor stay with him every year during Lent? Do you honestly think the two of them were playing cards?"

They drove over a narrow bridge. Worthy looked down to where a tiny trickle of water was spilling over the rocks, as if hurrying to escape something.

Sera glanced over at him. "Being a Penitente doesn't make a person crazy, Chris."

Worthy considered the point and realized there was nothing to be gained by arguing. "Okay, but remember what else we know. Victor told Alonzo that a devil was chasing him in Detroit. After leaving his uncle's place, he ran off to Colorado where he claimed he met an angel. Does that sound like your average normal kid?"

"All it proves is that Victor was having a hard time sorting things out."

"My God, Sera, he was hallucinating!"

"You don't know that. You're taking what Alonzo thought he heard and twisting it."

He stared at her. "I'm *twisting* it?" He ran his hand through his hair and stared at the road ahead. Victor's father had been a Penitente; his uncle was a Penitente. Why couldn't she see the obvious?

Sera spoke in a controlled voice. "Victor knew someone back in Detroit who was killed, and yes, he felt guilty. And okay, I grant you that it would have helped if he'd talked to a counselor. I won't even fight you about his wanting to play Christo in one of the old-style Brotherhoods. But how do you get from that to him being a killer?"

Worthy leaned back on the headrest. He thought of Jack Nicholson's line from one of the videos in his apartment—*You can't handle the truth!*

"Maybe I should shut up," he said. "We can go over this tomorrow."

"No, now."

"But if I tell you the rest, you're only going to hate me."

Sera turned toward him, color rising in her cheeks as she searched his face. "My father and grandfather were Penitentes, Chris."

He stared at her, open-mouthed. Of course. How had he missed that?

"Believe me, Sera, I'm not saying that I understand this group. And I'm not, despite what you think, simply out to blame them for what happened."

"Then help me, Chris. I honestly don't see how you get from Victor being messed up after Detroit to killing Ellie. We don't even know that the two ever met up, and here you have her dead."

"Are you hungry?"

"What?" Sera stared over at him. "We're talking about murder and you're hungry?"

"I'm in homicide. We deal with murder all the time, and we also get hungry." *Besides*, he thought, *I need more than ten minutes to explain the rest of this.*

"If you need Anglo food, McDonald's or Bob Evans, you're out of luck on this road. But if you don't mind—"

Worthy laughed. "Believe it or not, we have Mexican food in Detroit."

"I'm not talking about Taco Bell, and I'm not talking about Mexican food. I'm talking about authentic New Mexican food."

In the next town, Sera pulled into a roadside diner. They sat outside under a string of lamps, close enough to the highway to feel the trucks lumbering by. The canyon around them was turning a deep blue in the evening light, like a lake slowing filling up. A teenage girl, her hair as black as Sera's, came to take their order.

Worthy sipped on his beer and looked across at Sera as she ordered for both of them. From where he sat, her face was framed on one side by a road sign in Spanish, advertising what Worthy thought was flour, on the other, a tin church steeple from farther down the road. *This is her world*, he thought, *a tiny town where Anglos like me race by in their cars.*

"Okay, you got me to stop for food. So stop stalling," she whispered. "Why are you so certain Ellie is dead? How do we know that she isn't hiding in Santa Fe? For all we know, she really did send that letter to her parents last week." She drew her sweater closer around her and crossed her arms.

"No, she didn't. I wish that were true, but we both know it isn't."

She rubbed her arms. "But why are you sure she's dead?"

"Reason number one: she disappeared too quickly. She walks away from a city she doesn't know, without the medicine she desperately needs to even remember her name in the morning, and she leaves no clue?"

"That's it?" Sera asked. "Victor must have killed her because we failed to find her? I wouldn't try that theory out on Cortini. Just in case you haven't noticed, New Mexico's a big state. I prefer to believe that Ellie did find Victor, and they're still hiding out. Victor's grandmother said Ellie's mother was doping her with medication. Maybe Victor thinks he's saving her." Her gaze bore into Worthy. "And for all we know, maybe he is."

"No."

"But why? You said that was your number one reason for thinking she's dead. You have another?"

Worthy started to answer when a semi roaring through town cut him off. The candle on the table shook, its flame flickering. A toddler at the next table scooted off her chair and ran to bury her head in her mother's lap.

Worthy leaned over the table toward his partner. "Victor wouldn't have hesitated to kill Ellie," he whispered, "because by the time the two of them met up, he'd planned to kill or had already killed Sister Anna."

CHAPTER EIGHTEEN

———◆———

Flashlights in hand, Worthy and Father Fortis walked the dark road leading away from the monastery.

"Let me see if I understand you, Christopher. You're actually saying that Ellie VanBruskman is dead, and that Victor Martinez killed her soon after he killed Sister Anna? I ... I honestly don't know what to say."

Worthy looked out at the hills in the distance, with the blanket of stars rising above them. He thought of Sera, down in Santa Fe, having put her son to bed and now reconsidering every claim of his theory. No doubt she was cursing him.

Sera had reacted to his accusations against Victor as he should have expected, sitting mute for a moment before saying she'd lost her appetite. They'd cancelled their order and left the diner. In the car she'd remained silent, even after he told her where Lieutenant Choi should focus the search. Perhaps that was why he had roused Father Fortis for this late-night walk. He needed to share his thoughts with someone who had some faith in him.

Off to the right, he heard the river wash noisily over the rocks. Beyond that were the canyons. Maybe there were even more moradas out there. The more sites, the longer the search would take. But he knew what they'd find.

Now began the hardest part for him, the waiting. He knew that he'd sleep poorly, battle heartburn, and generally find everyone irritating until what he knew must happen finally did. He was especially irritated by Father Fortis's skepticism.

"Christopher, what I find the hardest to accept is how different your description of Victor is from the lost boy I'd been picturing. Just this afternoon, when I went to see Brother Andrew, I was struck by how much the two of them have in common. They're both young and both have some connection with the Penitentes. Most of all, both seem so fragile. I can't imagine Victor killing Sister Anna any more than I can Andrew."

"Fragile people can do a lot of damage, Nick."

"Maybe so, maybe so," Father Fortis said. "But don't they usually do that damage to themselves? Take Brother Andrew, for example. It turns out that he was the one who took Sister Anna's journal from my room and spied on me from the balcony. And because he was so afraid I'd discover his infatuation with Sister Anna, he tried to kill himself. You see, he tried to harm himself, Christopher, just himself."

The two walked the sharp rise in the road in silence before Father Fortis continued, "What about how bright a student he was, his loving family? And what about the kindness he showed Ellie back in Detroit?"

Worthy bent down and picked up a handful of gravel. "That was all before his breakdown at the college, Nick."

Father Fortis grunted. "And so he suddenly turned into a killer?"

Worthy heaved one of the rocks through the darkness toward the river, waited to hear the splash, and threw another.

"Why do I get the feeling that you'd like to throw one of those rocks at me, Christopher?"

Worthy lobbed one of the rocks into the air and caught it. "No, you're too close to be a challenge. I like to aim at things farther away."

"Then I'd better try to keep up with you," Father Fortis said with a laugh.

"It's just hard for me to understand why you and Sera don't see my point. Of course Victor didn't become a killer overnight. But he did begin to lose touch with reality. He left Detroit because he couldn't deal with the death of the Pakistani kid. That's not my imagination. That was confirmed by Ellie's psychiatrist and in a way, by the Catholic chaplain."

"Fair enough," Father Fortis conceded.

"For some reason, Ellie blamed the college for that, but the chaplain said that Victor blamed himself. And that guilt began to destroy him. First he said he was being followed by someone back in Detroit. Then, what's the first thing he does when he comes back? He heads up to Colorado, where his father's side of the family is from. Why? According to his high school buddy, Alonzo, he went up there to find a Brotherhood that would let him hang on the cross."

"The boy must have been in real trouble, I grant you that," Father Fortis said. "But to kill Sister Anna and then his best friend from college? Do you have any evidence that Ellie even found him?"

Father Fortis's disbelief seemed to echo in the canyon. Worthy knew what he knew, but explaining it was a different matter. "Look, the bottom line is this, Nick. We're going to find Ellie's body in a morada out there somewhere in these hills. That's where Victor has been hiding all this time."

From farther down the canyon, an insane howl rose. A coyote or wolf, Worthy reasoned, out for an evening of hunting. *When we find Victor*, he thought, *the boy could be howling like that. And we better find him soon, before he kills again.*

"Back up a bit in your scenario, Christopher. Something is troubling me about what you said about Colorado. You're saying that Victor went up there to find a morada?"

"Right. His father was a Penitente from up that way. So it makes sense he'd try there first. He had one thought in mind, Nick, to be nailed to a cross. The whole idea is so unbelievably crazy to me."

"Crazy to want to be freed from guilt? I don't know. If I were him, I might do the same thing," Father Fortis replied. "But for your theory to be right, Colorado must not have worked out for him."

"He probably got the same brush-off up there that he would have gotten a bit later from his uncle in Chimayó. I suspect that's when he started to hear the voices again, telling him to keep searching for other old moradas."

Worthy paused to see if Father Fortis was still with him, but only heard his friend's heavy breathing above the crunch of gravel.

"Listen, Nick, I know how this sounds. You and Sera think I've overreached myself this time. All I ask is that you don't pick at the details. The truth is in the big picture."

Worthy felt a hand on his shoulder. "No one knows better than I do how good your instincts can be, my friend."

"Then just hear me out. I know you think there's a huge gap between Victor hearing voices and suddenly killing a nun and then his only real friend from college. From what I can tell, Sera has the same problem with my theory. Well, I think I can explain that."

"Go on."

Worthy took a deep breath. If Father Fortis was having problems with his theory to this point, wait until he heard the next part.

"Victor is Native American on his mother's side, from a place called Acoma."

"Yes, you told me that," Father Fortis said.

"But he's Hispanic on his father's side. For me, that difference is very important. One of the brochures I picked up at Acoma talks about a massacre about three hundred years ago when the Indians there turned on their Catholic priests," Worthy said. "For some reason, the mix of Catholicism and their Native American ways didn't work. The brochure said that one day they stormed the church, took the friars, and threw them off the mesa."

"But that was a long time ago. How does that relate to Victor?"

"Picture Victor traveling from morada to morada and getting tired of being turned down. They probably told him he wasn't prepared or not old enough."

Father Fortis nodded, his beard bobbing up and down. "From what Father Linus said, they most likely told him the role of Christo had been given out long ago."

"Fine, fine," Worthy said. "But for the guilt-ridden Victor, all those reasons would have only frustrated him more. The voices in his head must have gotten a lot louder the closer he got to Good Friday."

Worthy thought he heard Father Fortis begin to say something, but then stop.

"Victor was probably always a bit of a spiritual schizophrenic," Worthy continued. "You see, he lived with his mother and grandmother, the Acoma side. He would have known the stories of his people rejecting Christianity, and his high school buddy, Alonzo, said that Victor used to make fun of the Brotherhood."

"But wait a minute, Christopher. I thought you said that his mother called him a little priest?"

"I know, but that had to be after he came back from Detroit, when he was swamped with guilt. That's the only thing that makes sense. Alonzo said he came back home a different person, totally obsessed with the Penitentes and his conviction that only they could save him. But time after time, when he reached out to them, they just rejected him. Finally, probably right after Good Friday, he just threw it all off."

"By killing the nun?"

"Why not? She did die right after Easter. It would have been like the friars on Acoma. One side within Victor turned on the other."

The two walked silently for a moment.

"And his motive for killing Ellie?"

"Who knows? Maybe he tried to explain to her why he'd killed or planned to kill the nun, saw Ellie's shock, and had another psychotic break. Maybe the voices in his head told him to kill again."

"But would a psychotic have the presence of mind to cover his tracks and leave no fingerprints?" Father Fortis asked.

Worthy took another deep breath. "Maybe he goes in and out of reality, Nick."

Father Fortis suddenly grabbed Worthy's arm. "Wait a minute, Christopher. Wait just a minute. Good Lord, you may be right. I remember what was troubling me before. When did you say Victor came back from Detroit?"

"The end of November," Worthy replied. "Why?"

"The Penitente brothers I met with Father Linus showed me pictures of moradas up in Colorado. They were vandalized about that same time. Could Victor have done that? Hmm, it would help to hear what your partner would say."

"You mean my partner who was raised in a Penitente family? I appreciate your sharing that bit of information with me, by the way."

"Christopher, I want to explain that, but let's turn back. It's getting cold out here."

The two turned around and headed back toward the monastery. "Yes, I admit it, my friend. I knew about Sera's past, but I also knew how you reacted to Father Linus and that painting. All I can say is that at the time her personal connection to the Penitentes didn't seem to matter."

Worthy's flashlight spotted a large pothole and the two men walked around it on different sides.

"So, what do you think, Nick? Have I convinced you?"

"Almost. There is one last puzzle piece that I don't understand. If you can explain that, then maybe I'll surrender."

"What is it?"

"It's something the old Penitente brothers showed me. In the vandalized moradas in Colorado, all the crucifixes were damaged in a very bizarre way. The body of Christ was ripped completely off, but the empty cross was left hanging on the wall. The brothers had never seen anything like that before. Can you think of a reason Victor would do something like that?"

Worthy looked up at the stars and pondered the question. Which voice in Victor's head would want him to do that? Suddenly, an answer came. "How about this? You say the body of Christ was ripped from the crosses, but the crosses were left."

"Yes, that's the odd part. It has to mean something, but what?"

"All right, think about it this way. What did Victor want more than anything?"

Father Fortis pulled on his beard. "According to his high school friend, to hang on a cross, rid himself of his guilt."

"Right. He told Alonzo that his angel, that voice in his head, was pushing him to find the right morada. So what would he do when no group up there would give him what he wanted? The big plan he'd hatched in Detroit was thwarted, stymied. It must have seemed as if the Penitentes were fighting his angel, fighting his God."

"But how does that explain the crosses?"

Worthy stopped and looked at Father Fortis. "Don't you see? If the Brotherhood wasn't going to let Victor be nailed to a cross, then no one should be. Not even Jesus."

Father Fortis turned the flickering beam of his flashlight on his friend. "So the empty cross was like his calling card?"

"Exactly, Nick."

"And after that, he came down this way, looking for other old moradas."

"Right. He must have been in a panic on Good Friday."

"In your theory, it was the end of all hope. No cross, no relief," Father Fortis mused.

"He probably knew he couldn't wait another year and try again. Imagine all that rage bubbling up with no place to go."

"And so that was when you believe he wandered onto St. Mary's land and found the retreat house," Father Fortis added.

"To him, it was just another old morada, which it had been once. Maybe he scouted the place before breaking into it. He was trashing it when Sister Anna returned."

Ahead, the lights of the monastery flickered through a stand of cottonwood trees. Father Fortis stopped and sighed deeply.

"Yes, yes, I am beginning to see it. I wish I didn't, but I do. That was exactly how the retreat house looked when they found Sister Anna's body. She must have come back from painting when he was in the middle of destroying the place or just waiting for her." Father Fortis shivered. "Oh, God, Christopher, how terrible it is if you are right."

✝

WORTHY'S BREAKTHROUGH HUNG LIKE A CLOUD over Father Fortis for the next two days. His research project with Father Linus seemed such a frivolous activity in comparison to the fate of the three young people. From Sister Anna's journal, he knew that she had made up her mind to leave the order and become a full-time artist. Ellie VanBruskman had run away in a similar hope of a new start. And less than a year before, a bright young man had left Acoma for a new future at one of Detroit's finest colleges. How terrible it was that such hopes could be shattered so quickly and finally.

His gloom reminded Father Fortis of how he'd felt in high school during his beloved aunt's ordeal. She and her husband were having difficulty getting pregnant, and so the impending birth of their child was anticipated as a national holiday in the family. But the week before her due date, they'd failed to find a heartbeat at her checkup. Within an hour, their hopes were destroyed. Not only had their baby died, but she would have to carry the baby until normal labor occurred.

That was how Father Fortis felt living in the knowledge of Ellie's death, and it didn't help to have Worthy underfoot. He seemed at loose ends, dividing his time between the library and the cloister, but always near a phone in case Sera or Lieutenant Choi called. When Father Fortis tried to make conversation, Worthy would snap at him or simply not respond at all. Occasionally, he would look out the library window to see Worthy sitting like an anxious novice by the garden fountain, throwing breadcrumbs to the koi.

On the morning of the third day, Father Fortis heard a knock on his door. Worthy peeked in, his eyes bright again as he announced, "It's nothing much, but I just got a call from Santa Fe. They solved the mystery of the letter."

"The one Ellie sent her parents?"

Worthy nodded. "We guessed right. One of the cleaning crew remembered finding it wedged behind one of the counters at a branch post office. It had a stamp on it, so the woman dropped it into the mail slot."

Father Fortis gazed out at shimmering heat rising already from the valley floor. "It fits your theory, doesn't it? Not good news for Ellie, though. They're sure it was the same letter?"

"The cleaning woman noticed it was addressed to Detroit. Ellie hid it intentionally, so it would be found, but not too quickly."

"To give herself a head start," Father Fortis added.

Worthy walked to the balcony window and fidgeted with some coins in his pocket. "But still no news from Choi on the searches."

Father Fortis remembered Worthy telling him once that the two worst parts of his work were coming upon the body and waiting for the big break. In this case, if Worthy was right, the two toughest moments would collapse into one.

"Have you told Ellie's family?" Father Fortis asked. "I suppose they're still considered her family."

"Hmm? I told them we're closing in, but I didn't tell them I know she's dead. And they didn't ask, which says something. So—"

Worthy was interrupted by another knock on the door. Father Fortis opened it to Brother Bartholomew.

"Another call for the policeman," the novice whispered.

"Can I take it in here?" Worthy asked.

Brother Bartholomew explained the process and left the room, shutting the door behind him.

Father Fortis took a deep breath as Worthy dialed the numbers. "This is Lieutenant Worthy. Can I speak to Lieutenant Choi? Yes, yes, fine," he said.

Father Fortis offered a short prayer for the soul of Ellie VanBruskman as Worthy answered in monosyllables to whoever was speaking on the other end.

"I guess that's it, then," Worthy said. "Is Lieutenant Lacey there? Okay, when you see her, tell her I'm on my way. Where? Just a minute." He took out a pen and began to write. "Off Forest Road 528, ten point four miles outside of San Ignacio. Pardon? Yes, I'll bring it."

Worthy hung up, his lips tight. "Get Father Linus. They flew over one of the abandoned moradas with an infrared camera this morning. Something there looks like a recent grave." He headed for the door. "I'll meet you at the Jeep."

"Where are you going?" Father Fortis asked.

"To get a sample of Ellie's hair I brought back from Detroit. They'll need some of her DNA."

Crossing himself, Father Fortis hurried down the hallway toward Father Linus's room. His legs felt like rubber. He paused to catch his breath before knocking on the old monk's door, remembering as he did so Father Bernard's parting comment, "St. Mary's pain might just be beginning."

Chapter Nineteen

———◆———

WORTHY PUSHED THE JEEP TO THE speed limit until he reached San Ignacio. Next to him sat Father Fortis. Behind them both, unusually quiet, sat Father Linus.

"You okay, Linus?" Father Fortis asked, gazing into the backseat.

"Yes, yes. Just a bit tired the past couple of days." In a louder voice, the old monk added, "I'm so glad you asked me to come along, Lieutenant."

Glad? Nick must not have told him what we're going to find, Worthy thought.

"Do you know this particular morada?" Worthy called back to the old monk.

"Yes, I think so. It's been many years, though."

At the correct mile marker, Worthy eased up on the pedal and turned onto a one-lane, rutted road.

"Are you sure this road actually leads somewhere?" Father Fortis asked as the Jeep bounced along. "Look at those boulders ahead."

"According to the directions, this has to be right," Worthy replied. "And from the cloud of dust ahead, we're not the first on it today."

"Guests at the monastery sometimes ask me where they can see a morada," Father Linus quipped. "I tell them to find a road that looks like a dead end."

Worthy glanced in his rearview mirror at his passenger. "So Father, how far are we from the monastery?"

"I'd say about twenty-five miles or so by foot, quite a bit more by road."

About the same distance as the retreat center, but in a different direction, Worthy realized.

Father Fortis twisted in the passenger seat again. "Linus, I couldn't help but notice how fit Father Bernard is. Does he exercise a lot?"

Worthy shot a puzzled look at his friend. Why that question now?

"Oh, I thought I told you. Bernard was in the military," Father Linus said. "And yes, he's very fit. I believe he entered one of those triathlon races a while back."

"Triathlons involve biking, don't they, Christopher?" Father Fortis asked.

"I think so." He turned toward his friend. "Why?"

"Just curious."

Obviously, but why? Worthy wondered.

At an intersection with another dirt road, Worthy slowed to a near stop and looked out his window. "Fresh tire tracks and more dust," he said.

"I don't know how you can tell—"

"Quiet, Nick," Worthy ordered as he turned off the throbbing motor. He craned his neck out the window and heard the faint rumble of generators.

Starting the Jeep again, he hurried toward the slight rise ahead. A mile of twisting road later, the Jeep rounded a bend. Before them was a scene out of a movie. Three banks of unlit floodlights peeked over an outcropping of rock, while police vehicles, both cars and vans, lined the sides of the road. Uniformed figures crawled back and forth over the rocks like ants.

"They're at the morada's cemetery. I hope they don't disturb innocent graves," Father Linus said.

They'll disturb one, Worthy thought. He inched the Jeep down the curving road to a gap in the rocks. From there they could see a simple adobe building, more like a barn than a church, surrounded by rows of wooden crosses. *Nicely hidden*, Worthy noted. Strangers happening down the road by mistake would be too focused on the potholes to notice what they were passing.

As he pulled off to the side, Worthy felt his stomach tighten. Men and women swarmed everywhere around the building and within a cordoned-off square at the edge of the cemetery. What if he'd made a mistake? What if this was all for nothing? He scanned the officers for the only two he knew, Sera and Sheriff Cortini.

"Do you want to stay here or come along?" Worthy asked.

Father Fortis didn't answer immediately. "We'll come," he finally said.

Father Linus leaned over the seat. "Perhaps a priest will be needed, Lieutenant?"

Worthy followed the two priests as they walked along the edge of the road toward the morada. Father Linus's medieval cassock, the tongue of his leather belt slapping rhythmically on his knee, only added to the surreal atmosphere of the scene. *High tech meets King Arthur*, Worthy thought.

He noted that some of the investigators were jumping from rock to rock like trained dancers. A few others scanned computer screens while another group worked in pairs with long tape measures. Abandoning the road and the two priests, Worthy climbed over a few rocks and walked toward the morada. The cracks in the building looked like wrinkles, as if the morada were an old and tired peasant.

Worthy tried to find Sera but didn't see her. He walked back to the road and looked into the line of police cars. In the third one from the end, Sera was curled up asleep on the front seat, a khaki blanket folded up as a pillow. Her eyes seemed closed more in prayer than exhausted sleep.

He shook her gently, and she squinted up at him.

"Hi," he said. "Have they found anything yet?"

Sera yawned as she sat up and opened the door. "A few fingerprints here and there, but not Ellie's. They're getting ready to dig up the grave."

Fine, Worthy thought. It wasn't Ellie's fingerprints he expected to find.

"I thought you'd be more excited," she said. "You all right?"

"I'm always nervous at this point, but more than usual out here. When I see all this equipment, I see budget overruns. I sure hope I'm right."

"We'll remember you if we don't get raises this year. Want to go for a walk?" she asked.

"Where to?"

She pointed to a line of vehicles down the road. "That last one is our forensic van. They're working on a blood sample they found about a half-hour ago, over by the grave."

As they approached, Worthy could hear the hum of the van's air conditioner and thought how welcome it would be to step inside. But Sera seemed to hesitate as she walked up the steps.

After knocking, she turned toward Worthy. "Brace yourself."

The door opened and a portly Hispanic man in stained surgical gloves looked out.

"Look who's here, Frankie," he said, gazing over his shoulder into the van. "It's my old high school sweetheart, the skirt who started all this." He belched, wiped his mouth with his sleeve, and eyed Worthy.

"Lieutenant Worthy, this is Manuel Parres, a pathologist, and as he says, a classmate from high school."

The pathologist took a step toward her. "Oh, Sera. Is that all I am to you? True, you refused to go out with me, but how can I forget the dance we had at your wedding?" Manuel pretended to hold her in his arms.

Worthy stood silently, the outsider from Detroit, impotent when it came to dealing with this jerk.

"Why do I need to say anything, Manny?" Sera countered. "Maybe nobody wanted to go out with you because your mouth never stops flapping."

"Hey, Manny, she's got you there," a voice from back in the van called out.

Manny leaned toward Sera and puckered for a kiss.

Sera stepped back. "How about cutting the crap and telling us about the blood?"

"Always in a hurry, Sera, even when you married Steve. Then, boom, along comes your kid. Sera, Sera, Sera, beautiful Sera with the angry black hair." He glanced over at Worthy. "Foxy lady, don't you think?"

Worthy stepped forward. "Like she said, are you running a lab here or not?"

"Ooh." Manny grimaced in mock fear. "Yes, sir, Lieutenant from Detroit. Your blood sample is fresh and it's human. Is that good enough for you?"

It is for me, Worthy thought. He took a step closer to the pathologist and handed him an envelope. "See if the DNA is a match for this."

Manny balanced the envelope in his hand as if he hadn't decided whether to cooperate. Finally he retreated in a stream of Spanish back into the van.

Sera walked down the ramp, her arms folded across her breasts, and started toward the morada.

"Heh, Sera," Manny called out from behind them. "I hear you're getting married again. Maybe I dance with you at Freddie's wedding, too."

For a moment, Worthy's brain froze on the thought as he stumbled down the road toward the crime scene. The next feeling was the memory of Sera on their first meeting using his back to draw him a map. *Why the shock?* he asked himself. She'd never given him grounds for thinking there was something between them, had she?

"I thought you knew," Sera said softly as Worthy turned his back to her. "But of course you wouldn't."

"What? No, I was thinking about something else," Worthy said as he scanned the mountains in the distance.

A sharp voice interrupted them. "Hey, you two, they're starting on the grave."

Sera turned and jogged toward the site, Worthy right behind. They approached two uniformed gatekeepers who let Sera through but blocked his path. A young policeman, kneeling on the ground, looked up at the men and nodded. Worthy stepped under the rope barrier.

That must be Choi, he thought. He watched as Sera pushed through the others toward the front. Two German shepherds pulled their handlers toward the mound in the center.

He turned around to search for Father Fortis and Father Linus and saw them well back beyond the yellow cordon. Father Linus dropped to his knees on the rocky ground and crossed himself.

"Bring me a long stick," Choi called. Someone stepped forward with a stick and handed it to the lieutenant. Gently, he moved dirt aside from what looked to be tiny holes along the edge of the mound. Another policeman stepped forward and laid a sling of tools down next to him.

"Turn off the generator," Choi commanded.

The whining motor sputtered to a halt, leaving the group in eerie silence. Worthy tried to catch Sera's eye, but her gaze was locked on the ground.

"My probe is hitting something hard, maybe rock," Choi said in a calm voice. "I think these holes were made by varmints, which means something down there attracted them. Who wants to start the digging?"

Choi rose to his feet and let two crewmen take his place. As he took his position next to Sera, he directed them to call out whenever they found something. Hands clasped in front of her, Sera looked like a student awaiting instruction. She answered a question from Choi asked too softly for Worthy to hear above the scraping sounds at their feet, but in a moment Choi walked over to him.

"Nice to finally meet you," he said evenly. "I wasn't too keen on your theory when I first heard it, but here we are. How do they say it? The proof is in the pudding. You should feel proud."

Worthy shrugged, angry that it was proving hard for him to get past Sera's news. What did that matter now? He'd be home by tomorrow.

In the afternoon heat, the methodical digging continued. The mound of dirt and stones, flat as tables, were removed first, exposing another layer of smaller stones. Everything was reassembled to the side, as if the group were archeologists, not police. The faces around the site changed as some wandered back to their cars and vans, and new diggers moved into the deepening pit.

Like sentries on opposite sides of the circle, Sera and Worthy remained as the afternoon dragged on. Beyond the cordon were Father Fortis and Father Linus, though the old monk finally sat on the ground and accepted water from a crew member. Choi's ever-watchful eye surveyed the scene as he sipped from a thermos and calmly encouraged his diggers.

Shortly after five o'clock, when Worthy felt his head would explode from the heat radiating off the rocks, one of the diggers suddenly jumped out of the pit and gagged. The other scrambled out after him and covered his mouth and nose with a rag. Choi jumped cautiously into the pit.

"Tissue decay," he announced, "but it's from beneath another layer of rocks. Get masks if you need them."

Worthy looked over at Sera, who shivered, despite the heat. He wanted to tell her that she didn't have to stay, that he could identify Ellie's body. There'd be no note of triumph in his voice, for it was a victory without any satisfaction. Sera glanced up at him sadly and shook her head, as if she'd read his thoughts. But she didn't leave.

Now minutes will seem like hours, Worthy thought as the sun moved behind a mesa and a stand of lights was brought to the edge of the pit. The generator roared back to life. The man in the pit was handed a broom, and minutes later he'd exposed a floor of loose rocks at least two feet across, six feet long.

That must cover the body, Worthy thought. The boy was certainly meticulous.

Choi looked around at his crew. "We're close, gentlemen, so be careful."

After the sixth stone had been methodically removed, the digger stood up and looked toward his superior. "There's some sort of tarp, I think. What do you want me to do?"

Choi licked his lips as he leaned over the edge of the hole. "Is the smell any worse?"

"Hell, yes," the digger replied.

"Any evidence of animals eating through the tarp?"

The digger knelt down again in the pit. "Hell, yes."

Choi handed the digger a smaller tool. "Take these scissors and see if you can enlarge one of the holes. Be very, very careful."

The crowd had re-formed around the pit, ready for the payoff. Worthy edged forward and knelt down by the lip. Suddenly the digger stopped.

"What the hell! It's made of wood!"

Choi jumped into the hole and fell to his knees as everyone waited for the verdict. *Wooden?* Worthy thought. He raised himself and watched as the message traveled through the crowd, past the cordon tape, to the two monks. The two looked at each other, and Father Linus crossed himself.

"It's wood, all right," Choi called up. "But it looks a lot like a body."

Worthy glanced over at Sera. To his surprise, she was gone, having retreated to the cordon tape where she spoke with the old monk.

Choi crawled out of the pit and dusted off his knees. "Anybody here have a clue about this?"

Sera called from the back over the roar of the generator. "Lieutenant, this priest knows."

"Bring him here," Choi ordered.

Father Linus stepped under the tape and approached the hole. Again, he crossed himself. "Lieutenant Choi, Father."

The detective didn't seem to remember the old monk who'd given him such a hard time at the monastery a week before. "What do we have here, Father?"

"It's La Muerte. The black cloth isn't a tarp, but a robe to cover the figure."

"Do you know what he means?" Choi asked Sera.

"It's a death figure, a wooden carving of a skeleton. The Penitentes use them."

"Shit, is this just a goddamn prank?" one of the diggers, wiping off sweat, called out from the side.

"Not with this smell," Choi replied. "Let's find out what we have here, but whatever you do, try not to touch the cloth any more than we already have. And I want Parres ready to check for prints as soon as we get it out."

Worthy walked around the hole and approached Father Fortis.

"Do you know what this is about?"

Father Fortis wiped his forehead. "A death figure was taken from a morada up in Colorado, one Father Linus knew about."

"So?"

"There's a cart that always goes with the death figure," Father Fortis added. "That was found in the retreat house next to Sister Anna's body."

"What? I don't follow."

"Don't let it bother you, Christopher. It fits your theory to a T. Other moradas, the retreat house, and now here. Victor Martinez is the common link."

It took two diggers to lift the wooden skeleton from the hole, the jointed arms and legs of the figure swaying eerily like a corpse's. The whitewashed wooden face was painted with black circles around the mouth, the eyes made of shiny shells. Worthy moved to his left to get a better view into the pit, expecting to see the exposed remains of Ellie VanBruskman. Instead, at the bottom of the pit, was an enormous wooden cross.

Only the stench emanating from the hole withstood the crazy thought that he'd brought everyone out here for a colossal waste of time. He noted the animal holes dotting each side of the cross's central beam. There had to be a body nailed to the other side.

As the fog in his brain cleared, Worthy saw that Sera had come around the pit and was kneeling next to him, her eyes wide.

"Oh God, I guess this is it," she said. "Even this morning, I didn't think it was possible. I guess I owe you an ...."

He touched her arm. *It's more than possible*, he thought. What they'd found was almost logical, in a crazy sort of way. Ellie VanBruskman's study partner, the boy she'd befriended and run away to find, had indeed found her. Driven over the edge by guilt, he'd killed his college friend and nailed her to a cross.

Behind him, even over the hum of the generator, he heard Father Linus begin to pray. No doubt Father Fortis would be joining him. *Too late*, Worthy thought. *Weeks too late.*

He thought of the girl he'd never meet, whose bad fortune it had been to find Victor just after he'd taken a final bloody step into psychosis. He thought of the phone call he'd have to make to the VanBruskmans and wondered if their anger would finally give way to grief. He imagined Victor's mother and grandmother on Acoma living out their last years in perpetual grief, as would the uncle in Chimayó.

The only remaining question was where they'd find Victor. Worthy glanced out at the hills, his eyes spotting a wooden cross set halfway up a hillside path. Was he up there somewhere, watching as they uncovered his handiwork? Or was he holed up in yet another morada, crazed out of his mind?

The shovelfuls of sand grew smaller with each passing minute. Finally, after a full half-hour, the lead digger asked for a small hand broom and began whisking the last remaining dust from around one arm of the cross.

Bending down, he called out, "I think I see a blouse."

"Be extra careful," Choi ordered. "We want to hoist up the cross without touching the girl's body, if that's possible. Let's get the winch in place."

First the top of the cross and then its arms …. The steel cables were secured. Choi waited until everything was in place before he gave the order. At his command, the winch groaned, and the cross was slowly raised. A photographer joined the last digger near the hole as first a sleeve full of dirt broke free, then the edge of a hand. Fingers caked with blood and dirt came free next.

"I see a ring," the photographer called up. "It's a pinky type. Looks like a horse head."

"Look again," Worthy called down. "I think you'll find it's a unicorn."

The photographer moved in closer to the hand. "Damn, you're right."

Worthy rose and sighed deeply. The only question remaining was whether Captain Spicer would let him stay until they found Victor.

His thoughts were interrupted by something on the body that didn't look right. The hand with the unicorn ring glistening in the floodlight seemed too large. *Of course*, he consoled himself, *Ellie's entire body would be bloated*. He'd have to remember to tell Arrol VanBruskman to prohibit his wife from ever seeing Ellie.

The digger's voice floated up from the hole. "I see the side of his head."

The comment drifted past Worthy like a bird until he caught the mistake. "Don't you mean *her* head?"

There was no response from the pit. Worthy edged closer to the hole, his shoe kicking sand into the pit.

"Then your girl has a peach-fuzz beard," the digger called back. As he started over the edge of the pit, Worthy felt a hand on his arm.

"Wait like the rest of us," Choi ordered.

With legs hanging over the hole, Worthy waited while Choi motioned for the winch to continue its work. The steel cables tightened, lifting the cross inch by inch toward an upright position. Despite the deafening roar of the generator, Worthy could have sworn he heard the sand as it rained off the figure. Suddenly, a gust of wind, the first relief of the day, blew the sand directly into his eyes, forcing him to look away. When the tears cleared, he opened his eyes to see the men behind him, standing open-mouthed.

Wheeling to face the crucified figure, Worthy lost his balance and fell sideways into the pit. A shot of pain radiated down his shoulder as he rolled over on the pit's floor, falling into the hole left by the cross. Through the floodlight's glare, he found the thin chest, then the slumped head, and finally, the face with the empty sockets and the swollen, sand-covered tongue. He heard Sera sob. Everything began to swim uncontrollably before his eyes, but just before passing out from pain, he recognized the face staring down on him from the cross. The identity of that face could not have been plainer if Victor Martinez had raised his lifeless head and introduced himself.

CHAPTER TWENTY

———◆———

FATHER FORTIS RUSHED TO THE EDGE of the pit and stared down at Worthy. The scene below him, his friend lying beneath Victor Martinez's outstretched body, seemed to be out of a nightmare. The smell of the exposed corpse knocked Father Fortis backwards, and he fought an urge to vomit. Out of the corner of his eye, he saw Sera trembling as she hovered at the edge of the grave.

Both jumped into the pit at the same time to attend to Worthy, still unconscious and lying in the hole left by the cross.

"Not this way, not this way," Sera moaned. "Oh, God, not this way. The poor mother …."

"We shouldn't lift him," Father Fortis cautioned as he noted the strange angle of his friend's arm. He could hear the policewoman's teeth chattering.

"We'll take care of him," a voice said from behind. As the two were helped out of the pit, two others in uniform knelt at Worthy's side. The first raised one of his eyelids while the other took his pulse.

Father Fortis and Sera watched helplessly as the cross, still holding Victor's body, twisted like a mobile above Worthy's unconscious body. With each swing of the cross, the smell of death wafted over those nearest the pit. A stretcher was passed down into the pit, and Worthy's limp body was lifted from the grave.

As the stretcher made its way through the crowd, Worthy regained consciousness and lifted his head. "But she's here. She has to be. The unicorn …," he moaned, before passing out again.

Sera huddled like a trembling bird beside Father Fortis. "I have to tell Victor's mother. I have to go now," she muttered. Father Fortis edged her toward the spot where he'd left Father Linus. But where was the old monk?

"Man down!" a voice shouted ahead of him. "Need medical!"

Father Fortis and Sera ran toward a group huddled over someone on the ground. A ball of fear rose in Father Fortis's belly as he sensed, even before he saw, that it was Father Linus.

The old monk lay prone on the ground, his legs twitching violently as he clutched at his chest.

"Cardiac, cardiac!" someone called out. "Get the cart!"

Sera weaved as she stumbled back toward Father Fortis. "His poor mother," she muttered again.

"We need a blanket here," Father Fortis called to one of the men running by.

"What the hell for? Oh, sorry, Father."

"I think she's going into shock."

"Shock over here!"

Personnel split into tight circles of action, as if the group had come under attack. Off to the side was the only still figure, Lieutenant Choi, conferring with a fellow officer.

Out of nowhere, a uniformed woman appeared with a blanket and covered Sera's shoulders before leading her away toward one of the vans. The ambulance holding Worthy and Father Linus already had its lights flashing. Father Fortis stood alone in the horror of the day and in the beauty of the evening light. He said a prayer for the dead boy, for the boy's family, for Sister Anna, for Father Linus, and finally for Worthy. *My God*, he thought, *the evil of this case is going to swallow us all.*

At the far end of the canyon the moon was rising like a balloon freed from a child's arms. Fiery contrails of airplanes crisscrossed in the deep blue sky above. He thought of the people flying high above in those planes, perhaps munching pretzels and sipping complimentary sodas as they looked down on the scene.

They probably think we're a small town, Father Fortis pondered, *or a Little League game being played underneath the lights.* They wouldn't hear of the strange story of the crucified boy until the morning papers arrived.

A crucified boy, he thought. *I can't believe it.* Victor Martinez had died a horrible death, and judging from the state of the body, not recently.

Father Fortis sat on a rock and felt the heat of the day still radiating from it. His friend Worthy had pictured the boy as crazy, roaming the hills for moradas, vandalizing and then finally killing. All that had been wrong. *No*, he corrected himself, *not completely wrong.* Based on what he knew, Worthy had predicted what they'd find at an abandoned morada, and he'd been right.

Yes, something had been right in the theory, even if the body was the wrong one. La Muerte, the death figure found with the body, proved Worthy's point—there was a link between the vandalism, Sister's Anna's murder, and now the boy's horrible death.

An officer approached him, explaining the logistics of getting him back to the monastery. Father Fortis stared at the sandwiches and water bottle left for him. Was there nothing for him to do but eat sandwiches and wait for a ride? He glanced around at the flurry of activity. Victor's body, still attached to the cross, was being carried as if in an ancient procession, while others were tearing down the equipment. No, there would be nothing for an outsider to do but sit and try to make sense of it all.

He thought of something Worthy had told him once, back in Ohio. He'd asked Worthy the question that had haunted him ever since they first met. "Why would anyone want to work on homicide cases?"

He would never forget his friend's unexpected response. "Murder is a lot like falling madly in love," Worthy had said. "Two people traveling on their own separate journeys bump into each other. There's a passionate meeting, an encounter, except with murder something goes horribly wrong. You see, Nick," he said, "when I kneel down over a body, I'm standing at a kind of intersection. People—sometimes my own captain—think my first job is to find the killer. But how can I do that until I know what led the victim to that spot, that meeting? Once I understand why the victim was there, I usually have a clue as to why a killer met them at the same spot at the same time. That's my job, and I won't apologize for enjoying the challenge."

Yes, two bizarre paths led to this place, Father Fortis thought, looking back on the morada. Nine months before, Victor Martinez had accepted a college scholarship and left this world behind. At college, his path had crossed that of a very rich, but fragile, girl. The death of a friend had rocked Victor and brought him home, but the peace he so desperately searched for had eluded him. Worthy's conviction that Victor had drifted from Colorado to Chimayó searching for forgiveness still made sense. From there, the boy had come to this lonely morada and met his end on a cross. That was one journey.

But what of the other journey? Sister Anna's killer had intersected with Victor Martinez at this morada and killed him. Similar ritualistic signatures had been left at both murders. Didn't it all add up to the killer being a Penitente or a group of them? Father Linus's nightmare had come true. No wonder his heart failed when he saw the boy on the cross.

Father Fortis unwrapped the sandwich and saw that it was cheese. The bread was cold from refrigeration, and he pressed it to his eyes.

He pictured Father Linus sitting next to him, defending his beloved Brotherhood. Was there still a chance the old monk was right? If the killer wasn't a Penitente, it would have to be someone who knew the Brotherhood's secret rituals and haunts. But why would an outsider hate a group of pious old men? Hadn't someone recently told him that the Brotherhood would probably expire on its own in a few years?

He took a long drink from the bottle. Who'd told him that? It took him a moment to remember that Father Bernard had been overheard saying those words to Brother Andrew. But the killer seemed unable to wait for these old brothers and their moradas to simply fade away. Whoever he was, the killer seemed to be in a hurry, as if time were running out.

In the fading light, he saw movement on the ground and looked down to watch ants swarm over his food wrapper. *We're like these ants*, he thought, *each of us on our separate journeys, bumping into one another, trying to find some way home. What a sorrowful lot we must be to God as He watches all the misery we put ourselves through.*

An officer called from the road and motioned him toward one of the cars. Father Fortis's feet and legs began to cramp, no doubt from standing on rocky ground for over six hours.

Stars were just beginning to peek through the band of turquoise in the western sky. Out here somewhere, in these darkening hills and canyons, Father Fortis prayed, Ellie VanBruskman was still alive and waiting for someone to find her.

✝

WORTHY HOBBLED SHEEPISHLY ACROSS THE HOSPITAL parking lot toward the waiting car.

"Get in, lefty," Sera called from the driver's seat.

Easing himself into the passenger seat, Worthy carefully arranged the seatbelt over the sling. "I didn't expect to see you. Someone told me you went into shock," he said. "You okay?"

"Better than you. What do they say about your shoulder?"

"It's just dislocated, nothing broken. They kept me overnight and worked on it this afternoon. I'm to give it a rest and have it checked again back in Detroit. Just don't make any sudden stops."

"No, I think we've had enough surprises," she agreed as she pulled away from the hospital.

Worthy sat quietly, wondering if he needed to apologize. He'd been so sure about Victor and Ellie. So sure and yet so wrong. He'd warned Sera at Acoma about the other side of his reputation, about his being a "flake." Maybe now she'd believe him.

As if to counter his thoughts, Sera said, "Cortini and Choi are pretty jazzed about yesterday."

"Jazzed? You mean entertained, don't you?"

"No, I mean impressed. Of course, they didn't have to drive out to Acoma to tell Victor's family. God, that was awful."

"It must have been," Worthy said, feeling somehow at fault. But why would Cortini and Choi be impressed? "Jeez, you have no idea how stupid I feel," he muttered, adjusting the strap on his sling and sending a twinge down his arm.

"Why stupid? Come on, Chris, think about it. You predicted that we'd find a body at an abandoned morada, and you also said the body would link Victor with the nun's murder. Cortini is calling you a genius."

"It's kind of him not to mention that we found the wrong body and that I have no idea where Ellie VanBruskman is."

"I might have a chain in the trunk that you can whip yourself with," she said.

"Sorry. I'm not very good company."

"Then stop it. We're here," she announced, as she turned off in an alley and parked behind a small cement block building next to some railroad tracks.

"Which is where?"

"Believe it or not, Chris, I'm taking you to one of the best restaurants in Santa Fe," she said. "It's not the kind in the fancy guidebooks, which makes it even better."

They walked into a crowded and noisy anteroom, where parents stood guard over small children playing on the floor. Sera excused herself to wend her way toward the hostess in another room, leaving Worthy alone. Several children stopped playing to stare up at his sling. Streams of Spanish flowed around him, and he realized as he looked into a far room of tables that he was one of only two or three Anglos in the place.

"Did a bad man shoot you?" a voice called from the floor. He looked down to a boy no taller than his knee, with eyes as black as Sera's. A woman said something to the boy in Spanish, but he continued to stare up at Worthy.

Worthy bent down. "No, I slipped and fell into a hole."

The boy bent down and pulled up his pant leg. "I fell down and skinned my knee. Want to see?"

"Ouch. That must have hurt."

He stood up and saw Sera's smiling face. "It looks like the two of us have something in common. We've both fallen," he explained. "He hurt his knee, while I mainly hurt my pride."

His shoulder started to throb, and he thought about the pain pills in his pocket. "How long is the wait?"

"We get the next table."

Worthy winced. "That should make us popular."

"They won't mind," she said, rising to her feet. "They can see you're injured."

In less than two minutes, Sera's name was called, and Worthy excused himself repeatedly as he threaded his way through those waiting. No one gave him the icy stare he'd have received in Detroit.

They were seated at a small table near a corner fireplace. The air, thick with the smell of chili peppers and deep-frying, made Worthy's mouth water. On the walls hung soccer banners from Mexico.

"I have some big news," Sera said as she sat down. The table wobbled on one leg, and she folded several napkins in half and reached down to steady it. "Choi is sending me to Colorado."

"Why?" he asked, but he could guess.

"To find out what we can about Victor. You know, where he stayed when he was up there, that sort of thing."

"When he met his angel," Worthy added. "I'd assumed that was all an hallucination, like the devil he said was chasing him in Detroit. A devil and then an angel. I don't suppose they could have been the same person."

She shrugged. "I don't see how. This angel seems to have been the opposite of whoever was chasing him back at the college."

He looked into the fire. "So, the two of us won't be looking for Ellie."

"Sorry, Chris, I can't. We're more than a little short-handed right now. Choi has everyone else headed south. The way he figures it, the killer is moving down the state. The first vandalism was up north across the border, the nun died near the monastery, and then Victor's body was found farther south. He's got everybody checking the known moradas south of here."

"How long will you be gone?"

"I'd say two or three days. Not so long. What will you do?"

"Go back to Chimayó, I guess."

She stared at him. "Chimayó? Why?"

"It was the last place Ellie visited. I'll take the new photos, the ones with the black hair, and ask around. But I'll need your car."

"My car?"

"I can't drive St. Mary's Jeep with this arm. I need an automatic."

"Welcome to *La Choza*," the waiter said. "Great food but shaky tables, as I see you've discovered. We blame the trains. Are you ready to order, or do you need more time?"

The waiter looked college age, clean-cut, and cheery.

Sera blushed. "Sorry, I guess we're not quite ready. Could we have a minute?"

"No, that's okay," Worthy interrupted. "You order for both of us."

Sera cleared her throat. "Hot or mild?"

"You decide," he said.

"Okay. You heard him," she said to the waiter, switching to Spanish to order.

To Worthy's relief, they managed to eat the chicken enchiladas, refried beans, and Spanish rice without ever mentioning Victor Martinez or Ellie VanBruskman.

"It wasn't too hot?" she asked, as they walked out to the restaurant.

"It was hot, but I got used to it." He wondered if the same could be true of New Mexico in general. Detroit and its urban landscape now seemed a miserable second to Santa Fe and its surrounding scenery.

As they strolled toward her car, Worthy said, "The kid who waited on us reminded me of Victor, at least as I've imagined him. They must have been about the same age. I like to think Victor was that confident and outgoing when he started college."

"Before things fell apart," Sera added.

He stood by the door of the car. "When I rolled into the grave and realized it was Victor, I thought I'd never get that image out of my mind. But maybe I was wrong. Maybe for Victor it wasn't … I don't know. Maybe it wasn't so bad."

They both got into the car but Sera didn't start the engine. "What do you mean?"

"Well, more than anything Victor wanted to be put on a cross, and in the end—"

The shocked look on her face silenced him.

"Oh, please finish," she said acidly.

Worthy felt the old chasm open between them. What did she think he meant? He was trying to say that Victor wasn't crazy. He was saying he had nothing but pity for how the boy had died. So why couldn't she see his point?

Sera looked straight ahead at the train tracks. "You were going to say that in the end, Victor got what he wanted. Right? God, Chris, Victor didn't want to die! He wanted to be forgiven."

"That's what I meant."

She turned completely toward him. "Oh, really? Chris, if you ever expect to understand people like Victor Martinez, you'll have to start with one very basic fact. Victor wanted that cross so that he could live again, not die! Have you considered for one moment that if Victor had found a willing Brotherhood, none of this would've happened? He'd probably be helping us look for Ellie right now."

Her face was flushed, her eyes flashing.

"What can I say? I'm s-sorry," he stammered, adding, "It seems we can't get through a meal without me upsetting you."

But Sera looked as if she hadn't heard him. She stared directly into his eyes and said nothing.

"I don't know why I'm bothering, but I want you to hear a story." She looked down at her hands. "When I was ten years old, I walked over to see my grandfather one day. He was in his tool shed making keys. It must have been in August because the day was like an oven. He didn't have a shirt on. I remember seeing his huge arms, and then he reached down for a tool and turned his back to me. That was the first time I had ever seen the scars, the two perfectly parallel slits between his shoulder blades. I knew enough not to ask him about them, but my mother told me later they were his initiation marks."

Sera's hand rubbed the upholstery of the seat as if she were tracing the marks on her grandfather's skin. "Do you know what an *hermano mayor* is, Chris?"

"The head honcho of the Brotherhood?"

She nodded. "He uses flint to cut the skin of the men willing to bear the cross on Good Friday," she said quietly. "Not the Christo, because my grandfather had done something too bad for that. But he carried the cross for Christo."

"What had he done?" Worthy asked.

Sera turned away, tears welling in her eyes. "He was a boxer, even a professional for a few years. But then he was just a fighter that other guys bet on. You know, illegal matches? One day—I must have been about seven or eight—he fought a big guy from another factory. No problem. My grandpa had the other guy in trouble right away. Unfortunately, the guy wouldn't go down, even when one eye was swollen shut. They didn't stop the fight until he lost consciousness. The next day, he died."

Sera wiped away a tear and cleared her throat. "That's when my grandfather started drinking really hard, so things got pretty bad for the rest of us. My dad had died a couple of years before, and the family needed my grandpa. The Brotherhood pulled him out of the bars and gave him a whip. Yes, a whip. My mother told me the hermano mayor sat with him every night for a month and sang Penitente songs to him while he whipped himself. Sometimes some of the other men would take him to their morada, and they'd all whip themselves. They said it was his penance for what had happened. My grandfather never drank after that, and he never fought again. The next Holy Friday, he carried the cross. He said it was the proudest day of his life." She paused for a moment. "The Brotherhood saved his life, and they saved ours."

Worthy didn't say anything.

"You probably think the whip and those scars are barbaric. But guilt is real, Chris, as real as the mountains or the river down there. In an hour, it's going to be so dark that we won't be able to see those mountains. But that doesn't mean they're not there. Look in any bar around here, and you'll know how guilt can pull a whole family into a grave."

Worthy nodded. "And Victor was like your grandfather, is that what you're saying?"

"Guilt had done a number on both of them. That's all I'm saying."

"So that's why you fought me so hard when I said he must have killed the nun and Ellie."

Sera wiped the tears off her cheek. "You had this picture of Victor all worked out. He'd come home from college disturbed about something," she said. "I had no problem with that, but from that point on, you and I were like two people pulling Victor in opposite directions."

"I already said I was wrong. I thought I had all the pieces of the puzzle, but I didn't. "

Sera shook her head slowly. "No, Chris, you still don't get it. I'm not talking about right and wrong. I'm talking about different ways of looking at the world. If a boy from Detroit wanted to be crucified, I would see it exactly the way you did. But Victor Martinez was from *here*."

✞

FATHER FORTIS HAD SPENT MOST OF the next two days at the hospital by Father Linus's bed. The old monk had, in fact, suffered a heart attack, but quick intervention at the scene had limited the damage. Father Linus was intermittently and groggily conscious, one minute insisting that the Brotherhood was innocent, the next dozing off. In one of those dozing moments, Father Fortis had made his escape and returned to the monastery. It was just as he was pulling into the parking lot and hoping for a quiet nap that Brother Bartholomew approached with another note.

Now what? he thought. But when he saw the name at the bottom of the note, he relaxed.

Are you free for the next two or three days? Please call. Lieutenant Sera Lacey.

He took the back way around the chapel to avoid the monastery's sudden rush of visitors. If a Trappist monastery could be so described, then St. Mary's was buzzing. The morning's headlines, "Boy Found Nailed to Cross Near San Ignacio," had brought the reporters and cameras back. Even now, he could see beyond the chapel to where Abbot Timothy was squinting into the lights of the cameras. As he quietly proceeded toward the dormitory, he heard the abbot promise that the community would be praying for Victor and his family. Abbot Timothy also pleaded with the killer or killers to come forward.

Not likely, Father Fortis thought. The killer was becoming bolder—or more desperate. The attacks had escalated in ferocity, bringing Father Fortis back to his question: what is this killer trying to accomplish?

In his room, Father Fortis closed the door and lay down on the bed before calling the policewoman's number. He was surprised when Sera explained her request.

"You want me to go to Colorado with you? Why?" he asked.

"Victor was up there before he came back and was killed. Somebody has to remember him. And I have directions to the morada near where some of his family still lives. I thought you might like to go along, and besides, I'd like some company."

As much as he wanted to sleep, Father Fortis had to admit that it would be good to get away from this media circus.

"What about Christopher?"

There was a momentary pause on the other end of the line. "Chris is going back to Chimayó. He's hoping he can pick up Ellie's trail again."

Of course, he thought. Victor's decayed body meant that Worthy was back where he started. No, worse than where he started. From the VanBruskmans' point of view, nearly two weeks had been wasted on finding the wrong person. Two weeks for Ellie's trail to grow even colder.

"When would we be leaving?" he asked.

"I can pick you up in two hours. What do you say?"

"I'd like to get permission from the abbot, but that shouldn't be a problem. With Father Linus laid up, I can't very well work on my research."

"He's going to be okay?"

"He had a heart attack, but it wasn't too serious."

"Thank God," Sera said. "So, I'll see you soon."

Father Fortis dragged himself out of bed and headed for the abbot's office, forgetting until he knocked where he'd last seen him.

A different voice answered from within the office. "Come in."

Father Fortis entered and saw Father Bernard standing by the window, looking out toward the rock face.

"Sorry, I was looking for Abbot Timothy."

"And you caught me hiding from the media," Father Bernard replied with a sheepish smile.

Or trying out your new office, Father Fortis thought.

"Is there anything I can tell Abbot Timothy?" Father Bernard asked.

Father Fortis weighed the question. On an impulse, he explained his plans and the purpose of the trip.

Father Bernard caught Father Fortis's eye and held it. Father Fortis noticed something new in the gaze, an eagerness and intensity.

"I'd like to come along," he said.

"I beg your pardon?"

"I'm asking to come along."

Father Fortis pondered not just the request but also his discomfort with it. Was it just that he was looking forward to some time away from St. Mary's and in the company of an attractive woman?

"May I ask why?" Father Fortis asked.

Father Bernard folded his arms across his chest. "I can think of three reasons. One, the two of us haven't had a chance to talk about Sister Anna's journal. Two, from what the reporters are saying, the boy's murder is linked to Sister Anna's." He looked down at the floor. "I feel a kind of responsibility to her to see what develops. And three, I used to have a parish up in southern Colorado, just across the border. The roads can be pretty confusing, so maybe I can be of some help."

Father Fortis hesitated, but in the end could think of no good reason to decline the offer. "We'd have to ask the abbot."

Father Bernard turned back to the window. "Of course."

Thirty minutes later, Father Fortis had his answer. The abbot did indeed agree. But more surprising was Father Linus's response when Father Fortis called him at the hospital. Claiming to feel much stronger, the old monk demanded to accompany them, especially if they were going to visit old moradas.

"Linus, we both know that's impossible, but I do need to ask you something. And please speak candidly. Father Bernard wants to come along. Apparently, he used to be a priest up there."

"And?"

Was it possible Father Linus didn't know of Bernard's comments about the Penitentes? "I'm asking if you think it's a good idea."

"Nicholas, if you won't let me tag along, then Father Bernard is the perfect person to go."

Father Fortis packed a small bag of toiletries and underwear, pondering the old monk's response. Father Bernard, St. Mary's spiritual director, was proving harder to understand every day.

AS PROMISED, SERA, DRIVING A POLICE van, picked up the two monks by early afternoon. She seemed surprised by the addition of a second person, but then Father Bernard seemed equally surprised to see that the police officer was a woman. When Sera revealed that her normal assignment wasn't homicide, but child protection, Father Bernard grew even quieter. He listened from the front passenger seat as the two others chatted easily.

For Father Bernard's benefit, Father Fortis asked Sera to explain the purpose of the trip.

"It's really Choi's idea, although I suppose I got him thinking about it. He's convinced the killer is south of here, and he's probably right. But we still need to know more about Victor's time up north."

"Sera, why would someone up in Colorado encourage Victor to head back down this way?" Father Fortis posed.

"I'm guessing some old Penitente brother took pity on him. Victor was obviously in pain, but no morada would let a stranger just barge in and play the role of Christo." Sera paused to catch a windswept lock of hair and thread it behind her ear. "So I'm thinking one of the old guys told Victor about a few of the more traditional moradas down by Santa Fe and Albuquerque. Anyway, my hope is that we can track down at least one person who remembers Victor. If I'm going to dream big, I hope we find the person Victor was traveling with."

Father Bernard turned abruptly in his seat. "You can't mean the girl. I read that the boy was dead long before she got here."

From the van's second seat, Father Fortis studied the monk's face, his piercing eyes and set mouth. Father Bernard ignored a line of perspiration running down from his mop of hair toward his eyebrow. *This is a different face than I've seen before*, Father Fortis thought. Father Bernard seemed on edge, no longer the calm spiritual advisor he'd talked to days before.

The challenge in Father Bernard's voice brought an air of tension into the van. Father Fortis knew from his own experience the trouble some monks had relating to women. But Father Bernard had been Sister Anna's confessor and had clearly liked her. And by his own admission, he'd served as a parish priest in Colorado. So why the new tone?

"Father, I'm not talking about Ellie VanBruskman," Sera patiently explained. "According to his uncle, Victor didn't drive. He must have hitchhiked north to visit his family's graves and their morada. At least, that's my theory about why he made the trip. And that's why I brought along Victor's mother's directions to the cemetery. If we're lucky, we'll find someone who met him. From that person, maybe a Penitente brother, we might get a description of the guy or the type of vehicle that gave him a lift south. If we can track that person down, we'll find out where he dropped Victor. We'll just keep going, doing our best to follow his trail south."

"But if he was hitchhiking along a road like this," Father Bernard countered, "wouldn't his rides have come from people just passing through?"

Sera shot Father Fortis a quick glance in the rearview mirror. It had been a mistake to let him come along, he realized. So why had he agreed? Simply because he thought it selfish to imagine that Sera wanted only his company? No, it had been more than that. It was Father Linus's assurance that Father Bernard would be the perfect one to go in his place. *This is perfect?*

Sera's eyes remained on the road ahead. "I'm not disagreeing. Of course it's probably a stranger who gave him a lift south," she said, slowly, as if explaining to a child, "but even if we uncover only one or two of Victor's contacts, we'll learn something about his state of mind. Don't forget, whoever we find is going to be one of the last persons Victor talked to before he died."

Father Bernard sat silently for a moment, looking out his window at the grasslands and sage bushes. But Father Fortis sensed that the man wasn't through.

"So, in the end, you agree with your superior," Father Bernard said. "The killer is in the opposite direction from where we're headed." His words were clipped, the West Texas drawl nearly buried in some inexplicable frustration.

"Look, Father," Sera replied curtly, "You somehow got the wrong idea about this trip. We're up here to fill in background. That's all."

Father Bernard ran a hand through his wiry hair. "The vandalizing of the morada, didn't that happen in Colorado?"

"Yes, but even if those incidents are connected to the murders, we're talking about something that happened four or five months ago. Let's say the killer or killers were responsible, although no one is sure of that. Where'd they go next? Down to St. Mary's where they killed Sister Anna. And Victor's body was found south of there."

Father Fortis could see Sera's neck turning red. He leaned forward and addressed his fellow monk. "Father Bernard, we've both met Lieutenant Choi, and I think we'd agree that he's clearly competent. If he's concentrating on the moradas farther south, I trust his judgment." *And why don't you?* he wanted to add.

"Fine, fine," Father Bernard replied. And with that, he pulled out his breviary and began his afternoon prayers. Ten minutes later, he leaned his head against the window, closed his eyes, and soon was snoring softly.

Why had he been so eager to come along? In the abbot's office, he'd promised to help. He claimed he wanted to talk about Sister Anna's journal. But now it seemed he'd tagged along for some other reason. Was it to play detective? Father Fortis of all people could understand the desire, but why was Father Bernard being so hard on Sera?

From his back window, Father Fortis looked down into a canyon lying hundreds of feet below the road. It would have been better to have Father Linus, even with his dogged defense of the Penitentes.

Sera caught his eye again in the rearview mirror. "I couldn't help noticing that our jolly friend was saying his prayers. Do you need to say yours, Father, or can we talk?"

He leaned forward on the back of her seat. "Please call me Nick. No, as I tell them at St. Mary's, we Orthodox say our prayers on Eastern time. Listen, my dear, I'm truly sorry. If I knew Father Bernard better, I'd apologize for him. But this isn't the man I spoke with back at St. Mary's."

"It's okay. I think I know what's going on. He's not the first man to doubt my abilities. Tell me, Nick, how convincing was I with your friend?"

"About what?"

"That I know what's up ahead in Colorado," she said, catching his eye again.

Father Bernard snorted and shifted in the passenger seat.

"Are you sure he's asleep?" she whispered.

Father Fortis leaned over the seat and studied the monk's face. "He's drooling a bit."

Sera laughed lightly. "The truth is, this is the first time I've worked a homicide. My usual job is to track down living people, children in trouble. Our sleeping friend's grilling really rattled me."

Father Fortis laid a hand on her shoulder. "Well, it didn't show, my dear."

"Thanks, but what he said is pretty close to what I've been asking myself all morning."

"What's your fear? Do you think we're headed into some danger?"

"Not really, but then I don't exactly have the training to know. Logically, everything points to the action being down south, just as I told him. And my head knows that if there was any chance Victor's killer is up in Colorado, Choi wouldn't have sent me. He certainly wouldn't have let me take two civilians along."

Father Fortis gazed out the window and spotted a wooden cross high on a hill. Father Linus had explained that such markers were Penitente stopping places used on processions to a morada or graveyard. Inexplicably, a chill ran down his spine.

"It's perfectly normal to be afraid," he offered, perhaps as much to himself as the policewoman. "I see nothing that you need to confess in that."

"It's not my fear, Father, but what you priests call pride."

"Pride?"

"Do you remember when I said a while back, about this trip being my idea? I hinted to Choi that Colorado might help us understand Victor better. I got that idea from something Chris told me on our way back from Acoma, something I hadn't considered before. He said that most problems on a case are caused by the investigation devoting too little time to what brought the victim to the place where he died."

"And few people ask witnesses what the victim was worried about the day and week before," Father Fortis added.

"I see he's told you his theory, too."

"Yes, and I've seen how accurate it can be in some cases. But how is that pride on your part?"

Sera gripped the steering wheel tighter. "Because after Choi agreed to my plan, he encouraged me to invite Chris to come along. And I didn't."

"Oh, I see."

Sera nodded. "When I told Chris about my coming, I had the perfect chance to invite him, but I wanted to do this on my own. It didn't seem difficult or dangerous at the time."

Father Fortis could feel the transmission lag as the van started its ascent. Ahead, vast horizons of piñon forests ran up toward snowcapped mountains, forming a perfect photo for a brochure. But today, the mountains seemed more like a wall.

He sat back in his seat and pondered Sera's confession. The most logical way to see the trip was from Choi's perspective. And wouldn't Worthy, if he'd sensed any danger, have insisted on coming along? Father Fortis couldn't deny that he wished for a fourth passenger in the van, one who had some experience when life suddenly left logic behind.

CHAPTER TWENTY-ONE

---◆---

"**H**OW THE HELL DID I MISS that?" Worthy muttered as he looked up from the desk to the canyon wall outside his window. But he knew exactly how he'd missed it. He'd had the news clippings about the Pakistani boy's death for almost a week, but in his certainty about Victor, he'd failed to even glance through them.

Sera had been absolutely right about him. He hadn't been completely wrong, but he'd wedded himself to a picture of Victor based on insufficient evidence. And that evidence had mainly come from two other outsiders, the college chaplain and Ellie's psychiatrist. Dr. Cartwright had never even met the boy. And he knew that his own aversion to the Penitentes had made him jump at the idea that Victor had plummeted from religious psychosis into murder.

Worthy realized that he'd neglected several basic questions. What had happened to make Victor and Ellie blame the college? What was it exactly that had sent Victor back home in desperate need of forgiveness and had brought him to die on a cross?

He stared at the name, dead center in the newspaper account, the one that condemned him. He should have seen it—if he hadn't been so quick to accuse Victor. Samir Romadji, the Pakistani fifteen-year-old, had fallen to his death while hiking at the Palisades. But he hadn't been alone. He'd been hiking with two other high school students. One was James Bidwell and the other was Aaron Stott.

Stott—the name of Victor's professor, the one who'd confronted Victor about his academic decline. With the evidence staring up at him from his desk, Worthy realized the truth was probably just the opposite. Stott hadn't confronted Victor about his studies. No, Victor had confronted Stott about what had happened out at the Palisades. That had to be the explanation for Ellie's odd line in her last letter, about the college being at fault.

Worthy remembered the chaplain's analogy, that Victor was the type who'd feel guilty over a distant tornado. What if the chaplain were wrong? What if Victor suspected something about Romadji's death, but no one would believe him? And could Stott or his son have been the "devil" Victor thought was tailing him?

Stott. The name appeared at least twice in every story, but he'd missed it. There was only one person who knew why Victor had felt so responsible, and she was still missing. If by some miracle Ellie wasn't dead, she could tell the entire story.

Worthy drove the back roads to Chimayó as fast as his bum arm would let him and arrived just before noon. As was true the first time, the lot was nearly empty. He looked up at the two steeples and their crosses, one tilting precariously as if it could fall at any moment. He wished Sera were with him. He'd like to tell someone how sorry he was for misjudging Victor. *But not the nosy nun*, he thought as he walked through the wooden doors.

In the dim light of the altar, he could see that he was alone. As he sat on the rough-hewn bench at the back, the famous church seemed smaller to him, as if it had sunk deeper into the ground since his last visit. When Father Fortis had been here with him, he'd felt his friend watching him, and he'd hated the place. But now the need to hate was gone. The busy altar, the milagros on the floor, and the saints looking down from the walls were as before, but now he knew how much the place was loved. The center of the world. That was how Victor had put it.

But some things hadn't changed. He still needed to understand Ellie VanBruskman's view of the church. What happened to her the day of her visit, the day before she ran away?

He thought again of the message she'd left. *Someday, Victor, I will find you.* As he glanced over to where the visitors' books were kept, he felt a hitch in his thinking. What had she meant by that?

Someday I will find you. The phrase had sounded perfectly straightforward just weeks before, but now it struck him as odd. Someday, someday, someday .... What did "someday" mean?

He jumped involuntarily off the bench as the answer came, the tip of his shoe catching on the stone floor. Almost falling, he stumbled toward the table of books, the word exploding in his brain. "Someday" meant some day, not this day, not tomorrow necessarily, or even next week. Ellie hadn't said, "Tomorrow, I will look for you," or "I'm coming for you right away," but "Someday I will find you."

Someday suddenly sounded like a hope postponed.

No wonder he'd never understood Ellie. Two weeks ago, he'd come here looking for a frightened, chemically dependent child. He'd pictured her full of loneliness and anxiety, maybe even panic, and desperate to find Victor. *That's what the VanBruskmans trained me to see*, he realized.

He sat down by the books, resting his wounded arm on the table. He closed his eyes. The sanctuary was quiet as a tomb. The words of Dr. Cartwright came back to him. Ellie had been improving, and was healthy enough to be angry with the VanBruskmans for their lies. But just as quickly, he remembered the psychiatrist's certainty that Ellie would regress without therapy.

What if Ellie hadn't regressed? What if she were like Allyson, able to live off the anger at her parents for weeks on end? But Ellie and Allyson were different. No, the psychiatrist's dire prediction couldn't be dismissed that easily.

Behind him the door opened, and he turned, half expecting Ellie to walk into the room, half expecting the nun. It was just the wind. But what was it that the nosy nun had told them? Chimayó was a healing site, not just for leg problems, but also for depression.

Depression. His mind drifted back to his kitchen in Detroit. Had that been the real reason he'd kept the dirt and given it to Allyson? *Oh, Ally*, he thought, *I'm so sorry.*

He willed his thoughts back to Ellie while he scanned the books on the wall. As he reached for one, a new thought, like a barely visible beam coming at him from the far end of a tunnel, lit up his brain.

No, no, it wasn't possible, he insisted, even as he admitted that the crazy thought would explain everything, even the new hope rising in his heart. If Ellie were too sick to survive on her own for more than a few days, she was either dead or somehow no longer sick—not as sick as Dr. Cartwright had believed, in any case.

What if Ellie had experienced something here? Was he saying a healing? No, but the nun herself had mentioned the phenomenon of temporary remission of symptoms. What if Ellie had heard of the church's reputation for curing depression and believed she'd been healed?

He pictured Ellie writing her promise to Victor from the very spot where he was sitting. Thinking herself cured, what would she have done next?

His eyes followed the wall in the direction of the altar and fixed on the strange saint in the glass case, the one with the funny little top hat, riding like a dandy on a toy horse. The animal looked to be a larger version of the one he'd purchased for Amy. *Add a horn*, he mused, *and it could be one of Ellie's unicorns.*

Where did you go, Ellie? The meager clues she'd left were like train cars needing to be linked. She had written the vague word *someday*. She'd felt something happen to her here, something so powerful that she'd felt hopeful, perhaps more hopeful than she had in years. *Not much to go on*, he thought. He looked around the sanctuary, waiting for the next train car to couple itself to the others.

His good hand tapped on the table, while his eyes scoured the books in the case. He glanced up at a cork bulletin board laden with business cards, notices, and small posters. A Catholic supply house in San Antonio advertised rose-petal rosaries from the Vatican, while a restaurant in Durango offered vegetarian dishes during Lent.

"Come on, come on," he whispered as he continued to scan the bulletin board. The eyes of an infant smiled down on him from a small, ragged poster pinned precariously to one corner. Squinting, Worthy read the tiny print of a pro-life poster, advertising Catholic hospices for pregnant girls willing to offer their babies for adoption. Below, the same message seemed to have been written in Spanish.

Adoption. He pictured Ellie looking at this same poster and realized that the tension in his belly was easing. He read the request at the bottom of the flyer for prayers, for money, and lastly for volunteers.

Worthy steadied himself with his good hand as the train cars of clues lined up, ready to move. Ellie had been adopted and was angry with the VanBruskmans for keeping that secret from her. She experienced some breakthrough in this church and left a message of hope that the future would bring Victor and her together. If in the next moment she'd seen the poster's plea for help, what would she have done? He reached up and pulled down the poster, having the odd feeling that Ellie had done exactly the same thing. His eyes scanned the small print at the bottom. Addresses were listed, two in Albuquerque and Las Cruces, one in Deming, and a fourth in Douglas, Arizona. The last stated a preference for Spanish-speaking volunteers.

For the first time on the case, he felt that he was beginning to understand Ellie VanBruskman. Hadn't Dr. Cartwright said her real mother was Hispanic, a Cuban from South Florida? Wouldn't Ellie have seen herself in the infant's face on the poster? Maybe he'd been wrong about the sequence. Maybe Ellie had seen the poster first, then written in the book. Maybe the baby's face on the poster had made finding Victor Martinez a someday goal.

He walked toward the altar and studied the santos wedged in its niches. Albuquerque, Las Cruces, Deming, and a place called Douglas. If he could pray, he would offer a prayer of thanksgiving. If he could pray, he would go across the plaza and buy a milagro and come back to leave it here. He would buy a milagro of a human leg, for the leg of a journey. He had found a trail.

✝

Father Fortis could not remember a more beautiful day since he'd arrived in New Mexico. They passed Abiquiu Lake shimmering in the afternoon light as they traveled along Route 84. Near the Ghost Ranch of Georgia O'Keeffe, Sera stopped at a pullout. While Father Bernard headed behind the rocks to relieve himself, Father Fortis stretched his legs and admired the cliffs, striated like Neapolitan ice cream.

He breathed in the cooler air of the higher elevation. In the car, Sera had explained that they'd just entered the high desert. As he stood admiring the tall ponderosa pines and groves of aspen, he nearly forgot his earlier dread.

Father Bernard's return from the makeshift toilet broke into his thoughts. The priest shielded his eyes, gazing out at the forested canyons. "Fifteen years ago I came down this very road to enter St. Mary's. Seems like another lifetime," he said wistfully.

"Oh, I imagine we'll run into some people who still remember you," Sera offered.

"Do you think so? People don't really know their priests." He stooped down and picked up some loose rocks. "We administer the sacraments, baptize their babies, marry them—sometimes in that order—but in the end we're just the guy with the funny collar in the family photo. Old what's-his-name."

"But the opposite is rarely true," Father Fortis posited.

Father Bernard gave him a sideways glance. "What do you mean?"

"I bet you remember nearly everyone in your parish."

Father Bernard nodded. "You know, that's true. Maybe not their first names, but I remember their problems, their struggles. I remember babies who died because the families couldn't afford basic medical care. Same with some of the older ones. I remember the young people getting married much too young and without steady work starting families. Most of all I remember wanting to do more than I could."

"Whereabouts was your parish, Father?" Sera asked.

"Just outside Alamosa."

"Not too far from where we're headed," she said. "Victor's father and grandfather are buried near Platoro. Do you know it?"

The monk looked at the stones in his hand. "Platoro? No, it doesn't ring a bell. You said that the boy's whole family was Penitente?"

"Just on the father's side," Sera replied as she returned to the van. "The mother is an Acoma Indian."

"Really. I didn't think Pueblo Indians married outsiders," Bernard said.

"They usually don't," Sera replied as she stepped into the van and restarted the engine.

"The moradas I knew up this way were filled with old men," Father Bernard said, taking the passenger seat again. "I don't suspect many of them are still alive."

Old men dying out, Father Fortis thought, recalling what Brother Elias had told him.

Two hours later, after Sera had turned onto Route 17 and crossed into Colorado, she pulled onto Fire Road 250 for Platoro. The town itself was higher in the mountains than those in New Mexico, but almost identical in poverty. Rusty trailers squatted on the valley side of the road, while a mountain chalet, complete with twin SUVs and hibernating snowmobiles, rose on the opposite side.

As the van crept along the bumpy road, Father Fortis sat forward in the second seat, trying to peer out the windshield in search of tire marks. The ground in front of them seemed simply dry and dusty, devoid of any discernible tracks.

Father Bernard sat silently as the van jostled its way down toward a creek and then up the other side. At one point, Father Fortis saw him gaze out at a line of trees on the right. Around the next pile of boulders, the road veered sharply in that direction as it climbed a rise. He wondered if Father Bernard knew this road after all.

Six miles farther, around another stand of pines and aspens, the morada and cemetery appeared. Crosses marking the graves were tipped at odd angles; some lay flat on the ground. The morada itself, sporting a cupola covered with a tin roof, was in less decay than the one Father Fortis had visited with Father Linus. Only the entrance of the structure, with its door leaning crazily from one hinge, suggested that it too was abandoned.

Father Fortis and Sera began in the graveyard, while Father Bernard walked toward the morada. A number of the names carved into the crosses were indecipherable, though it was clear that many of the Brotherhood had died during the flu epidemic of 1918. Father Fortis noticed also that Martinez was a common name.

He stopped by one grave. "Sera, I didn't know that women could participate in the Penitentes."

"Oh, yes. They're *Carmelitas*."

"What do they do?"

She stood next to him by the grave. "I was one of them once. We'd bring food to the Brothers during *Semana Santa*, Holy Week. And our procession would meet the brothers' procession on Good Friday."

"Meet them? Why?"

"The men carried their *bulto*, the statue of Our Suffering Lord, while the women carried the bulto of His Suffering Mother. We'd meet before we came to Calvario, and His holy mother would embrace Him and weep."

"It sounds impressive."

"It was pretty dramatic for a young girl. After that, we'd follow the men, and the Christo of course, to Calvario. After the Christo was taken down from the cross, we'd all go back to the morada for *Los Tinieblas*."

"A Tenebrae service," Father Fortis said. "Yes, I know something about that."

"Talk about something scary for a child. All that banging and those rattles in the darkness. The hymns were about Christ kicking down the doors of Hades, and it seemed pretty real to my sisters and me."

"Has your son witnessed it?"

"No, my husband didn't approve. I haven't seen it myself for a long time," she said.

Behind them, Father Bernard called out, "I found something in here." He walked into the graveyard and handed Sera a crumpled, stamped envelope. "What do you think …? I'm sorry, I forgot your rank."

Father Fortis looked over Sera's shoulder at the brief message written on it. "Room 16." In the corner was a return address of Souls' Harbor Mission, Alamosa, Colorado.

"I'm a lieutenant, but please call me Sera. Where exactly did you find this?"

"On one of the benches. The place is filled with trash."

"Let's have a look," Sera said, heading for the morada.

The room was as Father Bernard had described it. In the light of the policewoman's flashlight, it was indeed messy, though it clearly hadn't been vandalized. The plywood altar was dust-covered but bare. Benches, some facing the altar, others fallen over, were scattered around the room while leaves piled in one corner suggested an animal had been the building's most recent inhabitant. In the back, a collection of large crosses leaned on their sides against the wall.

They're just like the one that Victor was nailed to, Father Fortis thought with a shudder. Outside, the sun was descending behind the trees, and the cool breeze wafting in through the doorway rattled one of the window shutters. Father Fortis wondered how Father Bernard had found the envelope without the aid of a flashlight.

A quick search of the place revealed nothing more. "We can come back later if we need to," Sera suggested. "Let's get to Alamosa and see who's staying in Room 16."

During the forty-five minute ride, and now, as they drove down Alamosa's main street of bars, none of them was very talkative. The neon sign of Souls' Harbor Mission blinked on and off at the end of a garbage-strewn side street.

As the three walked from the van toward the mission, Father Fortis asked, "Father Bernard, do you know this place?"

Father Bernard stopped to do a couple of knee bends before replying, "If this is the same place, it's a soup kitchen and flophouse run by an evangelical group. I think I remember the sign."

As they entered, Father Fortis heard a pump organ laboring in the back, leading a few male voices through a chorus of "Bringing in the Sheaves."

An old man, his red hair slicked back with oil, looked up from the reception desk.

"Welcome, brothers. Oh, sorry, ma'am. Women can't stay here."

Sera showed her ID and asked for the mission's registration records. Without hesitation, as if he'd done the same for police before, the old man reached down and handed a large book across the counter.

"Please don't take it," he said. "You see, we get paid per person. If we don't show the names, the churches don't believe us."

Sera reassured him as the three gathered around the book. Sera's finger ran down the page and rested on room sixteen. The name Eladio Moldonado was printed next to it.

"Do you know if Mr. Moldonado is in?" Sera asked.

"He should be," the old man replied. "We eat in twenty minutes."

"Moldonado," Father Bernard muttered. "I think I remember that name. I could be wrong, but I think he worked for my parish."

"Worked for you?" Father Fortis asked.

"Garden work."

Sera turned back in the book until she found those from the previous February and March. She scanned down one until her finger stopped on a name.

"Look at this."

Father Fortis looked over her shoulder. There on the page was Victor Martinez's name. On the left margin were the dates February 13 through 15.

"Looks like he was here for St. Valentine's Day," the man behind the countered offered. "He must not have had a girlfriend."

After returning the book, Sera led the two priests down a hall reeking of disinfectant. Some of the doors they passed were no more than panels of plywood, but the door of room sixteen was solid, its varnish bubbled from age. Sera knocked, ID in hand.

The door was opened by a bleary-eyed, barefoot man who squinted at the offered badge. It was impossible to tell if he were Indian or Hispanic, thirty or fifty years old.

Father Fortis had the odd feeling he'd seen this man before, but where? Where had he been but at the monastery or at the airport?

Father Bernard stepped forward. "Eladio, is that you? It's been a long time."

The man shaded his eyes as from the sun to look up at the imposing monk. "Bernardo?" the man asked, taking a step back into his room.

Father Fortis peeked into the room, expecting to see the normal hovel of a flophouse room. To his amazement, the bed was neatly made with an open suitcase on top, as if Mr. Maldonado had been packing to leave. On a chair a pair of sandals waited, as did a serape with an eagle design. Above the bed hung a plaster plaque of praying hands.

That serape, Father Fortis thought, *I know that serape.* Slowly, the memory of his first day in New Mexico returned. The stop at the general store in Truchas to pick up some dental floss and mints, the derelict in a dirty serape who'd grabbed at his pectoral cross and muttered incoherently about the world coming to an end. "You're not my father," the derelict had said. That man had been Eladio Moldonado.

"Bernardo?" the derelict whispered, his voice trembling. He stared at the monk as if seeing a ghost. "I never thought it would be you who'd bring them to us."

CHAPTER TWENTY-TWO

———◆———

THE AFTERNOON SUN HAD ALREADY COOKED the steering wheel by the time Worthy finally pulled away from St. Mary's. It had been a frustrating hour. First, he'd failed to reach Sera at the police station, and then he'd failed to locate Father Fortis. It wasn't until he'd run into Brother Elias in the monastery library that he was given another piece of the puzzle to ponder. Father Fortis and Father Bernard had both left in the company of a policewoman for two to three days. Up to Colorado, the monk confided.

What in the world is going on? Worthy thought. So much for communication.

After a brief stop at St. Claire's Home for Girls in Albuquerque—the first on his list and a miss on Ellie, as he expected—he'd found himself stalled in the rush hour traffic out of the city. Heading south on Interstate 25 in the late afternoon light, he hunched forward in the seat, his back tense, as if he could urge the car to move faster.

"Relax, relax," he ordered himself. He glanced down to the well by the shift lever, where Sera had left a tube of lipstick. He leaned his wounded arm on the steering wheel and with the other opened the padded lid of the center console. Beneath tapes of Mexican music, his fingers found a piece of jewelry. He lifted the turquoise ring out and marveled for a moment at its beauty. It was exactly the type of ring that Susan would have loved. He turned the ring over and managed to read the inscription. He didn't need Spanish to understand the two names, Freddie and Sera, followed by the word *amor*. Feeling guilt with a touch of longing, he returned the ring to the box. *I hope their love, their amor, lasts*, he thought.

He refocused on the freeway, surprised at that time of day to see a cool mirage, a shimmering lake, still dancing on the road's horizon. He wondered what was waiting for him at the end of the road. He accelerated and aimed for the mirage ahead, as if desire alone were enough to make Ellie VanBruskman appear.

It was nearly three in the morning, nine hours later, when he cut the engine in Douglas, Arizona, and looked across the street at the last stop on his list. The motor pinged as if it, too, couldn't quite believe they'd finally reached the end. The ten o'clock stop at the two houses in Las Cruces had been repetitions of the first, though there had been a flicker of hope in Deming when an old nun thought she recognized Ellie's photograph. It turned out she had confused her with a girl from Mexico who'd given birth three months before.

He struggled out of the car, resting against it a moment to massage his sore shoulder. In the southern desert air, still hot despite the late hour, he could hear the pulsing sounds of insects.

For the past three hours, from Deming to Douglas, the certainty that he'd felt at Chimayó about finding Ellie VanBruskman's trail had nearly evaporated. Part of him suspected that he'd tricked himself at the church, while another part of him imagined Ellie coming this way, but instead of stopping, continuing on into Mexico. He pictured her as a bunch of bones in the desert, never to be recovered.

The porch light of the ranch-style home illuminated the now familiar sign: St. Claire's Home for Girls. He paused on the sidewalk in front of the house. *This is my last hope*, he thought. At the door, he squinted at the small print on the sign, hand-painted in two languages, asking anyone arriving after nine in the evening to knock softly.

Through the gauze curtain, he could see a lighted desk with a crucifix above it. He took a deep breath and knocked softly, reaching with his good hand for Ellie's picture. He was gazing at the timid, overgrown child with the blank stare for the fifth time that day when a sudden gust of wind off the desert lifted the photo from his hand and sent it drifting back toward the car. He bent down to retrieve it just as the door opened behind him. He stood, expecting to see yet another nun, but gazed instead into the face of Ellie VanBruskman.

✝

ELADIO MOLDONADO WAS A PUZZLE TO Father Fortis. The man paced his neat room one moment, then sat by his suitcase the next as if awaiting orders.

"Eladio could work wonders with tomatoes and squash. Peppers, too," Father Bernard said.

As the monk spoke, Father Fortis noticed the eyes of the derelict study the three of them, one at a time. Eladio's attention finally rested on Father Fortis's pectoral cross. He approached the priest as he had in Truchas and licked his lips as he examined it.

"Are you still gardening, Eladio?" Father Bernard asked.

The man didn't reply as he continued to finger the cross.

"I said, what are you doing with yourself these days?"

"Waiting," Eladio said, returning to the bed. "I'm waiting."

Father Bernard leaned against the wall. "So it appears. For what?"

The man's face flirted with a smile. "Just waiting. Same as you." He rubbed the top of his suitcase as he looked again toward Father Fortis's cross.

Sera handed a picture of Victor Martinez to him. "Do you remember this boy? He stayed here last winter."

Eladio looked at the picture, then up at Father Bernard.

"He's not here. He's gone."

"We know that," Sera replied.

"That boy was eager. Was I eager when I was young, Bernardo?" Before the monk could answer, Eladio turned toward Sera and said, "You can meet him."

"Mr. Moldonado, we know that's not possible."

"Not the boy," the derelict hissed. "Him."

"Who's that?" Sera asked.

"Phinehas. He helped the boy find his way."

"Find his way?"

"Who knows the ways of God?" Eladio asked.

The derelict caught Father Fortis's eye. "I see you looking around my room. The boy didn't stay with me. No, no. But Phinehas fed him. Gave him a place to live. He sent him on his way."

"Did this man travel with Victor?" Sera asked.

"No. I told you. He sent him on his way."

Victor's angel? Father Fortis wondered. Whoever Phinehas was, he'd have to be more helpful than Eladio. The derelict was making no more sense than he had that day in Truchas.

"Buy me supper and a drink—one drink, I promise—and I'll take you to see him tomorrow."

"Aren't they going to have supper here?" Father Bernard asked.

"I said food, not slop and coffee," Eladio said, continuing to rub the top of his suitcase.

"What do you have in the suitcase?" Sera asked.

The bizarre smile appeared again as Eladio looked directly at Father Bernard. "Just my secrets."

CHAPTER TWENTY-THREE

------- ◆ -------

WORTHY STARED AT ELLIE VANBRUSKMAN IN the doorway. Ellie, in turn, stared at her photo in the policeman's hand. Gradually, as the blood drained from his temples, Worthy understood how she'd managed to avoid being noticed. Ellie's hair was not only black, but cut short, nun-like, and the black-framed glasses added five years to her appearance. There were few similarities between the girl in front of him and the photo, aside from the panic in the eyes.

Ellie leaned unsteadily on the door before holding it open and motioning him to enter. *How long had she been expecting—no, dreading—this moment?* He reached for his identification, his hand shaking as he held it out to her. He was struck with her lips, how red and cracked they were.

Ellie took off her glasses and answered his unspoken question. "People here know me as Maria Sanchez, a volunteer from Florida. I told them my purse was stolen on the bus from Texas."

She led him to a couch in a lounge area. Large cactus plants guarded the corners of the room, while a picture of Jesus with children gazed down on them from over the vinyl-covered couch.

Worthy sat down heavily, bone weary. Over three weeks of searching in New Mexico and being harangued by the VanBruskmans back in Detroit had led to this moment, and yet he didn't know what to say. Was it simply that his line of work usually led him to find dead people, or something else?

"Do you have anything you'd like to ask me?" he began.

Ellie sat down at the other end of the couch and folded her legs beneath her. She looked out the window toward the street for a moment before turning toward Worthy.

She's as tired as I am, he thought.

"Can I get a pillow for your arm?" she asked. "It looks sore."

She started to rise, then fell back on the couch as if she might faint. When he moved toward her, she held out a hand. "I'm fine. Really, I am. Just tired."

Worthy knew she wasn't fine. She was too thin, as if she'd gone for days without food.

"Ellie—or should I call you Maria?—you don't look so hot."

She smiled weakly. "I'm fine," she repeated. "Even though I knew someone would come eventually, seeing you is a shock." She closed her eyes and ran her tongue over her chapped lips. "Did she let you see my room?"

"Who?"

"My mother."

"Yes, she did."

"Did you find the unicorns in my desk?"

He nodded again. "I thought maybe you used them for babysitting."

"No, I never did. You see, the unicorns were never my idea. She bought them for me, one after each of my setbacks. It started when I was ten. But even when I was hospitalized last year, she'd bring more in to show me. So you'll understand why I didn't bring them out here with me."

She put her head between her knees.

"Ellie, I need to get you to a hospital."

"This isn't fair," she moaned. "I was doing so well. I am fine. Really, I am. Or I was until I saw Victor's picture on the news."

"Are you out of medication?"

"No, I haven't touched the pills since I left the group."

Worthy was stunned. "Why not?"

Ellie looked up. "Because I'm fine! I know what it feels like to be depressed, and this isn't that. I just haven't been able to keep anything down since I heard about Victor. He was so scared, and then … and then to die that way …."

"You still need medical attention," Worthy insisted. "You have to be dehydrated at the very least. Hasn't anyone said anything about how you look?"

Ellie put her head between her knees again. "Sister Mary Grace did yesterday. She asked if something was wrong, said she'd take me to the clinic. But I can't do that. They'll want identification, though maybe now it doesn't matter." She groaned again. "I can't wait to see how many unicorns I get this time."

Worthy remembered Dr. Cartwright's wish, that against all odds he'd find Ellie alive and doing fine on her own. Well, he'd found her alive, though hardly doing fine. And he'd been sent to New Mexico for one reason—to bring her back. Did he have another choice?

"You don't know me, Ellie, and you have no reason to trust me, but I want you to know I've talked to Dr. Cartwright. I'm pretty sure she wouldn't want you to go back there to them."

Ellie looked up. "I thought you were working for my parents. And anyway, they fired Dr. Cartwright. So if you're trying to trick me, don't bother. You and I both know she can't stop anything."

The girl's face was turning paler by the minute.

"Will you let me take you to the emergency room?" he asked.

"But don't you see? I'll have to give them my name. I always knew that the first thing my parents would do, given my medical history, would be to alert all the hospitals out here. That means that once they type my real name into the computer, it's all over." Tears began to stream down her face. "Honestly, I'm not depressed," she pleaded. "I swear it on my soul."

Worthy assumed that if he ever found Ellie, his problem would be solved. Now here he was at three o'clock in the morning facing another decision. "I'm not saying you are depressed," he said wearily, "but we won't know what you need until you get some treatment. So let me offer a trade. We'll go to the emergency room, tell them you lost your ID on the bus, and—"

With her head down, Ellie moaned again. In a voice barely above a whisper, she said, "That won't work."

It was a tone Worthy remembered, one that he'd heard from Allyson as recently as a week before. "Then we'll do it this way," he said. "We'll say you're my daughter. You lost your ID while we've been traveling, but I'll show them mine. Trust me, a cop's ID goes a long way."

She looked up again. "You'd do that? You said a trade. What do I have to do?"

"If your condition isn't serious—and I don't see why they need to know your medical history—I promise to bring you back here. Then we need to talk."

"About going back to Detroit?"

"That, but something else. I want to know why Victor left the college last November. I want to know why he died the way he did. Do we have a deal?"

"Okay," she said weakly. "By the way, what name should I use at the emergency room?"

"I'm Christopher Worthy, and you're my daughter Allyson."

PERHAPS BECAUSE THE EMERGENCY ROOM STAFF was overwhelmed with victims from an auto accident, things went more smoothly than Worthy had hoped. Ellie was in fact dehydrated as well as malnourished. An IV was ordered, and by seven in the morning, she was released with a prescription in Worthy's name to ease the nausea. On the way back to St. Claire's, they stopped for breakfast at Denny's. The girl's cheeks were rosy, and her eyes were bright as she ate the scrambled eggs.

"So you can see I'm just fine," she said as they pulled into the driveway of the home.

"You're better, but you didn't exactly clean your plate back at the restaurant."

"Listen, for me that was a big meal. And my stomach got queasy because I kept expecting you to ask me about Victor. That was our bargain."

"It is, but I'd thought we'd do that back here. Is there someplace we can talk?"

"Around back in the garden." She opened a side gate and led him around the house. "Please try to remember that my name here is Maria," she whispered. "If we run into anyone, who are you going to be? Wait, I know. I'll say you're the father of my best friend from home."

"I now know why you got away so easily," Worthy said. "You're pretty good at lying."

For the first time, Ellie smiled. "You should talk."

They sat on green plastic garden chairs by a patio table. An aroma of lavender drifted up from the garden, where a statue of the Virgin Mary stood with her arms outstretched.

Ellie pointed beyond the cement block wall to the mountains beyond. "That's Mexico."

Worthy wasn't sure if the comment was an observation or warning.

"It's where most of the girls come from. They cross the border, wanting their babies born in the United States."

"Ellie, we need to talk about—"

"I know, I know," she said. "We need to talk about Victor, but that's not so easy. You see, there was more than one Victor. I like the one I knew last September. I was walking around Allgemein trying not to look like a mental patient, and here was this guy who was wowing all the professors. But I liked him, and he agreed to be my study partner. He was the brightest person I ever met. My own age, anyway."

"Then Samir Romadji died, right?"

Ellie nodded as tears began to flow.

"How did the two of them meet?" Worthy prodded.

"At one of these politically correct punch-and-cookie receptions at Allgemein. That's what Victor called them. He was clever like that. Victor detested functions where everyone in the room besides the college officials was a person of color or ethnic. The photographer would be shooting madly, and everyone knew they would see their faces on next year's brochures. It made Allgemein look like a miniature United Nations, which it definitely isn't."

"Did you ever meet Samir, Ellie?"

She nodded and pulled her knees up to cradle them. "What a sweet kid. I felt out of place at Allgemein, and I was from Detroit. He was from Pakistan, and yet he was so open to everyone."

"Do you know if Samir ever hung out in Victor's room?"

"Sure. He had a hard time making friends at the high school, and Victor could see he was in pain. Victor reached out to that sort—me included."

"And when Samir died?"

Ellie moaned as she had the night before. "Take about crazy timing. That happened just about the time I found out I'm adopted. Victor and I seemed like two people passing each other in some long hallway. But we were going in opposite directions. After that, Victor seemed to get so much ... smaller, I guess."

Worthy watched Ellie as she spoke, trying to figure out how healthy she really was. He thought of the rule that he taught to all new recruits at the academy. Is the subject coherent, alert, and able to show appropriate emotion? Yes, he admitted to himself, this young woman passed on all three counts.

"What I can't quite figure out is why Victor blamed himself for Samir's death," he said.

"That was because he was supposed to go hiking with Samir that Sunday, but by the time his bus got to Samir's house, the rest of them had already gone."

"You mean Aaron Stott and the other kid," Worthy said. "Stott's being there when Samir died ... was that why Victor went to see his father?"

Ellie began to rock back and forth in the chair as she looked down at the ground. "Victor called it the philosopher's runaround. Stott turned everything back on Victor, questioning why he couldn't accept life's unpredictability. He said Stott made Samir's death seem like a case study."

"But if the boy's death was an accident—"

"Was it?" Ellie interrupted. "That's what haunted Victor. Samir told him Aaron Stott was one of the guys at school who teased him. Victor had someone in his dorm doing the same thing to him. Victor couldn't get it out of his head that if he'd been there on time that Sunday, he could have saved Samir's life."

"Did Victor ever say he thought Aaron Stott pushed Samir over the cliff?" Worthy asked.

"Sometimes. But other times he just wondered if Stott had dared Samir to try the big cliff."

Worthy nodded. "So there was nothing provable." *No wonder Victor was so torn up*, he thought. Victor could have been right. Maybe if he'd been there, Samir would have lived. And if Samir had lived, Victor would have finished the semester and Ellie VanBruskman wouldn't be sitting in a chair next to him in Arizona with Mexico just beyond the garden wall.

"Ellie, was that when Victor said he was being followed?"

She stopped rocking. "His devil? Yes, it was, and I thought for a few days he might be right. I thought it could be the Stott boy. But then one day when Victor was talking pretty … crazy, I guess, I asked him what this devil looked like. He said it was a wooden skeleton with open eyes. I thought, oh, my God, he's hallucinating."

Worthy grimaced. "No, La Muerte."

"What?"

"It's a death figure, used by the Penitentes. There was one buried with Victor."

"Oh, God." Ellie sat for a moment and quietly wept. "Poor Victor. He wrote and told me the Penitentes were the only ones who could save him. That's why he came back here, you know."

Worthy sat forward. "He wrote to you? When?"

"In January, when he told me to meet him at Chimayó. I thought you knew. No, wait, of course, you couldn't. I tore it up and threw it away. In case you couldn't tell, my mother tends to look through my things."

January? Worthy thought. "Do you remember where the letter came from?"

"Colorado. He talked about meeting some guys at an old church or chapel up there."

"A morada?"

"Yes, that's what he wrote. He said one of the men was like an angel to him. The man let him stay at his place and even gave him some money."

Worthy felt needles pricking him in his chest. "He said the angel was a Penitente?"

"I think so. I think he said one of them had known his father."

"Did Victor say anything else about this angel?"

"Just that he was the first person to treat him with kindness." She looked out toward the statue of the Virgin Mary. "Wait, there was something else … the man told Victor to look for old moradas and to be sure to phone him whenever he found one."

Worthy felt his breakfast rise into his throat. "Did Victor say that he expected to see this man again?"

"Yes, yes, he did. He talked about waiting at one of those places for this man to …. Oh, God, was that his killer?"

Feeling lightheaded, Worthy rose slowly from the chair. "I need to use your phone."

"You don't have a cell?" she asked.

"It's a long story," Worthy replied.

Ellie rose from the chair and hurried toward the house. "I'll show you."

He called Sera's cell phone number. No answer. Next he tried the sheriff's department in Santa Fe. The desk sergeant told him confidentially that Choi's search of moradas south of Santa Fe had yielded new evidence. Gang-related vandalism had been found; besides, Sera wasn't alone in Colorado. Two priests from a monastery were with her. There was nothing to worry about.

The relief that assurance gave him lasted no more than five seconds after he hung up. Despite being reminded that Father Fortis was with her, he wondered what kind of gang would kill a nun and a boy. He called the number back, and after a few moments, convinced the sergeant to make every effort to locate Sera.

His mouth felt dry as he hung up the phone for a second time. "I need to get on the road but …."

Without speaking, Ellie led him back outside. They walked to the far wall and faced the mountains of Mexico.

"I should put you on a plane for Detroit," he said. "You know that."

Ellie crossed her arms across her chest and slumped. "If you do, they'll commit me to another hospital."

"No, they won't. You're much better. Anyone can see that."

"You don't understand. I'll be legally on my own in less than three months. Then I'll be gone for good, and they know it. They'll have to have me committed before that."

Worthy gazed at the mountains. If he trusted her, would he come back to find her sick again? Sick or well, would she even be here when he returned?

"If I'd wanted to, I could have run away last night," she said in barely a whisper.

"What do you mean?"

"After I was hooked up to the IV, all the nurses left for that car accident. I saw you sleeping out in the lobby. I could have left, and no one would have noticed."

"Why didn't you?"

Ellie turned back toward the house. "Because we have six pretty scared pregnant girls here right now. Two of them were raped. My real mother could have been one of them. I'm not going to abandon them."

CHAPTER TWENTY-FOUR

———◆———

FATHER FORTIS HADN'T SLEPT WELL. HE awoke early, bothered by the hum of the air conditioner, and so arose to offer his morning prayers. He prayed for Victor's soul, for the boy's family, and for Ellie VanBruskman before he showered and came down to the motel's coffee shop.

He wondered if his sleeplessness had something to do with their fruitless evening with Eladio Moldonado. As soon as the bartender recognized Eladio, he'd refused to serve him, but acquiesced when he saw two priests in the group. Although the mug of beer came at the same time as the hamburger, the derelict emptied the glass before touching the food. Any hope that he would provide new insight into Victor was washed away with that beer. Other than mentioning Phinehas again as the one who'd befriended Victor, Eladio spent the evening angling for another drink. When a pitcher of water was brought instead, the man sulked and merely picked at his burger. It wasn't until Father Fortis was in bed, trying to get to sleep, that he realized the derelict had been sizing up the three of them the entire time.

Father Fortis would have liked nothing better than to share his misgivings privately with Sera over breakfast. And not all his misgivings were about Eladio. Father Bernard had seemed preoccupied, hardly saying a word over supper. Throughout the entire previous day, the monk had never once brought up the topic of Sister Anna's journals. While Father Fortis had found the nun's story fascinating and her sarcastic wit oddly comforting, he'd found no clue as to why the abbot and Father Bernard had insisted on his reading it.

More curious to Father Fortis than the journal were the notes Father Bernard had added in the margin. Those and passages he had underlined appeared more frequently as the journal progressed, suggesting that he noted something developing. But what?

Any hopes for a private conversation with the policewoman were shattered when he entered the coffee shop and saw Father Bernard already sitting in the booth across from Sera.

"I simply can't believe the change in the man," Father Bernard said as Father Fortis squeezed in next to Sera. "He's not as old as he looks, probably no more than in his early forties." He shook his head. "Eladio had a real touch with gardens. Come to think of it, he was at St. Mary's once."

"You brought him there?" Father Fortis asked.

Bernard took a sip of coffee and smiled sheepishly. "I guess it was me. It's funny what you remember. As I recall, the first few days he worked for us were fine. Then he showed up drunk one day. That settled the matter for the abbot we had then, so in the end we put the pond in ourselves. Of course, the blasted thing has leaked ever since."

A gum-chewing waitress with a pencil behind each ear approached their table and sang out the specials. Father Fortis studied the menu as he pondered the new information. Eladio Moldonado had been at St. Mary's. Had he seen the retreat house?

After the waitress left, Father Fortis looked over at Sera. "The only thing I got from last night was that name Phinehas again. He's obviously pretty important to Eladio."

"He has to be the guy Victor told Alonzo about," Sera said.

"Who's Alonzo, again?" Father Bernard asked.

"One of Victor's high school buddies. Victor told him he met an angel up here in Colorado. So if Eladio can take us to this Phinehas, as he promised, maybe we can put some pieces together."

Father Fortis pondered how they'd gotten to this point—the envelope found by Father Bernard in the old morada that led them to Eladio Maldonado. Now Eladio promised to bring them to this Phinehas. Things were moving swiftly. Too swiftly?

"Phinehas seems an odd name, doesn't it?" he offered.

Father Bernard looked up from his coffee. "It's an Old Testament name, I believe."

Father Fortis watched Bernard pour cream into his coffee. The monk was dressed in civilian clothes, his short-sleeved shirt exposing the cords of muscle in his forearm.

"I think you're right," Father Fortis said. "Wasn't Phinehas a warrior?"

"I thought he was a priest," Bernard replied. "Maybe we're both right. A priest-warrior."

"Hmm," Father Fortis mused.

A half hour later, the three reentered the rescue mission. To Father Fortis's surprise, Eladio was waiting in the reception area, minus his suitcase. The derelict had made an attempt to tame his hair, borrowing oil perhaps from the man behind the counter. He wore the same serape and battered sandals Father Fortis recognized from four weeks before in Truchas.

As they left town, Father Fortis noticed they were headed out Route 370, the same road they'd taken into Alamosa the night before. The derelict sat up straight in the passenger seat, but said little except to offer directions.

Father Fortis caught Sera's eye in the rearview mirror. "Mr. Moldonado, are we by any chance going to an old morada by Platoro?" he asked.

The derelict twisted in the seat, glaring back at him, then at Father Bernard. "*Dios mio,*" he said, before mumbling something else under his breath.

"Because if we are," Sera added, "I can tell you there's nothing there."

"Phinehas will be there," he said, repeating himself several times.

"You telephoned him? You told him we're coming?" Sera asked.

The derelict shook his head. "No telephone. He knows."

Despite his previous association with the derelict, Father Bernard was quiet as he looked out his side window.

Father Fortis leaned forward. "Mr. Moldonado, if this Phinehas was kind enough to feed and house Victor, why did Victor leave?"

The derelict didn't turn around to answer. "To find his way, just like you and me. Even Bernardo has to find his way, don't you, Bernardo?"

On the spur of the moment, Father Fortis asked, "Does Phinehas have to find his way, too?"

Eladio Maldonado twisted fully around in the seat and glared at Father Fortis. His eyes drifted down from the priest's face back to his pectoral cross. "No, not Phinehas," he said. "He's found his way."

And around and around we go, Father Fortis thought. *Let's hope this Phinehas is more coherent. Of course, that assumes Phinehas even exists.* He envisioned the derelict leading them back to the abandoned morada and to a grave with the odd name written on it.

When Eladio told them to turn onto Route 371, then Route 15, Father Fortis confirmed that they were traveling the same roads as the night before. Sure enough, when they came to the turnoff for Forest Road 250, Eladio pointed in that direction. Father Fortis sat forward in his seat to study the road ahead. As far as he could tell, there were only two sets of tracks, which must be theirs from the night before. So how had this Phinehas gotten to the morada? Father Fortis sighed and sat back wearily in his seat. He studied the man in the passenger seat, the oily hair draping the collar of his flannel shirt. *We've come all this way on an alcoholic's delusion.*

For the first time on the morning drive, Father Bernard spoke. "We should have brought water. It's going to be hot today."

The derelict glared back at him, as if Father Bernard had insulted him. "There's plenty of water there. I told you!"

Father Fortis felt his mouth go instantly dry. Plenty of water there? Hardly. The morada was in the higher elevations, but no nearer to water than in the lower desert.

Ten bumpy miles later, they turned into the morada, pulling alongside the cemetery. The scene looked as desolate as it had the night before. *At least the wild goose chase will end here*, Father Fortis thought.

With sudden energy, the derelict jumped from the van and hastened toward the morada as if to catch a train.

"Wait here," he ordered over his shoulder. "I'll bring him out."

As the derelict jogged toward the building, the three stepped out of the van and stood in the morning sun. There was not a cloud in the deep blue sky. Father Bernard had been right. It would be a dry day in the mountains. Sera looked over at Father Fortis and shrugged. Father Fortis turned to see Father Bernard gazing intently at the cupola on top of the morada.

"Now that's odd. It looks like there's a camera up there," he said, pointing at the roof.

Before he could explain, an Anglo emerged from the morada, with Eladio following like a shadow behind him. The newcomer was tall, perhaps in his late fifties, and walked stiffly, with a limp. A brush mustache complemented the flattop, giving the man a military appearance. Large arms and shoulders protruded from the cut-off T-shirt. The stranger and Father Bernard looked as if they could have been on the same football team.

The man stopped, studying his visitors. He neither smiled nor looked surprised. The change in Eladio, however, was profound. He stood motionless behind the man, his arms behind his back. His eyes never left the back of the Anglo's head.

"Eladio, you know the drill," the man said in a crisp voice. "Hide the van and don't forget to blow out the tracks on the road."

Eladio stepped to the man's side and waited.

"While you're doing that, I'll make the introductions. I go by Phinehas, and you've met Eladio. We could have met last night, but you took me a bit by surprise. I blame myself. As Eladio knows, we've been expecting you, but in a different form, I should say. Yes, a very different form." He paused and bowed slightly, a smile playing across his face.

He was expecting us? Father Fortis thought. Had he been hiding nearby the night before?

With a mere flick of his hand, Phinehas brought Eladio to life. The derelict raised his arm from beneath the serape, exposing a semi-automatic weapon. He pointed it levelly from one of them to the other.

Sera muttered something in Spanish as she clutched at the crucifix around her neck.

She's a police officer, Father Fortis thought, *and that means she'll blame herself for not seeing this coming. That's what Worthy would do. But no one could have seen this coming.*

Phinehas smiled placidly at the three of them. Instinctively, Father Fortis knew he was facing the person who'd killed, then stabbed, Sister Anna in the retreat house and the man who'd tricked Victor onto a cross before burying him alive.

"It's a beautiful day to welcome the end of the world, don't you think?" the stranger said, the odd smile growing on his face.

The end of the world. That was what Eladio had muttered at the general store in Truchas four weeks before.

Father Fortis glanced toward Father Bernard, expecting the ex-Navy Seal to be determining how to counter the threat before them. He was stunned to see Father Bernard's hands stretch out toward the killer, his face enraptured.

FATHER FORTIS WIGGLED HIS FINGERS, FIGHTING the creeping tingle of numbness. Sitting across from him in the stark room was Sera, her ankles and wrists shackled like his to a steel chair, her wrists further confined by a chain wound under her knees. The lights on the motion detectors attached to their chairs blinked on and off.

The two of them wore khaki vests, their many pockets filled with explosives. Their vital organs were now only inches from military grade C-4, Phinehas had calmly explained when he and Eladio led them into the empty morada. The room looked just as it had the night before, until Eladio reached into the pile of leaves against the wall and pulled on a handle. A six-foot door rose from the ground, not one leaf on its top fluttering.

In handcuffs, the three had been directed down a stairway into a brightly lit chamber. Ahead, through another door, was a larger room of the same black metal walls and floor. Father Fortis had the odd feeling that they were entering some huge filing cabinet.

"Welcome to the ark of salvation, the new Jerusalem," Phinehas had announced as he motioned them into yet a third room. It was another box of black metal, but longer, perhaps twenty feet by ten feet. Identical doors with small windows were built into all three walls, suggesting the existence of rooms beyond.

How big is this place, Father Fortis wondered, *and how could anyone build it out here in the middle of nowhere?* Maybe that was the answer. The space-age bunker below the nineteenth-century morada was in the middle of nowhere, ten miles from the nearest well-traveled road. But could two men have built something like this? If not, were there others hiding somewhere in this metallic warren?

In the larger room, the three were bound securely to the chairs. In their explosive-laden vests, they looked like fly fishermen waiting for a ride to a trout stream. Father Bernard had been bound first, Father Fortis second, and Sera last. "Sorry to be so impolite, ma'am," Phinehas explained patiently, "but we need to neutralize the two bruisers first."

When Eladio was shackling and binding Father Bernard, Father Fortis noticed the two whispering. Eladio's hand stopped momentarily on the monk's wrists before finishing the job. Then, after Sera was bound, Eladio approached Phinehas and whispered something to him. The leader nodded, a grin forming on his face.

"Okay, here's the plan. We're going to drag you two," he said, pointing at Sera and Father Fortis, "into the next room. I'll be in to orient you to your new home presently."

"And Father Bernard?" Sera asked.

"You'll see him directly."

But neither had been true. It had been Eladio who'd come in to spoon-feed them a meal of canned hash. And it was Eladio who'd later unlocked the chains so they could, one at a time and still shackled, use the small bathroom off the room. But there'd been no visit from Phinehas and no reappearance of Father Bernard. Father Fortis didn't know whether to worry about the monk or worry because of him.

What amazed Father Fortis was how quickly his brain accepted the crazy situation and focused on matters closer at hand. When first bound and set in the room, he'd fought a panic attack of claustrophobia, but soon he felt air coming down from a ceiling vent above them. Funny, he couldn't hear a generator. *Someone has done a frightfully good job with this prison*, he thought.

"Do you think we can talk?" Sera whispered from across the room.

"If you're asking if I think they're listening or recording us, I'd say yes. It depends on how many there are, I suppose."

He studied the room. Fluorescent lights hummed overhead, while a desk in one corner held a blinking computer. Mismatched metal bookcases lined one wall. He studied the computer again. Had it been from this desk that Phinehas had notified the Missouri group about Sister Anna being at St. Mary's? He racked his brain to recall the name of the group. *Oh, yes, the Christian Warriors.*

Christian Warriors. Why did that sound familiar? It took a moment for the conversation from breakfast to come back to him. Father Bernard had been the one to suggest that the name Phinehas was derived from a Biblical priest-warrior. Coincidence?

He squinted at the books in the bookcase across the room. There were multiple copies of one titled *The Forgotten Books of the Bible*, while others near it concerned the Dead Sea Scrolls. A massive two-volume set farther down the row was titled *The Apocrypha and Pseudepigrapha of the Old Testament*. Below them, commentaries on the books of Daniel and Revelation were wedged in between numerous copies of worn Bibles. On the very bottom shelf were books related to engineering and construction. *So Phinehas is a fanatical Bible student interested in engineering*, Father Fortis concluded. The spotlessly clean bunker was certainly a testimony to someone's skill.

He tried to put the man they'd met outside into focus. One thing struck him. Father Linus may have been right. Phinehas didn't look like a Penitente, although he must have some twisted connection with the group. Another obvious fact was that Phinehas was a formidable adversary. He'd met them and led them down into this prison as if they'd been expected.

If Father Linus could see them, he'd bolt out of his infirmary bed and storm the place. No doubt his heart would give out, too, though Father Fortis knew old Linus would like nothing better than to spend his last breath screaming at the man who'd jeopardized his precious Brotherhood.

"I'm going to take a chance, but I'll whisper, Father," Sera said. "How are your hands and ankles?"

"Almost numb."

"Mine, too. Listen, Father, I shouldn't have gotten you involved in—"

"Don't say it, Sera. Nobody forced me to be here, and no one could have seen this coming."

"No one? I'm not so sure about your friend, Father Bernard."

He'd had the same thought. It had been Father Bernard who had advised Sister Anna to go to the retreat house, where Phinehas, Eladio, and perhaps others had been waiting. It had been Father Bernard who had gone into this same morada the night before and found the note that had brought them to Eladio. And now Eladio had led them to Phinehas.

"He called him Bernardo, did you notice that?" Sera asked.

"Who did?"

"Eladio. He never calls him Father."

"You mean like the two knew each other well?" Father Fortis asked.

"Or Eladio doesn't respect him."

"I saw Father Bernard whisper something to Eladio when he was being tied up," Father Fortis said softly.

"Really? So what are they talking about right now?" Sera bit her lip. "They're the killers, aren't they, Father?"

Father Fortis nodded and the policewoman slumped. He could hear her mutter something in Spanish, perhaps a prayer.

"You must be worried about your son," he said.

Without looking up, Sera nodded. "He's with my grandfather. My son already lost his father. Now it looks like he might—"

"Don't," Father Fortis interrupted. "The best thing we can do for ourselves and your son is to think clearly. Our hands and feet may be bound, but not our minds."

She looked up and nodded. "You're right. It's just hard to believe anyone is going to find us in this tomb."

"Don't underestimate Christopher, my dear. He has a way—no, a gift—for figuring things out."

Sera shook her head. "Chris is hundreds of miles from here looking for Ellie VanBruskman."

"But he must know by now Father Bernard and I came along for the ride."

"Okay, but all he knows is that we're somewhere in Colorado. How's he going to find us here? We're a needle—"

"In a haystack," Father Fortis finished the sentence. "Then that's what we should pray for."

With their watches removed and no clocks on the black metal walls, the two captives had no way of knowing how much time had passed since they'd been brought below ground. The only break in their isolation came when Eladio, every two to three hours, brought plastic cups of water or juice, or let them, one at a time, hobble to the bathroom. Father Fortis took note of the light on Sera's motion detector going off just before Eladio entered the room. *By remote control*, he reasoned.

The third time Father Fortis heard Eladio at the door, he craned his neck to peer into the other room. He saw neither Phinehas nor Father Bernard, nor did he hear anything. *How many rooms are down here*, he wondered, *and what is Father Bernard up to?*

During that third visit, Eladio removed Father Fortis's pectoral cross and put it into his own back pocket.

"Why are you doing that?" Father Fortis asked.

"You'll know soon enough," Eladio replied, moving toward the door.

"It's because Christ is still hanging on my cross, isn't it?"

The question had done its job. Eladio stopped in his tracks.

"Phinehas doesn't like crucifixes, does he?" Father Fortis pressed.

"Shut your mouth. He loves the cross!"

"Not ones with Christ dying on them. Am I right?"

"You're too nosy, that's what you are. You shouldn't want too many answers."

"How well did you know Father Bernard in the old days?" Sera asked.

"Bernardo? He's not my father," Eladio said, repeating the words Father Fortis had heard weeks before in Truchas.

"But he was your priest," Father Fortis said. "What do you think God will do if you let someone die who gave you the sacrament of His Son's very body?"

"Bernardo is only a sign from God. You are signs, too."

Phinehas's words, Father Fortis thought. "What kind of signs are we?"

"Phinehas knows the way!" Eladio whispered hoarsely. "You can't see that because you are blind. The Bible says so."

Father Fortis racked his brain to decipher Eladio's babbling. He looked over at the books in the case. Slowly, the thought came to him.

"Phinehas thinks we're signs of the end of the world. You believe that, Eladio?"

"In the last days, principalities and powers will rise up. But the Messiah will come to our rescue," Eladio said, as if reciting from a script.

"What if Phinehas is wrong, Eladio? What will God think of what you've done?"

"His words are true words. He is the teacher, the Teacher of Righteousness."

Father Fortis's brain hummed. He'd heard that title long ago, maybe in seminary. What did it mean?

"He's a killer, Eladio," Sera said. "You know that. He killed an innocent—"

"Shut up!" Eladio said, glancing nervously at the door before stepping toward the two of them. For the first time, the derelict looked frightened. "Everything you say is part of the plan. The plan."

"Was Sister Anna part of the plan? Was Victor?" Father Fortis asked.

"Judgment is near," Eladio whispered. "Those who question the truth must die."

"Is that what they did? Did they question Phinehas?"

"I've warned you," Eladio said, returning to the door. "The sons and daughters of death will perish from the earth. The plan says so."

"Is Father Bernard part of the plan? Is he questioning Phinehas?" Sera asked.

"No. I mean, yes," the derelict said, looking confused. "Bernardo has questions, but Phinehas, I don't know, he likes them. Yes, he likes them."

CHAPTER TWENTY-FIVE

———◆———

THE SHIMMY IN THE TIRES AT eighty miles an hour on I-25 as he headed north toward Colorado forced Worthy to ease off on the accelerator. What Ellie had said about Victor reconnecting with the "angel" from Colorado filled him with dread, as this "angel" must be the killer. But he could not explain why he was gripped with an even deeper sense of dread that the killer had returned to Colorado instead of heading south, as Lieutenant Choi believed. His head pounded with the fear that Sera, Father Fortis, and Father Bernard, in revisiting where Victor had been in Colorado, might inadvertently find themselves face to face with the killer or killers.

His shoulder throbbed, the pain shooting into his neck, but he couldn't afford the drowsiness that the pain pills would bring. Thinking clearly was his only hope, and the pain was now his friend, helping him to stay alert.

Maybe that's what the Penitentes know, he thought. *Pain keeps you alert.*

He told himself there could be many reasons why Sera hadn't answered her phone. The batteries could be low, or she might have left it in a restaurant, as he'd once done. Or possibly, he comforted himself, the three of them were in a mountain valley where her phone was useless.

Whenever he managed to take the edge off his fears, he'd ease off on the pedal and the car would cruise happily at seventy. But within a mile or two, he was back up to eighty again, trying to ignore the shimmy as he flew north on the freeway. Three times his fears boiled over, and he pulled off at a gas station and tried to reach her again. Nothing. *Damn cell phones*, he thought.

Above him, the cumulus clouds marched like loyal soldiers from one mountain range to another. By the time he reached Albuquerque, the afternoon heat had built to its peak. Sweat poured off him, drenching his shirt beneath the sling. The pain drummed from his arm up to his shoulder and into his brain.

"I need a plan," he said. "I've got to think of a plan." As soon as he crossed the Colorado border, he could contact the local authorities, ask if they'd gotten the message from the Santa Fe office. But southern Colorado spanned two full pages of his road atlas, and Sera and Father Fortis could be anywhere. No, if he expected any real help, he'd have to narrow his search.

He tried to remember Sera's exact words. Choi was sending her to Colorado to find Victor's "angel," assuming that this person had helped the troubled boy. Had she mentioned a town? He didn't think so. The three of them were somewhere up ahead, and Sera wouldn't even be carrying a gun.

He looked at his watch. Three o'clock. Heading up Route 68 out of Alcalde, he found the road flat and straight as it crossed a barren plateau. If all went well, he could make the border in two hours. That would still give him a couple of hours of daylight. But that assumed he'd have a trail to follow. He could just imagine what the local cops would say if he tried to tell them about Victor's angel. No, he'd have to do better.

He eased off the pedal again and set the car on cruise control. Finding Sera and Father Fortis, he realized, meant picking up Victor's trail himself. So where would he look?

The highway ahead gradually rose in elevation, and he heard the engine begin to ping as he tore past warning signs in the Carson National Forest for elk and deer. Miles of roads stretched out before him, and not one town listed on the road signs was familiar.

How absurd, he thought. *Of all people, I'm the one looking for Sera and Father Fortis.* If it were the other way round, they'd have a chance. Sera would know where to start, what to say, and what not to say. If this were Detroit, he'd have a chance, but here he was an alien. But what choice did he have? Choi and his men were convinced that the case would be solved hundreds of miles south of him. How he hoped Choi was right. How he wished for a message saying that Sera and Father Fortis were accounted for.

But wishful thinking wasn't a plan. He rubbed his eyes with his good hand, remembering that Ellie had mentioned a morada known to Victor's father. Was it possible that this angel had met Victor there?

He sped up again. Yes, that was a beginning. Certainly, the local police would know the location of such places. Moradas had to be on some map, didn't they?

A few minutes after he crossed the border into Colorado, he received an answer to his question. The overweight sergeant at the Antonito police station expertly rotated a toothpick in the corner of his mouth. "It's not like we have a map of that sort of thing. Hell, there's a bunch of those old places falling down all around here. And as far as I know, they don't keep records as to who they buried where. You're looking for a needle in a haystack."

Unless Worthy was mistaken, a pepperoni pizza had preceded him into the local police facility, clearly a former gas station. A desk, a counter, two file cabinets, and a coffee table accounted for the entire law enforcement operation of Antonito. Outside, the wall of the building assured passersby that the town stood one hundred percent behind U.S. troops.

The sergeant continued to work his toothpick as he conceded that he'd been notified by Santa Fe about a tan Ford van, but no one had reported seeing it.

"What the hell happened to your arm?" he asked, leaning on the counter.

"An accident. I fell into a hole."

The sergeant seemed to be eyeing Worthy's starched but sweaty Oxford-cloth shirt. "Where'd you say you was from?"

"Detroit."

"Where's that?"

Worthy stared at the man, too tired to know how to respond. This guy was going to help him find Sera and Father Fortis?

Worthy looked at his watch. It was already past five. He shook his head as if he could shake loose some idea. A fuzzy thought slowly emerged.

"What about recent reports connected with moradas?"

The sergeant continued to lean on the counter. "How recent?"

"Last couple of years."

"That would be vandalism," the sergeant replied as he moseyed over to a computer. "Hell, most of those old places are out in the middle of nowhere, just waiting for kids to break in. And then there're the folks who want to steal the art. God knows why. It's all ugly to me, but don't tell my wife I said that. Hell," he said, pointing to his name badge, "I'm Serbian."

As Sergeant Rakich typed rapidly on the keyboard, Worthy found himself reappraising the man. He couldn't find Detroit on a map, but he obviously knew his way around a computer.

After a few minutes, the sergeant's hands stopped. "Come around here and look for yourself, Lieutenant."

Worthy studied a list of break-ins, vandalism, and theft reports.

"Can we plot these locations on a map?" he asked.

The sergeant pulled a Baby Ruth candy bar from his pocket. He leaned back in the chair as he peeled back the wrapper. "All twenty of them?"

"Yeah, all of them."

Sergeant Rakich's eyebrows flared as he munched on the snack. He swiveled in his chair to check a clock on the wall. It was five thirty.

He's going to tell me he's got supper waiting at home, Worthy thought. *And then he's going to tell me they don't do things like that around here.*

"Oh, what the hell," the sergeant said. He reached into a desk drawer and pulled out a map. He unfolded it on the desk. "You want a candy bar or something?"

"Sure."

The sergeant opened the second desk drawer to reveal a mini snack bar.

"Pick your poison. Now, here's how we'll do this," he said, turning back to the screen. "You call out the location, and I'll mark it."

In ten minutes, the task was done. Several times the sergeant laughed at Worthy's mispronunciation of names. When finished, the two men studied the marks. All were within thirty miles of the New Mexico border, but other than that no particular pattern was discernible.

"Which ones were never solved?" Worthy asked.

The sergeant returned to the screen and began calling out names. Worthy marked the sites on the map. Eight fit that category.

"Still no pattern," Worthy said. He looked over the circled towns and forest roads. *So now what?* "Why do so many of these small roads just seem to dead end?"

"See those mountains out there?" the sergeant asked, turning toward the picture window behind him. "Those are the San Juan Mountains. The roads you're looking at dead end in the canyons."

"Mountain roads, then," he said, remembering Father Linus's comment. *Moradas are found on roads that seem to be dead ends.*

"Hell, there're some horrible roads up there. Most are switchbacks full of chuckholes. Rock slides have closed some of them."

Worthy looked out at the mountains turning dark blue in the fading light. "Any other reports from up that way?"

"In general, you mean? Some cattle rustling and poaching," the sergeant replied. "We specialize in minor crimes around here."

I hope you're right, Worthy thought. "Anything else?"

A few minutes of rapid key movements, and the sergeant stopped. "Huh, I forgot about this one."

"What is it?"

"An auto accident three years ago up a forest road outside Platoro. A real nasty one, if I remember the papers. One blind curve after another up that way. Some sheer drop-offs, too."

Worthy studied the report on the screen: three people died, two walkers and a person thrown from a vehicle. April 14, 2012, two fifteen in the morning. Victims identified as Oscar Silva and Leonardo Corrales, walkers who died at the scene, and Millie Coffman, a passenger who died later. Four other names of those injured, including a man named Porter Coffman. *Husband and wife,* Worthy thought.

"Why would people be walking a forest road at that time of night?" he asked.

The sergeant took another bite of candy. "You got me. Let's pull up the newspaper write-up."

"Thanks," Worthy said. He knew, to borrow the sergeant's words, he was looking for a needle in the haystack. Was this bizarre accident that needle?

A newspaper headline atop a grainy photo appeared on the screen. "*Old Rito Road Claims Two Lives, Another Left in Coma.*" The story was filled with insignificant details, including the make of the car, the distance the vehicle had rolled down the cliff, and the hospital where Mrs. Coffman had been taken. There was no answer to the one question Worthy cared about. What had drawn so many people to a desolate mountain road in the middle of the night? The more he read, the more the mystery deepened. Witnesses at the scene said the car had come around a blind corner. Witnesses at that time of the morning?

"This is crazy," Worthy said. "It's like somebody made this up. People out for a stroll at two in the morning?"

"Look at that," the sergeant interrupted, pointing to the photo. "Does that look like a banner leaning up against that tree?"

"So now we're talking about a parade?" Worthy asked.

"That's not a parade. This was in April, right? And you were asking about moradas. I think you're looking at a Penitente procession."

The needle in the haystack, Worthy thought. The two Hispanic men who'd died were Penitente brothers. His eye caught something else in the photo.

"Is that a body on the ground? Newspapers usually don't show that."

The sergeant squinted at the photo. "It looks like a …. No, it can't be."

Worthy straightened up, his heart racing. "You're right. It is something else. It's a skeleton, a wooden one. Black, with white circles painted around the eyes."

"You sound like you've seen one before."

Worthy didn't answer as he fought with his one good hand to fold the map. La Muerte on the ground, the fourth victim of the accident. Clues were flying out of the haystack. This was no coincidence.

"What happened to the woman?" he asked.

"According to this other clipping, she died a week later. You look like you're going somewhere," Rakich said, taking over with the map folding.

"I need a flashlight," Worthy ordered.

"You can't seriously be thinking of heading up that way in the dark."

Worthy ignored the sergeant's logic. "Find out what you can about this Porter Coffman. Oh, and two other things."

The sergeant raised both his hands in protest. "Look, I'm technically off duty, and then the station goes to on-call status. The little lady expected me a half-hour ago."

Worthy had an image of the sergeant's daily routine, filing reports on missing cattle before driving home to a wife at the window. The vision was immediately replaced by questions flooding into his mind. Somewhere out there a killer had begun his campaign of terror against the Penitentes. Was it this Porter Coffman? After killing Victor, could he have returned to where it all started? And had the killer crossed paths with Sera and Father Fortis, or were they safely far away?

"I won't hold you up," Worthy replied, "but can you lend me a cell phone in case you get a call?"

Worthy adjusted the strap of his sling and felt a twinge of pain run down his arm. A one-armed cop from Detroit driving a dangerous mountain road in the dark. *Not very smart*, he thought.

"You don't have a cell phone?" the sergeant asked in disbelief.

"It's a long story. Can you lend me one?"

The sergeant reached behind the candy bars in the desk drawer and pulled one out. "You said you needed two things. What's the other?"

"A gun."

CHAPTER TWENTY-SIX

————◆————

FROM THE CRAMPS IN HIS LEGS and the scratchiness of his eyes, Father Fortis guessed it must be six or seven in the evening. Other than waiting for Eladio to reappear with food, there was little to do but ponder what they knew. Conversation between the two captives came in shorter spurts, tending to double back on what they'd already talked about—Bernard's strange behavior above ground, his separation from them now, and the strange facility they found themselves in.

Father Fortis's failure to hear voices suggested that the underground facility was larger than they'd been allowed to see. The question returned—were there others down here as well? And like the tongue finding a sore tooth, Father Fortis's thoughts kept returning to Phinehas's comment about the end of the world.

For the past ten minutes, Sera had been singing softly. The melodies were mournful to Father Fortis, though not unpleasant. Even Eladio, when he came in the last time to feed them, had stood with his head bowed. At one point he started to raise his right hand to his chest, as if to cross himself, but stopped abruptly and left the room.

"They're very soothing, Sera," Father Fortis said. "Something we both need."

"They're songs from a long time ago, songs I learned as a girl. For years I did my best to forget them. I wanted the other kind of music, the kind we'd hear at school dances. Tell me if you want me to stop. I know my voice isn't so good."

"No, not at all. They're lovely. I just wish I knew Spanish."

Sera gazed down at her bound hands. "They're about dying. Christ dying, but also the death of those we love."

"Oh, I see," he said, pausing a moment. "That last one you were singing— what do the words mean?"

"I only remember a bit of it," she said. Softly, she began to sing.

Adios, adios, Jesus mio
Adios del cielo y la tierra,
Que moriste por el hombre
En una cruz verdadera.

"That's beautiful, truly beautiful."

"It means 'Farewell, farewell, my loving Jesus, farewell, from this earthly place. You who died for all of us, on the one true cross.' "

She looked at Father Fortis with tears in her eyes. "Father, I can't help feeling that this is all so unnecessary, all my fault."

"My dear, stop blaming yourself."

She shook her head. "I'm not just beating myself up. We're in this mess because I wanted to make my mark. It wasn't enough for me to search for missing children. And then Choi suggested I bring Worthy with us. If he'd been here—"

"Then he'd probably be tied up with us. As it is, he has to be out there looking for us."

"But how can he …."

The door opened, and Phinehas strode into the room. Neither Eladio nor Father Bernard accompanied him.

"I want to apologize for being such a poor host," he said, giving no indication that he'd overheard their conversation. "I've been tied up a bit." He frowned. "Sorry, that must seem crass on my part."

Father Fortis watched as the man limped toward the desk on the other side of the room. Whistling softly, he clicked the computer mouse. The screen changed, but Father Fortis's line of sight was blocked.

Phinehas turned off the screen. "Nothing. Well, I'm not surprised, though surprised is what they're going to be," he said, as if the three of them were confidants.

He turned the chair around to face his captives. "You must have many questions, as I do of you. Who wants to start?"

Father Fortis and Sera looked at each other.

"Perhaps I'll start then," the man said. His voice had the same commanding tone as above ground. He positioned his left leg straight out.

A war wound? Father Fortis wondered.

"I'm guessing from your get-up that you're some kind of priest," he said, looking intently at Father Fortis.

Father Fortis shook his head, trying to rouse himself. Although he and Sera had done nothing but think about this man, Father Fortis felt completely unprepared for this unexpected discussion.

"I'm a Greek Orthodox priest as well as a monk," he said.

"Really? Have you been to Greece yourself?"

"Oh, yes, many times," Father Fortis answered.

"To Patmos, perhaps? My wife always wanted to go to Patmos. Tell me about Patmos."

Father Fortis was struck by the oddness of the situation. It was a conversation that two people might have on a plane.

"Patmos is beautiful, though a bit touristy," he replied.

"We wouldn't have gone as tourists."

Have gone? Had his wife died?

"Tell me about the cave of John the Revelator," Phinehas insisted.

Father Fortis's eyes wandered to the commentaries of the Book of Revelation on the bookshelf. "You must mean the shrine built at the site of his vision."

The leader crossed his arms in front of him, a hand raised to finger his mustache. "I bet it's gaudy, like some of the old churches around here. Full of candles and incense. Pictures of saints, that sort of thing."

"Yes, of course."

"No 'of course' about it, mister. Painted up like a whore, I bet. Not what John would have known. He suffered on Patmos, a prisoner of another demonic government."

The man seemed to be watching Father Fortis for some reaction. Father Fortis sat silently, taking advantage of the opportunity to study the other man as well.

"But, praise Jesus, the truth washed over John despite his sufferings," Phinehas exclaimed. His eyes grew bigger as he stared at Father Fortis. "The raw power of God—that's what John felt. You just can't stop it, praise His holy name. Speaking of names, what's yours?"

"Father Nicholas Fortis."

"Fortis. What do your friends call you? Nick, maybe?" He flashed a sudden smile.

Father Fortis nodded.

"Well, we're going to get to know each other pretty well, so I'll call you Nick."

"And what should we call you?" Sera said.

"Pardon?" the man asked, as if he'd forgotten the policewoman was present.

"What's your name?" she repeated.

"Playing games with me, little lady? I know the police have been hunting me down."

"Eladio called you Phinehas. Is that your real name?" she asked.

The leader stopped playing with his mustache. He stared at Sera, his eyes cold. "My name is Porter Coffman, but I go by Phinehas. Nick, you must know the derivation of that name."

"I was told Phinehas was a priest-warrior."

"God's warrior. He killed two men who'd betrayed the covenant. You know the most powerful part of that story?" Coffman asked, addressing Father Fortis alone.

"I can't say I do," Father Fortis replied.

"God approved of Phinehas's zeal. You see, wickedness must be dealt with. God is raw power, and sometimes He needs us to be His instruments of that zeal. So I go by Phinehas Zealman."

"Your men call you that?" Father Fortis asked.

"Maybe. But I answer only to God, Nick."

Coffman rubbed his left knee. "It's your turn. Either of you," he said, looking from one to the other. "Just don't ask me anything about the nun. I've been talking about her for hours."

With Father Bernard, Father Fortis realized. Again, the same question pounded in his brain. What was Bernard up to?

"I've a question for you," Sera said, her voice strong. "What did Victor Martinez say when you shoveled the dirt onto him?"

The force of the question surprised Father Fortis. Sera's mood had changed dramatically since Phinehas had come into the room, and it worried him. He could see that Coffman's eyes danced wildly when he looked at Sera.

"You're a lieutenant, a pretty impressive rank for a woman. Are you in homicide?"

"No, missing persons," she replied.

"Must be easier to rise in the ranks in that work," Coffman said evenly. "No offense intended. Now, you asked what the boy said. I don't remember exactly, but I'll tell you what he understood by the end. He knew I'm a man of my word, and that I gave him exactly what he wanted."

Color rose in Sera's cheeks. "What did you say?"

"I said I gave him exactly what he wanted, Missy. You see, I pride myself in understanding people."

Sera's chair squeaked as it moved slightly toward the leader.

"Careful, careful," Coffman advised, a smile playing on his face.

"Victor wanted to be forgiven, you bastard, not die on a cross," she said.

The smile left Coffman's face. "I said the boy and I came to an understanding. I didn't say we agreed. The Bible never says we'll agree. But I gave him a chance, just like I'll give you."

Father Fortis could see the hatred that passed between Coffman and Sera. He had to find a way to divert Coffman's attention away from her.

"Bernard only wants to know about the nun, and you two only want to know about the boy. How interesting," Coffman said.

"You said you gave Victor a chance. What chance was that?" Father Fortis asked. The more Coffman talked, the more Father Fortis revised his estimation of the man. He'd thought Sister Anna and Victor's killer would be crazy, but Coffman wasn't that, at least in any obvious sense. There was an odd tone of confidence, even logic, running through the man's responses. *Our only hope is to keep him talking, to find in this logic some hope of escape,* Father Fortis thought. But with them bound and below ground, Coffman seemed to hold all the cards.

"It wasn't me who gave the boy a chance, Nick. God gave him the chance to turn from being a son of death and darkness to being a son of life," Coffman said. The leader extended his hand, palm upward, toward the priest.

"Oh, I see it now," Sera said. "You didn't find Sister Anna and Victor. They found you, asked to be murdered, and you simply agreed."

"You mock me, Lieutenant, but there's more truth in what you say than you know. Both the boy and the nun did, in fact, find me. That's what the Bible calls providence, right, Nick? I explained to both of them their choice, and they chose. You two will also choose."

"Choose life. Isn't that what Moses told the Israelites?" Father Fortis murmured.

The sound of Coffman's hands clapping echoed through the room. "Excellent, Nick! Two paths—the path of life and the path of death. You're a man of the Bible, though Paul says the devil also knows the Scriptures. Yet I'm an optimist. It's one of my flaws, you could say. It's clear that you understand me better than she does," he said, nodding toward the policewoman. "Who knows, perhaps you understand me better than Eladio." Coffman nodded to himself, fingering his mustache, as if the thought were worth considering.

"But I don't understand you, Mr. Coffman," Father Fortis protested. "I don't understand anything. Not these explosives, or why we're bound, or why you built this bunker under an old morada. And I certainly don't understand how you can believe God approved of your killing an innocent nun and a young boy."

The leader leaned forward, his hand massaging his knee. "Here's your mistake, Nick. You're looking at everything as separate pieces. The nun, the boy, you two coming here, not to mention what's about to happen …. It's all a whole, Nick, all a whole. If you knew your Bible, you'd see it."

Father Fortis glanced over and saw that Sera's face was flushed. *She's too angry*, he thought, *and a danger to us both.*

"But how did it all start?" he asked, trying to keep Coffman distracted. "How can you expect me to understand you if you don't tell me how it all started?"

Coffman rose and stood over Father Fortis, the captor's jaw clenched. *In trying to protect Sera, have I inadvertently pushed the man too far?* he wondered.

The leader paced the room, his body bobbing slightly on his left leg as if he were walking the deck of a ship.

"Did either of you notice two crosses about two miles back up the road as you came in?" he asked.

"No, I didn't," Father Fortis admitted.

"I did," Sera said. "I assumed it was an auto accident."

"That's what the police want everyone to believe. It wasn't an accident. It was the beginning of a war. No, it was the beginning of *the* war, though I didn't know it at the time."

"Who died?" Father Fortis asked.

"I don't say she died. No, I say Death stole her that night."

"Your wife? I'm truly sorry," Father Fortis said. "It's never easy—"

"No point to pity, Nick," Coffman said. "Not in Vietnam, and not in this war."

"Accept it as sympathy, then, not pity. To lose a spouse is always—"

"Stop twisting my words!" Coffman broke in again. "I told you, I didn't lose her. After the resurrection, we'll be together."

Father Fortis shot Sera a look. *Just let him talk.*

"Very soon, very soon," Coffman muttered, looking at the books on the far wall. "Christ will open her eyes, and we'll be together for a thousand years, then eternity above."

"So who are you blaming for killing her? Sister Anna or Victor? Or maybe it's both," Sera said.

"Has anyone ever told you that you have a very grating voice, ma'am? The boy was guilty, more than he knew. Once I learned who his father was, I realized God's mysterious purposes."

"Oh my God, you blame the Brotherhood ...," Sera said, her voice trailing off.

Before Coffman could answer, the door opened. Eladio peeked in, a look of alarm on his face. In his hand, he held the assault rifle. "Someone's snooping around outside," he said. "What do you want me to do?"

✠

WORTHY TURNED OFF ON THE BUMPY road and checked his odometer.

According to the accident report, the crash site would be six and two-tenths miles up the way. He switched on his high beams and steered from one side of the road to the other to avoid the potholes. With each mile, he was forced to go slower. At times, his tires came dangerously close to the road's edge, from where it dropped off sharply to the canyon below.

As he neared the six-mile mark, he momentarily saw something shiny ahead, like reflector strips. But the road curved away at that moment; it was not until he rounded another bend that he saw the two crosses, side by side. Plain, with shiny letters covering both spines, the crosses were encircled with plastic flowers. On one he read the name Oscar Silva; on the other, Leonardo Corrales.

Worthy got out of the car and studied the place where the two walkers had been killed in the accident. He used his flashlight to peer down the steep embankment for the third cross, the one commemorating where the woman died. He saw none.

He beat back the fatigue coursing through his body by trying to mentally recreate the accident. From one direction, perhaps the same way he'd approached the site, the Coffman car had come around the blind curve. Rounding the bend from the opposite direction must have been the Penitente procession, Oscar Silva and Leonardo Corrales leading the death cart.

He returned to the car and let the darkness settle in around him. His eyes slowly adjusted to the starlit sky. If it had been a night like this, neither the walkers, chanting as they marched, nor the Coffman vehicle would have seen the other until it was too late. He could almost hear the screams of the Penitentes as they were struck by the car, then the screams of the Coffmans as their car plunged over the edge. The tragedy would have taken only seconds.

Worthy pulled back onto the road. The voice of logic told him he'd found what he'd been looking for, and he might as well head back into town. But something in the back of his mind drew him forward. Then it came to him. The procession must have had some beginning point—a morada. Perhaps he'd already passed it without noticing, but he sensed it was still up ahead.

He stopped every several hundred yards to scan the roadsides with his flashlight. Nearly a mile and a half farther on, as the road leveled off slightly, his narrow beam spotted something that sent his heart racing. In front of him was a cemetery filled with crooked crosses. Behind it stood an old building.

Buckling the holstered gun to his belt, he jumped from the car. He trained the flashlight on the ground, looking for any clue that Sera and the other two had been there. If they had, he reasoned, it would have been within the last twenty-four to thirty-six hours—too short a time for the wind or weather to obliterate their tracks. His heart sank as he saw nothing more than the markings of a rabbit and another animal. Pine needles and dust had settled in powdery layers; it appeared that the place had been vacant for months. A gentle breeze fluttered the silver leaves of the aspens that ringed the site.

As the flashlight illuminated the crosses in the cemetery, he looked for something linking the place to Victor. Could the boy's father have been from this morada? The weathered condition of the crosses defeated the narrow beam of the flashlight. Some mounded graves held no markers at all, and only a few had the plastic flowers he'd seen back at the accident site.

Last of all, he trained the beam on the building and saw the door hanging crazily from the hinges. If the procession had started from this spot that night, then the accident had apparently destroyed the group's spirit as well as the two leaders. Judging by the evidence, no one had stood where he was standing for a long time.

He walked to the door of the morada and aimed the light into the darkness within. Except for a bare altar and a few benches lying on their sides, the room was empty. To his surprise, the walls were weather-beaten but unmarked, apparently unmolested by vandals. Maybe the place was too far from town.

His light found the mound of leaves in a back corner. The work of an animal, he concluded. The pile of leaves reminded him of happier days with Allyson when she'd been young. She always begged to dive into the leaves and cover herself. He felt an urge to lie down in them himself, to drift off to sleep. But wouldn't snakes be curled up in such a sheltered place? And he had no time for napping.

He could hear the wind whistling through the aspens outside the morada. Leaning back against the wall, he felt the day's heat still trapped in the adobe.

"Where are you?" he whispered to himself. "This is where you should have come." That was assuming, of course, that Sera and Father Fortis had even learned about the accident. Was it possible that there were other leads, other needles in the haystack, as tantalizing as this one? Every bone in his body, especially his aching shoulder, wanted this old building to mean something. Yet it clearly didn't. He'd wasted precious hours on a hunch. The beam flickered as it remained on the leaves, lying deathly still in the corner.

He must have jumped six inches when the phone rang in his shirt pocket. His shoulder radiated with pain as the surprise sent him crashing into the wall, but his mind was already racing past the pain to the only question that mattered. Had Sera and Father Fortis been found?

"That you, Sergeant?" he asked. Static buzzed from the dreaded cell phone, and he had to step out of the old building before the sergeant's voice could be heard.

"Sure is, Lieutenant. Where in the world are you?"

"Out at some old morada up the road from the accident site. I thought I might find something here, but it's totally empty. What've you got?"

"Two things. The van you asked about was spotted this morning in Alamosa."

Worthy's heart jumped in step with his feet as he headed for the car. "Where's that?"

"About forty miles east of where you are. Get on Route 285. Then go north into town."

"Where do I go once I get there?"

"To Souls' Harbor Rescue Mission."

A memory from his childhood floated back to him, of waiting in a locked car while his father dropped off a box of Gideon Bibles to a skid-row mission in Louisville.

"Fine. I'm on my way. There's nothing here."

"When do you plan to sleep, Lieutenant?"

"Soon. After I check things out at the mission. What did you say the name was?"

"You see? That's what I mean. Hell, you looked beat when you were at the station. And now you're going to drive down that road in the dark? I think you're in more danger than your friends."

As he started the engine, Worthy turned to take a final look at the morada. *Odd*, he thought, *that there's no static from the phone in the car but there was in the building.*

"More danger than my friends?" he repeated. "I sure hope so, Sergeant. Just tell me where I'm supposed to go, and then tell me what else you got."

"Souls' Harbor Rescue Mission," he repeated. "The other bit of info is about Porter Coffman. It turns out he used to work over at the National Science facility in Los Alamos. He was there about twenty years before he retired. You heard of it?"

"Sure. One of those top-secret places, right? Where's Coffman now?"

"He hasn't been seen for a month or two. That's not that unusual, apparently."

"Okay. Well, do we know what he did at Los Alamos?"

Rakich could be heard munching something. "He was what they call a structural engineer."

Worthy turned on his high beams as he again approached the accident site. "And that means what?"

"I asked the same thing of a buddy of mine who used to work over there. He didn't know Coffman, but said that they're the guys who specialize in the underground bunkers. Radiation-proof, that sort of thing."

"Great, just great," Worthy replied, as he looked out over the expanse of mountains and canyons. As if it wasn't hard enough finding something above ground … now Coffman might be hiding beneath it.

"Really?" the sergeant asked. "You think it might be important?"

Worthy didn't bother to answer. "Call me if you get anything else, even if it's in the middle of the night."

"It is almost the middle of the night."

Worthy drove back toward the highway, groping for the gun on his belt and the flashlight in the passenger seat. Why did he have the feeling that he'd left something in the morada?

CHAPTER TWENTY-SEVEN

——————◆——————

FATHER FORTIS COULD FEEL HIS HEARTBEAT in his ears as Eladio was directed to stand guard at the base of the stairs. Showing no panic, Coffman walked to the desk and swiveled the monitor so that the two of them could see.

Father Fortis watched the solitary figure walk into the cemetery. The sling on the visitor's arm could only mean one thing—Worthy had found them. He saw Sera's eyes transform into open circles, her tongue moistening her lips as she also stared at the screen.

"By the way, you can shout all you want," Coffman said. "We're completely cut off down here. But that won't keep us from watching our visitor's every move. Infrared night vision, state of the art."

Despite Coffman's confidence, Father Fortis felt for the first time since they'd been taken prisoner that they held the advantage. It seemed Coffman didn't recognize Worthy, so he couldn't know that his two prisoners were friends with the man above ground.

Outside, Worthy could be seen studying the graves. Suddenly, his flashlight beam panned toward the camera as Worthy approached the morada. Coffman hit several keys and a new camera angle, obviously from somewhere inside the dark building, showed Worthy approaching the door, then entering the room. Worthy was right above them, and yet there was nothing they could do.

Father Fortis quickly checked to make sure that Sera wasn't preparing to test Coffman's word. But he could see that her lips, although moving, were doing nothing more than whispering. Was she praying, or trying to magically communicate with Christopher?

He said a prayer himself for his friend's safety. The last thing they needed was for their last hope to be tied up with them in this bunker. In the morada above, Father Fortis could see Worthy's flashlight play across the walls before coming to rest on the fake pile of leaves. What would happen if Worthy came over to investigate? He pictured Eladio waiting with the assault rifle trained on the door, ready to shoot. "Be careful, be careful," Father Fortis pleaded under his breath.

"Everything is happening according to plan," Coffman commented. "This place is like a magnet pulling all of you to it. Can you see that, Nick?" he asked, turning from the screen toward his two captives.

Father Fortis didn't dare look at Sera.

"Be ready, Eladio," Coffman ordered. "Just a few more steps and—"

But something caused Worthy to jump. The figure stepped abruptly outside the morada. Father Fortis didn't know whether to cry or breathe a sigh of relief.

Coffman played with the keyboard, and yet a third camera angle showed Worthy talking on a cell phone. A cell phone? Since when did Christopher have a cell phone? Tears came to his eyes as he watched Worthy jog toward a car.

He risked a glance at Sera, her hands red from straining against the chains. He saw her lips move and read her message. *Goodbye, Chris. Goodbye.*

No, no, no! Father Fortis thought. *It can't end this way.* Yet to know that Worthy had stood right above them, only to leave, seemed to destroy his last bit of hope. He felt his hands relax as if they too had already accepted their fate.

Just as Worthy could be seen reentering the car, he turned to shine the flashlight one last time at the morada. Like a wave crashing on a shore, hope rose within Father Fortis. *Christopher suspects something*, he thought. *He suspects something!* He looked over and saw from Sera's tightly pursed lips that she knew it, too. Christopher would come back. But would it be in time?

✠

WORTHY PARKED IN FRONT OF SOULS' Harbor Rescue Mission in Alamosa, draining the cup of coffee purchased at a mom-and-pop store on the edge of town. The mission's neon-lit cross, blinking on, blinking off, sent rods of pain shooting into his dry eyes. Everything except his brain wanted to sleep. He squinted again as he walked into the brightly lit reception area.

It took a moment for him to recognize the man standing in his way.

"Sergeant Rakich, what are you doing here?"

The policeman from Antonito held out his hand, a tight frown on his face. "I thought I should be doing my job a little bit better. God knows, you must be worried about your friends."

Worthy shook the offered hand. What had happened to bring the man out at four in the morning? "You got something, Sergeant?"

"Not much. I got ahold of this photo of Coffman. I thought you might need it."

Worthy studied the face in the photo, a mug shot from some ID. The face was chiseled, the mouth dead, but the eyes seemed to hold contempt for the camera.

"No word on the van?" Worthy asked.

"No. Sorry. We're pretty sure it was here, but by now that was … yesterday."

Worthy adjusted the strap of the sling. The weight of his dead arm had caused his other shoulder to ache. He looked across the reception desk to where an old man was working a crossword puzzle. From another room, he heard the twang of a guitar and recognized a gospel tune from his childhood. "He lives! He lives! Christ Jesus lives today." One of his Dad's favorites.

"Have you talked to our friend over there yet?" Worthy asked.

Sergeant Rakich pulled a small notebook out from behind a candy bar in his shirt pocket. "He thinks he might have seen Coffman around here about a month ago, but he said the guy was going by another name. But he's not sure. And he said your friends were here the night before last, looking for some guy named Eladio Moldonado."

"Where is that guy now?"

"Gone. One of the other guys here said he saw Eladio leaving with your friends yesterday morning, but the guy at the desk says not to trust him."

"Do we need a search warrant to check his room?"

"Nope. A small donation to the mission took care of that. I was just waiting for you."

The two men walked through the recreation room, empty except for the tape player, on through another door into a hallway. The narrow passageway smelled of disinfectant, the reason becoming clear when they passed the common bathroom, which smelled of rancid alcohol and vomit. At the end of the hall, Sergeant Rakich stopped in front of a room and opened it with a key.

Worthy walked into a small, neat bedroom. All indications were that its most recent inhabitant had checked out. Worthy began with the bed, over which hung a plaque of praying hands, while Rakich checked a small chest of drawers. Finding nothing, Worthy rose too quickly to his knees and saw stars. *I've got to get some food,* he realized, though the thought of another candy bar or donut made his stomach turn. What he needed was sleep.

He sat on the floor as Rakich opened the bottom drawer and drew out a small suitcase. Laying it on the bed, the sergeant pried at the small locks with a pocket knife.

"This hasn't been opened for a long time," the sergeant said. Finally, one metal clasp sprang back, then the other. He pushed the suitcase toward Worthy.

Worthy got to his knees and reached into the suitcase. On the very top was a wooden crucifix of a bleeding Jesus, the type he'd seen at the monastery. The item directly beneath the crucifix seemed from a different world. A small whip made of rope with bits of metal tied in at uneven points lay curled like a sleeping snake.

"What do you make of it, Sergeant?"

Rakich shook his head slowly. "I'm guessing Penitente, but then again, I'm just an outsider. Anything else in there?"

Worthy's hand reached to the bottom of the box and pulled out an ornate certificate, all in Spanish.

"Can you translate?" he asked.

"If it's not too complicated. My wife's Spanish." He took the document, whistling softly as he studied the flowery script. His eyelids narrowed. "As best as I can make out, this says that Eladio Moldonado was a member of the Brotherhood of Jesus of Nazareth in a place called Arroyo Seco. That's Penitente jargon."

"And Arroyo Seco?"

"Down in New Mexico. North of Santa Fe."

"What else?" Worthy asked.

"It says he served faithfully as a *pitero* and a *rezador*. I don't know what the first word means, but I think that last word means he was a reader."

"Is the document dated?"

"Let me see. Yes, right here at the top," he replied, turning it in Worthy's direction. "It's from almost fifteen years ago."

"Anything else?"

"Some names at the bottom. One is a Felix Martinez, who's listed as El Hermano Mayor, but the other name makes no sense."

"Just a minute. You said Martinez?" Worthy asked.

"Yep."

He remembered Ellie's words the day before. Could that really have been only the day before? She'd said that Victor had run into two men; one knew his father.

"You said the other name makes no sense. Why's that?"

"The name of the *Hermano Coadjutor* is an Anglo name. I never heard of an Anglo being permitted into the Brotherhood."

"What's the name?"

"Somebody named Bernard Johnson. The cross after his name makes it look like he was a priest."

*

WORTHY FELL HEADLONG INTO THE MOTEL bed, fully dressed. He'd had the presence of mind to both set an alarm and leave a wake-up call for eight thirty, an hour later than the time Sergeant Rakich promised to be at the police station in Antonito. The two would meet there and then figure out their next step.

Worthy turned over in the bed to lighten the pressure on his shoulder. The next step. Was there a next step? He'd followed one clue out to an abandoned morada. From there he'd driven through the night to a rescue mission to find a suitcase of mementos. Were the two clues connected? Did either lead to some underground bunker?

If this Coffman was the killer, he was a meticulous and calm one. The clues he left were bizarre, but never obvious. Sera may have managed to fit some pieces together, but with each passing hour Worthy feared she'd also walked into his trap.

Worrying won't help, he scolded himself, turning over again. He tried to block out the sound of the semis rolling by outside, but they seemed to be driving through his head. What if he couldn't sleep? No, he had to sleep. He had no choice.

Closing his eyes, he pictured the pile of leaves in the morada, and saw Allyson as a third-grader diving into them. She was throwing the leaves over her head, holding up a large one for him to see. She put the huge oak leaf on her head and began dancing around the empty morada, her baby voice calling out, "See my hat, Daddy, see my hat."

He felt himself sliding down into the darkness of sleep. A final image, like the last frame of an old home movie, showed him raking leaves at their cabin, the same kind of leaves that he'd seen with his flashlight in the morada—tiny pale green and silver aspen leaves floated like feathers to the ground, falling on his head, covering his eyes, now his head.

"Daddy, Daddy, I can't make a hat with these," Allyson's baby voice complained as she tugged on his trousers. "They're too small."

"Daddy needs to sleep, sweetheart," he whispered. "I need to sleep."

But the little girl only pulled on his leg even harder. "Take me back to the little church," she said. "Take me to the big leaves or I'll … I'll run away!"

With a jolt, he sat upright in bed. His breath came in shallow bursts as he stared at the blank TV screen at the other end of the room. Big leaves in the morada. Tiny aspen leaves outside. Where had the big leaves come from? Could an animal have dragged them in? He tried to remember the road he'd traveled in the middle of the night. What kind of trees had he seen? Yes, there'd been piñon pine trees, then at a certain altitude he'd seen juniper pines and aspens. Pines and aspens, needles and tiny leaves.

But the leaves in the unmolested morada had been large, like oaks or sycamores. As he struggled with his one good arm to put on his shoes, he remembered Rakich's comment about the moradas farthest out being the easiest to vandalize. Why not that one?

His body, aching from his shoulder up to his head and down his back, yearned for the fluffy pillows. *Focus, focus*, he told himself. Why had that particular morada been left alone?

"Coffman was a structural engineer … he built bunkers," Rakich had said. He'd gotten that message on the borrowed cell phone, the moment he'd stepped outside the morada to clear the static. His brain leapfrogged to another fact. Both murders had been committed in or around a morada. And Coffman's wife had died down the road from that particular one.

Worthy was already closing the motel room door when a final thought came to him. What in an old adobe building would cause cellphone static? It had sounded like electronic interference of some sort, and yet when he went outside he could hear Rakich clearly. Was it possible that he'd been standing over something, perhaps a bunker?

✟

LIKE A WEARY SAMSON, FATHER BERNARD looked up blankly as Father Fortis and Sera, their chains rattling on the floor, were brought into the room. Eladio sat across from Father Bernard, as if the two had been sharing a secret.

The new room, a type of basic chapel, was smaller than the one that had held Father Fortis and Sera. At one end, in front of yet another set of doors, was a makeshift altar. Atop it was a large golden cross set on a square of white linen. The cross was empty, without Christ or any ornamentation other than golden flames attached to the top and at the ends of the cross's beam. The walls of the room were also bare except for two plaques. *Onward Christian Soldiers, Marching as to War* was balanced on the opposite wall by *Who Is on the Lord's Side?*

"Thank God, you're both okay," Father Bernard said. His voice was hoarse, as if he'd been talking for hours.

Coffman brought two chairs, the same metal types as those in the other room, and placed them on each side of Father Bernard. Once Eladio had secured them, the three captives and Eladio formed a semicircle in front of the altar. The only difference among the three was that Father Bernard's chains had been removed, and he was bound instead with layers of duct tape.

Coffman remained on his feet and hobbled to the door behind the altar. He opened it slightly. Father Fortis noticed that the man did this with reverence.

"What now?" Father Bernard demanded of the leader.

Coffman paced behind the group. "Actually, Bernard, it's time to set you free."

"Free?" he asked, looking from Coffman toward the other two. "Don't believe him."

"No, the truth is, we're tired of you. Right, Eladio?"

"Tired of you," Eladio repeated, his eyes not straying from his leader.

Sera's face was flushed but alert. Eladio could be heard mumbling in a mix of Spanish and English as if he were two people.

"Yes, we're bored with all your endless questions," Coffman continued. "Did this nun pray, did she resist at the end, did she say anything to Eladio or me before she died? Always about death, death, death. What is it with you Catholics?"

So only the two of them killed Sister Anna, Father Fortis thought. Very likely it had only been the two of them who'd crucified Victor as well. Eladio was only an alcohol-wasted derelict, a poor Sancho Panza, a fact that made Coffman all the more impressive. That Coffman had committed such horrific murders without leaving any telltale clues was sobering. The man's thinking was twisted, but he executed a plan with logical precision. Now their survival depended on finding a flaw in that logic and finding it quickly.

"These other two came as adversaries to battle me," Coffman said, gesturing toward Sera and Father Fortis. "That I understand. It is what we expected. It was what had been prophesied centuries ago. But you puzzled me, Bernard. You see, I believe that each of you was meant to be here, meant to come down our road and find us. Even before you met Eladio, you'd been to this place. A magnet. Didn't I tell you, Eladio?"

Eladio continued to mumble incoherently.

"Each of you is part of the plan. The only question I've had, Bernard, is why God brought you."

"But I told you," he interrupted.

"No, I heard what you said, but it took me a while to hear what was hidden in your words. And oh, so many words." He walked in front of the altar as if he were a priest and gazed down on Father Bernard. "Before Eladio frees you, I'm going to tell you the real reason you came."

Eladio stood up, his face drained of color. "Me? Free him? No, not me!"

"Settle yourself, Eladio. Let's not go through this again." Coffman turned to Father Fortis and Sera. "Did you know that Eladio and Bernard used to know each other?"

Father Fortis looked at Sera. Her gaze moved from Father Bernard to Coffman, as if she were as confused as he was. What did it mean that Coffman intended to "free" the monk? What was Father Bernard's game?

"I'm not ashamed to say that I was this man's priest," Father Bernard said, his eyes trained on Eladio.

"Half-truths, half-truths will never do, Bernard," Coffman chided. "Eladio, why don't you tell them the rest of the story?"

Eladio had returned to his seat. His hands were visibly shaking in his lap. "No, no. Too long ago."

Father Fortis watched Father Bernard. The ex-Navy Seal's face was set as if he, though helpless, was finally ready for battle.

"I'm not ashamed to say it. Eladio and I were brothers."

Coffman rested his hand on Father Bernard's shoulder. "Brothers. Yes, there's that term again. Brothers."

"What? You were a Penitente?" Sera asked, staring at Father Bernard.

He nodded.

Father Fortis watched Eladio, expecting him to deny it. But the derelict only kept repeating, "long time ago, long time ago." *No, this is preposterous,* Father Fortis thought. Brother Elias had described Father Bernard as an enemy of the Brotherhood.

"I see you don't believe me, Nicholas," Bernard said. "I thought Linus would have told you back at St. Mary's. As I said, I was a priest up here. Some of the men in my parish were members, and over time I came to believe. It took a while for them to trust me, but eventually they did. But the bishop got wind of it, and well, let's just say the hierarchy finds the Penitentes a bit embarrassing. That's when I was sent to St. Mary's."

If I can't go, there's no one I'd want to go in my place more than Bernard. That was what Father Linus had said. How could Brother Elias have been so wrong in accusing the spiritual director of hating the Brotherhood?

"Why'd you send Sister Anna out to the retreat house?" Father Fortis asked. He could feel Coffman's eyes on him, as if he were evaluating something.

"She was being tempted to renounce her vows. I couldn't let her do that," Father Bernard replied.

"So you sent her out to be killed?" Sera asked.

"No! What are you saying? I sent her on retreat to pray for direction. You don't think … Father, you, too?" He stared at Father Fortis.

"I saw you whisper something to Eladio when we were first taken," Father Fortis said. "I thought—"

"But I assumed you knew. You read her journal. The church needs to know as much as we can about how Sister Anna died."

"Why? We know how she died," Sera replied.

Not completely, Father Fortis thought. *Yes, that would explain everything.* "The church thinks that she might be a saint," Father Fortis muttered. "That's why you wanted me to read her journal, and that's why you tagged along with us, isn't it? You came along to begin to establish her ... what do you call it?"

"I'm only here to begin the process of establishing her cause," Father Bernard said.

"Boring, boring, boring," Coffman interrupted, as he started pacing again. "But not unimportant. Bernard, I will tell you something. I am going to free you, as I promised, but I want you to know that you're very much like the nun and the boy."

"Thank you. I only wish that were true," he replied.

"Thank you," Eladio repeated with an odd chuckle. "The cup is full, the cup is full. Father, but not my father."

There's that phrase again, Father Fortis thought. He studied Eladio as he wrung his hands and stole glances at Coffman. He'd first heard the derelict say it when he bumped into him weeks before at the store in Truchas. That must have been soon after the two men had buried Victor alive. He searched his memory. Had Coffman been with Eladio that day? *No*, he thought. *The derelict had been alone.*

"The final battle is between the children of death and the children of life," Coffman said as he paused in front of Bernard, their faces only inches apart. " 'Oh Death, where is your sting,' now?"

"Your sting now," Eladio mimicked.

Father Fortis strained in the shackles. Oh, what he wouldn't give to rise up just enough to string his chains around the man's neck.

Coffman raised himself to full height and walked behind the altar. Closing his eyes tightly, he raised his hands in the air. "Oh God of power and might, God of vengeance and zeal, hear us, we pray. The days are numbered, the very drops of blood to be shed in these final days are known to you alone. End this veil of tears, defeat Death we pray, judge the cup to be full in these moments."

Coffman opened his eyes, reached down to retrieve something from under the altar, and opened the door behind him another inch. "It is time to free Bernard, Eladio. Take the knife."

Eladio whimpered as he accepted a long fishing knife from Coffman. The six-inch blade was honed to a sharp point and glistened off the fluorescent lighting.

"Eladio ... I said, free him!" Coffman ordered from where he stood behind the altar.

Nothing about the scene made any sense to Father Fortis. Coffman edged back toward the door behind the altar as if someone would come out, while Eladio stood with the knife trembling in his hands. Father Bernard looked confused as he gazed down at the duct tape around his wrists.

"God is waiting, Eladio. So are the souls in Christ, including my beloved. And so is your friend, Bernard. Aren't you, Bernard?"

Eladio dropped the knife and ran toward the door at the other end of the room.

"Stop!" Coffman ordered. "Remember what I told you. When the end comes, the righteous will reign with the Judge. I promise you before God, Eladio, that I'll personally come and cut your eyes out if you walk out that door."

Eladio dropped to his knees, whimpering, as Coffman hobbled to pick up the knife. He bent down and looked into Father Bernard's eyes. "Before I free you, I want to finish what I was saying," he said in little more than a whisper. "When you started all those questions this morning about the nun, I thought at first that she'd been your whore. You told me you'd sent her to that house of death to paint those images, and I thought maybe that's where you and she fornicated. But then I realized you are just like her. You're just as much in love with death as she was. You all are, with your crucifixes of our Lord, as if he's still dying, and all your talk of saints and how they died. Death, death, death. Always death for you. That's when I understood. You weren't sent by God for me, but to test Eladio, to lure him back into that filth. He almost succeeded, didn't he, Eladio?"

Coffman turned his head toward Sera. "Pay attention, Lieutenant. This is why you and your type never had a chance of catching me. I've been given a gift of seeing into people. Case in point, I know you both want to kill me, but this big hulk of a man, the strongest of the three of you, doesn't. Bernard wants something else."

He started cutting the tape around Father Bernard's wrists. One at a time, the strands dropped free. Coffman paused over the last strand of tape and looked down into the priest's eyes. "Ready, Bernard?"

"She forgave you, didn't she? Yes, I can see it in your eyes. At the end, she forgave you," Father Bernard said, his voice clear and strong.

The knife rested for a second on the tape as if Coffman were pondering something before he took a vigorous step forward and sank the blade into Father Bernard's stomach. Father Fortis heard Father Bernard gasp as he looked down at his wound. Coffman took the knife's handle in both hands and with a powerful pull drew it upward. Father Bernard was lifted slightly in the chair by Coffman's strength, the priest's mouth trying to say something before his eyes rolled back in his head. Coffman pulled out the knife and in haste hobbled to the door behind the altar.

Father Fortis heard himself screaming. Sera had turned her head away to vomit, while Eladio had remained next to the far door, his eyes wide and fixed on Coffman.

The leader put his ear to the door behind the altar. "Shut up, all of you!" he ordered. He stood poised at the door, as if trying to hear something or waiting for orders.

After a moment, his head dropped to his chest. "More, Lord?" he asked. "Is the cup still not full?"

CHAPTER TWENTY-EIGHT

———— ◆ ————

FATHER FORTIS FELT A WAVE OF power surge within him as he watched blood flow down Father Bernard's shirt and pants onto the floor. He knew that he might be the next to die, but somehow, some way, he would go out in a blaze of glory that Coffman would never forget. He would bite, he would throw his whole body, chair included, at this man. He would make him pay.

Growing up with the stories of the saints, Father Fortis had always wondered how he would face death when his time came. He wasn't a saint, and he knew from the bottom of his heart, if he were to die in this bunker, he would not go out with forgiveness on his lips.

The drama in the room shifted to Eladio. The derelict opened the far door, even as Coffman seemed unwilling to leave the door by the altar. The leader shouted directions across the room, but it was as if Eladio could no longer hear him. Eladio's head was lolling from side to side as he mumbled a tangle of words.

"Father, he was a father ... not my father ... call no man father ... the cup should be full," and finally, "Lord, have mercy."

"Eladio, are you going to run away like last time?" Coffman taunted.

"Confess ... need to confess," Eladio mumbled.

Father Fortis caught Sera's eye. She spat mucus from her mouth, but her eyes sparkled.

The two watched as some unspoken tug of war was waged between the two captors. Eladio stood tall in the doorway, his whole body shaking. The next moment he was gone, slamming the door behind him. Father Fortis heard a bolt click.

Coffman jumped away from his post at the noise, hobbling hurriedly across the room and pushing against the door.

"The Judge sees you, Eladio!" he shouted. "Save yourself and unlock this door!"

There was no sound from the other side, and Coffman stepped back to inspect the door.

Father Fortis looked over at Sera, who nodded toward the door behind the altar.

"In there," she seemed to be mouthing.

What? he thought. Did she think the door provided some way out? They now outnumbered Coffman, but they were still shackled.

Coffman drew a utility tool from his pocket. Opening a long screwdriver blade, he began methodically working on the lock. "I built every inch of this place, every inch. Patience, my dear, patience." He soon pulled open the door and looked back at his two captives. "I'll be back with Eladio in a few seconds. Remember, I've got a detonator."

The room was utterly quiet as Father Bernard's blood pooled noiselessly on the floor. Father Fortis whispered to Sera, "What were you trying to say?"

"Can you hop in your chair?"

"I don't know," he said, thinking of the motion detectors. "Why?"

"If we can get through that door," she said, motioning with her head toward the altar, "we've got a chance."

"What? Didn't you hear what he just said?"

"I know what he said. I just don't believe him."

Had she gone crazy? "Sera, he just killed Father Bernard, and think what he did to Sister Anna and Victor. He'd kill us in a heartbeat."

"Not if one of us can get into that room."

"I don't understand."

"Nick, we don't have much time. Listen to me. He's not going to blow us up if we can get in there with her."

"*Her?* What are you talking about?"

"His wife. She's in there. I'm sure of it," Sera whispered.

"What?" he exclaimed, staring at the door behind the altar.

"Think about it. Why did he keep peeking in there? And he just said, 'Patience, dear, patience.' You don't think he was talking to me, do you?"

"But his wife's dead!" Father Fortis protested.

"Of course she is, but he's got her body in there. He thinks she'll come back to life."

"By killing others?"

Coffman's steps could be heard on the stairs.

"Just follow my lead when I figure this out," she whispered. "If I can find a way to get him out of the room for a few moments, maybe tell him I have to go to the bathroom, you start hopping."

"And do what?"

"It has to be dark in there, and you're a big guy. Fall on him, chair and all, when he comes through that door. I'll be in chains, but I'll …. Shh."

Coffman hobbled into the room and sat down wearily in a chair. Gone was the confident expression he'd worn all day and evening. He placed the detonator on the floor and began rubbing his bad knee.

"He'll come back. He always does. Not that it'll matter in a couple of hours. Nothing will matter then," Coffman said as he glanced up toward the altar.

✝

WORTHY DROVE ABSURDLY FAST, FIGHTING NOT only fatigue but the weird images in his head. He could force himself to stay awake, but how long would it be before he missed a stop sign or failed to negotiate a curve?

He contemplated calling Rakich at the station at Antonito, but imagined what the groggy sergeant would say. "Let me get this straight. You had a dream—no, a waking dream—about your daughter and big leaves!"

He turned off onto Forest Road 250 and drove as if he were the last man on earth. In the rearview mirror, he could see the first rays of sunlight peeking over the horizon behind him. Ahead, in a bunker underneath the old morada, could be his friends. Was it just another mirage to imagine that they were still alive?

He shook his head and fought the hypnotic pull of sleep. He would have to think clearly. He couldn't simply barge into the place as he had the night before. The static in the cell phone had to mean electronic equipment, cameras, maybe even motion detectors. That would mean Coffman had already spotted him. Why hadn't the man killed him then?

Forty-five minutes later, the sun now turning the mountains ahead of him from purple to gold, Worthy began the last rise toward the morada. He would leave the car short of the abandoned place and approach it carefully from behind. Somewhere along the way, he hoped, a plan would emerge.

As he rounded the curve leading to the accident site, he spotted something odd ahead. He pulled over and turned off the engine. If he wasn't hallucinating, a van was parked at the accident site. Not just any van, but a tan sheriff's van. He stepped quietly from the car and felt for the gun.

He hugged the cliff side of the road as he approached the vehicle. From a hundred yards away, he could see the yellow New Mexico license plates. The van's lights were on, but the motor was off. He drew out the gun and checked the clip as he stepped forward. *Stay alert, stay alert. Watch where you step, proceed slowly,* he ordered himself, as if reading from one of the training manuals at the academy.

But the manual would have disapproved of what he was doing. He should have walked a safe distance from the scene to call for backup. But then the manual didn't know that the entire area could be under surveillance and any communication might instantly make his presence known.

He crouched as he rounded the last bend, pondering the open space between himself and the van. Should he storm it or proceed slowly? What if he had to shoot? The echo through the canyon would surely alert everyone to his presence.

He looked down at the gun for a moment, then at the twenty yards of gravel he'd have to cross. He saw only one option. Holding the gun in his good hand, he sprinted across the road and prepared himself for whatever would happen.

But nothing did. There was no sound but the crunch of gravel beneath his feet and the sound of flapping wings as three ravens flew up from the canyon beyond the road's edge. He pressed himself flat and low against the passenger side of the van. Catching his breath, he rose and looked in. Empty.

Crouching down again, he carefully edged his way around to the front and rested his good hand on the grill. It was still warm. Whoever had driven this van had done so recently.

He ran toward the road's edge. More birds rose as his shoes spit small stones into the canyon. Why so many birds? He peeked over the edge and saw an odd shape ten feet below the road's edge. It was as if a man were leaning against a tree, studying the two crosses ten feet beyond. Worthy raised his gun to order the figure to turn around when it suddenly dawned on him that the man couldn't respond. The man wasn't leaning against the tree, but hanging by a belt from it.

✝

FATHER FORTIS TRIED TO MUSTER SOME belief in Sera's plan, but his brain kept stumbling over its flaws. He didn't have the strength to hop the fifteen feet to the door behind the altar. A loss of balance would mean he'd end up on the floor, as helpless as an upside-down turtle. Even if he reached the door, how could he and the metal chair attached to him ever fit through it?

But the plan seemed doomed by two even more serious considerations. First, how could Sera possibly distract Coffman long enough for him to do his part? If she feigned illness, what guarantee was there that he wouldn't simply kill her on the spot?

Second, and even more worrisome, Coffman had changed in the last twenty minutes. He worked silently as he dragged Father Bernard's body to the door from where Eladio had fled. Gone were the duels of conversation, gone the jabs at the police's inability to catch him, and gone was the confidence he'd exhibited when Eladio had been there. Coffman had clearly expected something to happen with Father Bernard's death. Eladio had felt it too, and when it hadn't, he'd betrayed his beloved leader.

Sera's entire plan was predicated on Coffman being a man of logic, an engineer and a systematic killer, a man with confident conviction. If Coffman were experiencing doubts, wouldn't that make him harder to predict? And far more dangerous?

Sera was as silent as Coffman, rarely catching Father Fortis's eye. *She's smart enough to see the same flaws*, Father Fortis thought.

He looked down at the chains that bound him to the chair and would likely ensure his death. How odd that the only prayer he could remember was one of his mother's. She'd taught it to him the very night she'd told him his father had lost his job in the foundry and that they would have to move to a rougher neighborhood in Baltimore.

Help me to face and endure my difficulty with faith, courage, and wisdom. Grant that this trial may bring me closer to You, for you are my rock and refuge, my comfort and hope.

Coffman paced the room, stopping occasionally to stare at the blood on the floor as if it would speak. He fingered his mustache nervously.

If we don't think of something quickly, we won't have a chance, Father Fortis thought. He hastily added a further petition to his prayer. *If this is to be my end, oh God, prepare me to face death without shame and in hope of eternal life.*

Was it the thought of death that made it more difficult to breathe? Perspiration started on his brow and began to weave its way down into his beard. He looked up at the vent above but felt nothing. Was this all his imagination?

He glanced over at Coffman, who seemed lost in thought. But there, on the killer's forehead, beads of sweat were also forming. Sera, too, was licking a drop of sweat from her upper lip. Coffman stood and hobbled over to the vent in the middle of the room. He raised his hand to the grill.

"Sand is in the filter again," he said.

Father Fortis felt his heart jump. The filter would have to be at ground level, which would mean they'd have a chance to try Sera's crazy plan. The two captives stared at each other, as if each knew the next minutes would mean life or death.

Coffman walked to the far end of the room, picked up the detonator from the floor and flashed it at them before leaving. Two seconds later, he appeared in the doorway again, an assault weapon in his hand. "I don't have to tell you to sit tight, do I?" Then he was gone.

Thank you, God, for miracles like sand in filters, for a chance to live or die with faith and courage. "Save us by your mercy," he prayed aloud in a whisper.

From across the room, Sera added, "Amen, Nick. But let's hope we have something else to be thankful for."

"Like what?"

"Like that clog in the filter being more than an accident."

"Are you saying Eladio did it?"

"No, I think Chris did," she whispered with the hint of a smile.

Instinctively, Father Fortis gazed up at the ceiling as adrenaline raced through him. He took a quick hop in the direction of the door. "Oh, God, Christopher, be careful."

✝

WORTHY READIED HIMSELF IN THE DARKEST corner of the morada. The sun outside was flooding the doorway with light, allowing him a clear view of the mound of leaves ten feet away. He'd had no trouble following the van's tracks back to the morada. He'd approached the place by way of the trees and rocks and in that way had found the air intake vent. It had been easy to jam sand and leaves down it.

He raised his pistol and waited, even as doubts as big as semis rumbled through his brain. There was indeed some underground structure below him, but what if it had several exits? And what if he found himself facing three or four armed men? Worse yet, what if someone brought Sera or Nick up with him as a shield? Yet another horrible scenario followed. What if Coffman had already moved his captives to another location?

He crouched lower, his arm shaking. *No, they have to be here*, he told himself. He'd get only one shot, and then whoever was down below would know everything. Sweat poured down his face despite the cool morning air. His stomach felt suddenly queasy. What if in trying to rescue his friends he caused their deaths?

He eased up on the gun as his brain scrambled to find a safer plan. Words he'd said not more than a month before at the academy came back to him. "There are times when the worst thing you can do is second-guess your plan."

Was this one of those times? Before he could answer that, he heard a click from the other corner of the room, as if a handle had been turned. He steadied his gun. Slowly, the leaves moved together, rising an inch, then several, before lifting as a solid unit toward him. Not one leaf fell to the ground.

He uttered a short gasp as he remembered his last visit to this place. The damned cell phone had gone off. What if Rakich called him again? Without looking at his watch, Worthy figured it must be nearly eight thirty, the time he'd promised to meet the sergeant at the station. *What if Rakich thinks I've overslept?*

The trapdoor stopped its upward progress. Had he been heard? His thoughts kept returning to the phone in his coat pocket. He might as well as be carrying a ticking bomb.

Take deep, slow breaths, he told himself, as the door remained poised, half-open. Whoever was on the other side of that door was listening. He shifted the gun to his injured hand and reached into the pocket for the phone.

Slowly, the trapdoor edged upward and the top of a head appeared. It was a flattop, military-style. Was it Coffman, or could it be someone else? What if the head belonged to the other priest from St. Mary's?

He glanced down at the phone and then at the gun in his useless hand. *What am I doing?* he thought. He pushed the off button on the phone and had just put it back into his pocket when he heard a faint tune coming from inside his coat. *Oh, God, no! The phone was telling him he'd shut it off.*

The figure emerging from the trapdoor swiveled toward the sound, and in the next second the air was filled with blinding flashes. He could hear bullets thumping into the adobe wall behind him as he returned fire. Other bullets, flying higher, sent splinters of wood raining down on Worthy as he fell to the ground.

The nightmare unfolded in fractions of seconds. The door dropped down with a bang, cutting Worthy off from the bunker below. But before it slammed shut, Worthy heard an alarm go off below ground.

"Oh, God, no," he repeated as he scrambled toward the leaves in the corner. Shoving the gun into his pocket, he felt for a handle, knowing his worst fear had come true. His friends could be dying at that very moment because of him.

His good hand found a small iron circle. Pulling on it with all his strength, he raised the door no more than a couple of inches. In the gap, he heard the beeping of the alarm below. He pulled harder. No good. He rose, yanking the sling from his bad arm. His injured shoulder and arm felt light, like a child's, as he reached down with both hands for the ring. But as he pulled on it again, he felt his shoulder shudder in disbelief, then scream in pain as the door rose six inches, then three more.

Stars flashed in the corners of his eyes, and his legs begin to buckle as he held the door open with his bad arm. Something tore in his shoulder as his good arm found the door's edge. He pulled upward with all his might. The door suddenly flew up, throwing him back on the wooden floor. On his feet again, he looked down at steps leading into a room below.

Pulling the gun from his pocket, he jumped down the stairwell. In front of him, the alarm sounded more insistent, but he listened only for the dreaded sound of gunfire. Instead, he heard Father Fortis's booming voice screaming out.

✝

"How dare you! How dare you!" Coffman yelled from far down the corridor. "Do you both want to die?"

"You blow us up, and your wife goes too," Sera yelled back as she hopped forward. She was already to the edge of the door.

Coffman stopped in the doorway to the chapel room. The bunker was eerily quiet until Father Fortis risked another hop in his chair, throwing him forward at a dangerous angle. If his torso hadn't landed on the edge of the altar top, he'd have fallen helplessly to the floor.

"Can you get up?" Sera asked breathlessly.

"You go ahead. I'll find a way," he replied. His clumsiness had sent the heavy golden cross atop the altar onto its side, and Father Fortis found the spine of it near his shackled hands. He grabbed onto it and turned it on its sturdy base for leverage. Pushing down on it with all his strength, he raised himself to a seated position.

"You whore!" Coffman screamed from the doorway. "You touch her, and I'll rip your head from your shoulders."

The anguish in the voice sent a chill down Father Fortis's spine. He turned his head to see Coffman, mouth wide open in a scream, hobbling toward them, the detonator raised threateningly in his left hand. The other hand was empty and hung limp, blood flowing from the shoulder to the ground.

Coffman is wounded. Father Fortis's joy at the sight was swamped by another thought. Where was Worthy? Had he been shot?

Coffman stopped five feet in front of the altar and stared at Sera. "Get away from her, you bitch."

"Come get me, you bastard," she yelled.

Coffman threw the detonator to the ground and charged the policewoman like a bull. His face was contorted with hate as he pulled the knife from the sheath.

As Coffman flew by the altar, Father Fortis threw himself forward to trip him. The killer started to fall and reached out, catching Father Fortis by the shoulder. The two men fell together, Coffman landing on top of the priest.

Father Fortis hadn't let go of the cross as they tumbled to the floor, and he felt it catch hold of something as he ended up on his hands and knees, his forehead smashed to the floor. He hadn't landed on Coffman, as had been the plan, yet he was still alive.

That was when he heard the strange gurgling sound. He pushed against Coffman and slowly the man rolled to one side. The cross went with him.

Father Fortis panted for air, still expecting the knife to come down between his shoulder blades and end his life. He made a feeble sign of the cross with his bound hands, trusting that God would understand.

But the blow didn't fall. Instead, he was being turned on his side and lowered gently to the ground. He looked across the floor and found Coffman's eyes staring blankly back at him, the sharp arm of the cross protruding from where it had impaled his throat as the two tumbled to the floor. Blood spurted spasmodically from the man's jugular vein and formed a widening pool.

Behind him, Father Fortis heard Sera scream out Worthy's name. He looked up to see his friend's face smiling down on him.

"Let's get out of here, Nick," were the last words he heard before passing out.

CHAPTER TWENTY-NINE

———◆———

For the next three days, Worthy was just another newspaper reader in New Mexico who drank his morning coffee over the story of the "Bunker Killer," as Coffman was now called. The first day featured the dramatic account of Sera's and Father Fortis's survival as well as a sketchy profile of the man responsible for the ritual murders of Sister Anna and Victor. Buried in the last paragraph was a brief mention of the deaths of Father Bernard and Eladio. In a sidebar piece, Worthy's own firefight with Coffman in the morada read like a scene out of a bad Western.

By the second day, when Worthy was wading through the legal forms that marked the end of any case, the newspapers were digging deeper into the story. Millie Coffman, Inspector Choi, and Sergeant Rakich were introduced, though Ellie VanBruskman's name was blessedly missing. Readers and viewers were also introduced to new terms—"apocalyptic" and "paranoia with religious ideation"—as well as the banter of religious studies experts, psychologists, and Internet scholars. All were trying to answer the central question—who was Porter Coffman, alias Phinehas Zealman?

For those first few days, St. Mary's provided little privacy for Worthy and Father Fortis. The monastery found itself again barraged with TV cameras and reporters as the monks processed to their prayers and prepared for Father Bernard's funeral. An apocryphal story began to circulate of Father Bernard offering confession to both Coffman and Eladio before his execution. Another story described how Father Bernard had died making the sign of the cross with his own blood. On the day of the funeral, Abbot Timothy wisely barred the road to St. Mary's.

The third day brought Lieutenant Sera Lacey's name and picture back onto the front pages. For courage and clear thinking under fire, she would receive a departmental citation. *She'll be offered a position in homicide*, Worthy thought as he packed his bags. He hoped, however, that she would work with child protection services for a little while longer.

Two days later, having said goodbye to Father Fortis at the monastery and after making a final road trip, Worthy showed up at Sera's office. She was emptying her bookshelves into boxes.

"So you're getting a new job. I expected as much. Congratulations."

"Thanks, Chris." She came around her desk and shook his outstretched hand. "They could be making a big mistake."

"No, they're not. You're very good."

Tears welled up in her eyes. "From you, that's really something. I still can't quite believe you came back for us. Which means I can't quite believe I'm standing here." She dropped her hand. "Any hints for a new detective?"

"Maybe just one. Trust your hunches. It's not always about logic."

She nodded. "I'll remember that. I know it won't be easy for you back in Detroit, your not finding Ellie, I mean. When do you leave?"

"In a few minutes, after one last matter is settled."

"Oh?"

"There's someone waiting outside. May I show her in?"

Looking puzzled, Sera shrugged.

Worthy opened the door for the newcomer, then closed it immediately behind her.

"Sera," Worthy whispered, "I'd like you to meet Ellie VanBruskman."

"What? No! Ellie?"

Ellie stood nervously, not knowing what to do with her hands. In the end, she folded her arms across her chest.

"But I thought you were—"

"Dead," Ellie finished the sentence.

Sera threw her arms around the girl. Slowly, Ellie's arms unfolded and dropped to her side. Sera began to sob and, after a few hesitations, Ellie tentatively hugged the policewoman back.

"Oh, my God, my God. It's a miracle," Sera said, stepping back to look at Ellie.

"No, it's just me," Ellie said, blushing.

"But when?" Sera asked, looking at Worthy.

"I found her downstate about a week ago. Ellie was the one who sent me up to Colorado, so she's really the one who deserves the credit for saving your life."

"But where's she been since then?"

"I left her there," Worthy said, looking at Ellie. "And that's where she was yesterday when I showed up again."

"You're going back to Detroit with Chris, then," Sera said. "I'm sorry, honey."

A smile stole over Ellie's face.

"No, she's not," Worthy said. "We both think she should stay out here."

"But her parents—"

Worthy interrupted her. "I'll tell them what I need to tell them. That all the clues led us to Victor, but Victor's tragic death ended the trail. In three months, Ellie becomes a legal adult. Until then, I need someone here in New Mexico who knows who and where she is. And Ellie needs someone to call in case of trouble. Am I asking too much of a new detective?"

"For the rest of this week, I'm still in child protection. Ellie, you'll be my last case. Okay?" She put her arms around the girl's shoulders. "Where will you be?"

"Over in Arizona, in Douglas, working with pregnant girls. I've put my number on this card." She handed Sera a small, handwritten note. "You'll see that my name is Maria. It really is, by the way. My mother—Ellen VanBruskman, I mean—changed it to Ellie to be like hers. But my real mother named me Maria."

"You sure this is okay, Sera?" Worthy asked. "She has her medication, though she hasn't needed it."

"It's better than okay, Chris. My hunch says it's the right thing to do."

Worthy nodded. "Email me, both of you, okay?"

Ellie approached Worthy shyly and hugged him. "I will, I promise. Don't forget to tell Dr. Cartwright I'm okay. And try not to worry."

Worthy walked to the door.

"Chris?" Sera called after him.

"Yes?

"Thanks for everything. And good luck with Allyson."

Ellie gave Worthy a puzzled look. "Allyson's a real person?"

"Sera will explain," he said. He closed the door behind him. Yes, Allyson was real, somehow more real to him than she'd been for a long time. He walked to the car pondering a new thought. Ever since Susan had called three months ago to tell him their daughter was safe and had returned home, he'd been waiting for Allyson to tell him why she'd run away.

He started the car and headed for the airport. He'd been asking a detective's question, and it had been the wrong one. Like Ellie, Allyson might have had a hundred reasons for running away. The question that he'd failed to ask, the question he now saw was the only one that really mattered, was why Allyson had chosen to come home.

That was a father's question.

Photo by Leif Carlson

DAVID **C**ARLSON WAS BORN IN THE western suburbs of Chicago and grew up in parsonages in various cities of Illinois. His grade school years were spent in Springfield, Illinois, where the numerous Abraham Lincoln sites initiated his lifelong love of history. His childhood hope was to play professional baseball, a dream that died ignominiously one day in high school.

He attended Wheaton College (Illinois) where he majored in political science and planned on going to law school. Not sure how to respond to the Vietnam War, he decided to attend seminary for a year to weigh his options. To his surprise, he fell in love with theological thinking—especially theological questioning—and his career plan shifted to college teaching in religious studies. He earned a doctorate at University of Aberdeen, Scotland, where he learned that research is a process of digging and then digging deeper. He believes the same process of digging and digging deeper has helped him in his nonfiction and mystery writing.

Franklin College, a traditional liberal arts college in central Indiana, has been his home for the past thirty-eight years. David has been particularly attracted to the topics of faith development, Catholic-Orthodox relations, and Muslim-Christian dialogue. In the last thirteen years, however, religious terrorism has become his area of specialty. In 2007, he conducted interviews across the country in monasteries and convents about monastic responses to 9/11 and religious terrorism. The book based on that experience, *Peace Be with You: Monastic Wisdom for a Terror-Filled World*, was published in 2011 by Thomas Nelson and was selected as one of the Best Books of 2011 in the area of Spiritual Living by Library Journal. He has subsequently written a second book on religious terrorism, *Countering ISIS: The Power of Spiritual Friendships*.

Much of his time in the last three years has been spent giving talks as well as being interviewed on radio and TV about ISIS. Nevertheless, he is still able to spend summers in Wisconsin where he enjoys sailing, fishing, kayaking, and restoring an old log cabin.

His wife, Kathy, is a retired English professor, an award-winning artist, and an excellent editor. Their two sons took parental advice to follow their passions. The older, Leif, is a photographer, and the younger, Marten, is a filmmaker.

For more information, please visit: www.davidccarlson.org.